Rave reviews
The

"In a grim world of medi____
tive surgery, E. C. Ambros_____ _____ ____ __ ___
man's humanity and courage. A gritty read for those who like
realism as well as hope in their fantasy."
—Glenda Larke, author of *The Last Stormlord*

"A vivid, violent, and marvelously detailed historical fantasy
set in the perilous world that is medieval England in the middle of a war. Elisha Barber wades through blood and battle in
his pursuit of arcane knowledge—forbidden love—and dangerous magic."   —Sharon Shinn, author of *Troubled Waters*

"Ambrose's fantasy debut depicts a 14th-century England in
which magic and fledgling science exist side by side. Elisha's
struggle to bring relief to those in need is complicated by his
own need for redemption and his innate fear of what he cannot
understand. This beautifully told, painfully elegant story should
appeal to fans of L.E. Modesitt's realistic fantasies as well as of
the period fantasy of Guy Gavriel Kay."
—*Library Journal* (starred review)

"*Elisha Barber* is at its heart a story of resilience, of why we
strive to be better, even when that journey seems pointless. As
the start of a new series, the book sets a half-dozen plates spinning, and not a one wobbles for a second."
—San Francisco Book Review

"E.C. Ambrose has created an exciting, adventure-filled world
that draws you in; you are able to picture not only the characters but the world they live in. *Elisha Magus* is fantasy at its
best and I can't wait for the next book by E.C. Ambrose."
—Fresh Fiction

"I am really enjoying this series. After reading the first book I
was eager to read *[Elisha Magus]*. It did not disappoint."
—Night Owl Reviews

"The historical milieu is detailed and brings the period into
sharp focus. . . . The magical battles rivet readers' attention as
Elisha fights for his life and sanity. Book three looms in the
wings as Elisha learns to wield his powers and protect his
chosen king."
—SFRevu

Novels of
The Dark Apostle
from E. C. Ambrose

ELISHA BARBER

ELISHA MAGUS

ELISHA REX*

*Coming soon from DAW

ELISHA MAGUS

BOOK TWO OF

The Dark Apostle

E. C. AMBROSE

DAW BOOKS, INC.
DONALD A. WOLLHEIM, FOUNDER
375 Hudson Street, New York, NY 10014

ELIZABETH R. WOLLHEIM
SHEILA E. GILBERT
PUBLISHERS
www.dawbooks.com

First Paperback Printing, March 2015
1 2 3 4 5 6 7 8 9

DAW TRADEMARK REGISTERED
U.S. PAT. AND TM. OFF. AND FOREIGN COUNTRIES
—MARCA REGISTRADA
HECHO EN U.S.A.

PRINTED IN THE U.S.A.

ELISHA MAGUS

"Since it is just that he who knows how to kill,
should learn how to die."

—CHILDEBERT

Chapter 1

The gray of the evening sky deepened as Elisha walked to the churchyard. The church itself leaned a bit to the left, its ruined steeple pointing up toward the duke's castle; accusing or beseeching, it was hard to say. Riders jangled by, talking and laughing, on their way to the grand masked ball, their chatter drifting over the walls into what should be a peaceful place. His business here would likely be brief, and he would be back at the castle in plenty of time to dodge the visitors and return to the comfort of his infirmary. He wanted to check on the scullion's new baby, not to mention that man-at-arms with the wounded leg. So far, no sign of putrefaction, but the fellow was terrified he'd have to lose his leg and his livelihood. Elisha hoped the noise of the ball wouldn't disturb them and that the flow of wine and ale wouldn't bring a flow of drunken nobles tumbling into his own domain.

The ribs of burned-out houses and barns still loomed over the streets, but a few had been dismantled, fresh stone laid for new foundations, and piles of cut saplings waited to be woven into walls. Two houses, at least, had already been built to the roofs, tiles gleaming dully with the rays of the distant sun as smoke curled from the chimneys. Elisha took careful stock of all that he saw, looking for movement, looking for new places someone might hide. Tension crept into his shoulders, much as he tried to keep it back, to focus on his duty. Nothing else caught his eye, but Elisha still stretched his awareness, allowing tendrils of his strength to move over the ground, aware of the families in each house, the sheep in each fold, the cat that slunk through a blackened barn in search of mice.

Even the graves lay unquiet after the battle, crosses askew, the handful of stone monuments broken or flattened by the bombards' blasts and the rumble of siege engines. Elisha picked his way toward the far side, where the low wall had been dismantled to expand the yard and a series of mounds, still high over the new graves, showed where the soldiers lay. A hunched figure bent over, shovel across his shoulder, examining the shrouded remains of the latest corpse.

The figure gave a twitch and turned, straightening as much as possible, the lumpish face curling into recognition. The fellow had been here through the battle, burying the dead of the king's army and of the hospital where Elisha did his best. Now he worked for Duke Randall's village. Gravediggers didn't choose sides.

Elisha gave a nod, but noticed the flutter of the shroud as if the gravedigger had been searching beneath it, not merely measuring the corpse for a grave. He narrowed his eyes. "Which side did he fight for?"

"Who can say, now? Anything worth money's been

stripped, eh? And his clothes don't tell much—been a month in the woods, ain't he?" The gravedigger grinned and shrugged, then set his shovel to the earth. "Didn't expect nobody but the priest."

Elisha moved past, facing the grave between them and the pale cloth of the shroud. The cracked bell in the crooked tower gave a thunk, then another, and a third, each with a groan of rope over pulley that suggested how hard the priest must work to get even that pitiful sound.

A week had passed since the last funeral, and he had thought it might be truly the last, until a few children found this sorry fellow half-buried in a blast pit by the trees. The first funerals he attended here included relatives of the deceased, the camp followers or nearby townsmen who still recognized their own. But time degraded the dead until their families would not have known them and most of the fallen had been already laid to rest. The gatherings dwindled to a few sympathetic townsfolk, and even then they wanted to know if the dead were of the king's army—which had set the torch to their homes—or of the duke's, as if the duke's bombards had spared them any grief. Elisha had effectively fought for both sides, impressed to the king's army before delivering the ultimate victory for the duke himself. He came as much for his brother's sake as for the soldiers', as if he could make up for that one funeral he had missed.

Father Michael crossed the yard, wringing his hands and shaking out his fingers, the lines of his face deepened by the sinking sun. He, too, nodded at Elisha. The three men stood around the grave as the priest crossed them and the corpse and spoke in Latin. Elisha's outspread awareness as much as the monotone of the priest's voice suggested that this task had moved from reverence to rote.

Father Michael led another prayer, followed by Elisha's quiet, "Amen," and the grunt of the gravedigger, then sprinkled holy water and turned away toward the church.

"Give us a hand, mate," the gravedigger muttered, waving Elisha closer with a flap of his wrist.

Pushing back his sleeves, Elisha came forward, squatting to lift the corpse's shoulders. The body gave in his hands, a softness foreign to healthy flesh, and Elisha swallowed the bile in his throat.

"Give 'im the toss." The gravedigger chuckled, but he moved carefully enough to lay his end of the body into the grave.

Still, Elisha stumbled and nearly slipped in afterward, the head and shoulders flopping heavily from his hands into the hole. A ripe odor drifted from the shroud, along with a few flies, and Elisha drew back, looking away for a breath of fresher air. Just to breathe in the stench of corpses opened one to disease. He straightened and tipped his head back, the clatter of hooves and merry voices rising from the road. The slightest thrill of interest touched him from afar and Elisha turned.

A bolt whizzed past, snagging the cloth of his shoulder with a sharp tug.

With a curse, Elisha leapt aside, tumbling into the half-filled grave as a second bolt whipped through the spot where he'd been standing and cracked against the dirt wall. His shoulder stung, and the corpse beneath him gave an exhalation of foul air. Recoiling from the stink, hand pressed over his mouth, Elisha froze. If he stuck his head up now, the archer might have a third shot. Damn it! His heart hammered loud in the narrow space. His eyes watered as the stench invaded his nostrils, but he held his stomach in check. Even without his extra senses, he heard the horses galloping off.

"Christ on the Cross, two in one grave!" The gravedigger peered down at him, a shovelful of dirt poised in his hands.

"Barber! What's happened?" Father Michael ran up. "I was checking the garden when I heard you cry out."

Elisha blinked up at the two faces silhouetted against the evening sky. "Someone shot at me," he managed. "Probably gone."

The priest paused a moment to look around then reached down. Elisha took his arm and climbed out of the grave, brushing off dirt and shaking his head. He frowned down at his shoulder where a thin line of blood marked the rip in his tunic. The evening breeze swept over him, wiping away the reek of death.

"In a churchyard, no less!" Father Michael frowned as well, or rather his lined face fell into the expression it seemed made for, then he bent to lift the fallen bolt, short and new, with a sharp head for piercing flesh. Holding it close to his nose to examine it, he said, "No fletcher's mark."

Hefting his shovel, the gravedigger started to scatter dirt over the corpse. "Woulda been convenient, eh, dying in a graveyard?"

"Not tonight," Elisha replied. He wiped his face and

took the bolt. The tip gave a chill tingle, marked with the intention of his death. A small crossbow could be carried loaded, easily hidden beneath a cloak or simply dangling at a horse's pommel, ready for use. Half the barons called for his blood, but they wanted a public execution. This wasn't an attempt at justice but an assassination.

"Come wait in the church—Morag here will send a boy for the duke's men to see you home."

The gravedigger huffed as he tossed in another shovelful.

"Go on," Father Michael prodded.

Morag gave a long look at the corpse, then put up his shovel and stumped off into the streets. A moment later, he could be heard banging on a door. Elisha kept glancing around as he followed the priest. His magical senses warned him, true enough, but they told him little else. A boy ran off in the direction of the castle, the gravedigger stumped back to his task, a pair of dogs snarled and tussled over something they'd found in a cellar hole. With a grand gesture, the priest ushered Elisha into the chilly church with its high, rectangular windows cutting bits of sky through the heavy stone. Father Michael paused to cross himself with a little bow, more like a lady's curtsy, then raised a brow until Elisha followed suit, then he shut the door at their backs with a solid thud.

The priest busied himself lighting a few tapers from the massive spiraled candle kept burning at the Lady altar—a donation from the duke, its curled length representing the number of dead.

"So . . ." Father Michael found a cloth and began to wipe down the altar. "Have you repented yet?"

"Sorry?" Elisha turned from the windows.

"Have you repented of your regicide?" The priest met his gaze, dark eyes reflecting the thin light of candles.

Elisha gripped the bolt a little tighter. Repented of killing a tyrant? At the time, he wanted all the killing to end: the deaths of the common soldiers and of his own friends, held hostage to the tyrant's will—not to mention saving Duke Randall, whom the king wished Elisha to kill. He had not meant to take magic into his own hands to slay the king, but the king's death had brought an end to the battle that caused so much pain. The idea of killing, and the manner of it, still disturbed him, but to regret that the tyrant was dead? "It's not a simple matter, Father."

"It is to God."

"Then I'll take it up with Him."

"Not if you are in Hell," the priest said, bracing his hands on the altar and leaning forward so the flame turned his wrinkles into crevasses. "Not if you are bound there sooner than you think. Myself, I have doubted the rumor of sorcery, believing that any man so devoted to attend to funerals cannot be so . . . diabolical. But if I am mistaken, Barber, then only true repentance can save you."

"I will repent of my actions when God repents of killing babies—or the mothers who would bear them." Elisha turned away, blowing out a breath, but his shoulders ached, the bolt wearing a line into his palm. He had not meant to speak so harshly, and he could sense the stillness of the priest at his back.

"It is not up to you to judge the Lord."

He could leave now—likely the archer was already in the castle, masked and dancing, camouflaged by a hundred others. If Elisha found a mask of his own, he might hide likewise and seek among the company for the one who sought his harm. He jerked at the knock on the door, then relaxed as Lord Robert, one of the duke's staunch retainers, stuck his head in.

"Father? Elisha! What's happened? The boy said somebody'd been shot."

"Nearly." Elisha held up the bolt. "One of the duke's guests, or somebody riding with them, tried to kill me."

"The prince's guests—surely his Grace wouldn't abide anyone who'd shoot his surgeons." Robert crossed himself and ducked his head then gestured Elisha toward the door. "No matter, we're with you now. I've got seven men."

"Think on what I've said, Barber," the priest called after them. "An eternity of torment awaits the sinner down below."

Elisha said nothing as he moved into the night. Ambushed twice on holy ground—the first time for his body, and the second for his soul.

Chapter 2

❖

An hour later, cleaned and clad in borrowed silks and a mask the duke had left for him, Elisha prowled into the ball, to look for his would-be killer. He felt awkward at events like this, which should be reserved for the nobility, worried that his low-born ways would offend some lord or other, in spite of the duke's warm welcome. A banner of the king's arms hung over the main door—a bit premature, given that Prince Alaric had not yet been crowned. Just below that hung a second banner marked with the French fleur-de-lis, a sign of welcome for the prince's foreign guests, at the ball given to impress them with the king-apparent and his solidarity with the duke whose castle hosted them all.

Elisha's mask pressed against his nose and cheeks, but he tried to keep from rubbing at it. Arches supported galleries down both sides of the Great Hall and sheltered the local nobility—knights, ladies, children who took up the benches or played beneath them, leaving the center of the floor clear for dancing all the way up to the raised table where Duke Randall sat with his guests as they finished their meal. Elisha'd been invited to the feast but declined, giving the funeral as his excuse and taking a cold slice of meat pie in the kitchen on his way out. Now, the scent of roasted onions dripping with beef gravy made him regret the choice—except for the company. Likely someone at that very table had hired out for his death.

"Are you the man who killed the king?" whispered a sly voice at Elisha's elbow.

He jerked, turning away from the spectacle of the ball to squint into the murk around him. He ought to have felt anyone's approach, but the accursed itching of his leather mask had distracted him. A small figure stood nearby, shifting one foot to the other, its face concealed by a mask with a grotesque nose. He sensed no menace, but a sort of eagerness instead. Glowering into the flickering torchlight, ignoring the swirling music and laughter around them, Elisha replied, "I am Elisha Barber." Not quite an answer, nor an evasion.

"Very good," purred the unseen mouth. "I speak for someone who has need of you."

"Sorry, I've been hired by the duke." Elisha sent a tendril of his awareness toward the hovering figure, seeking a deeper sense of the emotions behind the mask. Aside from the nervousness clear enough in the little man's movements, he felt little. Chances were he simply did not know enough about the man to interpret him. At least he seemed an unlikely assassin.

"Yes, well, some are prepared to offer you the sort of wealth and standing the duke has little taste for."

Uncomfortable beneath the eerie gaze of the bulbous

mask, Elisha replied, "I've little enough taste for it myself, sir."

The man raised his hands in a placatory gesture. "Think about it, Barber. What do you have a taste for? Women, perhaps?"

At that, Elisha laughed. After what happened with the last woman who interested him, he was hardly looking for another go.

With a darting glance around, the figure leaned closer. "Or perhaps boys? We are open-minded."

Shaking his head, Elisha said, "There's nothing you could offer me—and you've not even told me what you want."

"We understand you are a man of many talents." The man's accented voice reminded Elisha of the speech of the nobles, but his clothing was not so rich, his shoes well-worn. A garter with a little spear-like emblem hung a bit low on his leg beneath an over-sized tunic. "You would earn the gratitude of many," the man said.

A chill shivered Elisha's shoulders, and he crossed his arms, flimsy silk sleeves rubbing on the rich velvet doublet. "Who are you?"

"A messenger." The man gave an eloquent shrug, then the nose suddenly swung to the side. "I should talk with you later," he said, the words a little rushed.

Elisha felt a growing warmth to his left hand and smiled, sensing a friend's approach through the magical link they shared. "I wouldn't bother."

With a tiny bob of acknowledgement, the figure slid away into the darkness as the surgeon Mordecai drew up to Elisha's shoulder, his unmasked face looking pale and strange in contrast with the colorful masks around them. "What's that, Elisha?"

Frowning after the dim cloaked shape, Elisha wondered how the man had recognized him. Then he realized: the duke likely hadn't heard yet about the attempt on his life and had no reason not to point him out. His heart sank. Not only would he never locate his target in this crowd, it was just as likely the archer already knew where he was. In which case, only the crowd kept him from striking again. "I am unused to being a wanted man—aside from those who want me dead."

"I heard what happened in the churchyard." The sense of Mordecai's presence turned a shade concerned. He brushed his hand over Elisha's, and the next words echoed through Elisha's skin. *As for this, you've worked a powerful magic, the sort that makes the lords take notice, one way and another.*

"His master seems ready to offer me whatever I want, in exchange for unspecified services. I thought the nobles hated us."

With a wrinkle of his graying eyebrows, Mordecai replied without sound, *"They both hate and envy us, and more than a few depend upon the power of a magus."* He gave a nod toward the head table. Beyond the refuse of a rich meal, Randall, the Duke of Dunbury sat listening to his guest of honor. On the other side sat his wife, Duchess Allyson, a highly respected magus who had loaned her power to that impossible healing a month ago when he had stitched Mordecai's hand back on, rejoining flesh and bone and creating the bond between himself and his mentor.

Elisha glanced away from the dark-haired duchess to the young, self-declared king, Prince Alaric, who held forth on God knew what despite the evident irritation in the duke's posture. From the corner of his eye, he caught a glimpse of the lady who sat beside Alaric: Brigit, Alaric's betrothed. Elisha drew a deep breath, and let it out with a quiver of pain. His right cheek warmed as if her hand rested there, atop the mark her mother had placed in that same spot when he was a boy; had placed with the infinite wonder of her outstretched wing, before the fire claimed her.

With a sigh, Mordecai shook his head. "Many cures I've made, but that you must heal for yourself," he said aloud, breaking the contact of their skin.

Hoping his thoughts had not been too obvious, Elisha asked suddenly, "Do you know why they burned her mother?"

At this, Mordecai's eyebrows rose. "You don't know? Suppose not," he answered his own question. "She'd been the queen's lady in waiting. Queen died, king found her out, a witch so close to his wife."

"King Hugh, again."

"Really don't know politics, do you?" asked Mordecai dryly. "Best start learning, or you'll not last in this world."

Breathing in the scents of gravy and good wine, Elisha admitted, "It has its attractions, but I don't know that I want to be a part of this world."

"Not sure you'll have the option." The surgeon's dark, damp gaze settled gravely on Elisha's face. "Take care."

"Don't I always?"

Elisha felt the answering ripple of laugher in the air

around him. He could not feel most men this way, but since he had healed Mordecai, they shared a bond beyond even those of other magi. Not that Elisha had been one long enough to know what to expect. Still, his sensitivity extended beyond his skin, and he felt someone approaching, an unfamiliar touch. He flashed back to the little man in the bulbous mask, who had bid him a hasty farewell before Mordecai arrived. The little man was a magus—one both sensitive enough to feel the surgeon's approach and powerful enough to conceal his own nature. Elisha had dismissed the messenger too soon in his eagerness to seek out an assassin instead. He spun away from Mordecai, scanning the crowd around them, but the little man was nowhere to be seen.

"That emissary, he was a witch," Elisha murmured, but Mordecai cut him off with a gesture, and they turned as one to the newcomer.

Clad in a light gown of blue that neither emphasized nor concealed her ample bosom, the woman wore the mask of a bird, done in painted leather complete with exotic feathers twisting back over her dark hair.

Both men bowed, and the lady nodded in acknowledgement then held out her hand, palm down, to Elisha, who sucked in a quick breath. He felt the stirring of Mordecai's silent chuckle, and Elisha reddened beneath his mask.

He took the lady's hand on his palm, with the lightest possible touch, and bowed over it, blowing a tiny breath across her knuckles in the acceptable substitute for a kiss he was not worthy to bestow. Through the contact, he felt curiosity, attraction, and irritation in a strange jumble. Frowning, Elisha slipped his hand from hers. "To what do we owe the honor, my lady?" he asked, using the plural despite the fact that her attention was clearly all his own.

"My father speaks so highly of you, Elisha Barber, and I have cause to wonder why. I've not been home two days now, yet I've heard more about you than the rest of the battle and all his retainers combined. Why so?"

Elisha swallowed, leaned away from her, and shot a worried glance at Mordecai. This was Lady Rosalynn, the duke's daughter, whose denunciation by Prince Alaric had brought on the battle.

"*You seem safe enough now*," Mordecai said in a touch. "*At least from certain death.*" With the tiniest of smiles, he bowed his head. "My lady, if you'll excuse me."

When she curtseyed his dismissal, Mordecai went off with a lively step and left a wake of humor in the air.

Bristling, Elisha turned back to her. In his moment of inattention, she had slipped the mask from her face, and wiped sweat from below her eyes with two careful fingers. Rather he assumed it was sweat until he caught the flash of wetness in her dark eyes. Every line of her plump features showed her broken heart. How long could he look on her without his own becoming clear?

"I saved the life of the Earl of Blackmere, my lady, during the battle, when I was still in the king's service."

With a rough gesture, she pulled her mask back into place, folding her hands together. "Yes, I heard that story, from Lord Robert, in fact. He seems vastly amused by the fact that he held a sword to your throat for mistakenly thinking you would kill the earl. Now, he acts as if you are the best of friends, despite the fact that you are a barber and he is of noble birth. It was he who told me where to find you. None of which explains why my father should take such a liking to you, unless the rumors are true? That you are responsible for King Hugh's death, and thus my father's deliverance?"

She had her father's rounded features and shape, together with her mother's taller stature and a prattling tone Elisha could blame on neither parent. Perhaps it was no wonder Alaric had determined to put her aside. Of course, Rosalynn could never compete with Brigit in any case, no more than Elisha himself could compete with Alaric for Brigit's affections.

"Some rumors are more true than others, my lady," he said, tucking the silk cord that bound his cuff back into his sleeve.

She made a sharp noise, and the beak of the bird mask lifted as if it might poke his eye out. "I see. You are awfully brash for a low-born living off a duke's sufferance. Tell me, are you not enjoying my father's generosity?"

Elisha replied, "I am grateful for my position here, my lady."

"But I didn't see you at the head table, and I've not noticed you dancing."

He could hardly explain to Rosalynn, of all people, why he couldn't bring himself to dine at a table with the royal couple, so he pounced instead on the second query. "As you say, my lady, I am low-born. This music doesn't suit me, and I don't know the dances of court."

Tilting her bird's head, Rosalynn lifted her shoulders.

"I know them, but I don't care for them, either. The past few months, I've been at my brother's estate near Lincoln. They've got no proper musicians there but have to depend upon the local fiddlers."

Heavens, Elisha thought, nobles forced to dance to common music.

"If I can get them to change the tune, will you dance with me?"

"My lady, I'm not a fit partner for—"

"You are favored by my father, and that will see you through tonight, so long as you do not take advantage." As if she had crushed her sadness with sudden strength, Rosalynn thumped a fist onto her hip. "I have a mind to cause a stir for this king and all his fancy entourage."

Hiking up her flowing skirts, Rosalynn crossed the floor in rapid, manly strides, though the view he had of her was anything but masculine. She cut this way and that among the dancers, certain to be noticed although she took care not to interrupt any of the sets. Her mother spotted her from the head table and got a familiar little frown upon her face; the young prince turned slightly more pale but did not turn his head. And there was Brigit. If he danced with Rosalynn, the stir would be more than sufficient. He considered slipping off into the shadows, perhaps even retreating to his little chamber near the castle infirmary.

Then he thought of the tears in Rosalynn's eyes. She wanted to be daring, to dance with a peasant at her father's feast and pretend the gilded presence of the prince meant as little to her as hers did to him. During the battle, Elisha had the impression that theirs had been a match of power, not of love. Still, the prince had no right to wound her. He had no right to get his father into the battle that had left King Hugh dead. The younger prince pressed his own claim over that of his elder brother, Thomas, since finding evidence that Thomas had plotted their father's death. Faced with a choice between a liar and a traitor, Duke Randall supported the liar. But how would Alaric make any better king than his father, if he would break a vow and start a war over a woman? If this was politics, Elisha wanted little part in it.

Across the hall Rosalynn spoke earnestly to the lead musician, seeking a way to assuage her grief. Elisha had not got far in the search for his attempted assassin, and the crowd, for now, meant safety. Straightening his finery, Elisha strode over to meet her.

Chapter 3

—◆—

"**My lady?**" said Elisha, offering his hand as he had seen the lords do.

Rosalynn accepted, tightening her grip. The decorous dances of the nobility allowed only the slightest contact, never with the fingers closed about the lady's hand. The dance she had requested—and which the lead musician ran through slowly again for her approval—required a firmer grasp.

Elisha let her turn about his hand and lead him to the now empty floor. He hadn't danced in years and never in such company as now tittered and rumbled at the edges of the hall. He hoped it wouldn't be a disaster. "I'm not a very good dancer, my lady," he began, "I've no wish to embarrass you."

The beak of her mask turned sharply toward him, so that he pulled back from its tip. "Embarrass me, Barber? How can I be more humiliated before this company than I have already been, to see my betrothed sitting beside that? Don't worry over me—I'm for the nunnery after this. God is the only one left who'll have me."

Raw hurt flowed from her hand into his. He pushed back the foreign feelings, withdrawing his awareness until he barely felt her hand in his as she tugged him out, her steps determined and ungraceful. If the dance was a disaster, it mightn't be all his fault.

At the head table, the duke looked on, a vague smile playing about his lips, while the prince, unable now to avoid it, watched over the rim of his upraised goblet as he drained his wine. Brigit reached out and slipped her pale, slender hand about his elbow, leaning into him, her lips close to his ear. The party of Frenchmen, come for the new king's coronation and wedding, watched politely— not understanding what they saw.

They reached the center of the floor, and Rosalynn made an effort to draw herself up. Elisha drummed his fingers briefly on his ever-present pouch, full of emergency medical needs. Then he spun her to face him, clasping right hands to begin the dance. He grinned, and through the contact, he sent a quiet wave of resolve, and the sort of anger that lifted a chin, that made a deep breath the more enlivening. He tried to be subtle, so that she might think it was his smile that encouraged her, or the starting beat of the music that sparked her back to life. Indeed, if she were determined in her melancholy, he could not have moved her, not without her willingness to go along. But Rosalynn was willing. She wanted this little revenge, and his nudge gave her the strength to draw that breath and touch her toe to the floor, poised to begin.

A hand-drum gave the rapid beat, then the rebec player began. The dance had several forms, including lines, or circles, of couples, depending on how many joined in. Elisha and Rosalynn danced alone, forming a circle of their own.

From the moment the music started, his gaze never left her face. Would Brigit notice? Would she care? It didn't matter: he could imagine that she did.

They skipped forward, trotted backward, pulled together and apart. Rosalynn's skirts swirled about her as she spun a circle of her own.

When they came together, Elisha hesitated. For the second verse, they should take each other about the waist, repeating the series—an intimacy casually undertaken by his people and steadfastly forbidden by hers.

Rosalynn spun back to him, her arm slipping about his waist, her shoulder nestling against his own.

Again, he followed her lead, starting to pray under his breath that the duke would take it all in fun. He might have more than one enemy at the head table by the time the dance was done. His hand settled on her hip.

As they danced backward, she laughed aloud. As they pulled together, even closer, a tear trickled down past her ear.

They twirled apart, clapping with the music, and returned to the center, both hands clasped this time, arms stretched across one another in a near embrace. This time, they pivoted at each change, performing all the steps in reverse. Listening, Elisha caught the trill of music which signaled the last pattern, and he released their left hands, turning her against him and dropping down on one knee.

Startled, Rosalynn nearly lost her balance but landed

neatly on his knee, her head thrown back, laughing louder now, wiping at her cheeks as she caught her breath.

Elisha, too, gasped, his heart pounding in the rhythm of the dance. Someone applauded, and others joined in. Shaking, Rosalynn clung to his hand, her fingers kneading his.

Elisha drew her to her feet, rising along with her and bowing over their hands. He led her away, knowing without probing, that if he let her go, she would collapse to the floor in a quaking puddle of grief.

Elisha brought her quickly through the crowd and shook off her hand. Rosalynn fled into the darker hall beyond. He hoped no one else had noticed her tears. Her revenge would not be so rich if it were tempered by other people's pity. Including his own.

"You dance with passion," murmured a voice nearby, and Elisha turned to find a tall man tucked into the shadowed arch. He wore a tunic that seemed stitched of rags and embellished with soil, complete to a simple mask of cloth that draped his face, holes torn out over his eyes.

"Desperation, more like," Elisha replied. "If I dance fast enough, I won't fall on my face." The stranger held one arm over his stomach as if it ached, and Elisha noted that he'd even wrapped his palms with rags. The set of his shoulders and the lift of his chin showed his noble bearing, or Elisha might have truly believed him a beggar. This garb didn't have enough layers to conceal much of a weapon, but still . . . Elisha unfurled his awareness, sensing exhaustion and fear in the stranger—at war with desire. For Rosalynn? She would be as surprised to hear it as he was surprised to find it in such a costume. "An excellent disguise, my lord."

The man drew a sharp breath, his eyes flaring, his glance darting about before returning to Elisha's masked face. "It should be, for what I paid." It sounded like a jest but for the grim tone of his voice.

"Not so much, I hope."

The stranger let out a sound somewhere between a laugh and a cry. "By my faith, it was a princely sum."

A group of revelers, singing loudly, stumbled through the arch toward the yard beyond, and the stranger drew back from them then plunged into the darkness himself, leaving Elisha frowning after him. With his regal bearing and woeful garb, the stranger felt like Elisha's opposite, as if they had traded places, leaving the nobleman masquerading as a beggar while the barber played a lord.

A flourish of horns turned him from the arch to find the French delegation rising, filing carefully around the table. Each man of the party, and the two women, wore fixed smiles. The lords went unmasked, but their parti-colored gowns were of rich brocade with fleur-de-lis shimmering in gold on one side. The same symbol the messenger had worn, though his was woven coarse and barely recognizable. Elisha scanned their group of attendants as the lords approached from the floor—he did not see the mask or tunic, but one among them had a drooping stocking, that garter-ribbon still in want of adjustment. Elisha sucked on his teeth. The French? Just to speak of hiring out to them was dangerous. No wonder the little man tried to hide his identity. Elisha sought the source of one danger only to stumble upon another.

"My lord prince—and soon, may we hope, the proud king of our sister nation," pronounced the leader.

"They must really mean it, if they're not speaking French," muttered a young man on the other side of Elisha's pillar, only to win a cuff from his mother. He scowled but subsided.

"In token of our friendship, we bring you this." The man bowed stiffly and stuck out a hand, but the bearer hesitated and had to be waved forward. A smile from one of the women turned briefly genuine, as if she were amused by the whole affair, but Brigit's eyes narrowed at them from her side of the high table.

The servant knelt, holding up the offering, and the lord swept off an embroidered velvet sash to reveal a miniature church complete with a tower and angels, gleaming with gold, sparkling with silver. At its heart rested a crystal vessel, though Elisha could not make out the contents at such a distance.

"A relic of the blessed Saint Louis, to guide you upon your reign." They all bowed again.

Alaric stared down at the gaudy thing, his jaw tight. He answered in French, a fluent little speech, in which Elisha caught a reference to the sainted king Edward the Confessor. Saint Louis had been king of France only fifty years before, and now was beatified, but Edward's cult had been venerated for hundreds of years. The rest of the high table tried to conceal their amusement, but the French ambassador's face seemed rigid. The lady beside him gave a deep curtsey—along with a view down her low neckline no doubt—and answered with a suspicious lightness in her voice. Elisha did not need to understand her words to know what else was on offer.

"Thank you, I'm sure," said Brigit, pushing up from her chair. "It is a lovely gift and a fine addition to our chapel." She emphasized "our," and the French lady rose, recoiling a little with a swish of her silken headdress.

"Another dance!" cried the duke. "Please. Our pages shall parade the relic so that all may see the generosity of our neighbors." He urged two boys to take up the cushion and make a slow passage down the table, the bishop, as well, rose to join the procession.

Distantly Elisha heard a new tune, one of the slow and courtly dances played toward the end of an evening, and the soft shuffle of slippers as the assembled nobles resumed their fun. A gaggle of children emerged around their parents' skirts and ankles and rushed up to view the saint's bone in its tiny gilded hall. Alaric gazed at the French lady a moment too long before Brigit seized his hand, and Elisha chuckled. Brigit hadn't learned from the experience of Lady Rosalynn if she were expecting faith from her prince.

The duke's hand settled on his shoulder, with an eddy of concern.

Elisha immediately began, "Your Grace, I'm sorry, she asked me, and I didn't—"

Much to his dismay, the duke laughed. "I've not come to rip you limb from limb, Elisha, you can calm yourself about that. I'm only hoping we can settle the French and the prince without anyone having to invade." He gave a sigh, then glanced up at Elisha. "Saint Louis is the patron saint of Paris. It wasn't a gift, it was a threat."

"My guess was they hoped it to be a nuptial gift, but not for Brigit."

"Some things a man doesn't need a knowledge of French to understand." Then his glance turned speculative. "So what do you think of our Rosalynn?"

Flushed from both the dancing and now the question, Elisha managed, "She seems pleasant enough."

"Pleasant?" The duke looked vexed. "From the way you danced, you might've thought her a ravishing beauty."

Elisha hesitated, wondering how to remove the insult.

"Don't be so concerned, Barber, I'm not out for blood, truly." The duke exerted a gentle pressure, prodding Elisha into motion away from the crowd into an open-air yard. "In fact, I enjoyed it. I little imagined Rosalynn would dance again, never mind with such . . . exuberance. She's been in a black mood since . . ." His gesture completed the sentence. "I thought the time at her brother's would help her get over it and give me time to sort out Hugh and Alaric, besides. Now look what it's all come to."

Elisha slipped off his mask, rubbing the sweat from his face. "I don't follow you, Your Grace."

He tapped his fingers together, then sighed. "Hugh and I were cousins. It's why he advanced me during the confusion after King Edward's death." He crossed himself briefly at the mention of the old king. "Hugh needed those around him who'd support his claim to the throne."

"Cousins? Good God, I am sorry." Elisha felt he was still back in the hall, dizzy with dancing.

"Sorry you killed him? Don't be. Someone had to cut down the treacherous bastard. I'm only sorry it was not I who did the deed."

This time, Elisha held his tongue. The night air chilled his skin, despite the stillness of June all around them. Lately, he felt cold all the time, indoors or out. Ever since the day he had invited Death into himself, and it had not entirely left him.

"In fact," the duke continued, "I amazed Alaric right then when I failed to take the crown for myself, by right of arms aside from the ties of blood we shared." He shrugged. "So here comes Alaric to be sure I support his claim over Thomas's."

On second thought, perhaps Rosalynn had gotten her conversational style from her father—neither of them seemed to require his participation, only his attention.

"It's all about alliances, who can summon the strongest allies." He cocked his head to study Elisha sidelong. "Have they started in on you yet?"

Elisha had almost forgotten the small man in the ugly mask. "Someone sent a messenger, offering wealth and power."

"Not what you want?" The duke smiled. "Someone'll find out what you *do* want, Barber, and offer you that. All these factions will want you for themselves."

"What for, Your Grace? As you say, I'm just a barber."

"Not just. You killed the king, apparently by magic, though few were close enough to know the truth, and every tavern and brothel from here to the border will be abuzz with stories. Every soldier you ever healed will claim himself a miracle—or a curse. Oh, no, Elisha Barber. As far as the barons are concerned, you are the most dangerous man alive, and you'd do well to remember that. They just can't be sure what you'll do next."

Duke Randall, too, wanted something from him, something more than his medical skill, and Elisha regarded him warily. "Without the talisman, I'm just a man."

"A magus, still, and the talisman is nothing without someone who has the insight and wherewithal to use it."

That stung. Insight had nothing to do with the desperation which brought him to kill. Elisha walked a few paces away, arms folded against the chill. The talisman—the sorry remains of a tragedy for which he was at least partially responsible—had lent him the power of Death, the power to kill the king. But when he woke from the long exhaustion which had overcome him after such a spell, the talisman was gone, stolen by the woman he loved. He meant to get it back, before the innocent life it represented could be twisted again to harm.

The duke pursued him but stopped short, a soothing note creeping into his voice. "I know you don't like to be reminded, Elisha, but you must face the consequences of what you've done."

"What," Elisha snapped back, "will they hang me again?"

"Holy Rood, that's not what I meant. You stand there, swathing yourself in guilt that you, the healer, have taken a life. Have done, Elisha. Men die, you know better than most, and sometimes men must be killed so that other men can live." He closed the distance, coming to face Elisha in the moonlight. "You've done no more than a thousand others in your place, but the way you did it was nothing short of spectacular."

The word took Elisha by surprise atop the other tensions of the night—as if he and the duke had never understood each other. "If you think that, then you're no better than the man I killed," Elisha retorted.

The duke slapped him, hard and fast, his hand drawing back as if the blow had stung his palm, then retreated two steps immediately. "Sweet Jesus, Elisha, I am sorry."

Elisha reeled at the blow, no more than his due for speaking too freely to nobility. He'd been expecting to offend someone—just not the man who presented himself as Elisha's protector. Elisha's fingers trailed over the new ache. His jaw clenched. "You are all the same. Sitting at your head table, looking down on the rest of us, smiling kindly and ready to strike."

Dropping his head, the duke revealed a bald patch that winked in the moonlight. "I am sorry, but I know that changes nothing. Before you, I had never considered that a common man could be worthy of my friendship. It's hard to overcome the training of a lifetime." He put up his hands, his face drawn tight. "Please do not mistake me. Little more than an accident of birth has placed me higher than you on the chain of being. The money, the land, confer on us a chance to be educated, to think beyond our daily bread—nobility is not about blood, it's about being at liberty to raise your eyes from the dirt at your feet and see the sky."

Unwillingly, still stinging, Elisha understood. The first day he had come to Dunbury, he climbed the broken steeple which became his lodging and gazed out over a landscape he had never been able to see before, a place of valleys and towers, not of ditches and walls.

"We travel, we study, we take up art and music because some servant or another will provide our meals.

Most of my peers think we've earned it by the blood of our ancestors." He gave a harsh laugh. "You and I both know, if it's blood that counts, then your ancestors have spent a lot more of it than mine. All I mean to say is that I don't know how to be your friend—which makes what I would ask of you that much harder." He ran his hands through what remained of his hair.

"And what is it you want from me?" Elisha asked, squaring his shoulders.

The duke let out another sigh, then a weary chuckle. "I want you to marry my daughter."

Chapter 4

Elisha blinked, then said, "I don't think I heard you right."

The duke laughed again, with more humor this time. "Oh, I believe you did. I've never seen anyone look so dumbfounded since I told Allyson I knew she was a magus, and I didn't care."

Dry-mouthed, Elisha repeated, "You want me to marry your daughter."

"Just so," said the duke, then his smile slipped away, and moonlight etched the lines a little deeper around his eyes. "Not that you'll be willing," he said. "Not now."

Elisha plopped himself onto one of the benches. For a moment, he even forgot that he was cold. "But why?"

"A variety of reasons, really." With a half-shrug, the duke held his hands at his back. "Because I've seen you work, both medicine and magic. You're a good man, Elisha, you have a kind of integrity I don't see very often. For damn sure, Prince Alaric hasn't got it. As I told you before, I want you on my side, not just because I know what you are capable of but also because I know what you are not capable of. Yes, you killed a man that day, but how many could you have killed, Elisha? Ten, a hundred, a thousand?"

Elisha wanted to say that he would have killed at least one more—Prince Alaric himself—but he wasn't sure it was the truth.

"From a practical standpoint, you'd argue that I'll have a terrible time finding someone else to marry her." He flopped his hands into a gesture of despair. "It's true. The only men still eager for her hand are those with little to offer in return—they want to bind themselves to me. They act as if I should be glad to have her taken off my hands." A suggestion of anger returned to his voice. "She might go to a convent, others have, in her position, but I would like to see her happy. There's another thing, too," the duke said, his hands gripped together almost in prayer. "Both princes will be courting your power, and there are others in the kingdom eager to cause the sort of havoc they will see in what you've done. Someone has already begun bargaining for you."

"And someone else has tried to kill me." He briefly told the duke about the scene in the churchyard.

Randall's head bowed as he listened, then he murmured, "You are a valuable weapon, a powerful threat. Do they kill you for your own sake, to take the power from me, or as justice for Hugh?"

Elisha met his gaze once more, expelled a breath. "But I only did it to save my friends—he would have killed them all. I don't kill people, I heal them."

"I know." The duke's smile twisted. "I know that, Elisha, but they don't, and they will not believe you when you tell them. They are so used to lying that they can no longer hear the truth. If they can't buy you, they will kill you."

The words echoed in the night and inside Elisha's skull, redoubling until they filled his awareness. The cut at his shoulder, slim though it was, stung in mute reminder, and Elisha sighed, "Then I'm a dead man."

Lowering himself carefully to his knees, Randall looked up into Elisha's face. "As my servant, they'll kill you—someone has already tried. As my friend, they'll simply hurt you more. These men will imagine I won't pursue them over such a matter. But if you were my son, well, they already know I'd go to war over an insult to my daughter." Gazing at him steadily, in the posture of a supplicant, the duke said, "I would have you as my son, Elisha Barber, but I would wish for you a better father."

Still steady, he reached out his hand and lightly touched Elisha's.

A wave of sincerity and hope and despair washed over Elisha. Through that contact, the duke laid himself open, his fears and needs warring with a genuine respect that crept into Elisha's skin. Regret colored the contact, and a fierce fatherly love. Just for a moment, Elisha saw himself through the duke's eyes, dancing with Rosalynn, and the swell of joy took his breath away. The duke feared that she might never recover, and to see her dance with such abandon—he knew it was born of jealousy, but still the vision gave him hope. Except when Mordecai had shared a vision, Elisha had never seen so clearly through another's eyes. Perhaps living with Allyson had clarified the duke's sensitivity.

Then, overlaid with the image of Rosalynn, another woman danced, a small, round girl full of life and love, in the arms of a handsome lord. In a moment, she had gone pale and drifted away like a mist of sadness. A sister who had thrown herself to her death over a lover lost. A secret from all but a very few. For a moment, yet another face flashed before Elisha's view, that of his own brother, Nathaniel, who felt responsible for his infant's death and had believed his wife, Helena, dead along with the child. Nathaniel had killed himself, and Elisha concealed it to save his brother's memory from the stigma of suicide. Elisha swallowed around the lump in his throat.

The touch withdrew, and the duke's eyes flitted over Elisha's face, frowning slightly, as if he might have felt in return some of Elisha's own memory.

Elisha snapped his attention back to the matter at hand: Nathaniel was dead and buried, his widow was healing in her own way, and as for his baby, Elisha still must make amends. The first step would be to take back the talisman he had lost, the small pot containing the stillborn child's head. Before Mordecai confirmed that the mystical Bone of Luz did not exist—the Bone said to lead to resurrection on the Day of Judgment—Elisha had hoped he might use the Bone to bring back the stillborn child. That was before he knew he could perform magic and the horrors it might cause if he did. Death was not a thing to be given or taken lightly. If the priest down in the village would condemn him for taking a life, how much more so would Elisha be damned for giving back a life that God had claimed?

Behind them, the festivities had risen to dull roar of

enjoyment and drink, the king's retainers succored by the duke's wine. It seemed unbelievable that Elisha could matter to such people—better that he retreated to his patients, to the grubby streets of that city where he could not see the sky, leaving the kingdom to its new tyrant. He imagined himself grumbling as he used to do, sharing the complaints of his neighbors over a bit of ale, powerless beyond that limited space.

"I'll think about what you've said, Your Grace," Elisha answered softly.

"Thank you," said Randall. "For that and for the dance." With a sigh and a creak of his leather boots the duke got to his feet. "Time to bid goodnight to my guests."

Elisha, too, rose, smoothing his palms over the fine linen of his trousers as the duke moved back toward the hall.

Standing alone in the moonlight, Elisha's mind reeled. Everything the duke told him sounded reasonable, and the contact they shared only re-enforced his belief in the duke's sincerity. The slap still stung, but Elisha should not have taken his own guilt out on the duke, not when his benefactor was forced to entertain the man responsible for his daughter's misery. Both the duke and the prince struggled to maintain an air of civil friendship. The self-declared king had to cement his authority before his brother came home from the north, leading an army—whatever army would follow him.

Politics. Elisha snorted. Perhaps he should pack his surgical tools and sneak off into the night, disappearing back into the obscurity from which he had been torn and thrust into battle. He turned reluctantly back to the Great

Hall. Returning to the head table, Duke Randall greeted the royal couple and made some remarks that were hard to hear over the crowd. Elisha edged up closer. He had to figure out what Brigit had done with the talisman, and she surely wouldn't tell him outright. Perhaps the drink and the company would soften her defenses, and she would let something slip if he could get close enough.

"If you really loved him, Your Grace," bawled a young lord as he swayed to plant his elbow on the table, "you'd execute his father's killer."

The room grew quiet, the French ambassadors suddenly keen.

Duke Randall's round face hardened. "My lord Mortimer, a moment later and I should have killed the king myself—or been killed by him. I challenged King Hugh to personal combat, and my champion prevailed."

It was not quite a lie but certainly a view of the events that Elisha had never considered.

"You submitted a barber as your champion? You expect us to believe that?"

"The brute Goliath was leveled by a child with a stone."

"A child who later rose to be king!" Mortimer lurched forward, swaying against the table, out of the grip of those who might protect him.

Lord Robert and two of the guards leaned close, hands upon their swords, but Duke Randall waved them back, spreading his hands in a conciliatory gesture. "His Royal Highness has expressed his wish to leave the battle behind us and let matters rest. Given that you, Lord

Mortimer, are his companion and a member of his household, I suggest you do the same."

"To let a barber strike down a king, and live to tell of it? Hah! No wonder they're thinking they can plant their dead on English ground," Mortimer exclaimed, waving his arm toward the fancy reliquary. With his wild swing, the golden miniature pitched from the table and smashed onto the stone. The French leapt up with a burst of fluttering words.

With a desperate lunge, Alaric intercepted Mortimer and grasped the back of his neck, whispering as he thrust the man back into the arms of his companions to be led away. Then he gave another little speech to the French, this one more gentle, as he gestured toward the bishop, priest, and pages who reverently collected the bits of crystal. The incident left them all looking as sour as Elisha's stomach felt.

Duke Randall embraced Prince Alaric, who beamed his most charming smile. Then the duke bowed low over Brigit's hand, before the prince escorted her away. Everything that happened up there had another meaning, or three, a mummer's show Elisha could not hope to understand. The best way he could get on in this world of nobles would be to get out of it, taking up his tools in a distant town where no one had heard his name and neither assassin nor benefactor would bother to hunt him down.

But first, his brother's child must be laid to rest. Shaking off Mortimer's demands for his execution, Elisha damped his awareness, his very presence, down to nothing.

He passed a couple kissing in an alcove, their masks resting on a nearby bench, and casually took up one of the stifling things to slip over his face. As he walked, he cast a slight deflection, calling upon the law of opposites to send out the idea of his absence. He made it small and local, not wanting to arouse too much suspicion. Elisha merged into the crowd as it departed through various arches and came to where the royal party said their farewells and good-nights.

"I'll need my horse in the morning—early," Alaric was saying to the duke's steward.

"As you wish, Your Majesty."

Brigit smiled thinly as the man bowed away from them, then she remarked, "I thought you would accompany me to the lodge, my lord." These last words were a purr so sweet that Elisha knew she was furious. Pregnancy often heightened a woman's emotions, and he wondered if she were feeling the effects and if her lord had noticed.

"Randall's support is a good start," Alaric responded, "but I have many other barons to meet, not to mention the Commons. And as you see, I'll have to keep the various factions from killing one another if I'm to bring them together in my support. The French wish to pay their respects at Canterbury, and I'm hard-pressed to make excuses *not* to go with them. Come, darling, I'll escort you to your room."

A small cadre of knights and ladies fell in with them, allowing Elisha to dodge Brigit's glance. "Those are not the only allies we must court," she replied, maintaining her overly pleasant demeanor. "And a word from the king could win them over."

"I'm sure a word from the future queen will be sufficient." He, too, smiled, but fiercely. "The king has many obligations."

"Not least of which are his promises to me."

"I will be there as soon as I might," he replied firmly, then added, "I have no wish to be separated from you any longer than I must." Alaric caressed her shoulder as they stopped before a door, the knights and ladies separating, leaving Elisha lurking beyond the light of the last torch. Brigit glanced around, frowning, but Alaric's palm moved up to cup her chin. "Do what you can and assure your friends that I'll do what I can, when the time is right."

"Of course, my lord," she said, accepting his light kiss. "Let us talk again—very soon."

"As soon as I may." Alaric drew back. "I'm leaving early for London. Take the carriage when you go to the lodge."

Her expression turned sour. "The carriage will take forever."

"You are the lady who would be queen." He touched the tip of her nose, as if admonishing a child, and Elisha briefly thought she would snap off the end of his finger. "If you must go, then you must go safely and with all due privilege. Sleep well." Alaric gave a slight bow and turned with his guards to the room across the hall—the duke's own chamber, given up for the occasion.

"What, should I fear bandits, my lord?" she called after him.

Alaric's back went rigid, his jaw knotted, and Brigit nearly smiled. "Don't worry, my lord, I shall take every precaution." He shoved through the door and let it thump to behind him.

Brigit stared after him while the ladies made pretenses of yawning or stroking down their skirts. This little power play, though made of riddles, gave Elisha a hint of satisfaction. Brigit may have won her place, but all was not as settled as it seemed. She lifted her head at last. "Attend me." She swept into her room with the ladies in parade and the last one shut the door. All due privilege indeed, but Elisha could hardly deflect the eyes and ears of half a dozen women in such close quarters in order to follow her and perhaps learn more.

Elisha turned away, at last, for his own bed in the dispensary, alongside the infirmary. This business about the lodge seemed a promising lead. Brigit apparently planned to meet with her supporters, other witches, from what she said. Yet Alaric didn't deem her contacts important enough for his own presence. With that on top of his obvious interest in the woman the French were apparently offering, it was no wonder Brigit was furious. The important thing was she would be away from her prince and in the company of friends—Elisha's as well as her own. If she took the carriage as commanded, Elisha could even be there ahead of her, to search for the talisman and prepare to confront her more directly if need be, if he could figure out where she was going.

He had not gone far past the Hall when a quiet step fell in with his, and Elisha stopped and turned swiftly, his guard returning with the sting in his shoulder.

The little Frenchman stood there, once again in his mask and tunic.

"If you're trying not to be recognized, sir, you'll have to take more care with your garters." Elisha pointed, and the man's exaggerated mask aimed downward, sagging. Then he reached up and slipped off the mask, sliding back his hair.

A bit younger than Elisha, with hair the color of flax and an angular face, the Frenchman squared his shoulders. "You are in danger here, too alone."

"I don't want what you're offering, nor will I go to Paris." Elisha started moving again, and the messenger caught up.

"You do not know what I offer! Nor for whom." The accent grew suddenly stronger, the voice sharper, and Elisha slowed unwillingly. The man looked around quickly and drew closer, his face in the weak light of the distant torches looking sickly, his eyes too dark. "The voyage of the ambassador was a fortunate timing for me. It is not on the king's behalf that I ask, but for the rest of us."

"If you're going to ask me to kill your king, then best go now," Elisha snapped, adding an edge of menace, but the little man stumbled, his hands reaching, his breath caught. "Good God," Elisha breathed, "not really."

The messenger looked around again. "Do not speak so, I beg of you." He swallowed and shook himself.

Elisha, too, lowered his voice. "I spoke in jest. Or rather, I thought I did."

Steeling himself, the man knit his fingers together. "Is it permitted to talk another way?" Elisha must have looked confused, for the other extended his hand a little, inviting contact, then finished the gesture, placing his fingertips lightly on Elisha's hand. He could feel the effort of will to craft the words, the sense of another language running underneath, before the man spoke at last, skin to skin. "*Our king is gone strange. I am of his household, and I see many things.*"

"*My own country has enough trouble without adding yours.*" Elisha suppressed his next thought, that Alaric, as king, would be trouble again, even without Brigit at his side. Unless Elisha were willing to become an assassin in truth, there was nothing he could do about that.

"*Our king will make trouble for yours, if he suspects weakness. The ambassador will tell him all, and already he has agents here to find his chance.*"

"*I'm not the one you should be warning.*" Elisha moved as if to shake him off, but the messenger hung on, coming with him almost to the door of his room.

"*He has been killing us. We cannot see how he can know who we are—we have done nothing, made no act, and yet the arrests come, or simply the knife.*" The man still shielded his emotions from the contact, but couldn't hide his fear. His dark eyes searched Elisha's face.

"*Then what do you want from me? I will kill no more kings.*"

"*Help us to come here. Help us to know who to trust.*"

Elisha almost laughed. "*Oh, you have come to the wrong man.*"

The French magus shook his head. "*When I came to you, I pushed you, to see what kind of man you are. You have committed a great act, and with a great magic, yet you live at liberty. It seems this country may be more favorable than our own land.*"

Elisha's own position was precarious, but he might

know others who would help, if he had the freedom to think without worrying that he would betray his thoughts. *"My room is here. We can talk in the air."*

He pushed open the door to usher the stranger inside, the messenger giving a little nod as he stepped through, then a horrific shriek as a pair of blades hacked through him, blood spattering from his lips as the sound died.

Chapter 5

❖

The messenger collapsed backward as the blades tore out again, grating on bone. Elisha caught him, swinging with him toward the floor. The shriek reverberated against the stone, and a voice called out. The attacker moved swiftly, metal gleaming, knives shone against the bare skin of his chest. He glanced down. "Shit." Then he lunged with a strange creak and clatter.

Elisha scrambled sideways, carrying the Frenchman with him, and the weapon slid along his arm, thunking again into the messenger's chest. The messenger jerked and shuddered against him as the blades ripped free again.

"Shit." The attacker lurched into motion, running, blood dripping, back down the corridor Elisha had just come from.

"Hallo! What happened? Holy Mother!" yelped the night attendant emerging from the infirmary.

"A man attacked us. He ran for the Great Hall—shirtless and bloody. Stop him and send help. Go, go!" Elisha shouted as he rolled the Frenchman to the floor, already stripping off his own doublet and tunic to staunch the wounds. He held the magus on his side, pressing the silk against the pulsing wounds at his back. The man's hand groped up his arm, clinging. Elisha opened all his senses, searching for the wounds with practiced hands and the awareness of the magi. Nine blows penetrated the man's chest. Elisha brought to bear all his anatomical knowledge, following each blow almost as if he moved with the weapon. Five thrusts cut the man's heart as if slicing it for a feast.

Blood gushed over Elisha's hand, soaking the shirt. Too much, too fast. The magus's grip tightened, burrowing into his flesh, and Elisha stilled. A burst of images sprang through the contact—a king at prayer, a witch dying, castles and towers, the king again, meeting with several others, a grand figure with a hat like an arched door, who blessed the king in a church so magnificent it dazzled the viewer. Then cold, an ebbing away. Elisha reached back, tried to cling to that fading life as he sought for the means to stop so many wounds. He urged the flesh to heal, fumbling in his pouch for the slight talisman he carried, a scrap of cloth given to him by a friend and returned to him after he had applied it in a more traditional healing. The talisman, endowed now with the strength of friendship, the urgency of his earlier need, and even the blood of the nobleman he had bandaged with it, magnified his talent. Power warmed his hands, the wounded flesh rousing, twitching to his urgency. The slashed heart gave a thump and a shudder, and blood sluiced over Elisha's knees. The weapon must have many blades, for he swore the attacker had struck only twice.

Blades in both hands? Maybe. Bare-chested? Had he imagined that? The Frenchman's erratic heartbeat grew still, and the slight response of his own healing instinct faded, the flesh releasing all tension. A magus could be strongest in death, but even then he must live long enough to use it.

Elisha crumpled the cloth talisman in his hands, slumping back on his heels. He had lost many on the battlefield, but at least he'd had a chance, a knowledge of what was coming, if nothing else. This . . .

"Elisha." Mordecai's hand was on his back, and others came near.

"A man was hiding in my chamber. He had a knife, a handful of knives—I don't know."

The night attendant returned, hurrying along with a pair of servants from the Hall. "What can we do?" he called, then swallowed and stopped as he took in the scene. "Nobody covered in blood, sir, though some of 'em are sleeping without their shirts. I don't see how he could've got out, but maybe through the arches, if he dodged the king's men."

"Bare-chested and bloody? He'd've had to cross the breadth of the hall, and nobody noticed?"

"Not so's we've heard." The attendant tipped his hands. "Anything taken, sir?"

"I'll check," Mordecai said, slipping back the comforting heat of his hand to lead the attendant inside. After a moment, a candle was lit and their voices murmured.

"That's one of the Frenchmen," one of the servants said.

"The ambassador will need to be told, but the duke

first." Elisha dripped again with another man's blood. He was careful not to wipe his face.

"I'll go to his Grace." The young woman trotted off.

"A few of the containers are missing, some expensive things," Mordecai said. "Looks like robbery." It would explain the clatter of the man's emergence. Elisha searched his memory for any detail of the man's presence, chill and cutting and angry: not enough to identify him. "Who is this?" Mordecai held out a sheet and the two of them covered the dead man, leaving a square of linen pale against the stained stone of the floor.

"The man who approached me earlier. He came to ask me some questions." Elisha rose stiffly, bloody garments still clutched in his hands, his branded chest spattered as well. "He was already in fear for his life." Elisha stared down at the covered corpse, the day's second, and both times his own life had been at risk. Robbery? Or a second murder attempt? And what to make of the jumbled images the magus sent him with his dying breath? "I need to wash up. Could you ask his Grace to meet me in the chapel, if he's willing?"

Mordecai's eyebrows rose, but he gave a nod. "We'll see to the body."

Down a short flight of steps from the infirmary was one of the castle's three wells, with a trough alongside, easily filled. Elisha scrubbed as best he could and pulled on one of the damp shirts that always hung nearby. He knew it had been a slow time in the infirmary if the shirt he'd worn at the last surgery had time to dry. His trousers would be stiff with blood, but he'd deal with that later.

Something in the messenger's sending was bothering him, something he hoped the chapel would help him understand. Taking a lantern from its loop, Elisha crossed the lower and upper yards to the little church that served the duke's retainers. A few candles still flickered on the side and main altars, but not enough to reach the painted ceiling. Elisha held up his lantern, illuminating the half-dome flared with gold around the figure of Christ. To either side stood a pair of Evangelists, and there—he saw the man he was looking for, a man in the same hat he'd seen through the Frenchman's eyes: Saint Peter.

"Elisha? I've just left the French ambassadors. First their gift is ruined and now this." Randall spread his hands and let them drop.

"The pope," Elisha said, pointing up. "That's the hat, isn't it, Your Grace, the one Saint Peter wears?"

Randall clenched his teeth, and gave a nod. "I am talking to you about quelling a war with the French and you are asking me about Saint Peter's mitre."

"The dead man was a magus, he came to me to ask for help in immigrating here—for all of the magi he knows in Paris. Their king has been killing them. He showed me a series of visions, memories. One of them showed the king meeting with the Pope."

"Yes, well, they're both French, aren't they? If his critics are to be believed, the king is the Pope's master, even before the Lord. Is this all you know about the killing?"

"He feared for his life, Your Grace, and now he's lost it. Maybe we should be asking the French what they know."

The duke groaned. "I have no intention of leading

them to believe I think them guilty of killing their own. I've already had to invent a twisted ankle to explain his being in the infirmary in the first place. It seems to have been a robbery, and that should satisfy them, though it would look better if we'd caught the man. And I don't expect anything will placate them but for a long visit with His Royal Highness, Prince Alaric." He sat heavily on the single pew, reserved for his family, and ran his fingers through what remained of his hair. "I had thought to send you to them in the morning, to tell the tale. In light of what you say, it seems better I should keep you away. Perhaps find an urgent mission to send you on for the time being."

Elisha stared down at his master, his almost-friend. To him, the death was personal, an affront because he could not prevent it, but to Randall, it was something else entirely: a tiny move on a vast field. Lowering the lantern, the bloody trousers sticking to his legs, Elisha came forward, trying to remember everything that had happened. "He told me their king would be eager for war, if he spotted weakness, Your Grace. I'd wager the killer was a magus as well, and he concealed himself from the searchers."

Randall gave a slight nod. "That's something. Allyson might be able to look. I'll tell her what you've said about the magi of France, as well. I believe she may have kin across the channel."

"Thank you, Your Grace." Elisha gave a bow of his head, but Randall waved it off.

"I'll have to face them all in the morning. Many of the barons still hold land over there." He set his hands on his knees and pushed himself up. For a moment, their eyes met, and the duke shook his head. "We both need our rest."

"Aye, Your Grace," Elisha murmured as he followed the older man out into the night.

When he tumbled into his own bed, it was not his own king he dreamed of, and the branded skin of his palm and chest itched like the Devil, looking for a way in.

When he prowled into the solar too early the next morning, in search of breakfast, he found the duke already there and nearly withdrew at the relief on the man's face. "Then we are still friends, in spite of everything—come, sit," Randall called out. "I was rather harsh last night. It's been a dreadful spring, and summer looks no better." He waved Elisha toward a cushioned seat, a breadknife still in his hand. "Have you recovered from last night's trouble?"

Elisha gave a slight shrug. "Hard to say, Your Grace, but I'd feel better if they've caught the man."

Randall shook his head. "Great Hall was still full of the prince's knights—sorry, the king's—and half of them bare-chested, but none bloody. The blood trail just . . . stopped." He met Elisha's look. "Allyson has started looking, in her own way."

At that, Elisha nodded, glad to have the duchess's magical prowess at work on the question. "I want to examine the body again. I may be able to learn more about the weapon."

"Knives, wasn't it?"

"Some sort of blade, but nothing I recognized."

"The poor fellow's been taken down to Saint John's in town. He's been washed and wrapped already." Randall prodded something on his plate. "Don't let the French catch you at it." He glanced sharply up, waiting for Elisha's nod before he carried on with his meal.

Elisha moved to the sideboard laden with food, the silent servants fussing over every tray. The idea of the search reminded him of his own goal, set aside in the excitement and disturbed sleep.

"Prince Alaric's off for London, I hear, Your Grace." Elisha took a slab of bread and piled it with cheese, trying to think how to ask.

"London? Leaving me to deal with these French, I suppose. Well, he'll have to wait once he's heard about the death."

"Mmm." Elisha took a breath and said, "His lady is spending time at a lodge. Would you know where?"

The duke set down his knife and shook his head. "Elisha, you must know—"

"Your Grace, she's taken something from me, and it may be there. That's all I want from her. If I know where she's going, I can leave ahead of her, and we might not even have to meet." He stared down at the trencher, piled now with more cheese than he could possibly eat. "You suggested I should leave for awhile."

Randall stared at him, his eyes ringed with the effects of more than one sleepless night. "A lodge? Most likely she means one of the royal hunting lodges in the New Forest. Do you know any more than that?"

"The prince suggested she take his carriage, Your

Grace, so there must be a road nearby, and she said something about bandits, so I gather it's in the forest proper."

"That'll be the old lodge then. I thought they'd sold it, actually. Little place, hardly seems royal at all, and nobody's been out for a couple of years, not since the princesses, God rest their souls." He crossed himself.

"The princesses," Elisha echoed, "I remember." It had been the talk of London a couple of years ago: the horrific news of Prince Thomas's young wife and child slain. A bloody business. Perhaps Brigit should, indeed, be afraid. But it would be the perfect place for her to use his talisman, given the history of bloodshed. It reminded him of the French magus who died on his doorstep, and he pushed his plate away.

"I can tell you a faster way to go, avoiding the carriage road." Randall settled his thick fingers together. "If you'll take Rosalynn with you."

"What about the bandits?"

Randall waved this away. "The verderers strung them up. Besides, you needn't take her into the forest, just to the abbey. Beaulieu's not far from there, and she might be able to spend some time in healing. She's started murmuring about taking the veil. Being a guest there might help to convince her not to. I can still find her a worthy match, given time."

Elisha extended his awareness toward his benefactor, meeting his hooded gaze. "So long as it's not a way to convince me to spend more time with her, Your Grace."

"It's not a bad thought." The duke pursed his lips and gave a dismissive shrug. "She knows the way, and I'll send a small entourage with her. If anyone from Brigit's camp hears about it, it'll provide you cover."

Sighing, Elisha conceded the point. Escorting the lady to an abbey was a perfectly honorable excuse for travel. "If she can leave immediately, Your Grace, then I accept."

Chapter 6

❖

Æfter packing a few things for the journey and leaving them with the duke's grooms, Elisha walked toward the battered town. On a low hill against the rising sun, a windmill's tattered sails groaned as if sorry not to be able to catch the winds. A pair of workmen hammered on the scaffold being built to repair it. Dawn's light gave the valley a golden cast, highlighting the edges of burned beams and broken walls. A few shepherds moved out to the fields, their dogs giving Elisha sharp looks. The leaning church rose over all, reminding Elisha of his narrow escape the night before. He kept his senses extended, but he guessed nothing would come of it today. In order to catch him, the hunters must know where to look and when. Funeral notices were posted, in case anyone still sought their unburied dead, and many people knew Elisha had been attending them all. As for the "robbery," it had been his own chamber. It might have been truly a crime, meant to take advantage of his presence at the ball to steal medical herbs, though the strange weapon suggested otherwise. Two possibilities remained: That the Frenchman's fear had come to pass and his mysterious betrayer had noticed him with Elisha earlier or even seen them meet again. Or that Elisha's enemies were willing to lay more than one trap, perhaps counting on catching him off balance after the first attack failed.

Hopefully, his examination of the dead magus would point him toward one answer or the other. The idea of another magus as the killer left him disappointed, as if all magi were above vengeance or murder. He should know better—just look at Brigit.

Elisha went around the side of the little church to the crypt door where he expected the body had been kept until a funeral could be arranged. In addition to his medical kit, Elisha carried a strong cloth needle and some plain thread to stitch up the winding cloth when he had finished. With care, no one would know he'd been there at all.

A wooden door set down a few steps from the street led beneath the church. Trotting down to stand beneath its little roof, Elisha tried the latch, but it did not give. He glanced about, thankful that he was at least on the shaded side of the building and most of the damaged buildings around him remained empty. He would have to enter using his other skills.

Setting his hand to the lock, Elisha drew in his awareness, honing it as a hunter hones his spear. He could not see into the darkness of the iron hole, but his awareness, focused in this way, reached inside like tiny fingers, feeling out the edges and tumblers. Awareness alone had no force to move things, but it gave him the means to create an affinity. He withdrew the infirmary key from his belt and touched the talisman cloth he carried. It took a moment to understand the lock, then to translate this knowledge into the shape of a key that might work it. The infirmary key in his hand grew warm, then twitched and twisted, pulling itself longer and pushing out a new shape. He tried this in the lock to no avail, and had to give it a few more refinements before the tumblers clicked and the bolt drew back.

Replacing the altered key, Elisha stepped inside and shut the door softly behind him. Utter darkness enveloped him, and Elisha cursed under his breath. A few minutes groping along the wall of the entry and his questing fingers found a shelf with waiting candles for the priest or his assistants. It took longer to strike a flame to one of them, but at least the sudden light showed a table just inside where a wrapped corpse awaited its final resting place. Elisha crossed carefully and set the candle on a ledge that stuck out from the wall above the body. It cast a square shadow over the table, superimposed upon the pale stiffness of the corpse.

At least they had chosen a simple shroud, the sort where they laid the body at its center and brought up the sides to be sewn. It might even be the very sheet he and Mordecai laid over the man the night before. If the body had been truly wound, he should have struggled over unwrapping the whole man just to get to his chest. As it was, Elisha set to work with the scalpel from his medical kit, snipping the stitches from the vicinity of the stomach up close to the throat. That should give him enough room to view the wounds, though he might have to peel back the covering on the man's face to take a look at the back, where the blades had entered. He remembered the solid thunk of blade into flesh, jolting against him as he tried to swing himself and the Frenchman out of the way. A short blade, not long enough to pierce them both.

Elisha took the edges of cloth and separated them. The fabric came away from the body with a sticky sound. Given how much the man bled in the hall last night, he expected little blood, so the glossy sheen of the corpse surprised him. At the very least, the man's damaged clothes should be there—if one of the duke's servants stooped to stealing from the dead, Randall would need to hear about it. Elisha picked up the candle holder to get a better look.

He yelped and jumped back, the candle rocking from its holder to tumble to the floor, plunging him back into darkness. His breath shuddered, his heart suddenly at his throat. Elisha took a moment to steady his nerve, then stooped and groped for the candle again. His hand closed around it, trembling, and he rose slowly. The wick was still hot and took only a moment's magical encouragement to re-light, but Elisha stared at the flame a few minutes longer, soothed by the heat and the glow. At last, he steeled himself for a second look at the dead man.

The shoulders and head above as well as the pelvis and legs below remained wrapped in cloth. In between, the gap Elisha made showed the firm musculature of a young man's torso, the grain of the muscles striating

across pectorals and abdominals, yellowed blobs of fat
riming below the ribs, thin veins of white fat interlacing
the muscles. Naked flesh. The corpse had been skinned.

Elisha turned away more deliberately this time, walking a few paces to stand by the marble sarcophagi, bile
burning in his throat. Skinned. Like a rabbit for the
duke's table. He swallowed hard, trying to master his
stomach. Years of medical experience inured him to almost any reaction to the wounds of the living except to
consider what he must do to save them. This felt different. Someone violated the tomb, cutting the thread just
as Elisha had done, stripping the victim of his clothes,
then stripping him still further, peeling back the skin
from his damaged chest. For what?

Elisha pressed a hand to his mouth, his own breathing
too loud in the stuffy space beneath the church. Thank
God nobody had heard his cry of discovery. He could
only imagine how it would look if someone found him
here, in a crypt, stooped over the mutilated body of a
murdered man. How much time had passed already? He
had to finish his examination, stitch up the shroud and
get out of here before they came for the funeral.

Raising the candle, Elisha turned back to the dead
man. He forced himself into motion, holding the candle
over the bared muscles, the vulnerable fat and flaccid
stomach. In addition to the two punctures that pierced
the chest, he could see the nicks of the flayer's knife as it
had drawn down the sternum to the navel, cutting barely
deep enough to get the job done. The skinner's hand was
practiced, his blade sharp. A brief lifting of the cloth in
both directions showed every inch of muscle stripped of

its skin. He gagged at the thought of viewing the dead man's face and tugged the cloth closer together.

Such an intimate, awful deed, it had to be personal. Some sort of vengeance, perhaps for his betrayal in seeking to leave France? The man told him magi were marked for execution; if any in the French party suspected him—not even that he was a magus, but only that he sought to betray his king . . . was this the punishment for traitors across the channel? A French matter, disguised as a crime to cast some embarrassment upon their English hosts, and so they didn't have to explain themselves to foreigners. It might explain, as well, the unfamiliar weapon used in the slaying: a brutal custom from across the channel.

Elisha brought the candle in close. He no longer dared to roll the victim and examine the entry wounds at his back, but studied the two marks clearly visible at the front. They resembled bowshot more than anything else—round passages, still slightly open, instead of the thin slits of traditional blades. But the weapon was hand held, certainly, thrust with the strength of the attacker's arm. It had a round profile, thick, perhaps like a stitcher's awl but of great size.

The flame shivered in Elisha's grasp. He replaced the candleholder on its stone, then took out his needle. It, too, trembled. He forced it steady and brought the thread to the eye with infinite care then held together the edges of cloth. His stitching was a bit clumsy, stitches hastily far apart, then closer together as he made himself slow down. At last, he made the knot, cut the thread and straightened. He crossed himself, bowing his head over the man whose name he never knew, a stranger who hoped to leave his troubles beyond the sea, only to be caught by them when he thought he was safe.

Elisha took up the candle and turned at the tumble of the lock. He flinched and took a breath to calm himself, then squared his shoulders as the door opened.

Father Michael gasped in turn. "Barber!" The two men behind him, carrying a coffin on their shoulders stopped abruptly, the box shifting forward until the leader slapped it back with one hand.

"Forgive me. I cannot attend the funeral, and I wished to pay my respects."

The priest frowned furiously. "Here?"

"I have an important mission for the duke—I'm leaving right away."

"These dark events do seem to seek you out." Descending the last few steps, Father Michael approached him, daylight streaming down behind. It illuminated Elisha's face, and the priest's expression shifted. He laid a firm hand on Elisha's shoulder. "I can see you are troubled. Return to the fold of the Shepherd. Repent now, before it is too late."

The warmth and urgency of the priest's piety flowed through their contact, a curious application of a near-magical skill. In spite of Father Michael's stern commandment, his touch was strangely comforting. "Thank you, Father. I'll do what I can."

Elisha nodded to the men on the steps, stepping aside to let them come in and set the casket down with a hollow thunk, ready to receive its occupant. Then he climbed the few steps to the road and hurried back up the hill before the priest had time to wonder how he'd gotten in. Which made him wonder how and when the flaying had occurred. Probably last night before the body was brought down. There could be only a few people with keys to the crypt, aside from the priest himself, and the castle infirmary likely had one to facilitate transporting the dead without rousing the priest. Breathless, he came into the yard to find the duke's family already there as Mordecai explained that he expected Elisha at any moment. Mordecai broke off as Elisha skidded to a halt, remembering to bow to Duke Randall, his wife, and daughter.

"Are you ready?" the duke asked.

"Nearly, Your Grace. A word with Mordecai Surgeon."

"Very well, then," said Randall, but he frowned, and Lady Rosalynn, clad in a long, dark traveling dress, frowned with him as she watched Elisha pass.

The surgeon followed him a few paces away, but Elisha took his arm as if giving a hearty farewell. "*The Frenchman's been skinned.*" He sent a brief glimpse of what he had seen, and Mordecai's grip tightened with shock. "*Duchess Allyson is searching for the killer, but they think it's an outsider, a criminal. My guess is he was slain and skinned by his own people, as a punishment.*"

"*For talking to you? Good thing you'll be gone.*"

"*Don't I know it. Watch yourself—and let the duchess know. They may have the skin among their things. They'll want to warn off the other magi.*"

"*A bone when they came, a skin when they go. Hope they don't mean to stay long.*" Mordecai shook his hand,

and Elisha let him go. "Take care," said the surgeon aloud. Elisha nodded and gave a wave as he made for the cluster of horses.

If he were right about the killer and the cause, that would be the end of it. And if he were wrong ... Elisha found himself absently itching at his sternum, visualizing the attachment of muscles moving just below the skin.

Chapter 7

⟡

By the time they reached Netley Abbey, a sister cell to their destination at Beaulieu, Elisha wished he could simply leave Lady Rosalynn there and walk on alone. His back and legs ached from riding, his hands and arms from clinging to the reins, his head from practicing courtly manners. Surely Netley was near enough? The whole ride was consumed by the minutiae of a lady's concerns, which seemed so small compared to everything else happening, that he wanted to shake her. Except, of course, that she had no idea what else was going on; her own concerns must seem large enough. It was hardly her fault if her position and gender protected her from the darkness beneath the day.

"Netley Abbey is famous for its hospitality, but I've not stayed here for years," Rosalynn said as they entered the grounds. "Primarily sailors, isn't it, but lots of other travelers, too." She leaned close to him, confident in her saddle while he held on for dear life. "They've had a bit of bother with the king, in the past. He's meant to support the Abbey, but sometimes the money doesn't arrive."

"At least we have, my lady." He slid numbly down from the horse and stumbled on his weary legs.

"Yes, but we could ride a bit further. The gate's not till we pass these trees." She waved a hand.

"You go on ahead. I need to stretch my legs." He clung to the reins, not trusting his legs just yet, and his horse stamped and snorted.

Rosalynn smiled brightly. "I shall walk with you." To her escort, she said, "Go on ahead and tell them how many we are and that we require dinner." She slid down easily, handing her reins over to one of the mounted guards.

"Shall I stay, milady?" asked her maid, eying Elisha suspiciously, as she had for every hour of the past two days.

"Go on. We're within view, aren't we?"

In the gathering dusk, whatever view the maid had would be obscure at best, but she went on with the guards, the last of whom stopped to take Elisha's reins. He tried to seem grateful as he took a few creaky steps and winced. How the nobility ever got used to such a thing as riding, he should never understand.

Rosalynn plucked up her skirts just enough and glided a few steps ahead of him through the tunnel of trees. "Beaulieu Abbey, on the other hand, answers only to the Pope himself. His Holiness has even granted it special privileges of sanctuary throughout the grounds, not just in the church itself."

She kept talking, or rather, he assumed that she did, but he practiced his attunement and succeeded in blocking her sound from his mind, focusing instead on the tangled trees that set off the road from the fields on one side. Bells rang out across the countryside, summoning the monks and laymen from their work. Laborers propped hoes over their shoulders and trudged back toward the moated monastery. The scene brought Elisha back to his childhood in the village, with its daily rhythm of fields and bells; men and women plodding home from their work, children carrying the baskets leftover from a lunch, beneath the round, full tolling of the bells that ruled their lives. London had bells, of course, but they meant nothing to Elisha's work and merely echoed among the half-timbered houses that buttressed the twisted streets.

The light grew suddenly warm, and Elisha turned to find its source. The trees ceased some distance from the walls, leaving a slope that led downward to the water. Pink and gold drenched the sky and painted the clouds against the darkening vault of heaven. Above, indigo, not quite as deep as night, and before him, a scene of such splendor that he crossed himself. The duke's castle commanded quite a view of the surrounding towns and country, and Elisha would never forget the first time he climbed the tower at the ruined monastery and could see for such a distance. But it had not prepared him for this.

The colors of the sinking sun glowed across the water between their vantage and the opposite shore. Beyond stood thousands of trees, thick as London houses, interrupted here and there by fields. Hills rose up after that. Looking the other way, he found a few boats making their way to the port, their wakes turning over darkness, their sails gilded, the fishermen made more ruddy by the light. He breathed in the slightest taste of salt. Somewhere in the distance—closer now than he had ever been—swelled the boundless sea.

A warm hand clutched his arm, and Elisha jerked away, staring into Rosalynn's face, her brows furrowed. He shook himself and pushed his awareness back out until her voice came clear.

"Are you well? It's like you've not heard even a word I was saying! I was that afraid for you. Or is it a witch thing?" She glanced around quickly to be sure no one was near. "My mother is, and keeps expecting that I'll be, too, but there hasn't been any sign of that. My brothers aren't, but you know it's more likely to carry through in a child of the same sex, isn't it?"

"I wouldn't know, my lady." He looked back to the scene below, hearing the splash of oars and the slap of water against the shore, the distant song of a crew on their way home, but his eyes rose again to the miraculous sky so wide above the water.

Rosalynn laughed then. "What, haven't you ever seen the sun setting before? You grew up in a village, didn't you? And of course my father has a western tower."

Elisha spun about to face her. He took her arm and turned her toward the gloomy fields, the trees, and the darkness that hung beneath them. "In the village, that's what you see. The dirt, the fields, the rows you have yet to tend. When the sun sets, you'd best drag yourself to bed because when it rises again, you'd best be ready. In London, the sky flows like a river between banks of rooftops. It gets narrower every year as the merchants add more gables."

She pulled away from him. "You don't have to be rough with me."

He took a deep breath. "Forgive me, my lady. It has been a long journey."

With one hand, she tucked a few strands of dark hair back beneath her travelling veil. In a voice very small, she said, "You do not care for me."

Shame burned at him, and Elisha did not know how to answer. There was nothing he could say without lying or hurting her more.

"My father will be disappointed." She glanced away, her fingers knotting together. "He had hoped . . . but you know—oh." Her chin fell.

"I know what he hoped," Elisha echoed, "but I little thought he shared it with you. Not such a distant hope as that."

"I hadn't gone far that night, had I? I did not mean to hear, it was just, well, it was hard to avoid. And it touched upon me, didn't I? So I had the right." For only the second time since he had known her, she fell silent without prompting. "He worries about you. About both of us. It might be a good match." She watched him sidelong, with the eagerness of attraction, as if their single dance had kindled some hope within her. "Only I get worried, too, and then I tend to chatter." She swallowed hard, and her eyes glistened as she looked away.

"I'd like to go down to the water, my lady. Why don't you go on ahead, and I'll be there in time for supper?" He touched her arm gently, trying to add a sense of comfort that overlaid his touch.

"Yes, very well. By tomorrow noon, you shall be shut of me." She crossed her arms, tipping back her head as if to keep the tears from flowing.

Resolutely, he turned away, finding a narrow path that led down in a series of angles. He could not decide now if he wanted the peace of silence, or the comfort of other magi he could reach through the water. Silence seemed very appealing, but he also wanted word of Brigit, to be sure they were ahead of her. Rosalynn's broken heart and ruined life were really nothing to do with him; it was not something he could heal except by sacrificing himself, and that he was not willing to do, not for her or even her father. He pictured himself bound to the stake while Rosalynn circled around him, talking, and he begged her to simply light the pyre. Grim and unworthy. She'd told him that she chattered when she worried, and goodness knew she had plenty to worry over.

Elisha crossed the wider trail at the bottom of the slope and came at last to the water's edge. He sank down gratefully and pulled off his boots with a groan. Turning to place them behind him, he glimpsed the figure of Rosalynn above, just far enough that he could not clearly see her face. The sunset touched her skin with a rosy glow, and she looked regal in her gown of blue, the creamy veil rippling over her shoulders. She should marry some crusading lord who would see her this way always, gilded and strong.

The cold water at first shocked his toes, then numbed them, finally easing away the aches and sweat of the road. He edged his presence into the water. Water enabled a weak sort of contact among the witches, enough to send their voices and sometimes sensations across greater distances. He opened himself to this contact, and tension struck through him sharper than the cold.

"—she only needs us to support Prince Alaric's claim to the throne, in whatever way we might. We needn't per-

form any castings at all," one voice said through the water, with a sense of exhaustion.

"She wouldn't be my first choice. No more would he, for that matter," another voice snapped back. *"Neither of them shall fly the banner of justice."*

"This could be our best chance to be heard, to be free, don't you understand?" That voice felt familiar. Briarrose, wasn't it? Brigit's friend. Strange how Elisha could know what someone was like when he'd never met her. *"We'll finally have a magus on the throne."*

A deeper voice put in, *"I just don't think the time is right. We're being rushed into this, and I don't like it. There's been inquisitors in France for years, there's a mess in the Holy Roman Empire. Even the Pope himself fears to return to Rome. Too much is happening."*

And the magi of Paris were so worried they were seeking a new home. Allyson knew, but neither she nor Elisha knew enough to do anything with the news the dead man had brought, except to be even more vigilant about the Channel.

"It's our own place we need to worry over, Watercress. But I agree with you in principle. We are being pushed. Somebody wants this done and quickly. For that very reason, we ought to stay quiet."

"We don't have to cast any spells," the first voice protested again. *"You're all so used to hiding in fear that you don't recognize the chance we've got before us."*

"Listen to Foxglove," Briarrose urged. *"Or think of Rowena if you doubt us. She pointed to the signs, she prepared the way for this."*

"For her daughter to be queen," Watercress pointed

out. "*That hardly seems the mark of an altruistic plan to elevate the magi.*"

"*She gave the signs, as clear a prophecy as any could wish for. And now here he is, and with a magus prepared to assume the throne—as queen, at least. It's time for us to come together. The time is now!*"

"*Bittersweet is hardly the harbinger of light we might wish him to be,*" said Watercress's friend. "*Or have you forgotten his crime?*"

"*Why not ask what he thinks? I believe he's joined us,*" said Briarrose. "*Who's there?*" she called out, almost playfully through their watery contact.

"*Watercress,*" in a worried tone.

"*Briarrose.*"

"*Foxglove,*" wearily.

"*Thyme,*" said Watercress's friend.

"*Bittersweet,*" Elisha announced, using the herbal name that would protect him if any of those gathered were questioned about the other witches.

And so softly he nearly missed it, "*Chanterelle,*" in a quiet voice but with a clarity of presence indicating the speaker was very close by. There was another presence as well, or rather, the echo of a presence, as if he felt the silence between breaths.

Immediately, Watercress said, "*We can't talk with him around. He's one of them!*"

"*Tell me you're not starting up about necromancers again,*" said Foxglove. "*We can't even be sure there are any.*"

"*Of course there are! Why do you think the desolati fear us so much? They think we're all necromancers!*"

"*I've never seen any evidence of such a thing. And we*

prefer not to use the term 'desolati.' Many of us have spouses without talent—there's no need to be insulting."

Elisha wanted to protest that he was no necromancer, that he wasn't even sure what it meant, although he knew it had something to do with conjuring the dead. If any here might be accused of that, it would be him. *"Whatever I have done, I did it alone and without instruction. I never meant—"* What? To hurt anyone? It would have been a lie.

"You see? And Marigold trusts him," Briarrose offered, sending a thread of comfort through the water.

"He withered the king and turned weapons to rust! If he's not a necromancer I don't know what is."

"Even if he isn't we cannot afford to have the king's murderer on our side. Sorry," said Thyme.

"He's not one of them, he's one of us," whispered Chanterelle.

"What was that?" Watercress demanded. *"Speak up, child."*

"He's one of us, the indivisi," she said, but no louder than before.

"He's an accursed necromancer!"

Foxglove broke in at a shout, *"I told you, there aren't any necromancers. They're just a story told to frighten people. Just believing in them gives our enemies power to suppress us."*

"I wasn't sure there were indivisi either," Thyme said, *"and now we seem to have one."*

"The mancers're real," said Chanterelle. *"And so close by. I've heard them in the earth."* Her voice grew a little louder. *"Do you feel that?"*

Elisha spread his awareness around him, catching the edge of fear in Chanterelle's presence. He had not fully attuned himself to the place and started to do so now, sending his awareness into the earth and air, reaching out with his other senses to the darkness. The sun had nearly gone, but moonlight fell around him, turning the scene from gold to silver. The air remained warm, the water chill, but there was a cold beneath the cold, a force that did not flow like water. "*Yes,*" he answered her. "*I feel it.*"

In an instant, she was gone, her presence lifted from the water. With his senses fully alert, Elisha heard a rustle across the water, wide though it was. He rose in time to see a figure spring up from the water's edge. Slight and long haired, the figure ran through the reeds over the rocky verge to the grass and dove into the earth. It swallowed her up with a tiny spit of dirt, just as a splash of water marked a cormorant's dive.

"*Just as well she's left,*" said Watercress. "*The indivisi are all mad, every one of them.*"

"*It comes of too much knowledge. They devote themselves to one thing so thoroughly they can't relate to anything else,*" Foxglove replied.

"*But that's not what we came to talk about,*" Briarrose began.

"*She's not mad,*" Elisha cut in, "*she's frightened. Didn't you feel it? It was like ... like an eel slipping through the water to find her.*"

"*Maybe he really is one of them,*" Thyme said.

Then a shriek shot through mud and water, jolting from Elisha's soles to the crown of his head. He cried out in echo.

From the bank above, Rosalynn's voice called, "Elisha? Are you hurt?"

He shook himself, casting off the sense of the other's terror and searching the darkening shore for any sign of her. She seemed to have vanished into the dirt, but how far could she go? Something glimmered—a torch in the hand of a thick figure hard to distinguish from the shadowy trees at its back. The torch dropped as the figure moved away into the trees. Smoke furled upward from a dozen places in the earth, then flickering cracks of flame crept across the heath beyond. That dark figure had set the very ground on fire, kindling the peat which might burn for weeks. Orange and crimson flames worked their way inward from all directions, converging like hunting hounds, tiny flames, but quick and driven. A woman hid beneath that earth, but her enemy was already upon her.

Chapter 8

———◆———

Elisha splashed into the water, but it was quickly up to his thighs and pulling hard against him. Damn it! Chanterelle was trapped, might already be burning, and he was helpless.

"Elisha!" Rosalynn stumbled to shore, breathless. "What's going on? What are you doing out there and why did you cry out like that?"

"A woman's in trouble—over there!" He jabbed his finger toward the opposite shore. "Where's the bridge?" He spun about in an arc of water, but Rosalynn caught his hand.

"This way!"

Aside from a few buildings further on, he saw nothing to span the water. "There's no—"

"This way," she insisted, tugging at him. "There is no bridge, not for miles. There's a ferryboat." Rosalynn pulled and Elisha ran after until they ran together along the bank.

The cottage door stood open when they got there, an old man peering into the twilight, his own fire in the hearth behind him. "What's on? Thought I heard a scream, I did."

"There's someone in trouble on the opposite shore," Elisha told him. "We need to cross."

"No night crossings," the man said stiffly and started to pull the door shut.

"We'll pay double," Rosalynn announced. "I'm Lady Rosalynn of Dunbury. We need that crossing, right now."

He looked her up and down, then stepped out and preceded them around the cottage to a dock at the waterside, only to stop again and peer across the water. "Looks like smoke. Peat fire, eh."

Elisha steeled himself for another refusal, but the man went on, "Just you stay on the river path when you get across, eh?"

"Yes!" They scrambled into the boat, and the old man cast off, setting his hands to the oars. Elisha leaned out from the bow, willing the boat to hurry. He searched for some way to use his power to speed their passage, some way that wouldn't result in a wreck. He doubted Rosalynn could swim any more than he.

"Do you know, I have a cousin whose keep guards a ferry crossing, and he got quite close with the ferryman," Rosalynn said suddenly. "The fellow had to quit when he got older, of course, he couldn't really pull as strongly then, could he? But we used to have the most fun visiting and seeing just how fast he could get us across the lake, my brothers and me. And I'm sure he wasn't as strong as you."

She leaned earnestly toward the ferryman. Elisha couldn't see the man's face, but he noted the tightening of his neck and the quickening of his strokes. Rosalynn's admiring chatter undertook to inspire the man, and Elisha nearly smiled. He clung to the edges of the boat as it swayed with wind, water, the pressure of the oars. So quickly, the movement made him queasy, and he clamped his jaw against the roiling of his stomach. The shore grew closer, the flames still low and fierce, crackling through the earth, weaving back and forth. Smoke carried toward them on the breeze, then away.

When they were a few feet off the dock, Elisha leapt from the boat into waist-deep water and ran, his feet slithering over muck and submerged stone.

"Here, you!" The ferryman called. "Mind the peat! It'll be burning below, where you can't even see. Your man's gone off his course, he has," he added to Rosalynn.

"Never you mind," she replied stiffly. "You may go once I'm ashore."

Their voices fell lower, then splashing followed by the creak of oars told of the ferryman's retreat into the gathering darkness. Elisha ignored them and ran for the burning earth. Several acres between the reeds and the forest edge crackled with heat and shifting smoke. He gasped and coughed hard, doubled over.

"Elisha?" A gentle hand caught his shoulder. "I don't see anyone."

"She's here," he gulped. "I have to find her." He spread his awareness, this time reaching deep into dirt. He had a little knowledge, thanks to the farm where he was raised, but it still felt like breaking untilled soil with his fingers. Then his spreading senses reached the edge of the peat. The deposit was dense and crumbled, layer on layer of moss and bog myrtle compressed, dry from the growing heat, most of it already smoldering. It throbbed with fear and pressure, and presence, more than one. Old and new. He tried to call to her, but his voice could not pass. The twisting mass of earth defied him. Already sweat streamed down his face from the heat, and his lips felt dry. He searched the area with his eyes and found no sign. His hands and knees grew hot, and his wet clothing dried in seconds. The fear that thrummed beneath him grew to terror. He drew breath in gulps of smoke that seared his throat. He had only moments left before he could stand it no longer.

"Elisha?" Rosalynn kneaded his shoulder. "There's nobody here."

Summoning. If he could not get to her, he could bring her to him. He pulled out his talisman, a strip of cloth given by a friend, used to bind the wound of another. Gripping it in his fist, Elisha called out again through his awareness. In the strength of the memories it carried, the talisman resonated with his power. If his senses were right, there was more than one presence in the earth. Chanterelle and her enemies? But the land was a confusing mix of cold and heat, dead and living, and he could not tell where she was or who the others might be. It was as if the other presences screened her from him. Even if he could not hold them, he might force them to be seen. "Whoever you are, I call you to rise," Elisha growled to the earth. "Come to me," he whispered. "If you be willing, come to me."

Willingness was key. If Chanterelle were reaching back, she could break free, but if she denied him, he

could do nothing to touch her. The confounded peat
gave him contact: her need must do the rest. The power
rushed through him, redoubling with his talisman, and
he pushed it out through his hands and feet into the
earth all around him, trembling with it, shaping the urge
to reach the surface.

Rosalynn's fingers dug into his shoulder, and she
started screaming. Elisha raised his head and started
back against her legs, her arms wrapping him as she, too,
dropped to her knees, her scream rebounding in his ears.

The peat before them bubbled and broke, and a body
emerged, tumbling dirt to lie on the surface as if it had
just fallen in a dreadful war. Crushed sideways, its ancient face stared at them with empty eyes beneath a ragged drape of hair. Brown, withered skin wrapped the
twisted limbs, and a leg dragged behind, shards of bone
rattling free.

Another emerged beyond that, a fragmented torso,
with hands bound fast by sinew across a broken chest.

Elisha forced himself to stare. As each body broke the
surface, he shed his contact with it, abandoning them to
the flames as quickly as he knew what they were. An arm
here, a skull there, a leather shoe still clasped around a
foot.

A body broke the surface with a moan, and Elisha
sprang up, shaking off the sobbing Rosalynn. He shattered his contact, snatching back his spell as he sprinted
over the burning ground, leaping the remains that spread
about his feet. A woman—a girl, really—writhed before
him, flames streaking toward her. Elisha swept her up,
and she wailed as he touched her burned skin.

"I'm sorry, I'm sorry," he said as much as sent into her. The forest edge was nearer now than going back and he ran for it, his feet sizzling with every touch of the ground. Her trailing hair sparked as a flame leapt nearby. He spun away from it, stumbling, and fetched up against a low stone. Digging his arms and elbows and toes against the rock, he pushed them both up, dragging his feet as far as he could from the burning ground, coughing hard over the girl. He let her roll onto her side on the stone, scrabbling up beside her as soon as the coughing subsided. Even then, his lungs and throat felt raw, and his muscles shivered.

"Elisha!" Rosalynn wailed from across the cackling flames.

"My lady! I need your skirts. Wet—and hurry!" He shifted position, crawling around Chanterelle until he could get a better sense of her injuries. Thankfully, though she was singed all over, she had few bad burns. She must have been aware enough to protect herself, at least for a time.

"Elisha." More like a whimper this time. "There's dead men. Burning."

Elisha had nearly been one of them. Evidently, Rosalynn wasn't coming. He had to find a different way to soothe the girl's burns. Carefully, he rose, balancing on the stone to look around. They were on a great rectangular rock, dragged here by the heathens of old. It lay tilted but relatively smooth at the edge of a road that bordered the trees. Another pathway branched off into the woods to the south. The heat and smoke of the peat lay before him and to both sides but did not extend too far, from what he could see. It must be a small deposit. Hopefully, the woods and adjoining heath were still moist enough to withstand the smoldering fire. Here and there among the low flames, the ancient dead twitched and stretched with the heat, contributing the smell of burning bone. Had those men brought the stone here—or had they been sacrificed to the unholy spirit it represented? Elisha swallowed and looked away. Toward the river, he heard sloshing and strange noises, then a woman's silhouette came into view, edging around the smoke, keeping to the path as the ferryman advised.

"Bring mud, if you can," Elisha called out to her. She paused, then moved nearer the river and scraping sounds followed.

Elisha knelt at Chanterelle's side and touched her with his barest fingertips. He sent her comfort and soothing thoughts as he attuned himself to the changing dusk. Slowly, he became aware of her body, how she lay, how she breathed, everything that might indicate her condition. The last rays of sun showed her nakedness, her body barely a woman's. She might be old enough to marry or not, but her face looked old beyond her years, even in this uneasy rest. Dirt rimmed her short nails, both hands and feet, and edged every line and wrinkle.

"Good gracious!" Rosalynn stopped short, staring at the girl, her outer skirt hugged in both arms. "But she's— did the fire burn off her clothing then? My goodness!" Her tone was faint. She leaned down to let the sodden lump of fabric onto the surface of the stone. "Mud, plenty, I hope. I'm not strong."

"You were strong enough when we needed you," Elisha told her. "The ferryman wouldn't have rowed for me." He flicked back the top fabric and scooped some of the oozy stuff gently over Chanterelle's limbs. Her arms seemed to have the worst of it, as if she had kept them before her after her dive into the earth. She sighed as he smoothed the mud over her burns, and some of the tension left her.

"It's not really proper, is it? You, touching her, like that." Rosalynn hugged herself.

"I am a barber," Elisha pointed out, continuing his ministrations.

"Yes, but—"

"I'm what she has," he growled. "I don't suppose the ferryman is waiting to take us back?" Although if the man had witnessed this scene, he'd take Elisha for the Devil, surrounded by the burning dead.

"No," she said timidly. "Well, no. He's going to the abbey to let my maid know I'm fine."

"We can't stay here, my lady. This was an attack, and they might return."

"An attack? Somebody lit the fire to burn her?" She drew a deep breath and squared her shoulders. "I'll be back in a moment."

She turned away and moved behind a screen of trees. Behind this cover, she grumbled as fabric strained and sometimes tore. Elisha finished with his mud-daubing and sat back, puzzled. Then Rosalynn re-appeared, carrying a pale shift. Her remaining undergown, stained with mud and smoke, splashed with water and now torn along one side, hung askew from her shoulders. "She can't go ... like that. Here." Elisha carefully helped the girl sit up, and Rosalynn pulled the yards of fabric down over her unresisting arms and head, then drew back as Elisha let Chanterelle settle back against him. She stirred and mumbled. "Better, yes." Lady Rosalynn nodded to herself, holding the torn side of her dress closed. "These things are not meant for me to do on my own, you see? I ought to have my maid with me, or it's a bit much to manage. But I trust they shall bring over my things in the morning, and I can be properly assisted then."

"In the morning." Elisha met Rosalynn's eyes over Chanterelle's lolling head.

Rosalynn looked away quickly. "I asked the ferryman to tell my maid that we would meet them at Beaulieu Abbey. Really, though, the lodge you're looking for is nearer. If you need to tend her, that would be easiest. We just need to go along the path, there, and—"

"What will it mean if you and I are over here without your maid or any soldiers?" Elisha asked firmly.

"Perhaps they would think we are together," she whispered. "You are a handsome man, and I am a duke's daughter. They might think you . . . wanted . . . to be with me. But it's fine. I shall go to the convent. I could be happy there. With God, you know."

"If you would act with courage instead of fear, as you have tonight, my lady, you would find someone who wants to be with you." Elisha held her gaze as her eyes widened. "In the meantime, take us to the lodge."

"This way." She gripped the torn fabric and started toward the trail. "Courage. Do you really think so?"

"Talking less might also help." Elisha edged over the rock and dropped down to his feet, nearly overbalancing as his singed soles struck the packed dirt. He bit down on the pain.

"Yes. I know. I've known it's a problem, it's just—" She hesitated, then finished firmly, "I know."

In his arms, Chanterelle stirred again, then cried out, shoving against him. They both fell, him to his knees, her tumbling onto the pathway, then trying to scramble up again. "Wait!" he shouted, "You're hurt."

She froze there, her eyes flashing white. "Don't touch me."

Elisha spread his hands. "I won't. No more unless you ask it."

Her glance darted from him to Rosalynn and back, then she grabbed the chemise and ripped it off, flinging it aside and staring at her limbs. Rosalynn made a startled sound, but the girl ignored her, touching the mud. The cloth had smeared away some patches, but her skin already looked smoother and less red, as if the healing were well on its way. "Thank you," she mumbled. "I should say that." Her toes dug into the earth—no, more than that, they seemed almost drawn into it, her feet following, small stones and grasses shifting aside to admit her.

"Please wait." Elisha reached toward her. "Please."

"I can't wait. They'll come."

She did not look around, but he felt the furtive ripple of contact in the earth beneath him, then it was gone, a glance indeed, but in the dirt. "The necromancers."

Quickly, she nodded, her hair scraggling about her face. "Mancers. Close by all the time now. The others don't believe."

"But you know better. How?"

She spread her fingers into the dirt, her flesh growing dark with the contact, matching the color of the earth. "I feel where they meet. I've begun to sense that they feel me, too. They look for places—like that. Places of the dead." She did look at him then.

He stared into her dark eyes and said what he needed to know. "But I'm not one of them."

She nearly smiled. "You're one of us. *Indivisi.* You don't seek death. It's already with you."

"What is with you?" he asked, but she was vanishing before him, sinking into the earth without a ripple, until she was gone. And he did not need her to speak to know the answer.

Chapter 9

"**My goodness,**" Rosalynn breathed as the space between them settled again into an empty pathway.

Elisha rose slowly, brushed off his palms, and took a few limping steps nearer to his guide. His hands felt loose and numb. "Please," he said, "I need to rest."

"This way." She started walking again. "Do you know, some monasteries have vows of silence. Perhaps I should try that?"

Exhaustion and giddiness rose up through him. "Tell me about your brother's home," he suggested.

She glanced at him sidelong. "Not silence?"

He managed a slender smile. "It would be a help to me to have something else to think about."

After a moment, Rosalynn obliged, describing the fine estate in the north country where she had so recently stayed. Elisha let the sound of her voice wash over him and keep him awake enough to move, focused enough not to give in to the light-headedness of spell-casting. The walk, accompanied at every step by the stinging of his feet, seemed to help fend off the aftereffects of magic, even as the gloom under the trees set in. Rosalynn chose this trail, then another, tending south toward the sea. The ground rose and fell gently, then the stands of oak and willow gave way to the crooked shapes of apple trees, like hunched old men but with the new, tall shoots that showed they had not been tended for some time. Mist crept up between them from the river Elisha heard down below. The vague shapes of buildings clustered at the other side, against the trees.

"Oh, we're here! But it occurs to me, we may not be able—"

A huge dog barreled out of the trees, baying like the Devil, and they instinctively jumped together. With the long muzzle and powerful build of a deerhound, the beast's head came as high as Elisha's chest.

"There it is again!" cried a voice from the darkness. A door banged open, and the firelight within gave shape to a small house. "I'll get the brute this time!"

"Leave off, Patric—don't hurt it! If we catch it, we'll make good money." Two brawny men burst through the door with a clatter of mail.

"Who goes there?" shouted the first. Patric, presumably. Rosalynn leapt behind Elisha, but the dog veered off, snarling, and lowered its head. Patric sprang to the attack, a sword in his hand, while the other man shouted at him from behind. The dog leapt, clamping its jaws round his gauntlet, but Patric flung it aside. The dog fell hard, skidding, and lay still. The second man ran up. "What've you done? That's a valuable animal, I tell you."

"You've got a soft spot for dogs, Ian, and none for

your companions." Patric shook out his bruised hand and turned his eye on Elisha. "Who're you? What do you want here?"

"I'll have you know—" Rosalynn began, but Elisha caught her arm, giving it a squeeze.

"Weary travelers," he said. "On our way to the Abbey."

"Ye should've turned right," Patric rumbled, eyes narrowing as he moved a little closer.

"We're a bit lost," Elisha said carefully. He scanned the man's clothing for any heraldry, any symbol of his master.

"See, it's got a collar and all." Ian removed his belt and looped it over the dog's collar, leaving a long leash which he gripped as he rose. "Maybe get a reward from the owner. Not surprising ye'd get lost, given it's so . . ." He trailed off and took a few steps nearer, the leash drawn straight behind him. "Cor. It's that barber."

Patric's sword swung up to point directly at them. Elisha tensed, but he tried to keep his voice even. "You have the better of me, good sirs. Who are you?"

"Hands up," barked Patric. "You—come out where I can see you." He directed the sword at Rosalynn, who carefully stepped out. "Closer. Bloody Hell—Lady Rosalynn."

Ian and Patric shared a glance, then Ian led them in bowing to Rosalynn. "That's interesting," he chuckled. "Wouldn't've expected to see you out here. Say, Barber, can you take a look at the dog for us?"

"Dogs aren't really my trade. Besides, I must get the lady to the Abbey." He kept his hands spread and visible; not that he had any weapons.

"Everything good?" called a voice from the darkness, and another soldier appeared from down behind the house. A fourth gave a call from the slope of the orchard as well, and Elisha gritted his teeth. Whatever they'd walked into, there were too many of them to simply walk back out again.

"Now, Barber, it's awfully late and the lady looks a bit worn from her journey. Surely it's no good taking her off into the dark." Ian gestured toward Rosalynn with another slight bow that set Elisha's skin tingling, but Rosalynn smoothed her gown with her free hand, the other still holding shut the torn side, her noble manners returning. "We'd be happy to offer you what hospitality we can. Least for tonight, eh?"

"Do you think—" Patric began, his heavy brows furrowed, but Ian flapped a hand at him without turning from Rosalynn.

"Lord knows we ain't got much, but there's a warm bed and something to eat, my lady. Any man can see you've had a rough time of it."

"Well, yes, that's true enough." She glanced at Elisha. "You did want rest, after all, and surely . . ."

Elisha drew her toward him, leaning in to whisper, "We don't know these men or who they serve, my lady. What are they doing here?"

She stared at him a moment, then turned away. "As grateful as we are, good sirs, we can't presume upon the hospitality of your home."

"Oh, not our home, my lady, we're just care-taking for a little while before the new owners arrive. It'd be un-

Christian if we'd let a lady go off in the dark with no proper escort."

Rosalynn's eyes lingered on the open door, all hint of tension sliding from her shoulders as if she'd put off that mantle for the night. With every gentle word the soldier spoke, she moved from the resourceful woman back to the child of lords. "You see, Elisha, there's no need for us to be uncomfortable. And who knows what might be lurking in the darkness?"

Who, indeed? And that was the argument Elisha could not deny. Whatever might be out there, he was too tired to handle it alone. These men clearly recognized Rosalynn—they wouldn't dare to mistreat her. "Very well, my lady," Elisha told her, "As you wish."

She beamed at him, and Patric bowed her toward the entrance, bright and warm with firelight. "We've been trying to get the place clean, my lady, I'm afraid you'll not find it ready for visitors."

"Nonsense. I shall take matters in hand." She plucked up a bit of her skirt to mount the front steps.

Ian looked up at Elisha from a bow of his own, the makeshift leash still clutched in his hand. "Would you . . . ?"

"Let me see the dog," Elisha sighed.

"All's well, you lot, but you'd best keep a better look-out!" Ian called to the shadowy shapes of the other soldiers as he motioned Elisha toward the dog.

"Thought I saw that beggar you mentioned, captain, and I was following a bit, but no sign of 'im now," one of them replied.

"Mebbe you've run him off for good. Get back to your posts."

The other soldiers moved away. Shaking his head, Elisha came up and dropped to one knee beside the dog. With their clean, well-kept clothes and quality swords, these men were no bandits; it couldn't hurt to cooperate, at least for now. The new owner they spoke of was likely Brigit herself. Elisha's weariness ebbed away, replaced by a sense of doom. He didn't want to be here when Brigit arrived, but he didn't know how to talk Rosalynn back out of the house. There was nothing to be done for it until morning, and maybe he could find a way to search the house and grounds in the meantime.

Before he laid a hand on the dog, he reached out in his mind, feeling for the energy of its presence, a warmth palpable at this distance.

Mentally urging it to keep still, to trust him—best yet, to stay unconscious until he was through—Elisha edged forward. Wetting his lips, he murmured the sort of soothing noises he used to use on the farm dogs when they lay whelping. His first medical experience had been assisting the delivery of puppies, soothing the mothers. He lay his hand on the dog's fur, stroking softly, then pressing a little more firmly, finding the pulse beneath the matted fur. A collar nearly as broad as his hand encircled its throat, with spikes of metal sticking out at intervals.

The dog breathed with a wheezy note, and Elisha worked his hands down through the fur, carefully, carefully, exuding all the comfort he knew how. Stunned, yes, and with two ribs broken from the impact. Still stroking the rough fur, Elisha looked up to where Ian stood, trying to make him out in the darkness. "Could use some rest, but he'll be all right. He broke a couple of ribs, I think."

With a grunt and a nod, Ian told him, "Bring him out to the barn and tie him off to something. Let me know when he wakes, and I'll have a go making friends. Meantime, I'll get your lady her supper."

Elisha gathered the dog in his arms and lugged it into the barn. A few horses stood in narrow stalls, chewing on hay thrown down for them, and he found a larger stall on the opposite side, the straw inside disturbed as if it had already been used as a bed. Likely the dog had been sleeping there when they showed up. Good—it would be familiar.

A torch stuck into a holder on the outer wall gave some flickering light, enough to make out the rows of hooks for harness and bridles. Here, Elisha found a stout length of rope and made his way back to the dog.

"Leave it!"

Elisha jumped, spinning to face the speaker, a ragged silhouette in the queer light. "Who're you? Is it your dog?"

"I said leave it!" The man moved forward, thrusting out a long, curving knife.

Holding up his hands, Elisha took a step back, only to thump against the wall. "All right, take the damn dog." Ian would be none too pleased, but Elisha had nothing with which to fight back, not even his boots.

Hunching down, without taking his attention from Elisha, the man called out in a low voice, "Cerberus!" Then he gave a soft whistle.

No response.

"Dear Lord, don't tell me they've killed you, after so long." He fell to all fours and crawled up to the dog, digging his fingers into its dense coat.

The man looked familiar, and Elisha placed him as the lordly beggar at the duke's party. Apparently, more beggar than lord now, but what was he doing here? Slowly, Elisha lowered his hands. "Get him to keep still, if you can. He's got two ribs broken on the right."

"What do you know about it?" the man shot back.

To Elisha's ears, the anger sounded false, a deliberate attempt to hide—what? The stranger hadn't recognized him, thanks to the mask and finery he'd been wearing that night. Now, he might pass for a beggar himself. There were too many questions, too many people suddenly involved with this place. The men outside must be Brigit's advance party, with this man trailing them. For what purpose? Elisha tried to calm his own jangled nerves and attuned himself, feeling the weary weight of the horses, the blank warmth of the dog, then sending his awareness to the complexity of the man.

Fear came first, seeping from him like that mist creeping up from the river. Pain followed on the fear, both a sharp, physical pain and a long-time desperation of spirit. Tied up in these, he felt exhaustion, grief, and worry, reaching out toward the dog that meant more to him than a mere hunting beast. Tears hovered close.

The raw emotions surprised Elisha. Few men carried their feelings so close to the surface, certainly not when they were in full command of their faculties, and to get such a clear impression without even touching the man—but that desperation might tell all. How long had this man gone without sleep, without a proper meal? The fear drove him, and the pain pricked him constantly.

Elisha had never felt anything like it. It seeped through him, and he shook himself, withdrawing to the confines of his skin, taking a few breaths to settle his own emotions before he carefully unfurled his awareness again. He couldn't afford to let the man stir him up like that, not until he knew what the stranger was about.

He took a step nearer, and the man jerked, the knife coming back to his hand though he gasped in pain as he lifted it. Still, Elisha held up his hands. "Who are you?" Elisha asked, his tone coming from that same place of comfort he had called on for the dog.

"Nobody." The man trembled ever so slightly, then forced himself still. "A beggar, no more than that."

A beggar, with a dog so fine. Not likely. "You were at Dunbury a few days ago, at the ball."

The man's eyes flared, he took in Elisha's face and clothing, then he relaxed a little. "You danced with Lady Rosalynn. I remember."

Elisha nodded. The swirl of emotion twisted toward guilt, and a hint of something lighter: desire. Rosalynn had at least one admirer, even if he had fallen from his rightful place. "I'm Elisha Barber—"

The ferocity of the attack knocked the wind out of him, even as the butt of the knife slammed into his head.

Chapter 10

❖

Elisha blacked out as he tumbled away, then his vision flashed back, blurry, as his attacker pounced on top of him. Gleaming gold, the knife dove toward his chest.

Elisha threw up his arm, catching the other man's wrist. Still, the knife edged down, slashing his shirt and cutting a groove against the bone. Slamming his left fist into Elisha's temple, the man let a cry of pain escape between bared teeth.

The knife pressed against Elisha's ribcage, blood and pus oozing down the hilt from the man's hand, dripping to mingle with Elisha's blood. Pain cut the shock that had struck first, and Elisha gasped. The face above him snarled its hatred, bearing down against his protective arm. Exhausted, yes, but still strong.

Elisha visualized the ribbons that tied his shirt cuffs, and the rope he had found to tie the dog. Affinity. His wrist circled by the ribbon, another wrist circled by the rope. He still carried the cloth talisman he had used at the fire. Drawing strength from it, he fumbled on the ground and found the rope. Contact.

The rope leapt to his command, snapping around the man's right arm.

Crying out, the stranger struggled, and Elisha rolled him aside, sending the other end of the rope tight around a pillar of the barn, then back to find the other wrist. The rope wound itself around the ragged man, jerked him back against the wood, and secured itself in knots Elisha imagined with his pain and shock.

Edging away, gasping, Elisha demanded, "What the Hell did you attack me for?"

"You killed the king," his captive spat.

From the house, Ian's voice called, "Here, what's going on out there?"

Staring at the man before him in the uneven light, Elisha saw the pain drawn in the dirty face. He didn't want to speak, not until he knew what was going on himself. "I tripped in the dark," he called back, noting the narrowing of his captive's eyes.

"Take care with that dog, mind you!"

Tilting his face to the sky, Elisha replied, "Aye, soldier," and was answered by the thump of the door.

"You are a witch," his prisoner hissed. "They ought to burn you and scatter the ashes where even God won't see."

"I'm sure they'll get to that in time," Elisha said. He untied his cuffs and stripped off his shirt, turning to face the torch so he could examine his wound.

Elisha heard the intake of breath behind him and ignored it. In the curly hair of his chest, the brand of his punishment showed smooth and darker than the surrounding skin, a barren patch as big as his palm, reminder of the interrogation he'd undergone at King Hugh's demand, the interrogation where he protected Brigit at the cost of his own pain. Blood seeped from the freshly carved valley that cut across the scar. It stung with his every breath and reminded him of the French magus in his shroud, skinned, his muscle laid bare by a sharp blade and a steady hand.

"God's blood," Elisha cursed.

The wound was short and shallow, given that it touched the bone, but the already scarred skin would not knit well, and was too stretched to permit him to stitch it back again. There was nothing to do but keep it clean, and hope for the best.

"What happened to you?" the prisoner asked, interest mingling with enmity.

"Which, the back, or the chest?" Elisha shot back, facing him again, his chin high. "I was lashed for saving the prince, and branded for loving the wrong woman. And hung for treason—I'll give you that one for free." He grinned. "How about you?"

The prisoner's face had gone pale beneath his dirt and a month's growth of facial hair. "The prince?"

"Well," Elisha allowed, "I didn't know he was the prince at the time. He was disguised as a commoner to carry the king's messages. Not that he's helped me out much since. Who are you, and what are you doing here?"

The man shook his head, forehead furrowed. "But you killed the king."

"If it helps to know, I didn't mean anything by it." Elisha sat back on his heels, studying his prisoner, who slumped against the pillar, breathing heavily and watching him in return. "I never set out for treason, but he was threatening some people very dear to me. I didn't see another choice." The rush of excitement had pushed away his own aches. "I gather you heard about it, and me, and swore to avenge him, am I right?"

"More or less." The man made an effort to straighten.

From the end stall came a low whimper. Both turned to stare.

"Cerberus!" the man hissed.

Claws scraped on the dirt as the dog heaved itself to its feet.

With a triumphant smile, the captive urged, "To me, Cerberus! Attack!"

Immediately, the dog burst around the corner, head lowered, teeth bared. It stopped short, skidding in the straw and whining as it slid up very near. The dog lowered its head again, but with the ears half-raised, the tail out straight. Interest rather than threat. Elisha let himself relax and smile. Cerberus on his feet was higher than the seated men and had to look down to shift his gaze from Elisha to the prisoner and back. The dog whined, his tail giving a slow wave.

Elisha held out his hand to be sniffed. Gravely, Cerberus pushed his wet nose against Elisha's fingers, then gave him a single, long slurp, and lay down at his master's side.

Casting a quick look at the dog, the prisoner turned as quickly away, his eyes shining. "What have you done to my dog?" he whispered, his voice cracking. "You've cast some accursed spell on him."

At that, Elisha laughed, shaking his head. He had gotten a fright from that knife brandished against him, but, try as he might, he couldn't see the danger now. Here was a man loyal to his king, seeking justice as he saw it, heart-sick because his dog seemed to have deserted him. Letting go his irritation, Elisha said, "It's nearly impossible to cast a spell on a being with willpower of its own. All I did was try to help him, to make him comfortable, nothing more. If that's a spell, I believe it's commonly known as kindness."

"All witches are liars," the man said, his neck arched as he turned his face away, his throat trembling with shuddering breaths.

"Maybe I'll cast one on you, too," Elisha murmured, and the man stiffened in an instant. Creeping behind the dog to avoid the prisoner's thrashing legs, Elisha unfolded the fingers on one bound hand.

Rags wrapped the palm, but blood escaped around the edges and had bonded them into a single thickness. He had seen the bindings at the ball, and thought them a clever touch to finish the disguise. After a moment's search, Elisha found the discarded knife.

With a soft moan, the prisoner mumbled, "*Pater noster, qui est in caelis . . .*"

The stranger went on, the Lord's prayer tumbling from his lips in Latin as naturally as his native tongue. Elisha recognized the sounds and the sense of the words from the daily masses of his youth, and his estimation of the stranger's position rose. He put the prayer from his mind, cutting away the foul bandage. Attunement, he was learning, worked both ways, enabling him to sense more than usual, or to selectively block certain elements to better focus on the task before him.

At the center of the man's left palm, his right as well, as Elisha shortly confirmed, a patch of smooth flesh darkened the skin, with cracked skin all around, oozing and giving off the odor of infection. Wrinkling his nose, Elisha remarked, "You ought to take more care with your bandages."

The man broke off his prayer, flinching at Elisha's gentle touch.

"If I untie you, will you promise not to kill me before I've had a chance to see to these?"

"I'll rip your head off," muttered the prisoner, "before I let you curse me."

Placing his elbow over the man's shoulder, Elisha rolled the arm palm up, revealing the burn mark that scarred his palm and the trail of identical wounds leading from his wrist to his elbow. "You've been branded. Someone should take care of you before you lose both hands."

The beggar averted his eyes. "I would've killed you— why do me any favors?"

Withdrawing his hand, Elisha said, "Because it's just possible that both of us are good men doing what we must to survive. Who are you? Why were you branded?"

He kept silent, his head bowed.

"My guess would be theft," Elisha continued. "That's what they burn your hands for." As he spoke, he loosened the rope, easing the strain of his prisoner's arms, sending all his good-will into his hands. "But if you'd stolen something valuable, they'd've cut them off instead, even though you're of noble birth." The man stirred beneath his touch. "I'd bet you stole food. You've been on a long journey, and a hard one, that's plain. Whatever has happened to you, you can't count on your old ways, or on the brotherhood of your fellow nobles. If there is such a thing." Elisha edged around the pillar, sitting shoulder to shoulder with his prisoner.

Again the prisoner turned his face away.

"Why do you any favors?" Elisha asked of the night. "To prove to God and man that I'm no killer." He leaned over and found a few millet seeds not sprouted, rolling them between his fingers. "Yes, I am a witch. It doesn't make me evil any more than does the fact that you're a thief."

That brought his head up, his dormant pride sneaking back in. "Don't speak of what you do not understand."

"It's good advice, my friend," Elisha said, closing his hand over a seed and opening it to reveal an egg, "but it cuts both ways, wouldn't you say?"

The lashes flickered as a wary glance came his way. "Where'd you get that egg?"

Holding up another seed, Elisha pictured it similarly transformed, and let the new egg rock in his palm.

"Get away from me with those." He used the loosened bonds to push himself toward the dog, turning his back to Elisha, the rope shifting against his wrists.

"Don't you think, if I wanted to kill you, I'd have a better way than a couple of eggs?" Elisha set the eggs down, then ripped one sleeve from his shirt—he'd have had to explain the slash and the blood anyhow, might as well put the thing to use. Taking the man's arm, he exposed one hand, the taut muscles resisting and finally submitting. He carefully cleaned away the ooze from each wound, steadying the injured hands as much with his presence as the physical touch, sending comfort, trust, calm through the contact.

"What're you doing?" the man demanded, but his voice showed that weariness again, and his sense of defeat flowed through his skin. He'd been weary at the duke's hall, but nothing like this, as if that party had been the final humiliation.

"Cleaning the wounds, then I'll make a poultice from the eggs. It would be better if I'd not lost my herbs, but this should—" He broke off, considering.

"What? What is it?" Tension flooded the contact.

"I thought I saw some vines by the door. I wondered if they're roses."

Automatically, the man began, "No, that's—" and stopped himself, his body going rigid, his skin trembling against Elisha's.

Elisha looked up, the warmth of the other man's hand cupped against his palm. "It's your house, isn't it?" Duke Randall had mentioned the royal family giving up the lodge, but he hadn't said the name of its new owner.

Again, the head drooped. "The doors were all bolted, and I didn't have the heart to break the locks."

"Or the strength," Elisha murmured, rubbing egg white gently over the brands.

The man gave a bitter laugh more a movement than a sound. "You're a clever man, Elisha Barber. It's no wonder you were able to kill him."

"I told you I meant nothing by it." Deftly, he wound

strips from his shirt around the injured hands. "Take care, would you? Don't try to kill anyone until your hands have a chance to heal."

Another laugh, a little closer to a sob.

Elisha sat back and considered the man before him. He was tall but gaunt, now, with whatever grief he carried. His birth showed in his speech and carriage, even in defeat, and in the fabric of the torn clothes he wore, ruined though they were. The calluses on both hands took the pattern common to soldiers, but without the ground-in dirt also common. He was more than a captain, then. He wore no shoes—too easy to sell when you needed money—but his bare feet looked worn out. Unlike Elisha, he wasn't used to walking unshod.

After a moment, Elisha set his fingers to the knots and untied them, lifting the rope from the man's chest, easing his arms forward, the newly bandaged hands draped in his lap. He came around to study the young lord's face, turned away in shadows, always averted as if he feared being recognized. He had dodged the question of his name once before; Elisha would not ask again now. "Look, they've got supper on inside. Will you let me bring you a meal?"

Chapter 11

———❖———

Elisha ducked into the kitchen, watching out for the low beams, dangling with betony and primrose—both said to be proof against witches, he noted wryly. The scent of rich beef stew reminded him he hadn't eaten in quite a while.

A handful of soldiers gathered around the table with Rosalynn at the head, full bowls in front of them. She pushed back when she saw him, her face brightening, then going dark. "What's happened to your shirt?"

He turned away, hiding his fresh wound, to fill a bowl from the pot hanging over the coals. "I used it to bind the dog's ribs. He'd come awake and clawed at me, so the thing was torn up anyhow. I had to put him back out to deal with him."

Ian gave a hearty laugh. "Aye, he's a feisty one, then. He'll fetch me a fine price if I can't find the owner."

"For a dog? All of this for a dog?" Rosalynn dabbed at her mouth with the only napkin in sight. They'd given her a napkin. Her hair was combed, and her dress held with a few pins. Evidently, the soldiers were upholding their bargain. "You should see the rest of the house. It's lovely, but it's clear nobody's lived here for a long while. The whole place needs to be cleaned, and I haven't any idea how to go about it without my maidservant."

"You'll get on fine, I'm sure." Elisha smiled inwardly, suddenly eager to escape again to his wary captive and the silent Cerberus. With that thought, he plucked another bowl from the mantel and filled that as well.

"What'd you need two bowls for?" Rosalynn asked as he turned.

"Well, we don't want the dog to go hungry, do we?" He looked to Ian, got his approval and more.

"Get a bigger bowl, then," Ian ordered. "That's a mighty beast we've got ourselves."

Following the command, Elisha poured the contents of one bowl into another three times bigger and topped it up. "Maybe I'd best stay with him—make sure he recovers."

"You can't mean to sleep in a barn!" Rosalynn set her hands on her hips, but Elisha stared at her, then gave a little tip of his head, drawing her close.

"I'm looking for a copper pot that would just fit in this bowl," he told her softly. "It's got a sealed lid. It's what I came here for. While you clean, will you look for me? I'll be looking outside."

Her eyes brightened with a conspiratorial smile. "I see. Of course."

Elisha met Rosalynn's gaze and mouthed the word "courage." She lifted her chin and looked away. "I'll see you in the morning then," she remarked over her shoulder, not noticing the speculative glances that passed between the soldiers. They thought he was her leman. All the better if it meant they would leave her alone. Before taking up the bowls again, he tucked a half-loaf from the table under his arm and carried his booty out the door.

He entered the open end of the barn, carefully bearing the hot bowls toward the back.

The man started up, scrambling to his feet, his right hand flying automatically to his hip.

"Just me, the murderous witch," Elisha said, with a slight smile. "If you want anyone to think you're a beggar, you should be ducking your head rather than going for your sword."

The man straightened, a deal taller than Elisha, then sank back to his knees, staring as Elisha set the huge bowl before him. "How on earth—?"

"It's supposed to be for Cerberus, so you'd best share with him." Elisha ripped the bread in two and handed some over.

As the man reached out to take it, he looked up, his eyes a vivid blue beneath their overlay of pain, his hand shaking. His eyebrows pinched together, and he let his gaze drop.

For a moment, their fingers brushed together. A rush of gratitude flowed through Elisha like the glory of that sunset, sweeping away the last of his doubts and his worries about what was to come. Suddenly, he understood what made monks give away all they had, and what made the nuns work so hard in the hospitals. Others might work for the glory of God or the glory of the church, but sometimes, it was enough to make a difference to one man, even for just one evening.

Settling at a pillar opposite the stranger, Elisha slowly ate about half of his stew. He set the bowl aside and turned a blind eye when Cerberus's questing muzzle dipped in. Meditatively, he chewed on his bread, letting one hand stroke the dog's coarse fur. "You weren't with the king's army, then."

Glancing up, his mouth full, the man shook his head. "Up north," he said, taking a bite of bread.

"With Prince Thomas."

The man jerked, his gaze suddenly sharper. "The traitor."

"So I'm told. Are you sworn to kill him, too?" Elisha asked lightly, surprised by the twist to the man's lips.

"An enemy of the king is an enemy of mine." The stranger raised his bowl to take another swallow.

"I take it my life is forfeit when you've finished dinner?" Elisha crossed his legs, leaning back against a pillar.

"I've not decided yet." Another swallow finished the bowl, and he cast a guilty look at Cerberus, who lay content enough. No doubt the dog had been able to supplement his diet with rats and other wild things his master would have disdained. Settling himself, the man said, "I confess I don't know what to make of you. You killed the king, and with witchcraft, both capital offenses in this country, yet apparently you're free and happy in the company of the duke and his daughter."

"Perhaps we are neither of us what we seem," Elisha replied, rubbing his arms.

The man shook his head, tangled hair wreathing his shadowed face. "You don't know who I am?"

"A nobleman—or you were—on the run, for some reason. The king's man, the owner of this house. What else should I know?"

The stranger drew back a little, and asked a question of his own instead. "Are you cold?"

Self-consciously, Elisha dropped his hands, but the gooseflesh showed plain enough, even in the dim light. "I'm always cold. A man doesn't invite Death and expect it to leave again without a trace."

The man gave a low whistle and a toss of his head.

Ears perked, Cerberus rose and padded over, draping himself against Elisha's side.

Wriggling his fingers into the dense fur, Elisha felt the warmth of life and company. The dog was all this man had left, and still he sent him to comfort another. "Thanks."

A half-shrug. "You say that it's hard to cast a spell on a creature of will."

"Nearly impossible, unless his will is bent to helping the witch."

The stranger looked away, drawing up his knees and hugging them. "I don't know that I believe you. Or that I want to."

"You've had dealings with witches before."

"A long time ago."

Edging back from the chill in his voice, Elisha asked instead, "Tell me about Cerberus. It's a strange name."

This brought a small chuckle and a shake of the head. "You don't know Greek legends?"

Irritated to be caught again in his ignorance, Elisha said, "Well, I don't have much call for that in my line of work."

Instantly, the stranger's manner changed, the haughtiness turning to contrition, his hands falling aside in apology. "Of course, of course. It's the name of the dog who guards the gates of Hell."

Turning to Cerberus, Elisha remarked, "Then you watch out for me, I'll be bound there some day soon." He scratched the long muzzle, receiving a contented sigh. The dog's presence drew away the cold, replacing it with a warmth of more than simply life, of friendship. "Did you raise him?"

"Yes." Pride evident, then sorrow. "The puppy was a wedding gift."

Keeping his eyes on the dog, Elisha felt the wave of grief and worry begin to rise all over again. "I didn't realize you were married," he said quietly.

"Anna's dead," the stranger whispered. "They're all dead, all of the women who loved me." Huddled there, wrapped up in himself, the man looked more like a child than either lord or beggar, a child who found his way home only to discover that home no longer held any comfort for him.

Quietly, Elisha said, "I don't know how long we'll be here, or how I will be leaving, but, if I am able, I'll leave the door open for you."

The stranger drew a ragged breath and looked away. Then his head sank to his arms, and his shoulders quaked as the tears finally fell.

Cerberus raised his head, and Elisha lifted his hand. They rose together and crossed the few paces.

Once again, this man had touched him, the torrent of his sorrow stemmed for just a moment and released by

Elisha's offer. Elisha didn't know how to approach grief of this magnitude and mystery. He had no more words— even his attempt at kindness brought only more pain. It seemed ages ago when he had spoken to Mordecai, when he knew him as a magus called "Sage," pouring out his frustration, and Mordecai had answered him, "*Each of us is as God has made us, cursed and blessed in equal measure.*"

Cerberus sank his belly to the floor and burrowed his nose in his master's lap.

After a moment, Elisha sat down, his arm brushing against the stranger's. His fingers laced together in his lap, Elisha leaned his head back against the post. He shut his eyes and searched for peace. Cursed and blessed.

Instead of attuning himself to this place, the sounds and scents of the barn and all it held, he attuned it to him, reaching out to draw on the familiar scent of hay and the warmth of the dog's steadfastness. He found again the glory of the sunset and the wonder of the moon, and took strength from the beauty all around them. He softened this strength with that familiarity and comfort, and let it all seep from him into the other man, a silent current of faith that swirled into the other's pain. As he had done when he danced with Rosalynn, he did not try to guide it but sent it on with all of his good wishes, the only gift he had.

Eventually, the torch guttered and died, a trail of smoke drifting their way.

The man's sobs, too, died away. He breathed deeper and let it out without that rough edge. After a while, he raised his head, expelling a long breath into the night.

"My God." His shoulders shifted back. "I hardly know who I am anymore."

In spite of himself, Elisha laughed, just a little, with that bittersweet air. "I know just what you mean."

And the other man laughed, just a little. "I'm glad I didn't kill you."

"Not as glad as I am."

Another laugh. "Aren't you supposed to go in some time? The duke's daughter is waiting for you."

"No, not for me, nor for any man, I think, thanks to the one who wouldn't have her."

"That bastard," cursed the cultivated voice.

So perhaps he'd guessed right about the man's attraction. Elisha smiled into the darkness. "A king's man, but not a prince's?"

He laughed again, longer, and with a suggestion of real humor Elisha had not felt in him before. "No," he said at last, "Not that prince." He yawned.

"You two should get some sleep," Elisha said.

When he hesitated, the tension flowing back, Elisha added, "I'll keep watch."

With an awkward smile Elisha felt as a warmth against his skin, the other man said, "I should not trust you."

"Probably not," Elisha agreed. "But your dog does."

"Yes, well, he's rather daft, isn't he?" Pushing the dog's head from his lap, he got slowly to his feet and walked toward the far stall, his bare feet crackling straw and dirt. He placed a hand on the wood of the wall, bowing his head for a moment, a figure shown silver by the moon and stars. "You cannot possibly know what it means to me to feel safe, even just for tonight." He tapped his fingers on the wood then slipped into the stall, the huge dog stalking after, with a wave of its tail.

Elisha's throat ached. He settled on a mound of straw, trembling from the force of the other man's emotions. Shaking himself free of the compulsion, he stretched out all of his senses. It seemed he could reach further every time, as if the exercise of the power made it stronger, like a muscle he had never known he possessed.

His awareness brushed the lives around him, light and serene. Four horses dozed in their stalls, whuffling in their sleep. A low fire burned in the kitchen, a lone man awake, prodding it to occupy his watch. Rosalynn tucked in an upstairs room, sleeping soundly. He could watch over her, even from here. It gave him a measure of comfort. Had she found anything in her search? That answer, and his own search, must wait the length of his promise. Outside, small animals prowled the night, something died silently, something else was born. He thought of Chanterelle sinking in the embrace of her beloved earth.

And in the last stall, a man slept curled against his one companion. Slept at last, for the first time in days. Elisha reveled in this, taking the power to comfort another even when his own situation was far from safe. Into the night, Elisha guarded the trust his spell had earned him, his simple spell of kindness.

Chapter 12

＊

Even before the sun rose, Elisha could feel her coming. He felt the lifting of his spirit first and thought it only the aftermath of last night's accomplishment. Then the anticipation grew stronger until he could not imagine it was only for the coming dawn. And at last, he sensed her presence drawing closer, riding at a good pace through the woods. She had abandoned the carriage then. He should not be surprised. He could flee under cover of a deflection spell, but Rosalynn was still inside, and the soldiers would tell Brigit he'd been there. He hadn't even had a chance to search for the talisman that brought him here, and he had a new trust to protect as well.

He got up and stretched, considering what to do about the man and dog, still sleeping. A dreary gray sky greeted him, lightening ever so slightly and promising rain. The kitchen door popped open, and Patric came out, yawning and scratching under his arm. He walked to the edge of the road and pissed on one of the apple trees.

Disgusted, Elisha turned away. With a forest of trees to choose from, the man was pissing at another man's food. His body ached a bit from assuming a wide variety of uncomfortable postures to stay awake. He had allowed himself to doze lightly, his heightened senses jerking him out of it when a horse shifted in its stall, when Rosalynn moved restlessly indoors, or when one of the guards experienced a dream that sent a rush of pleasure out into the night.

The sound of hoof beats rose from the road. Patric got his britches tied and trotted a bit down the road to meet them.

A wiser man would have spent his night searching for the talisman, knowing that Brigit was on her way. Well, if Elisha were such a fool, at least it was for a worthy cause, letting a battered man sleep peacefully before he faced his next day. Elisha retreated to the shadow of the barn door as Patric escorted the riders up the road.

"Good work, Patric. He's tending a dog, you say?" Brigit's voice cut the dawn, shrill after Patric's revelations.

"Aye, Highness, huge one, with a spiked collar and all." He waved his hands about, exaggerating Cerberus, but not by much.

Brigit frowned. "That sounds like Thomas's dog, Cerberus. Alaric's always complaining about that beast."

"Dogs are known to find their way home, Highness." Patric smiled up at her as he helped her down. "Maybe that means the traitor's already dead."

About to step from the shadow of the barn, Elisha

froze, a chill sweeping over him. Brigit knew about Cerberus and his master: Thomas.

"Oh, my sweet Lord," Elisha breathed. Immediately he clamped down on his shock, pulling back his tendrils of awareness as if he had been singed. As carefully as he could, he retreated to the back of the barn, hurrying when he knew he was out of sight, and dropped to his knees in the straw.

Awake in an instant, Cerberus drew himself up and stretched out his long legs, giving a yawn full of pink tongue and sharp teeth.

"Wake up," Elisha whispered, giving his voice an edge of power drawn from the talisman at his waist.

The man stirred and rolled, then sat bolt upright, his hand at his hip, then searching the straw until he found his knife. Shaggy dark hair hung down past his shoulders, and the ragged beard concealed his jaw, but those eyes were vividly familiar, a deep blue, almost as sharp as Elisha's own—eyes that he'd been told reminded people of the king's.

With a puff of breath, the man relaxed. "Is it dawn?" He rubbed his face.

"You've got to leave, out the back, right now." Elisha thrust out his arm and helped him up, keeping a hand on his arm.

"What is it?" He glanced quickly toward the door.

"Your brother's betrothed is here."

His eyes flared in a panic that sprang through the contact. "You know who I am." He searched Elisha's face.

"I just found out."

Prince Thomas stiffened, pulling away, his grip on the knife tightening. "Will you reveal me?"

"God, no." Elisha took a step forward, reaching up to touch Thomas's knife-hand, sending his assurance.

"I'm accused of treason." He trembled, ever so slightly, his eyes darting to the door and back.

"I don't care. Maybe you plotted to kill him and maybe you didn't, but I'm the one who did the deed, remember? Trust me for a little longer—please."

Wiping a hand over his face, Thomas nodded once.

Elisha thought furiously, listening for the sound of approaching feet. "Can you get Cerberus to run? Through the orchard, maybe?"

"Yes, of course, but—"

"Good, we'll make a diversion." He slipped from the stall and found the rope from last night. With a quick spell, he weakened it, breaking off a piece which he tied to the big dog's collar. "We draw them off, you get out of here, yes?"

Prince Thomas swallowed and nodded again.

"Go."

Running a swift hand over the dog's back, Thomas murmured, "Cerberus, river," and put out his hand.

The dog sprang forward like an arrow from a bow.

Elisha yelled, cursed, and ran after. "Get back here, you bugger!" He never looked back.

Cerberus burst through the startled crowd, pulling away from Elisha with every enormous bound, bent on his master's bidding.

His hands balled into fists, Elisha ran after, brushing

past the guards. "Curse you, Hell-hound!" he shouted, flinging himself into the tall grass of the orchard in the wake of Cerberus's passing.

"Elisha!" Brigit cried as she jumped out of the way.

Elisha ran for all he was worth. Bounding ahead, Cerberus let out a bark that rattled the branches above them. A deer sprang up from the lee of the riverbank and fled, with Cerberus in pursuit.

Grinning, panting, Elisha stumbled over a stone and slithered down the rest of the slope, rocks scraping his back and arms. For one blessed moment, his bare feet found the water. Into it he sent all of his triumph and all of his hopes, for he heard the pounding of booted feet coming after and shouts of dismay. Somewhere in the woods, his prince was slipping back into the shadows.

Elisha had never given allegiance to any man. He was subject to the Master of the Barber's Guild and the burghers of the city and, more distantly, to the king with his knights and barons. For the most part, he ignored them all and did as he must. Now, he risked his neck in the most literal sense for the traitor prince, a man who had tried to kill him. He felt as drawn to Thomas as he once had been to Brigit herself.

Rough hands grabbed his arms and dragged him back. They hauled him up the slope, their help a little too harsh for men apparently assisting a fallen guest. They shoved him before Brigit, waiting on the verge.

"How did you get here?" Brigit demanded. "What are you doing here?"

Elisha stared up into her dazzling green eyes. She was

beautiful in her fury: a dangerous beauty. "I'm taking Lady Rosalynn to Beaulieu Abbey. We got lost."

At the mention of Rosalynn, Brigit's eyes narrowed. He wondered if she might be jealous. "You are taking her?"

"There's just the two of them, Highness," Ian offered. "Showed up last night, and the dog tipped us off. We gave 'em supper and beds. We knew you'd want to see them."

"Sorry about the dog," Elisha offered. "He broke the rope and bowled me over."

"Shut up about the damned dog," Brigit snapped, her cheeks colored as she regarded the house and orchard around them.

"Sorry," he murmured again. A hundred little scrapes and bruises plagued him. Small price to pay for a man's life. He had once paid twenty-seven lashes for Alaric's own. The irony of it lifted his head, and he met Brigit's fiery gaze.

"I don't believe it," she said. "I don't believe you. It's no coincidence you being here."

"Perhaps I came for love of you," he murmured.

She stared at him, glancing at the scar upon his chest, her hands knotting into her cloak as if confused by what he meant. "Last we met you swore you would never trust me again."

"They do go best together, trust and love, but I'd rather have one than neither."

Brigit flushed and glanced away, leaving his heart thundering from more than his run. Flushing was another sign of pregnancy, though her body showed no change yet. She looked to be in good health. On behalf of the child, Elisha approved. Trying to steady his nerves, he looked back toward the barn, but it eased him not at all. In the shadows of the wood beyond, he saw a face, arrested in flight.

Thomas stood turning back, his lips parted, his face pale, his expression shifting between fear and wonder. He stared at Brigit as if at a ghost. Damn it all, the fool would get himself hung.

"Brigit," Elisha blurted, and her eyes snapped back to his. "Why not tell your men to back off?"

"Yes, of course." She waved a hand at the soldiers, who grumbled but retreated.

Elisha moved forward until he stood inches from her, her head tipped slightly to meet his eyes. "I think you know what I came for." She started to look away again, but he seized her hand. *"Brigit, if you ever cared for me—"*

"I did. I do. But I don't—"

"You can't bear to give up the power, even if you can't use it."

"You don't understand," she said aloud. "Thomas is mounting an army against us, and—"

Elisha felt his denial before he spoke and drew it back—for how could he know she was lying?—but already her touch grew colder.

"You know something, Elisha. Tell me what you know."

"There's division among the magi," he began, hurrying to cover his slip. "Some of them would support you, some are afraid to. They're afraid your actions will reveal them to those who hate us. My killing the king has made things worse. If you use the talisman, they'll never trust you."

"It needn't be so theatrical as what you did," she replied.

"Some of them are calling me a necromancer."

"No one could think that who's ever met you." Brigit smiled, but there had been something else, a fleeting suggestion of desire. "Necromancers thrive on fear and pain; death isn't the enemy to them, it's what they live for."

"So they are real."

"I only know what I've been told." She curled both hands around Elisha's, wrapping him in heat. "You could master the power. I know you could. You could use the strength of that talisman to serve our common cause."

"Not if I don't know where it is," he pointed out with a gentle squeeze.

Brigit's lips curled, and her eyes sparkled as if he had promised her the world, and he wondered how anyone ever resisted her. But there was a hint of calculation in that gaze. After a beat of silence, she replied, *"I'll bring you there."*

Elisha took a moment to realize what she had said. She would bring him to his talisman, so easily? *"Brigit, you'd give it to me?"*

Aloud, she said, "Come inside and break the fast. I must meet your lady-friend."

"She isn't mine, and you know it." He would have broken contact, but she tugged his arm, sliding her own hand about his elbow as if he escorted her.

As they walked up to the house, Elisha managed a glance toward the barn and the forest. Prince Thomas had vanished as if he had never been, and Elisha wondered if he would ever see him again. He stumbled on the step and rested his hand upon the lock, ever so briefly, slipping Brigit's hand as she preceded him. A thought, a bit of rust and contact. Elisha sent a spark of magic like a wicked key, and Thomas's door could never again be locked against him.

Chapter 13

"I see you have made yourself at home," Brigit purred, and Elisha moved up behind her to find Rosalynn in the solar against a wall painted with diamonds and roses, a bound volume in her hands. She slapped it shut and dropped it on the desk.

"You have found her then, Elisha. I take it she is the mistress of the house, now?" In her muddy gown, missing her chemise, underskirts, and veil, Rosalynn could not help but look dowdy. Her shoulders hunched, and she clutched the torn side of her gown, seeming to shrink as Brigit approached.

Brigit smiled graciously. "Oh, I do hope you enjoyed our hospitality. You are free to go, and I suggest you do so. Come, Elisha." She flicked her fingers at him. "We started off early, and I am starved."

Elisha's stomach rumbled agreement, but Rosalynn pressed her trembling lips together. Her chatter was her most terrible defense and apparently she feared to use it. Her damp eyes traced Elisha's scarred chest and looked away. "Yes, well," she said at last. "I'm sure I can find the way to Beaulieu on my own."

"You can't go alone," Elisha said, shaking off the hand that Brigit put out to him. "She can't. I'll bring her to the abbey and return. It's not far, is it?"

"I'll send my men, and you can stay with me." She reached out again and stroked his arm. The touch sent a tingling warmth through his flesh.

"Yes. That's fine." Rosalynn brushed past them along the corridor and pushed her way outside.

Elisha took back his arm but slowly, his body responding to Brigit's touch while his duty urged him to go. "I swore an oath to her father."

Brigit's eyes narrowed, and her hands clenched briefly, then she trotted past him and leaned out the door. "Lady Rosalynn, please wait!" Her voice dripped sweetness, and Elisha wondered if it were a spell. "Elisha shall attend you, of course. But he does need something to eat. And a new shirt, I think. You've been cleaning, haven't you? Do you know where one might be found?" She drew Elisha back with her while Rosalynn stood in the yard, wavering, head bowed against the drizzle.

"I'll go with you a ways," Brigit murmured. "We can get the talisman as we go." Her touch on his arm was soft, almost tentative. "But we won't tell her that I'm coming along until after we breakfast. I think she doesn't like me. I can't say I blame her, of course." Was it a hint of sadness in her voice?

Elisha nodded, ever more convinced that Brigit was trying something; perhaps a glamour she cast upon herself, to appear the more tempting. "I thought you would fight me for it."

"I've had it for weeks, Elisha, and I cannot do what you have done." Her nails brushed his skin.

With an effort, Elisha turned from Brigit to the yard. "Please, my lady," Elisha said. "Let's be as comfortable as we may."

Rosalynn squared her shoulders, glancing back at him, and finally nodded. "I shall find you a shirt. There are a few chests of clothes upstairs, hunting things, mainly, but I think there is something that will do."

He put out his hand to help her mount the steps, the sort of unnecessary gesture the servants of nobility performed all the time, and she laid her hand over his with a tremulous smile.

"Very good," Brigit said. "I shall make things ready." But instead of heading for the kitchen, she slipped out the door behind them and hurried to meet with her men.

"I suppose she has soldiers for servants, but she really ought to have a proper retinue." Rosalynn pushed back her damp hair, her hand hesitating, then she turned from him. "The shirt. Yes." Hauling her bedraggled skirts, Rosalynn mounted the narrow stairs, her footsteps creaking the floor overhead.

Elisha stood in the hall, frowning. In spite of the desire she still kindled in him, Brigit's change of heart did not sit well, nor did her easy offer to get him the talisman. She must hope to seduce him to her cause, if not to her bed, and she probably thought her sudden kindness toward a woman she clearly despised would soften Elisha's determination. She was wrong.

Elisha stalked into the solar to wait for the two women. He took in the chairs—sturdy, but elegantly carved—a desk with quills and inkpots that must be long dry, a broad fireplace that would back up to the one in the kitchen beyond. Over the mantle hung a painting of the Madonna and child, a lovely blond version. The Madonna wore a cloak of ermine, the child stood beside her. Elisha drew closer. With long, blond locks and bright blue eyes, the child was clearly a girl. Not a Madonna, then, but a portrait. Thomas's two princesses. Elisha wished that he had shown the man more kindness. Surely there was something else he could have done.

"Here we are, then." Rosalynn settled a creamy silk tunic over his arm. "It's a bit long; I gather the owner here is taller than you, but I think it will do. I found some travelling cloaks as well—I do hope they won't mind our borrowing them. Perhaps I should write a note to explain the matter? But your Lady Brigit must know them." As she spoke, she hung the cloaks on pegs in the wall.

"I don't think she does, my lady." The eyes of the little princess in the painting gazed back at him, so like her father's. He gathered up the cloth of the shirt, though it caught on the little nicks and calluses of his hands. It slithered down over his chest, stroking the cut its owner had made above Elisha's heart, and he winced. The sleeves hung over his hands and he bound them back with silken ties. As fine as his garments had been for the ball, this shirt was worth the lot of them. If he found Thomas again, he'd hand it over.

"A note then. Oh, good, there's still ink!" Rosalynn settled herself at the desk and found a bit of parchment. Her quill scraped lightly over it, but for a jump when the door popped open, and Brigit returned. Her brows pinched briefly, then she bustled past, carrying a few bundles. Of course: more provisions.

Elisha followed her to the small dining room, where he sliced wedges of cheese to lay out with the bread Brigit unwrapped. They worked side by side, the hanging bundles of herbs brushed his hair from time to time, letting out the scent of lavender. Rosalynn and a few soldiers soon joined them, warming the place and steaming the windows as their rain-drenched clothing dried. Ian and Patric must have taken their turn at guarding the perimeter. Elisha hoped they hadn't gone after either the dog or its owner.

Talk was of the weather, the hunting, the great stag these men had brought down yesterday, and how pleased they were to be able to hunt here, in the king's own forest, thanks to their master Alaric's change of status. It was not until they all rose again after eating that Brigit announced, "I shall accompany you a little way, my lady, if you don't mind. There's something of Elisha's I need to fetch for him."

Instantly, Rosalynn's face reddened, and Elisha set his hand near hers, not quite touching. "It would be a service to me, my lady. It's what I came here for."

Her dark eyes darkened a bit more, but she managed a smile. "Yes, of course. And I thank you for your generosity to us both."

"I'm pleased that my men were gracious on my

behalf." The two ladies, one pale and bright, the other damp and dark, stared at each other across the table, matching one another's regal guise.

"Yes, thanks," Elisha said, rising. "But we must be going. I'm sure Lady Rosalynn's escorts are already wondering where we are."

He draped a cloak over the lady's stiff shoulders and scooped up the other for himself, flinging it about him and securing the clasp as he left the house. As lovely as it was, the place felt haunted, each room and everything in them remembering the rightful occupants. Elisha's little magic with the lock would not be enough to make this place a refuge.

Two of Brigit's men trailed after the trio as they departed, ready to escort their lady home again, but Brigit took the lead, bringing them up the road a bit, then onto a trail through the woods. Although the first part of the forest had been tangled with vines and undergrowth, the trees here stood tall above them, thick oaks buttressing the rainclouds, with the occasional hazel down below. They spooked another deer which bounded off and started the guards whispering behind them. The drizzle set in properly now, not strong enough to sting but so thoroughly coating them that Elisha's green woolen cloak clung too tightly and weighed him down, the rim of the hood dripping onto his nose.

The rain worsened when they emerged from the trees onto the heath, a broad and tumbled plain thick with gorse and heather. Round mounds rose up nearby, fanning out into the distance, and gooseflesh rose on Elisha's arms: the burial mounds of the ancient heathens. If

Chanterelle were right about necromancers meeting in the places of the dead, then this forest would welcome them like a grave.

Brigit led them onward, weaving between these mounds, and Rosalynn drew closer to Elisha, hunching into her cloak. They came at last to a hillock that rose above their heads, pink with tiny blooms bowing under the ceaseless rain. On the far side, stones framed a dark hole, and Rosalynn stopped short, murmuring a prayer.

"It's just here," Brigit said. "You needn't go inside."

The chill seeped in beneath Elisha's hood and through his hands, a creeping cold stirred by the darkness of the open tomb. It was only a resting place, nothing more. Hadn't the souls moved on long ago? The bones that remained were only the structure of a form once dear, now departed. Flesh and bones formed his livelihood— to fear such things was foolish. Yet Elisha hung back with Rosalynn, as if to protect her. From the moment they crossed the water, the earth of the forest grew dense with the dead.

Brigit ducked into the darkness, vanishing inside with a swish of her cloak upon the ground. Outside, rain dripped from the lichened lintel. Chances were the large stone that defended Chanterelle and Elisha from fire in the bog had been the capstone of another grave, its corpse prevented from rising by that great weight, but Elisha had not thought of it until now. Brigit no doubt enjoyed bringing them there to discomfit her one-time rival in Alaric's affections—no, the thought was uncharitable. Rather, in a place like this, the talisman's own menace would be muffled, shielded from any effort he made to find it—which implied that such a magical search was possible. The idea quickened Elisha, taking his mind from the damp, as he considered how it might be done. An extension of the attunement he used to dispel the mystery of his surroundings during spell-casting? But how far could his awareness reach before it grew so thin that even his sensitivity failed?

A rustle at the opening brought him back to find Brigit emerging on hands and knees. One hand, really, for the other carried a wrapped bundle close to her chest.

She shook herself off, cradling the bundle, then walked to where they waited. "I'm sorry about this. I should not have taken it."

The bundle seemed too small for so much ceremony and concern. Elisha took it with both hands, its weight both slight and inconceivable. It contained the weight of tragic death, his love for his brother, his guilt and grief: it contained the head of his brother's still-born baby. His brother, too, died that day, cutting his own throat in anguish, believing his wife and child both dead. At one time, Elisha believed he might find the legendary Bone of Luz, said to shelter in the skull, and use it to bring the child back to life, restoring to its mother some of what she had lost. The surgeon Mordecai assured him there was no such bone. Elisha wondered if the necromancers might know otherwise.

A piece of cloth bound with a bit of rope concealed the copper jar with its wax seal and terrible contents. In spite of the weather and the talisman, Elisha felt the touch of warmth on one finger and turned the bundle. "There's blood on the wrapping. Are you hurt?"

"Just a scrape." Brigit held up her hand for him to see, a short scrape marring the pale skin, oozing blood. "I stumbled in the dark. It's nothing."

"Let me attend it." He fumbled beneath his cloak for the pouch of medical supplies he always carried.

"You have other things to attend to." Brigit inclined her head toward Rosalynn whose gray cloak and solemn posture made her look like a funerary sculpture far from its proper sanctuary. "And I should return to the lodge."

Elisha gave a slight bow. "Thank you." He searched for more to say to her, while they had this moment free of court and her royal husband-to-be.

She gazed back at him, eyes moist, lips parted, as if she, too, would say more. "Think of me," she said at last. "Your help could mean victory for all of us."

And like that, the moment broke. She asked for his support in a war that would not come, a war between brothers, when one of them was already broken, branded as a traitor, bereft of crown and country, and the other already as good as king. She was lying, but he did not know why.

Chapter 14

❖

"There's a road ahead, my lady, that aims the right direction," Elisha pointed between the mounds, but Rosalynn headed resolutely back the way they came.

"I saw a branching just in the woods that will take us there. I know it's a little farther, and a little darker, but it will get us out of the rain."

And away from the mounds, Elisha thought, but he followed in any case, understanding that her dread of the ancient burial mounds overcame common sense. Brigit and her men disappeared into the forest ahead of them and turned away toward the lodge.

As he followed Rosalynn through the woods, the rain and their footsteps the only sounds, Elisha carried the talisman in the crook of his arm, beneath his cloak. He left the wrapping on, remembering too well the way his fingers froze to the metal the first time he touched it as a witch. He wished he could carry it a little further from himself, but he had no satchel. When they reached the abbey, the duke's men would be waiting for them, ready to turn back to Dunbury, and he could accompany them;

aside from simply leaving the forest, he wanted to know if Allyson had learned anything more about the slaying. But first, he must endure another long ride to remind him of his aches. In the rush of seeing Brigit again, he put aside all of those annoyances, but they returned now with a low but constant pain, the aches of riding the day before, the singed soles of his feet, the stinging wound upon his chest. No doubt the pretty silk tunic would be stained with blood as well: unworthy of a prince, even an outcast. There must be an enemy—at least, Brigit believed there was—even if Thomas was in no position to raise an army.

Then he had the thought that stopped his breath. In befriending Thomas, Elisha made himself her enemy. She was set to marry Alaric, to become queen. Under no circumstance could Alaric allow his brother to live. And as much as he hated to admit it, Duke Randall was right: The power Elisha had drawn upon was no trifle, even if the way he had used the talisman could never be repeated. Everyone who knew what had happened to King Hugh must believe that a man who had Elisha on his side was a formidable opponent. If they found out—

Rosalynn screamed.

Three men emerged from the trees before them, bows in the hands of two, the third thrusting out a sword. "Give us your cloaks and your money," shouted the leader.

A quick glance showed three more behind, fanning out to form a circle. Elisha extended his awareness. At least three more presences hid in the forest, he could feel their heat and sense their stillness. Brigit and her men must be well away by now, too far to hear Rosalynn's cry, for he felt no sense of them. He did feel something strange, like a distant echo, but Elisha hadn't time to consider it as the men advanced on Rosalynn.

She leaped back, grabbing Elisha's arm. They both had knives, but no other weapons, aside from the talisman he carried.

"Your cloaks! Quickly!" Each word was emphasized with a jab of the sword. Two of the men behind ran up, pulling Elisha and Rosalynn away from each other. Elisha's hand found the hilt of the surgical blade tucked at the back of his pouch.

"Yes! Of course. Don't hurt us!" Rosalynn fumbled with the clasp and struggled the wet garment off her shoulders, flinging it toward them. But she didn't let go of the hood, and it swung out from her, smacking the leader and knocking free the arrow of the man on his right before slapping itself around the man who held her.

"Christ on the Cross!" shouted one of the men. Then she was running.

Elisha slashed the hand of his keeper, stabbed for his arm and dove beneath it as he drew back. Before he'd taken three steps, his own cloak jerked back against his throat, and he was down, a brigand on top of his legs, twisting the fabric to keep hold of him. In his memory, he fought the hanging rope, doused by a cold rain just like today, his feet flailing, his arms bound, and he cried out against the constriction. Stone scraped his cheek, returning him forcefully to reality.

A bow string twanged, and Elisha kicked at the man

sitting on him. "Run, lady," he gasped. He pulled free his blade, then an arm clamped around his throat, dragging him back. Another hand clamped his wrist, twisting until Elisha dropped his knife.

"Get back here, bitch, or he dies on the road!"

Run, Elisha pleaded in his mind, but he couldn't breathe. Pain shot up his right arm, and his left felt numb from clutching the thing he could not drop. His vision throbbed around the sight of Rosalynn, pulled back by her hair, wailing.

"Hasn't got no purse, boss. Few rings and some hair-pins."

"No purse?" He touched the flat of his sword against Rosalynn's cheek, bringing her to face him. "None but what's beneath her skirts."

"I'm the duke of Dunbury's daughter," she stammered. "If you hurt me, he'll never rest until he's got your heads."

"Only if he finds a witness." But as the men laughed the leader shared a sharp look with one of the archers.

"'Sides, the duke's daughter ain't traipsing the woods without a proper escort. This one ain't no fighting man." The leader flexed his muscle, twitching the sword against her face.

Elisha's pulse thundered in his skull. Rosalynn knelt weeping, framed by a rapist and his sword. The man twitched his head toward the forest, and they pulled her away, shrieking, leaving four men on the road with Elisha.

He choked and struggled, his lungs already burning.

"What's he got there?" one of the men asked, drawing near and pointing with his sword. "Might's well search him 'fore it's our turn."

Elisha gripped the talisman tighter. Through his pain and panic he felt the awful burden inside, the child he swore to return to its rightful resting place. Who but a necromancer would use the child's death for sorcery? Then Rosalynn screamed.

Thrusting aside his shame, Elisha called upon Death. It was not a stranger and never far from his thoughts or his work. To work magic, he needed contact with whatever he would affect, he needed knowledge of the change, and he needed to grasp the mystery: to acknowledge what he could never know. Death, he knew. Through his years as a barber-surgeon, through the battlefield, through the horrible day of the child's birth and his brother's suicide, all the way back to the moment he watched Brigit's mother burning on the stake. Oh, yes, he knew Death better than he had known any lover.

Creeping up from the talisman, chills feathered his arm, even through the wrappings, piercing him like thorns as Death reached back, entwining into him, and his spirit answered, as if he were the talisman, resonating to the witch's call, welcoming the familiar numbness. Elisha tried to hold it back this time, to force the cold to do his bidding and no more, but it strained against him with a murmur of power. He could kill the man who held him. He could wither the man to dust, through the agonizing contact at his throat. The sound of rain and the creak of leather and sinewed bows died back to nothing. The taste of his own blood on his lips faded, along with the smell of damp earth and the sweating bastard who held him. Death dominated his senses. His pain grew numb, his burns cooled, the thunder of his heart slowed to the beating drum of a funeral march.

Elisha tipped his head as a chill wind touched his shoulder, followed by the swift crack of dying. Strength flowed to him where a man fell dead in the forest. It surged up from the ground through his body to circle round his heart.

"Where's Joseph?" a voice on the wind. "Joseph! Did you hear that!"

The arm at his throat jerked the cloak tighter. Elisha turned his chin into the elbow and breathed out Death. The fabric of the man's garments parted, scattered to threads, and fell away. His skin beneath blackened and shook, then Elisha was free, a mindless howl rising up at his back, another before him as the bandits lunged with their weapons drawn. Something stirred in the calm that infused him, a quiver of interest, first from one side, then another, as if a choir suddenly heard the note that told them to be ready. It was an awful alertness, an eagerness that stretched in his direction, drawn by the dreadful thing he carried and the dreadful things he'd done.

Elisha's stomach clenched and his calm was shattered by a rush of shame. The heat of it shot through him, and he pushed away the icy strength that filled him, forcing it back into the talisman which suddenly shook in his hand. Raindrops trickled down his face and arms, dripping from the bundle as if the child inside it wept.

The man at his back staggered, clutching his arm, and

crashed into Elisha. The talisman tumbled from his grip, and a sword slashed at his chest.

A shaggy, gray form burst from the leaves and barreled into the swordsman, its teeth snapping into flesh as they rolled together across the ground. A wolf? No—Cerberus.

Elisha fell and instinctively drew back his aching wrist. The sword swung over his head, then jabbed at his stomach.

A second blade clanged against it, swept it away, and followed through with a backhand thrust that spattered blood across Elisha's face. He dimly felt another death and gasped, arching his back as the dead man's blood seared him with cold.

A third bandit sprang to the attack, his blackened arm dangling as Elisha's defender feinted around him, drawing his blade. The great dog snarled to one side from bloody lips. Swords clashed and slid.

With tearing, desperate fingers, Elisha finally freed himself from his twisted cloak and gulped for breath. He lay on his side, head throbbing, then pressed his palm to the dirt and tried to rise.

A shriek and a curse. The injured bandit backed away from Elisha's ragged defender, who faced him with a sword in one hand and a curved knife in the other. A dodge, then the bandit leapt to the attack. The ragged man ducked and twisted with exquisite grace, taking the blade on his dagger and sliding it away, bringing up his sword to the other man's gut. He straightened with the thrust, letting the bandit fall free of his weapon, then glanced back. Sharp blue eyes found Elisha's gaze. Thomas.

"Rosalynn," Elisha struggled to speak, though his throat burned. He pointed toward the wood beyond.

Thomas gave a tiny nod and swung away, lunging between the trees.

Elisha groped to retrieve the talisman and took up his fallen knife, forcing his hand to close around the grip. Then he staggered to his feet to follow. In the clearing beneath a towering beech tree, Thomas circled with the leader. A second man gripped Rosalynn's arm, holding her up beside him. Her gown hung open, the bandits having finished the tear that her own efforts had begun. She fumbled with her dress, trying to cover her nakedness, sobbing breathlessly, but she and her keeper both watched the fight.

Treading carefully, Elisha thanked God and the king for the wide spacing of the well-tended trees. Elisha sidled nearer to the bandit and his captive. Rosalynn took a sharp breath, then flopped forward, causing her captor to stumble ahead with her fall. Elisha's medical mind performed a quick calculation—the dozen places he could thrust and incapacitate the bandit. He aimed low, to cause maximum pain without killing, but a chill ripple passed through him, a moment of wanton lust for blood as if the needs of Death still lingered in his flesh. With all the strength he had remaining, Elisha rammed the dagger home into the brigand's heart. Skin and muscle parted beneath his blade. The hilt twisted as the knife struck bone and he shoved it past, then a spurt of blood, hot and sticky, gushed over his fist. A successful surgery, Elisha thought bitterly.

The bandit's tiny cry gave Thomas the opening he

needed to slice through the leader's doublet and shove him away to groan out the last of his life. Thomas withdrew, panting, shaking back his dark hair.

Setting the talisman among the tree roots with shaky hands, Elisha crawled to where Rosalynn sprawled on the ground, hair tangled over her face. Her hand crept upward, tugging at her bodice. He found the cloth for her and drew it over her quaking chest, concealing her breasts and bringing her hand up to hold it closed. With the blood on his hands and on the knife, kneeling once more over a fallen innocent, Elisha thought of the French magus who died in his arms.

"My lady, are you hurt?" His voice rasped. He kept his hand over hers, lightly touching the pulse at her wrist, reaching for some measure of comfort and calm that he could share with her. He had none.

"Who's there?" she cried, and Elisha tightened his grip, letting his warmth and stillness tell her he meant no harm.

He swallowed hard, and tried again, "It's just Elisha. Are you hurt?"

"No," she whispered. "They ... touched me, they started—I'm not hurt." She lay there, panting, her knees drawn up.

As gently as he could, Elisha brushed the wild tendrils of her hair back from her face, but she turned away, her eyes clamped shut. He wet his lips, controlling his breathing. If he kept his voice low, it didn't hurt so much. "My lady Rosalynn." She stirred vaguely. "You are the most courageous woman I ever knew. Ever. We will take care of you."

"Who's with you?" she said, almost a whimper.

"A friend," Thomas answered, and his voice was soft and strong as he knelt on her other side.

"He saved your life, my lady. There's nothing to fear."

Very slightly, she nodded, but her face remained pale, her lips trembling.

She'd be all right, Elisha felt with a rush of relief. Not like the Frenchman—she would recover. "We'll bring you to the abbey, my lady. I can help you rest. Would you want that?"

"Please."

Elisha settled his hand over her forehead, making the contact strong. Gently, he sent her the need for sleep, to let her tired body relax, and her fear ebb away. He sent the image of the abbey as a peaceful place of stone, a place she would have shelter, warmth, and healing. Beneath his touch, her breathing eased. When her hand softened beneath his, he released the contact, shifting his touch to a careful examination, moving his hands over her limbs, checking for blood that might be her own.

Cerberus pushed his muzzle toward her, sniffing, then withdrew, content to watch. While Elisha worked, Thomas moved away. He returned in a moment, the sheathed sword at his hip, Rosalynn's cloak in his arms. Spreading the damp garment beside her, Thomas murmured, "Will she be all right?"

Elisha remembered the sense he'd gotten so briefly at the dance, of Thomas's attraction. "I think so. She's had a difficult time of it since—"

"Since my ass of a brother discarded her."

"She doesn't seem to be injured, just tired and

terrified." He lifted Rosalynn's head and shoulders, Thomas moving automatically to gather her legs, and they shifted her onto the cloak, wrapping it around her. "She had an awful night, met someone she hates, and now this. The abbey's the best thing for her."

"You did not tell me you were among enemies," Thomas remarked, giving his dog a pat.

Elisha nearly smiled. "It seemed churlish for me to complain to you, Your Highness. Even before I knew who you were, it was clear to me you weren't well off. At least I was clean and dry, and not too hungry."

"It's been better than a month since anyone called me 'Highness,' and then he was calling me to meet an assassin's knife. I was lucky to escape with my life."

"No luck, Your Highness—I've seen you fight. Speaking of which, we should check your hands. That must have hurt." Thomas glanced at his bandaged palms as Elisha reached out, but pain shot down Elisha's arm, pulling him back as he stifled a groan.

"They seem well enough, thanks—" Thomas began, checking the bandages.

Elisha examined his own wrist. It throbbed but hadn't swollen. Likely no significant damage. He tugged free the strip of cloth he called upon as a talisman and set about wrapping the joint awkwardly with his left hand.

Thomas noticed his action. "Blessed Mother, I am a fool." Thomas crouched by him, finishing the binding with a quick but gentle hand. He glanced up beneath the fringe of his hair and touched the side of Elisha's jaw, searching his throat where fresh bruises overlaid the scar of his hanging. "You're the one who's injured."

The touch sent a wave of heat and concern Elisha felt in no way worthy of bearing. He turned aside and saw the body of the man he'd stabbed. The first man he had killed in cold blood and sound mind. The creeping, awful cold of Death still dwelt within him. "It's fine," he said. "Nothing broken. No blood lost." He gulped a breath. "I'm fine. I will be—"

"You're an awful liar."

Elisha shut his eyes, pressing the heels of his hands into them.

"It's the killing, isn't it. I trained all my life for it, but you . . ."

Silent, Elisha took a breath that caught at his throat and hitched inside his chest.

Thomas's hand rested on his back, then moved slowly, as if stroking the breath back into him. Thomas's sympathy returned to Elisha a thousand times the gift of his own kindness.

Chapter 15

━━━━━◆━━━━━

Elisha waited until he could speak without shaking. "We should go," he said at last, loath to break the moment's peace.

"If you can carry her, I'll guard your back." Thomas rose to one knee, briefly gripping Elisha's shoulder. "If you're able. If not, I can take her."

Evading his touch, Elisha gathered Rosalynn into his arms, resting her head against his chest. "You can't come with us. It's not safe."

"Not safe?" Thomas gave a sharp laugh. "You're not safe without me, given her condition, never mind yours."

Slowly, Elisha rose, focusing on his balance. He could do this; he must. Rosalynn was his responsibility, and her father would never forgive him if anything more happened to her. He might already be unforgivable. Elisha imagined that he had hidden his own pain and weariness until he saw Thomas regarding him with eyebrows raised, his head slightly cocked, a hand resting on the hilt of his sword. He stood for all the world like a master waiting for a student to tell the truth, both knowing the student had lied.

"No," Elisha said quietly, "you're right. I do no service to her to deny it, even for your sake." He turned away from that steady gaze. "If anyone sees you, Highness, anyone who knows you, they'll kill you."

"I am the prince," Thomas said, "They might allow me the grace of a trial."

"You know your brother better than I do. What orders would he give?"

Thomas's shoulders sank. "They'll kill me," he agreed. "They've already tried once and turned my generals against me."

"That bundle by the tree, Highness. Would you carry it for me?"

Thomas gave him a curious glance, but did as he was asked, using a bit of its wrapping to tie the talisman to his belt. At least Elisha would be free of it for a little while. Elisha started to walk, cradling the weight of the sleeping Rosalynn close to his chest. At a whistle, Cerberus went before him, head up and ready.

"Why did you go to Dunbury?" Elisha asked. "That was an awful risk." They came back to the road, and he found Thomas had dragged the bodies off to the side to be picked apart by scavengers. A few crows were already clustered in the trees, watching.

"Well, I didn't expect my brother to be there. I've not been close enough to towns to receive news of the royal progress. Dunbury has been my supporter in the past; I hoped he would be again, but I could not approach him, not in all that crowd. When I saw him embrace Alaric, there seemed little point in trying to speak to him."

So he had come home to the forest, to find his house barred against him.

"Here's your cloak." Thomas retrieved it, and gave a slight smile as he looked at it. "My cloak, actually." He made as if to drape Elisha's shoulders, but Elisha shook his head in spite of the damp.

"That thing nearly strangled me," he said abruptly.

Thomas stared at the garment for a moment, then draped it over his own broad shoulders, keeping his sword arm free. Elisha, for whom any bit of clothing represented a goodly investment, walked with a man who owned so many cloaks he could afford to leave them unused in chests in empty houses. Back at Dunbury, before he knew him, Elisha had admired Thomas's beggar's guise, and Thomas told him he'd paid a princely sum. It was a jest he only now perceived.

Their steps scrunched the stone and grass of the pathway. The big trees parted from time to time, brightening the walk and giving misty views of the heath with its burial mounds. "Actually, I've been to the abbey, for alms. I draped my face and wrapped my hands a bit more. They think me a leper." Thomas started to pull ahead then paused and shortened his stride to stay abreast. "Lately I've felt that I am."

Elisha stared ahead, the weight of the sleeping Rosalynn dragging at his arms. "If they kill you, Highness, Alaric will be king."

"He's declared himself so already, and I can't see a damned thing I can do about it. I'm marked for a traitor, regicide, in fact, and he's got my every ally already supporting him."

A realization struck him, and Elisha sighed, suddenly more weary than ever. "If they find us together, they'll believe I was your agent in the killing. Damn it all! I'm sorry."

"For befriending me? By the Cross, Elisha, don't apologize for that, of all things. When you first arrived, I thought the Lord brought you to me to kill, to win justice for my father. But you seemed bent on healing me—one of His little ironies. Then you shared your supper with me and offered to let me back into my home."

Elisha remembered his own sense of wonder at earning the gift of Thomas's trust and gratitude.

"Before my fall, I had servants for my every whim. Since then, I have been alone as never before in my life, Elisha. I've had nothing." They walked a moment in silence, then Thomas glanced at him and whispered a few lines in Latin. He paused and spoke again, reverently, "'For I hungered, and you gave me meat; I thirsted, and you gave me drink; I was a stranger and you took me in.'" His voice rose in strength. "'I was sick and you visited me; I was in prison, and you came to me.' It's from the Gospel of our Lord."

Thomas crossed himself with such grace that Elisha murmured, "I'm not a devout man, Your Highness."

"Even a goat can be an instrument of God."

Yet the Devil was often depicted with a goat's hooves and horns, Elisha thought. Thomas found him a symbol of faith, a reason to hope. Thomas had not witnessed the full scene upon the road. He had not seen what Elisha could become, and he did not know that terrible twist that transformed Elisha's medical precision into a murderous stroke.

"That woman, at the lodge, who was she?" Thomas asked.

Heaven and Hell or Brigit. Elisha did not know which topic was the worse for him.

"I'm sure I've seen her before," the prince continued, his strides again taking him ahead, "but never at court."

"I doubt she's welcome there. Lady Brigit is the image of her mother, who died on the stake when I was a boy."

Thomas's steps faltered. "Saints preserve us, I should have known. Seeing her, it sent a shock straight through my soul."

"Mine, too, Highness, the first time I saw her."

"You were there at the execution? I couldn't watch." Thomas gave himself a shake that sent water shivering off his hair, as if he cast off more than rain. "If we shall be executed together, you might at least call me by my name."

They walked on together, mostly silent, with Elisha focused on each step so as not to fall. Before long, stone walls appeared to either side and tended fields replaced the heath and woodland, where every step increased the danger of being seen. Beaulieu Abbey must be just ahead. Elisha's steps slowed. "You have to leave us, Thomas," he said, the first time he had spoken the prince's name. "You have to live."

Thomas examined the dirty toes of his bare feet. "I've got little enough to live for."

"If you can't find hope for yourself," Elisha shot back, "then do it for her." He turned, facing Thomas, still cradling Rosalynn's still form. "So that she, and all of us, don't suffer another tyrant on the throne."

Thomas's gaze fell to the woman, then rose to linger at Elisha's throat, and finally back to his face. "I don't know that it is in my power."

"I don't know either, but it's no reason not to try."

A flight of crows burst from the nearby wall and flew cawing into the rain. Voices rose in a murmur, approaching from the abbey road, and Thomas's eyes flared. Then he tipped his head to Elisha, acquiescing with the grace of majesty. "Then I leave it, and you, in God's hands."

Elisha watched him hurry back to the forest, his cloak flaring out around him, rain glinting silver on the darkness of his hair. Fitted with a fine cloak and a sheathed sword, he had begun to leave the beggar behind, and, for a moment, Elisha glimpsed the king he could be. Cerberus gave a little whine and a wave of his tail, then trotted gamely after his master. The voices grew louder at his back, then someone called out, and the footsteps broke into a run as Thomas disappeared into the forest just as those from the abbey spotted Elisha on the road.

Saints and Martyrs: Thomas still carried the talisman at his belt! Elisha drew breath to call out to him, then a voice from behind shouted, "My God, what's happened?"

Elisha bit off his words, turning to find a pair of men in the duke's livery sprinting to halt before him.

"Bandits," Elisha said shortly. "We fought them off.

She's not hurt, but she'll need rest." He stumbled, placing her into the arms of one of the soldiers, the long night settling heavily into his bones. He wanted to turn immediately and go after Thomas, but his knees trembled with weariness, and he had yet to see his patient truly safe behind the abbey walls. He must trust that Thomas could hide a while longer. The talisman would have to wait— but Elisha's heart rose a little to know that they must meet again, if only so that he could retrieve it. He hurried to keep up as the duke's men finished the last of the journey. The men called out for aid, and a party of nuns and lay servants quickly enveloped them, with Rosalynn's maid cutting through the crowd, crying out for her lady.

Elisha kept his feet all the way to the well where he slumped onto a bench to wash the blood from his face and hands and drink until his lips and throat, still aching, no longer felt parched. He was no good to anyone in this condition. His own Master Barber would have ordered him to bed. Stifling a yawn, Elisha found his way to the guests' dormitory, where he collapsed onto one of a line of pallets and let himself sleep.

Some hours later, his stomach was growling as he woke to the sound of a baby's cry. But any thought of hunger left him immediately, along with his exhaustion. Thomas did not know what he carried on Elisha's behalf, but when Elisha had used it on their assailants, he had perceived someone else—several someones'—interest in the use of it, their extended awarenesses quickening at the sense of magic like weary travelers at the sight of a cathedral's lantern-tower. Was it the talisman or himself that drew their interest? Brigit's care in hiding it had told him it might be sought by magical means, but he had ignored this vital clue. Could the searchers find it when it wasn't in use? What might they do to Thomas if they found it and realized he was not its master? Or if—Heaven forbid—they knew Thomas for who he was? It was not he, Elisha, who needed God's hand, it was the prince himself, and Elisha had set him up. Idiot!

He rolled out of bed, wiping off a few bits of straw, but he hadn't the first idea how to look for Thomas. He wasn't the one who hunted these woods all his life. He did not know his way nor less where a prince might hide—but he knew someone who would, if she were awake and feeling talkative.

A lay servant bustled down the aisle between the pallets, and Elisha stopped him with an outstretched palm. "Lady Rosalynn of Dunbury. Do you know where she is?"

The man's gaze arrested at the sight of Elisha's throat, and he stammered, "We've had a cottage made up for her, my lord." He recovered himself to ask, "Are you Elisha, her companion? She's asked for you." The man turned on his heel, rope belt swinging, and bustled back the way he came. "Come along then!"

Stepping lively, Elisha caught him up and passed between the tall, gray buildings to a little house on the grounds apart from the church and cloister. The man knocked and showed him inside, but Rosalynn's maid rose up from her stitching and glared.

"You were to keep her safe, Barber. First you ran off with her in the darkness, and now this. It's to God alone that she's not badly hurt or worse!" Her sharp face grew sharper in the shouting.

Elisha spread his hands, wincing at the protest of his sprained wrist. "I hardly need to be reminded of that, mistress."

"It's what we get for trusting a commoner. One of the duke's soldiers has already ridden off to let him know she's missing, and now another to let him know she's found, and in what state—"

"Please, Mary, is that Elisha?" called Rosalynn from beyond the passage. "I can't imagine who else you would berate in such a fashion while I'm at my rest. Bring him through, if you please."

Mary's eyes narrowed even further, her lip twisting, but she bobbed a tiny, fierce curtsey and lead the way through the passage and up the stairs.

Rosalynn lay propped in a wide bed, snuggled about with blankets, her hair combed out around her, a fur robe drawn up to her chest. A fire crackled in the grate, with a jug set nearby. "More cider, Mary. And for Elisha."

The maid poured two mugs from the waiting jug. She snatched a poker from the flames and jabbed it into each in turn, until they steamed, then slammed the poker onto its hook and thrust a mug at Elisha.

"Thank you, mistress." The scent of cinnamon warmed his face, and he drew it in. In spite of Mary's ill will, his gratitude was unfeigned.

"Here, Elisha, come by me." Rosalynn gave a roll of her hand to summon him close, gesturing toward a small chair set at her bedside. "The infirmarian has been here, and many other people besides. It was a wonder I got any rest at all. If I did, it was due to you." She raised her own mug to him, her cheeks pleasantly pink once more.

"I'm glad to see you looking so well. I wish," Elisha shook his head, "I know there's nothing I can do to make amends for this."

"As if it were your fault." She studied him, and her round face grew serious. "Elisha, you have done what you must, first to save that other woman—Chanterelle, did you call her?—then to come for me. It was not you who put me in those places, but I myself for my stubbornness." She shot a look at her maid. "I shall atone for that later in the church. But I should like to give my thanks to your friend as well." Rosalynn nibbled on her lip, then shrugged. "He seemed familiar somehow, but I cannot place him. Perhaps you've had him to my father's keep?"

"It's about him that I've come, my lady—"

"Do call me 'Rosie,' please."

Mary huffed, and Elisha bowed his head. Twice today, he had been given the name of someone so far beyond his birth that not two months prior he should have been beaten just for speaking it. He used Thomas's name, and only once, to try to convince him of what must be.

"You may return to your stitching, Mary. I shall ring the bell if I have need of you."

"But my lady, to leave you with him! Of all people!"

"He has seen me at my worst, Mary—at least, I trust the Lord that was as bad as it shall ever be. You may go."

Mary went, scowling and muttering, shutting the door with the merest curtsey to her lady. "She is a good maid, truly, but she's been all upset over my disappearance, and for me to return again in such a fashion. You can imagine what it's done to her. Like you, she believes she is responsible."

"My friend," Elisha began, "I need to find him, but he knows his way around these parts, and I don't. I hoped you would have some ideas where a man might stay who did not wish to be seen."

"Is he a criminal? I hope not! He ought to come here for sanctuary. Wait—he's a deserter, isn't he? Such skilled swordsmanship, he's no mere footman if I'm not mistaken. He—"

If she kept talking, Elisha realized, she might well talk her way around to the truth. "Please, my lady, there may not be much time."

"Is he another spy then?"

Elisha shook his head. "Another spy?"

"Like the woman in the dirt. I may not be of the magi, but I have been raised by one. My mother's been worried about rumors of dark magic." Rosalynn crossed herself with a shiver. "Even so, it took me this little while to understand that that woman in the dirt was one of your spies. The magi, I mean."

For a moment, Elisha sat breathless with astonishment. He travelled with her for days, groaning inwardly as she talked of minor things, and it never occurred to him that she might know anything he needed. That, in fact, it might pay to listen to her. "Tell me about the necromancers, lady."

She hesitated, pinching her lips together. "It's not really a proper topic, is it? I suppose it can't be helped. They are like magi, aren't they, but they use only, well, murder," — another cross over her breast — "and their victims, or parts of them. They can create fear, nightmares, and so forth, but they can't make spells beyond what they know, and all they know is killing."

No wonder he was accused of being one of them. The chill of Death never quite left him, not since the king. And even his brief use of the talisman this morning had given him a rush of power, threatening to overwhelm whatever faith, love, or reason kept a man from killing.

"It's why a lot of magi don't believe necromancers exist," she went on. "For one thing, why would you limit yourself that way? There are the *indivisi*, of course, but they're mad. For another thing, necromancers are the whole reason why people like me are afraid of people like you and the other magi."

"What about the *indivisi*?" Elisha prompted.

"They have made themselves indivisible from their talismans. They know all there is to know about it and they can even define its mysteries — so much so that they take on its aspects. They're not quite . . . people anymore. Your woman in the bog, she could just go into the dirt, and she abhorred the touch of clothing, that was plain. It's not quite normal, is it?" Suddenly her eyes flew wider. "Oh, dear. You're not thinking of becoming *indivisi*, are you? Only I don't actually know all that much about you. Perhaps if I did not do all the talking." She trailed off, plucking the edge of the fur with her fingers.

"I asked you, my lady. You were hardly taking advantage." *Indivisi.* Utterly devoted to one thing. If a man could know Death in such an intimate way, did that make him *indivisi*? But if he used that knowledge, he became a necromancer, a wielder of terror. If a man could know Death . . .

"No," she said, studying him sidelong. "You asked me where a man would hide. There's a village close to here, or rather, there was a village, but the Conqueror had it cleared out when he claimed this land back for the crown. Not much left of it, I guess, but it would be a dry place, if a man didn't have another place to go."

"Nobody's using it?"

"Just beyond the village is the heath, with all of those pagan burials. Who'd want to live there?" She shivered, then took another swallow of her cider.

Elisha remembered his own cup, cool enough now not to scorch. It tasted sweet and wonderful down his bruised throat.

"If you leave Beaulieu to the west, you can take that road for a bit, then you'll turn at the pond." Scooting down into her fur and blankets, Rosalynn tipped her head toward the window where rain had left behind the steely sky of late afternoon. Her knuckles whitened on the mug. "There was a sweep of the forest after the princesses were killed, and I think any bandits in the village were routed. Except, they're coming back now, aren't they." She faltered, moved to sip her mug again, and found it empty. "Elisha."

His name echoed softly from the empty mug, and he had to lean forward to hear what she said next.

"The man who seized me, today, he said something strange. Their captain had torn my dress, and the man, he asked if I were a part of the price, and the captain laughed, and he said, 'No, mate, she's a bonus.'" She stirred as Elisha put his hand on her arm. "I don't understand."

For a moment, he didn't either, looking into her dark, puzzled eyes and thinking of the men who held him, who did not merely slit his throat and take what they would. "They weren't bandits," Elisha said. "They were mercenaries. They were hired to kill us."

Chapter 16

After taking his leave as gently as he might, Elisha pelted down the stairs and burst out the door.

The startled Mary shouted after him, "At least take the filthy boots I carried for you!" When he glanced back, she flung them at him, catching him in the shins, causing him to stumble.

Ignoring her triumphant air, he snatched the boots and winced as he stuffed his aching feet into them, then hobbled back into a run. The moment he put the truth to Rosalynn's words, he knew who would hire out the attack and why. It wasn't their deaths the brigands sought, but something else—something that required subjecting Rosalynn to their foulness, something that made them hold Elisha without killing him, even after Rosalynn admitted their poverty and tried to escape. They didn't want him dead, they wanted him frightened and furious—desperate enough to save Rosalynn that he would summon up the very essence of Death from the talisman he carried. So that the woman who had marked it with her blood could learn how to use it herself. Brigit.

He ran all the way to the gate of the abbey grounds, dodging a drift of people moving in the opposite direction, before he realized that speed would avail him little: it had been hours since the attack, and Brigit would have been ready for the next step, whatever that might be. Even if she kept contact with the talisman from the comfort of the lodge, she could have mounted up in pursuit once the attack was over. But she need not hurry either. She would be expecting Elisha to carry the talisman as far as Beaulieu. Once she knew he had defeated the bandits, all she needed was an excuse to come looking for him. She knew he was a sensitive. She wasn't—she didn't know what little it might take to alert him of her interest. She would not, therefore, risk maintaining her contact with the talisman when she already knew where they were going. She would expect to find Elisha taking the talisman away with him. If she did search, it would lead her directly to Thomas.

In this one foolish act, allowing another man to carry his burden, Elisha had aimed all of their enemies in a single direction.

Elisha turned for the stables and stopped short. A large party of riders milled about there, dismounting and handing off their mounts to the grooms. A stocky fellow hesitated, then glanced in Elisha's direction. He put out a hand toward the nearest horse, where its rider waited for a stable boy. The rider looked sharply up and smiled.

"Why, Elisha! The very man we've come to see." Prince Alaric's smile, spread upon his youthful face, was nearly contagious. "I was surprised to find you gone so early, but it did not take much work to find out where." He kicked free of his stirrup, the other man still holding his mount, and slid down, straightening the layers of his sumptuous clothing, ermine close about his throat beneath a golden chain.

Another member of the party glared down at Elisha before sliding from his own mount. "Please tell me we needn't violate sanctuary to gain satisfaction, Your Majesty." Mortimer—the drunk from the ball—rested his hand on his sword, his own dark woolens replete with golden stitching. Elisha liked him better drunk.

A boy hurried up, hands out for the reins, but Alaric gave him a resounding slap across the face with the short crop in his fist. "You're late."

"Sorry, my lord," the boy piped up—and Alaric threatened the crop again as the boy cowered.

"Do you not recognize your king?" Mortimer snapped, and the boy dropped to his knees, head bowed nearly to the earth.

"Forgive me, Your Majesty." He huddled at the prince's feet. Elisha's hands clenched of their own accord, his wrist throbbing. He had once had much the same view of the royal boots of King Hugh, and he noticed Prince Alaric wore his father's silver spurs.

"What do you want of me?" Elisha took a step forward, drawing their eyes from the quaking stable boy.

Alaric tossed down his crop and gloves and strode over. "You left me with a foreign mess, Barber. I intend to know why. You have done me service in the past, for which I am grateful, but I will not be tolerant forever." Behind him, the boy gathered up Alaric's riding things and scrambled for the horse. A sharp, red welt crossed his face.

"My lord king," called a monk as he hustled toward them, bowing, a trio of other monks at his back. "The abbot is clearing his house for you, Your Majesty, but it won't be ready for a little while. Is there another way we might accommodate you? There is a fine solar in the—"

"We need a private place to talk." He reached out and slung his arm through Elisha's. "Immediately." Six of his men moved forward as well, with casual menace.

The monk scowled at them. "If you will join us for Vespers service, Your Majesty, the brothers shall to bed, and you may have the Abbey entire."

"We must away shortly after Vespers, for an appointment at Compline. Pray you leave the gates ready for us on our return," said Alaric with a gracious smile. The monk's lean face failed to show any change of expression though the king-apparent planned to claim the very church and bend the monastery to his own regimen. The bells had nearly finished, and Alaric tugged Elisha with him toward the church, Mortimer following close at their back with the retinue of soldiers. They joined the press of monks, lay brothers, guests, and townsfolk. Elisha spotted Rosalynn and her maid among the crowd, not far from a ragged gathering of beggars assembling in the hopes of offerings from the parishioners. Was Thomas among them? Elisha felt chilled. Pray God he had not chosen to return tonight.

"Come, Elisha, join us in the abbot's row," Alaric murmured close to his ear. "If you look penitent enough, perhaps people will stop calling for your head."

Mortimer gave a snort, eyes narrowed as they met Elisha's.

"This is absurd, Your Highness," Elisha said. "Tell me what you want from me. There are a thousand other places we might go."

"Don't you want to go to service? Why not? Are you afraid of God?" But Alaric's throat bobbed as he said it, his glance sneaking up to the cross they passed below. With a twitch of ermine, he swept the crowd with his gaze as they entered the church then moved toward the rood screen beyond which the monks would be gathering. Then he hesitated and his smile twisted. "Her? Are you trying to protect Rosalynn? Lord, Elisha, tell me you've not fallen for that baggage. You've already got Randall's favor, and I can't imagine any other reason a man would court her."

Elisha gritted his teeth. "You may not know her as well as you think, Your Highness."

Alaric chuckled. He stared in Rosalynn's direction and tipped his head towing Elisha past to stand in the front. Once there, Alaric glanced around a bit, his grip tightening. "I ought to have sent my rider on earlier—then at least they'd have set out a chair."

The prince's men crowded close by Elisha's other side, hemming him in. Their entry had been so public that even the strongest deflection wouldn't allow him to slip from the church. Nothing short of an earthquake would free him from Alaric's oppressive grip.

The abbot, resplendent in his dark habit and gold-embroidered chasuble, emerged from behind the rood screen to the monks' chanting. His voice rang in prayer through the church, then changed mode, calling out over his congregation. Latin, of course. Alaric stared up at him, listening, frowning, one of the few on this side of the screen who would understand Latin. His fingers gripped Elisha's arm from time to time, as if the abbot's words were aimed at him, and he did not like them.

As the abbot droned on, Elisha studied the statue of the Virgin Mary, placed to one side; a lovely wooden figure, brightly painted with a gown of red and mantle of blue. She balanced the chubby Christ child on one hip and held out a lily in her other hand. Beneath her benevolent gaze, Elisha grew warm, Father Michael's injunction to repent resounding in his skull. She was a mother—*the* Mother—why did she not intercede on behalf of the mothers he had known? Helena had prayed to her for her own child's safe delivery, and that, like so many other births, turned to grief. The statue's pretty face and attentive look concealed a heart of wood. She reminded him of Brigit, herself a mother-to-be. Would the baby soften the mother's heart?

From behind the screen, the monks began to sing, and Elisha caught his breath. The choir of masculine voices resonated through the grandeur of the church, giving that attentive Madonna something worth listening to. They sang in unison, but with a range of tones, from the fluting of the youngest novice down to the sonorous depths of his elders. The stone hummed and echoed; some monks, glimpsed only through the elaborate gilded carving of the screen, swayed with their song. Glory,

Hallelujah, Elisha thought—there was some beauty in the church yet, and some who still found their distant God worthy of all praise.

The office at last wound to an end, though the song reverberated a while longer, and Alaric herded him up to receive communion, the prince kneeling first among all for the wafer. "Interesting service, Father Abbot, especially for a sanctuary. A den of thieves, indeed. I hope you didn't extemporize the whole thing." He gave the abbot a hard stare.

The abbot merely stared back down his long nose and crossed the prince's forehead as he intoned a ritual blessing, but the prince's face softened, his lips a-tremble, as if every word of God were reaching him tonight.

Then came Elisha's turn. The body of Christ tasted dry, the Son's battered figure sagging on the cross above them, the Frenchman's flayed chest overlaying Christ's own wounds in Elisha's mind.

Mortimer came next, his eyes closed in a reverent expression as the wafer touched his tongue. While the others accepted their communion and retreated outside to the remnants of day, Elisha stood with Alaric and his soldiers, waiting, his wrist and throat aching, the Body of Christ still clinging to his tongue. Rosalynn and her maid moved up with the line, her glance darting toward Alaric and away, barely resting on Elisha. He moved to speak to her, but Alaric caught the back of his neck, a gesture that might have looked friendly, but he let his thumb and fingers dig in painfully against the fresh bruises. Elisha winced. He wanted to knock the prince's hand away, but it would avail him nothing. The service felt like his mother's warning after bad behavior, ushering in the long wait until his father decreed what punishment should fall.

Behind the rood screen, the monks shuffled away toward the south transept leading to their cloister and their beds. They'd be up in a few hours to do it again. Mortimer strode about, trailing the monks and the congregants, giving the abbot a smile and nod and shutting the door firmly behind them.

When the church had emptied but for Alaric's men and the radiant, mocking glow of the stained glass windows, Alaric pushed Elisha in front of him and gave a gesture that spread out his men around them. "You were talking to the French. Why?"

"A man came to me at the ball, he wanted my help. I wasn't talking to the French, I was talking to him."

"Don't listen to this miscreant, Your Majesty," Mortimer said, jabbing a finger in Elisha's direction. "Why else did he kill your father? I'll wager he went over to the French before he ever saw that battlefield."

Both noblemen had a few inches over Elisha, with Mortimer given to leaning in. Elisha caught himself cringing slightly, obeying some memory of childhood when the lord's reeve came to loom over his father, searching for a way to squeeze out more work or more tribute. Elisha forced himself to stand straighter. He spoke carefully. "I believe, my lord, that the prince knows exactly why I killed his father."

Alaric made a low sound, but Mortimer cocked his head. "Indeed? I'm sure he knows what you want him to think. The Duke may claim you as his" — a wrinkle of the lips—"champion, but the laws of challenge were not met, nor do you qualify for such consideration. You expected more protection than that, I'm sure, before you did the deed. Protection the French offered to supply? Is that why the Frenchman sought you out? A masked ball is a perfect place to betray your king."

Elisha's throat ached as if he were about to be hanged all over again. "I didn't even know the man was French until after he was dead. If anything, he wanted my help against his own king."

"Really? What did he say to make you believe that?" Mortimer stared him down.

"He feared assassination."

The lord laughed sharply, dismissing this with a slice of his hand. "A servant in the house of the king? I'm sure King Phillip runs a tight household. The man could've been punished at any time."

Alaric stilled Mortimer with a touch. "We have no need to make more enemies," said Alaric softly, and Mortimer drew back.

The Frenchman was thought of as part of the ambassador's retinue, not directly tied to the king, though he had told Elisha about his royal connection. Perhaps Mortimer had learned about it after Elisha's departure from Dunbury. Or did he know more? Elisha met the lord's haughty gaze.

"Don't let mercy weaken you, Your Majesty. He's already an enemy." Mortimer drummed his fingers on his sword hilt. "A man cannot fraternize with sorcery and remain godly."

"Peace." The prince spread his hands and smiled. "I have more powerful allies whom I trust even less." He pivoted back to Elisha. "You said he wanted your help, Elisha—with what?"

Mortimer and the soldiers stood watching, and Elisha said, "You wished for privacy, Your Highness. This hardly seems private enough."

For a moment, Alaric sucked on his lip, then he waved Elisha over to the north transept, motioning for his men to stay where they were. From that side crossing, they could still see the soldiers, but were unlikely to be heard. Mortimer growled and stalked back toward the altar, receding around the corner.

Elisha stood a few paces from Alaric, considering him. His regal attire looked a bit loose, the gold chain of office quivering with his breaths. The prince tried his smile again, but it had lost the youthful carelessness that Elisha remembered. There were echoes of his brother's face about his brow and nose. "The man who spoke to me was a magus. He told me the king was against them, was hunting them down. He was looking for a place he and his companions might be safe. Apparently, he didn't find it."

In turn, the prince watched him carefully. "And the ambassador?"

"I never spoke with him. Or with the French lady."

Alaric nodded slowly and shifted his weight, looking toward one of the recessed chapels. "I am inclined to believe you, given our history."

"Then may I go, Your Highness?"

"You went back to view his body—why?"

"Did you hear about the other funeral that night?"

Alaric frowned. "Another funeral? What's that got to do with the French?"

With a shrug, Elisha said, "We found another body on the battlefield and the funeral was held that afternoon. Someone tried to shoot me with a crossbow during the burial. I thought the robbery might have been another attempt. Besides, the robber had an unusual weapon. I wanted to know more about it."

"An unusual weapon? I don't recall hearing about this." Alaric's profile was calm, but his Adam's apple bobbed, and Elisha made himself relax, spreading his senses to envelop the prince's nervousness.

"The Frenchman was in fear of his life, then he lost it. That doesn't seem coincidental to me. I assume the weapon was something foreign." Something about the slaying put the prince on edge, but why should mention of the weapon attract so much interest?

"You think the French ambassador had him killed?"

"As a traitor, Your Highness, with the added benefit, perhaps, of embarrassing the duke or yourself."

"I see. Well, the more they fight among themselves, the less likely they are to bother us." Alaric tapped his lips. "So what did you determine about this weapon?"

The prince was not the only one nervous about this line of questioning. Beyond him, in the church, Mortimer was nowhere to be seen. Elisha unfurled his senses further, and found him lurking just past the corner, holding his breath. "It has more than one blade, perhaps as many as five, not flat, but . . ."

Elisha had been shaping it with his hands, and now he

watched them. A glove, perhaps? Like a gauntlet with sharpened fingers? "But perhaps my lord Mortimer has something to add?" he said, raising his voice.

"What?" Alaric swung about. "Mortimer?"

The lord appeared around the corner and gave a short bow. "Forgive me, Your Majesty. I cannot countenance leaving you alone with a traitor and a witch. Everything he says is tainted. Don't you think the French ambassador had more important issues to hand than watching where his servants went? No doubt you simply had a robber with quick blade."

"Issues to hand," Elisha repeated, and Mortimer twitched. He knew more about the weapon than Elisha did, and he knew too much about the dead Frenchman: Somehow Mortimer was involved. Mortimer was antagonizing Elisha now to distract Alaric's attention from the Frenchman's death—but the assailant's cursing suggested something had gone wrong, that it was not a successful assassination, not carried out as planned. What if he had hoped to kill them both?

Would Mortimer try again to kill him, even on hallowed ground? Heaven knew the other barons would be pleased at Elisha's death—all but Randall and a few of his supporters. And even Randall's strength might be outweighed by the rest. Something stayed Mortimer's hand, forcing him to work in secret. That suggested Alaric did not know what his man was up to, and Mortimer wished to keep it that way.

Aloud, Elisha said, "A robber with a quick blade. No doubt. If that's all, Your Highness . . ."

Leaning against a marble pillar, Alaric regarded him,

his face no longer boyish. "It's hard to say. The French are very unhappy right now. My retainer"—he shot a dark look at Mortimer—"ruined their nasty little gift, their own retainer was killed on our watch, and I'll have to refuse their princess." He was scowling, but the expression looked pensive rather than angry.

He needn't refuse the princess, Elisha thought, but he said, carefully, "I've told you, Your Highness, that I have had nothing to do with them, and I intend to have nothing to do with them."

"What *do* you intend, Elisha?" Alaric held his name with a speculative accent. "You're a barber, still a commoner. Randall's taken you in, but he can't change what you are."

"It's always been enough for me," Elisha replied. His secret senses found Alaric warm and closed, any effort to sense beneath his skin foiled by some internal armor, slippery as a fish.

"Perhaps you should be seeking higher employment. A king could use a man with your talent. What do you say, Barber? Duke Randall and I have reached an accord. As his servant, your fealty will follow his at any rate—but I am prepared to offer you a place a bit nearer the throne."

At his side, Mortimer stiffened. "You can't do this, Your Majesty."

"You do not know what's at stake, Mortimer," Alaric said softly and precisely.

"I'm not ready for such high service, Your Highness." Their eyes met, and both men were silent a long moment.

"You know me, Barber. I held back my father's men that day. One might even say we worked well together: I, rescuing his hostages while you took care of the man himself. I'm curious what else you might undertake in the name of justice."

"A man who hires his father's killer can hardly claim that virtue, Your Highness." Elisha took the sting from the statement with a smile and a shrug. "Your barons are unhappy enough with me alive, never mind as part of your household."

"At least he's not a dullard," Mortimer put in.

"They don't have to know you work for me. Nobody else has to know."

"What of God, who knows all?" Mortimer demanded.

Waving away this remark, Alaric shoved off from the pillar and strode over, his ermine-edged cloak slithering over the ground. He had dressed to display his kingship—not to Elisha, surely. Then to whom? Who would he be meeting at Compline? Alaric leaned close to Elisha's ear and whispered, "You can do things even my lady cannot."

Elisha swallowed, and the duke's voice echoed in his head—if they could not seduce him, they would kill him.

Drawing back, Alaric went on, "Certain missions require the utmost secrecy, a surgical skill, one might say. You could travel, see some of the continent, enjoy much more luxury than you do now."

"In the name of justice," Elisha said, and Alaric gave a nod. "Because the assassin you already have has failed you. At least once."

And Alaric froze while Mortimer slid his sword a few

inches free of its sheath, his hand firm and face impassive. "My assassin?" the prince blurted. "I don't know—" he stopped and gave a sharp breath, his face lighting up almost as it used to. "Oh, my good Barber, you don't think I've been trying to kill you? If I wanted you dead, I'd call for your execution. Mortimer here would—"

"With pleasure," the lord said.

Alaric swung about to face his retainer. "You didn't. Tell me you didn't, Mortimer."

The lord hesitated, his sharp chin brought up, then, at last, Mortimer's lips bent into a grudging smile and he bowed his head. "I thought you would be pleased, Majesty, even if you couldn't bring yourself to do the deed."

"The crossbow?" Alaric pressed. "And the Frenchman?"

Sheathing his weapon once more, Mortimer lowered his hands and lied so palpably Elisha could see it the stiffness of his face. "Regrettable, Your Majesty. And the more so if his death cast any aspersions on yourself. It was a clumsy attempt, Your Majesty, and the hireling has been duly punished."

Alaric relaxed, shaking his head. "You can't take these decisions for yourself, Mortimer. Don't do it again."

"Of course, Your Majesty. Forgive me." He watched Elisha from the corner of his eye, and his posture of lordly penitence seemed a bit too languid, the confession too easy. Nor did his admission of guilt ease Elisha's nerves. In apologizing for the Frenchman's death, Mortimer claimed the crime to be an accident, deflecting interest from the mysterious assassin with his strange weapon. If he did not work on Alaric's orders, who, then, was Mortimer's master? Far off, a door opened, echoing in the stone interior.

"Have you been thinking on my offer?" the prince asked suddenly, interrupting Elisha's line of thought. "I can't guarantee that Mortimer here is the only one with ideas of his own. A foreign residence might be just the thing for you."

Thinking on it? As if Elisha should simply overlook the fact that the king's retainers wanted him dead.

"I'm sure our enemies already have agents here, working against us," Alaric went on, his gaze focused with a curious urgency. "I could use a man of your talents, to counter whatever threats may arise."

In fact, Alaric's whole being focused with a need Elisha could not understand; tension in his hands, in his shoulders, in the straining expression on his face. He looked so taut that Elisha wanted to soften, to speak soothing words, as a healer to his patient, to reassure him that the condition was not so dire as all that. What threats? he wanted to ask. Were the French so great a worry? Or did Alaric still fear his fallen brother? It was too late. Elisha's heart, and hand, would serve another. "Do you actually mean to buy me, Highness, or are you only trying to figure out my price?"

In the nave beyond, voices rose, and Rosalynn's voice called, "Elisha!"

Alaric spun on his heel and stuck his head around the corner, jerking back almost as quickly. "Oh, Barber. You work too cheap."

"Your Majesty, she just—came in—should we . . ." The guard looked at a loss, gesturing down the nave.

"I don't believe we have any more to say." Elisha bowed curtly and stepped past the prince, walking swiftly.

Steel hissed behind him, and Alaric spoke in a low voice. "I did not give you leave." Mortimer's long shadow came up with a firm stride and a second blade.

Elisha's heart hammered, the tension at his shoulders making his throat ache all the more. If he had thought an honest refusal would earn his freedom he was mistaken. The seduction was over.

"Elisha!" Rosalynn pinched up her skirts and hurried toward him, her cheeks flushed, eyes darting to the soldiers, to the prince, back to his face.

For a moment, Elisha dearly wished she were a witch, but he must speak to the air and be quick. He stepped up boldly, evading the hesitant guards and cupped the lady's cheek. She stiffened, eyes going wide. "Forgive me, lady," he whispered as softly as he could, their cheeks pressed together, his lips to her ear. "I have need of you."

"I'm listening," she murmured in reply, breathless now, but not frightened.

"Would you know my friend if you saw him again?"

Rosalynn gasped and clasped her hand over his, trembling. "But he's outside—he's looking for you."

Elisha bit down on an oath.

"We are not done here, Barber," Mortimer snapped behind him.

"He must not come here. Not for anything. Nothing at all, my lady, do you understand?" He sent his urgency, perhaps too sharply, for she flinched, her dark hair brushing against his face.

"But how could I stop him?"

For a moment, their hands clasped, cradling her head, and he had to admit, "I don't know. But you have to try." Then he released her, stepping away. Rosalynn gave a shiver, her eyes still wide.

"Then I'll take my leave," she said, her voice a bit shrill. She took in the soldiers around them. "You will not attend me, Elisha?"

"I think not, my lady." Alaric's words fell like hammer blows at Elisha's back. "Give my regards to your father, would you?"

"Yes, of course, Your Highness." She made a pretty curtsey, turned, and walked away down the long nave.

"Don't know her as well as I thought, eh, Barber?" Alaric spoke too loud, letting his voice echo from the stone arches. "She is every inch the slut I claimed her for."

"There's no call for that, Your Highness." Elisha glanced back at the prince. "Don't you have what you wanted? Everything you've wanted? Why taunt the rest of us?"

The door gave another creak, and a guard shouted, "You there! Be gone!"

"It's all right, he's just checking on me," Rosalynn called over her shoulder and then hurried her pace, going to meet whomever the guards had spotted by the door.

Elisha's heart sank, and he snapped back his awareness, gathering his strength.

"Get out of here, the both of you," Mortimer called. "The barber is no more of your concern."

Like the wandering stars, they stood for a moment aligned, Elisha at the crossing, surrounded by armed men, Rosalynn nearly at the door, Thomas framed inside of it. He must know his brother was here—had he come for some stupid, hero's battle, or would he take the coward's role and walk away? And what could Elisha say to make him leave without revealing him?

"You heard the lord, my lady," Elisha echoed. "Get out of here."

"I don't like this, Majesty," Mortimer muttered. "If she is no slut, then why did she come back?"

At this distance, in the dim light of the church, Elisha could just make out the figure of Thomas by the door, but his face remained in darkness. Rosalynn was near enough to see him, but she stumbled to a halt, then turned back to Elisha. She grabbed her skirts and started to run—directly toward him.

"No, Elisha, I won't leave you!"

"Guards," roared the prince. "Stop that woman—and shut her up!"

"What are you doing?" Elisha howled at Rosalynn, as the guards seized him, pulling him back. Three men sprinted past toward Rosalynn.

Her face pale but strangely resolute, she fell, full-length, and started to scramble up again.

Then, in a few long strides, Thomas sprang from his place. Elisha wanted to scream and rage at the both of them, but before Rosalynn had quite gained her feet, Thomas swept her up over his shoulder and ran for the door.

For a moment before they vanished outside, Rosalynn raised her hand, and they were gone.

Elisha gaped after them. She wasn't a fool, not really.

Her feet had been perfectly stable—she had fallen on purpose, giving Thomas time to rescue her. Elisha wanted to laugh aloud, but the guards were pulling at him.

"Who was that?" Alaric demanded of no one—then he flung himself in front of Elisha. "Who was he?"

"Some charity man she's taken on," Elisha replied.

With a wave of his arm, Alaric sent his other soldiers scrambling. "Get them. Bring them back here—I don't like this."

"I warned you, Your Majesty," said Mortimer. "I said you couldn't trust him. Whatever it is, she's in on it, too."

Elisha's euphoria vanished. He dropped to his knees, pulling free of the confused guards, and slapped his hand to the marble floor, his wrist still bound up with the purple cloth of his talisman. Silk again. Contact. He snatched at his knowledge—strong, smooth, foreign—stone as smooth as silk. He stretched his power into it, as if he wove through the pattern of tiles, then he gave a tug. The floor rippled like fabric, tossing upward. Men skidded and clattered to the ground, swords sliding away from them on the sudden wrinkles. Mortimer landed with a crack of his head and a groan. Elisha tugged again, sending the wave out behind him as well. He whipped off his right boot and stood up, maintaining contact through the sole of one bare foot.

"Damn it, Mortimer, where's Farus?" Alaric cried, his fancy cloak swirling about him as he tried to maintain his footing.

But Mortimer only groaned the louder as he struggled to his knees and tumbled again.

"Said you didn't want him here, Majesty," blurted one

of the guards. He slithered sideways, leapt a hump of marble and fell to his knees. "Went to see his sister!" The words grew louder as the man wobbled in a slick arc, clearing Elisha's path.

Elisha leapt up and ran, each strike of his left foot keeping the floor briefly steady, before the right made contact and set the floor to shaking. He made for the south transept and the cloister of the monks, for a hundred men who'd call down the pope if any man—even their king—dared shed blood in their precinct.

A man's length short of the door, an agony of horror snatched his throat and hurled him down, clawing at his neck, his breath cut off and lungs already burning.

Chapter 17

Elisha writhed on the floor, bewildered, power of speech and spell both ripped away. The rope tore into his throat, his feet kicked free of the earth—No! He was in the church at Beaulieu, his throat was bare, but his flesh remembered the grip of the rope that had hanged him at Dunbury weeks before. His head throbbed, and he struggled for breath. Each time he rocked against the floor, it drew him back into now, but his body recalled fighting the rope, fighting for his life. Pain streaked through him from the terrible grip, but there was no rain to carry his cries, no way to force a word from his constricted throat. No one to save him. Elisha sobbed.

Then, just as it had those weeks ago, Brigit's face came before his eyes. Tears blurred her, a halo of stained glass lighting her from behind. His agony eased, and he gasped a breath that seared him. His shoulders hitched with effort, his bare foot shaking.

"You see, my lord king, you need me." Her face briefly vanished, only to return, joined by Alaric's.

Elisha blinked the tears away, the spasms passing.

Brigit's brows pinched together, her lips pressed hard, as if she knew some echo of his pain and sorrowed for it. She bent nearer, and looked him over carefully, as he might search a patient for signs of injury. Her frown deepened.

"What in God's name did you do that for?" Alaric bleated. "Now we'll have to kill him!"

"What?" Brigit's attention shifted in an instant.

"Pick him up. Don't let him touch anything," Alaric directed, the mask of his majesty returning to his face. Had Elisha glimpsed his terror, or was it his own terror projected on another? "And get your bloody swords!" the prince snarled.

Brigit rose away from him as the guards moved in. Her hands drew apart, one of them concealing something that she slipped away beneath her surcoat. One of the men yanked the wrapping from Elisha's wrist and bound his hands together. Six guards grabbed Elisha's arms and legs, letting his head loll, so that he stared at a dizzying image of the door as it retreated from him. Bits of colored light swirled over him, candle flames and the Virgin Mary's face.

"He shan't be capable of much magic for a little while," said Brigit. "But I don't think he's badly off."

"I had this well in hand, Brigit, what are you doing here?" Alaric murmured, taking Brigit's arm and closing behind Elisha's bearers, cutting off his glimpse of safety as the procession moved toward the north transept, with its door that would lead to empty fields. At least, so his disoriented memory informed him.

"Looking for something. I thought he'd brought it here."

"You're not still after that accursed talisman, are you? You don't need it. You are strong enough without."

"In our realm, my love, a witch can never be strong enough. What do you mean, 'now we have to kill him?' Weren't you already trying?"

A door at Elisha's feet pushed open, releasing them into a world of chill twilight, the sky still bright overhead. His bearers crunched over stone, then grass. Patric and Ian appeared, bowed, with greetings gruff but pleasant enough for the prince and his lady.

"You're sure he can't act against us?" Alaric glowered down at Elisha, the prince's face swimmingly upside down.

"Look at him. He hasn't even figured out what happened to him."

Alaric gave a sharp gesture, and they dropped Elisha onto the clipped grass, near a mound of sheep dung. He rolled to his side, retching and gulping at the air. The familiar smells of sheep and hay refreshed his battered throat as he took his first deep breaths. Hadn't figured out what happened to him, but the memories of the past still chilled his flesh. Only the hanging rope itself could conjure such a vivid horror, the rope Brigit had taken for a talisman the day it almost killed him.

"Should we go after Lady Rosalynn now, Your Majesty?"

Sucking on his teeth, Alaric considered, then shook his head. "Her behavior's been so wild of late. The lady I knew would never allow herself to be handled by a commoner, never mind two in one day. After this, I can't imagine anyone short of her father will listen to her— seems she'd do anything to get a little barbering."

Brigit gave an exasperated sigh. "I can't explain where that attraction came from—he didn't strike me as so eager for the duke's favor."

Mortimer loomed up then, blood matting the right side of his hair, his nostrils flaring. He nudged Elisha with a boot, pushed him to his back and pinned him firmly beneath his foot, sword extended. "So, Your Majesty, now may I do the deed?"

"Kill him," said Alaric, and Brigit began to speak, but he overrode her, "He'll never trust us again—never."

The sword shifted, pressing harder, but another voice interrupted.

"Now, you don't want to be doin' that here, Majesty, begging your pardon and all." A thick hand patted Mortimer's sword hilt, then clasped over it, giving it a friendly wiggle that nicked Elisha's chest.

"Where did you come from—and who the Devil are you?"

"Humble gravedigger, Majesty, at your service, all that. But I do know my work." The lumpish face of the hunchback from Dunbury loomed into view with something like a smile. "Didn't expect all this to-do. Jest looking for work myself, y'know." He smacked his lips together. "Plenty of criminals hereabouts. Plenty to keep busy."

Mortimer gave a little shake of his head, then glanced at his king, looking for guidance. Alaric, too, started at the man's approach, but his eyes went round as if the gravedigger frightened him.

"Now, don't say nuffin', Majesty, jest you let old Morag take care of this, eh?"

Alaric's brows leapt, his lips parted as if to speak, then he scowled instead, drawing back from the intruder, masking his brief concern in his royal air.

Elisha felt a whiff of fear. His chest shivered with pain, each gasp pressing the sword into his skin, but this fear was not his own. Was this what Alaric had somehow sensed to startle him like that? It drifted around Elisha, up from the earth perhaps, a sudden sense of watchfulness, of his own insignificance. He wanted someone else to take charge, to make the hard choices and do the dirty things. Elisha, too, shrank from this queer blend of desires, but the chill, at least, felt familiar, and he focused on Morag. Was he real, truly the gravedigger from Dunbury? Or had Elisha's addled mind imposed Morag's face upon a stranger?

Elisha squeezed his eyes shut and popped them open to the same sight.

"Back 'ere's a better spot, where they do the sheep for table. Nobody's like to notice more blood, eh?" The gravedigger leaned down and grabbed Elisha's upper arm, causing the startled Mortimer to pull back his sword and his foot rather than fall over as Morag lurched into motion, dragging Elisha with him across the grass. "Come on, Majesty."

"My lord king, you can't do this," Brigit insisted softly. "Some of our friends will be furious."

"Then don't tell them," Alaric snapped. He hung his hand on his sword, following the gravedigger.

"As if I would—but they will know. They will find out. If we are to bring our peoples together, we can't simply flout their wishes like this."

"How will they? These are my most loyal men." He stared at the gravedigger moving ahead of them, Elisha's view bouncing as he thumped over the grass. "Even that one, it seems." Alaric nodded at Morag, who gave a sickly grin in reply.

"Too true, Majesty." He gave Elisha another yank, and the chill of death seeped up from the dirt through Elisha's back, the smell of slaughtered sheep filling his skull.

"Please, Alaric, listen to me. I only wanted to stop him running before you'd finished, don't you see? We can control him. We can find another way." Brigit clung to his arm, but he gently set her aside, with a shake of his head.

"I am sorry, Brigit, truly. When you're thinking more clearly you'll understand. If you knew all that I know—" he broke off with a sharp breath. "Go back, find the talisman, whatever you need, darling. You don't need to watch this." He rubbed her arms, smiled fondly, kissed her forehead.

Her troubled, green-eyed glance fell briefly on Elisha, then she stepped away, Ian and Patric falling in with her. If he had voice enough to speak, would he thank her for trying? The gravedigger, Morag, bowed politely as the lady withdrew.

Then Morag tightened his grip on Elisha and jerked him into Hell.

The smell of brimstone reminded him of the bombards' smoke on the battlefield. The world snapped apart, filled with shrieks and terrors, a thousand icy winds tore at Elisha's clothes and hair, wrapped his throat, and stung the brands of his punishment. For a moment, he felt suspended in a tempest, mad wails whirling about him, streaks of light like shooting stars. His head pulsed with the crazed rhythm. He tried to open his eyes, and found they were already open, garish colors writhing in his sight. His ears throbbed with every sound of human misery, and his throat burned with foul mists. Faceless tormentors trailed pain and pleading across his skin.

The world blinked back. Elisha reeled as the grave-digger turned about with him. Elisha lay once more on a marble floor, staring up at a church ceiling, but one with enormously high painted arches, red stone and three ranks of galleries. He gaped at it. Hell to Heaven in the space of a breath.

"Naw, bad idea," Morag muttered.

Hell snapped them up and spat them out once more, under trees and a twilight sky. Tall, pollarded oaks that smelled like home, and a bed of acorns that nubbed into his back. The New Forest? Elisha blinked up at the branches.

Finally, he wet his lips and swallowed past the pain. "What was that?" he breathed.

"Tossed 'em a smoke bomb and ran like the devil. You've been out a little while, friend."

"No, I haven't," Elisha managed, but he had smelled smoke, hadn't he? He pushed himself up on his elbows until he could sit, wavering slightly. Then he grabbed the knotted cloth in his teeth and tugged until it came free. He rubbed his aching wrist and re-wrapped it slowly, this time without help.

"Prob'ly thought you'd gone to Hell for a moment, eh? All in your head." Morag reached out and gave Elisha's skull a rap. "When you think you're dead."

He recoiled from the touch. Had he been close to death? He hadn't had any visions at the hanging tree. Absently, he rubbed his neck. The memory had receded far enough that Elisha felt himself returned fully to the present. Certainly, he had not been quite lucid since Brigit nearly strangled him with a scrap of the same rope. How could she choke the life from him with her magic, then claim they shouldn't kill him? But then, she had not yet gotten what she wanted, and she would give up no advantage until she had—even the symbol she had made of him to rally the other magi. It wasn't as if she wanted him free. "Thanks."

"Pffff." The gravedigger tossed off his gratitude with a careless flap of his hand. "We're not far from where we were—close enough that you'll have a deal of running afore you leave him behind. And he's the king and all, so that makes it tricky."

Elisha nodded vaguely.

Morag scratched the stubble under his chin and eyed him sidelong. "Might be, a man had some friends, some with . . . similar interests, he might get out all right."

Recalling the wave of anxiety that came over him when Morag appeared and how, by force of his presence alone, he had pushed away the prince's men, Elisha said, "You're a magus."

Again, Morag gave a dismissive flop of his hand. "Y' could say." He moved surprisingly well for a hunchback, and Elisha wondered if his deformity were some kind of skin condition or growth rather than a problem with the skeleton itself. "Y'did something in that church, eh?"

"Something," Elisha agreed. Now that he had returned to his faculties, he began the process of attune-ment, letting his awareness creep out into the duff on the forest floor and up to the trees, and over to the strange man who saved him; a man who felt like nothing at all. Elisha glanced at him, to find the sunken eyes staring back.

"Without no talisman."

"A minor one." He held up his sore wrist with its pur-ple binding. Elisha could see Morag, feel the moisture of his breath, smell the slightly putrid presence, and knew the strength of the arm that had dragged him here — through what means, he could not quite be sure. But with his other senses? Nothing. He felt tempted to touch him again, to see if closer contact might reveal more.

Morag reached out and flicked the purple cloth at his wrist. "That? Pffff. How d'you get a spell from a thing like that?"

"Same as any other talisman." Elisha shrugged. "As I said, a minor one."

"You got a fuckin' earthquake from that?" Morag gave a hoot of disbelief, then he glanced around Elisha, as if expecting to see something else. "No jest?"

For a moment, Elisha sensed interest, the same kind of questing he had felt when he called upon the power of that other talisman. "I appreciate your help back there, but I really must go."

"So the king can lop your head off, and I don't get nuffing?"

Elisha rose, a little lopsided with one foot bare and one booted. The ground felt warm. "Can you point me back toward the abbey?"

The gravedigger shoved himself up, dusting off his sloppy tunic. He grabbed Elisha's shoulder before he could dodge the reaching hand, and pushed him about. A river gurgled at the edge of the trees. Beyond that, a high stone wall with a steeple poking out. Morag leaned into him and rumbled, "What if I told you it was Rome you saw, not Heaven?"

Rome was where the Pope should be, far to the east. Weeks away at best. "If Rome is Heaven, then what was Hell?" Elisha twisted away from the hand, not wanting this fellow behind him, especially on a riverbank.

"Hell's what you make it—you just ain't thinkin' right." He hooked his thumbs into a belt. "But you're thinkin' now, eh?"

"You took me to Rome and back in an instant? It's not possible."

"Not for most." That grin returned, smelling of rotten teeth and gapped by those already gone. "You strangle your own strength, playing w' scraps like that." Morag pointed to the talisman cloth. "You've had more. The kind a power gets a man up in the morning."

"I made the earth move with this."

The gravedigger bobbed his head side to side. "Gonna tell me you're happy with that? Bullshit." Elisha scowled, and Morag let out a guttural chuckle. "I coulda ripped the place down. Like that." He snapped his fingers, and the gesture flashed in Elisha's awareness with a sudden leap of cold. "Coulda smashed them soldiers like lice between my nails." The blunt fingers pinched and the cold snuffed into nothing. "Part of your trouble is just you ain't workin' at it. Hardly done any magic, nuffin' big.

Well—one thing big, eh?" Morag reached out and gave his shoulder a friendly slap.

A different riverside sprang before his eyes, King Hugh trapped there, his face shriveling to dust and his crown rolling away, Death leaping from the shrunken man to Elisha's hand. And the thrill of power afterward. He tasted again the visceral joy, a rush of strength that flamed through him, when he could have done anything, been anything, and no man had the power to hurt him, ever again. Elisha recoiled from the memory, shaking himself.

Morag licked his lips and sighed. "Can't believe you let that one get away."

"Get away? I killed him," Elisha blurted.

"Wasted. Y'could've had so much more. Any idiot can kill somebody." He hitched his thumb toward the great oak at his back, a stocky stone at its base. "Y'see that? William Rufus took an arrow to the lung right here." He thudded his fist into his chest and made a grotesque face while his other hand imitated blood squirting from a wound. "You ain't the only one as killed a king." Morag leaned his shoulders against the rock, his hump compressing awkwardly. "Wisht I coulda been here then. Wisht I coulda brought yon prince out here. We'd show him what happens to kings, and mebbe he'd show us a little more respect, eh?" Morag settled into the stone like a cat on a hearth, but the hearth was cold with the sense of the dead, stained with blood, probably from the butchering pit in the yard where Morag had snatched him.

Now, the other magus watched him from slitted eyes. "Saw Hell, did you? Lemme show you again." He waved his hand in the air, beckoning.

"I don't want you to show me anything," Elisha murmured, but some part of him did, the part that could suck down a man's death and spin it into power, into armor, into weapons, into whatever his need required.

When finally he allowed Morag to grip his hand, he focused, intent on what was happening. Again, it happened too quickly, as if without thought, and they passed from the world. This time, Morag held the passage. It howled around them with the thousand voices of the dead—cries of torture, tears of despair, unheard prayers to distant saints. They were not souls, exactly—at least, they had not the sense of presence that a living person embodied. Rather, they were shadows, cast by the dead and captured in their pain.

But Morag twisted what he heard, and the maelstrom blasted into a sudden wind, the sort that sailors and millers admired. The gravedigger threw back his head and laughed. "Yes!" he shouted. "Yes!" Power flooded through them. Through his grip, all the strength of this vast and dreadful world flowed to Elisha's hand, strength to break steel. His presence expanded, an awareness so full he could not drink it all, so rich, he could not take in all that he could know. It suffused him from toes to tingling scalp, such medicine that a man might never know sickness. By God, if he could channel that—

His knees trembled with the rush, and he would have collapsed if not for the grip of Morag's hand. Unlike the heat of Mordecai's healing, this grip was solid and void at once, like a physical deflection—the strength of the lashing wind of Death outweighing the slender life of man.

Outside was rage, horror, pain; inside, Morag kept it at bay. It swirled and eddied through him. Elisha stared at him, brought his every sense to bear upon him, the heightened, extraordinary awareness Morag's very touch allowed him. The crowds of the dead, flickering like Hell's inferno, resolved around the misshapen man, casting him in shadows. Four shadows or more stretched and shrank and clung in tatters about him, springing from his hands and shoulders. He touched the howling throng through these, the shades that never left him. They filtered the powerful wind, fluttering. Enslaved, they fed Morag on the pain that shrieked around him.

Elisha reached back and some of the shades stirred toward him, twin shadows, thinner than the others, that stilled at his presence.

Morag's head snapped up, his body tremoring and he let go the door with a reluctant twinge. It slammed in an instant to a thunderous silence, an afterimage dancing in blue against the trees until Elisha could blink it away.

Elisha sank to his knees, gasping. His heartbeat filled the silence. He wanted to vomit, to purge his stomach until he had forgotten all he saw and heard and felt, forgot the way the shadows reached for him. He wanted to know how it was done—how Morag stepped through this place of horrors all the way to Rome, how to gather the strength of a world, how to spread his awareness through a shifting sea of knowledge.

Slowly, the chatter of crows, the distant neigh of horses, the calling of a shepherd emerged from the stunning quiet. Elisha quivered and worked to calm his breathing. Slowly, he raised his head.

"Hell, may be, but I'm the master." Morag grinned, his grip tightening. "Hell's all mine. Who needs Heaven?"

But the strip of cloth cradled his wrist with the pledge of the friend who had given it, and Elisha let that slender strength seep back into his bones. It felt the more slender now that he had felt what Morag possessed, what he offered to share. The gravedigger summoned and dispelled his passage with so little effort, even Elisha had not sensed it. He might be weakened by Brigit's spell, but still, Morag's agility struck him with a terrible awe. Morag's mysterious talismans drew down a power almost unimaginable, a power that strained his senses to contain it. Elisha thought of all his teachers, of Brigit, Mordecai, Allyson—nothing they ever said or speculated had suggested this.

Elisha's little scrap gave him the skill to tame his racing thoughts and seal his emotions back in his own skin. It gave him strength to lift his head and look up into the eyes of the man who would be his master, the man who claimed to master Hell. The necromancer.

Chapter 18

◈

Morag stared back at him, his eyes dark and cold beneath his furrowed brow. The hairs on Elisha's arm tingled as if spiders crept from Morag's sleeve, but he had sealed his emotions—or thought he had.

After a long moment, the mancer growled. "Never shoulda got me for this, he shouldn't. Don't ye feel it?"

Elisha bit back the obvious question. Morag searched him, looking for a reflection of his own fascination with the power of the dead. Elisha felt that power. He knew what it might do, and he even longed for the world that might lie open to him if he seized it. But Elisha's work, his heart, was with the living.

"Bloody sensitive, my arse." He jerked Elisha's arm so that Elisha had to scramble up to alleviate the pain. Then Morag swung him against the stone, leaning over him, reeking breath blowing out in Elisha's face. "Anybody's got a baby head in a bottle for a talisman's got to be one of us, he says. Somebody got to go see, and seeing's you awready know the fella—" Morag snarled. "Ye didn't even make that talisman a'purpose, did you?"

"On purpose? Are you mad?" Then Elisha caught his breath. The necromancer thought Elisha was already one of them. Or he had believed it, until now.

"Are *you*?" Morag roared. "We're the masters! We're more than kings! Ye've got the strength, ye've got the skill, and ye want to be a bloody barber all yer fuckin' life?"

He had—ever since he'd seen an angel die. Now, dared he hope to be a surgeon? To be a doctor in the eyes of all? To tame his wild power and be the man who saved a king, setting Thomas in his rightful throne? Morag offered him a place in the palace of Hell. He might earn it through his sins, but it would not be for want of striving. Morag's dark eyes bored into him, and Elisha knew his answer was writ plain upon his face.

A shock of cold blasted Elisha's hand, first shaking, then numb, creeping up toward his elbow. He called upon the power of his cloth, remembering Martin who had given it to him and the long affection between them. Heat urged his flesh back to life. Pushed back against the stone, he brought up both feet and kicked hard, catching Morag in the belly and thigh. The mancer stumbled, pivoting so that they nearly changed places.

"Why'd I show myself for you?" the gravedigger shouted on a howl of dark wind.

The blast knocked Elisha flat, finally breaking the grip on his arm. He scrambled up again, finding his surgical knife. A pathetic weapon, but it had killed before.

Morag lunged for him, then stopped short, eyes narrowing as he looked at the knife. Afraid of its puny blade? No—in the space of breath between them, Elisha felt the cold that clung to the blade, the vestiges of murder that caught Morag's attention.

"Mebbe not a fuckin' waste of time." the mancer muttered.

"I'm grateful for your help—now I will be grateful if you leave me alone." He was grateful, too, that his hand didn't shake as he held out the knife.

Morag snorted. "Can't do it. Can't let ye walk from here, now ye've seen. But I'll be happy t' carry you." From his belt, he slipped free a knife of his own, a broad, half-moon shape, dark with blood. He moved it back and forth and grinned.

A wave of horror that curdled Elisha's stomach spread from Morag's presence and made the evening sky go dark. Their breath came in clouds, pale in the shifting darkness. They circled like brawlers, but the leaves overhead cackled together and the ground crunched with frost. Morag lunged, Elisha dodged and feinted, turning to keep his enemy in sight. The bandit's death stained his blade, and while he moved, he conjured, bringing up the echoes, allowing the knife to become a talisman unto itself. When Morag pounced again, Elisha was ready, ducking but surging inward, closer to the mancer, thrusting not only with the blade but with the focused anguish of a man's destruction.

Morag stumbled back, letting out a whoop as if a game were on, and he was sure of victory.

Elisha pressed the advantage. Morag fell to his left, his arm swinging up, and Elisha froze. This was no chill in the air, no creeping sense of doom, but a slap of ice against his chest. He gasped for breath, his lungs pierced, his heart working too hard. He felt slick with blood, unable to scream, and clutched at his chest. Aside from the narrow cut left by Thomas's blade, he bled no more. What he felt was a memory—but not his own.

Elisha tried to cast off the phantasm, drawing from the cloth, but its tiny heat withered. Then Morag was on him, flinging him back against the stone, the breath knocked from his lungs as if pierced in truth. The mancer shoved up against him, trapping him with his own bulk, his knife trapped as Morag brought up his own. Morag shifted his grip, setting the blade not crosswise for a quick slash, but vertically, one tip of the crescent tucked beneath Elisha's chin.

"Where's the fun in that?" Morag muttered, eyes narrowed as if he calculated dark designs.

Blood dripped from the blade to trickle down Elisha's throat. Pierced chest, blood streaming. The French magus who died in his arms.

"You skinned him," Elisha breathed very carefully. "Did you kill him, too?"

The gravedigger's thick eyebrows twitched up, then he smiled, his rank odor curling into Elisha's desperate lungs. "Could kill ye now—but ye'll be sweeter by and by." His off-hand seized a handful of Elisha's shirt and shoved him backward.

Elisha braced for the crack of his skull on the stone. Instead, they plunged into the howling abyss. One of the gray shadows at Morag's shoulders flashed toward him immediately, and Elisha reached back, feeling the rush of power in spite of Morag's snarl.

"*You wanted the abbey—here ya go.*" The words

seared a cold pathway down the curving blade into Elisha's skin.

The world split open, and Morag plunged him through, dropping him as the world snapped shut again. He tumbled onto the bloody field, gasping, his knife drawn, his being charged with that final blast of cold. He sprang to his feet, searching. No one. Alaric and his men had gone, and Morag had not followed.

For a moment, Elisha worked to catch his breath. The mad magus saved his life from Alaric, only to think of taking it himself—then he held back. Why? Elisha would be sweeter soon, he'd said. What that meant Elisha did not want to know, but he needed to. Morag wanted to recruit him on behalf of another, and Elisha's refusal made them his enemies, so why let him go? The release was nearly more frightening than the threat of murder. Like Morag's whoop of battle joy, it suggested they had absolute certainty that they could take him when they wanted. Duke Randall thought Elisha the most dangerous man in England. The duke had been very, very wrong.

And that brought him back to the problem of the princes. Alaric came dressed for an audience, not for Elisha's benefit and not for a mere abbot, surely. Alaric wanted to impress someone—or to keep his own confidence—for the meeting he faced clearly terrified him. What then? No matter. Elisha had to focus on the primary talisman and get Thomas out of danger as quickly as he could. Brigit was not the only one searching, and not even—Blessed Mother!—the most dangerous. Elisha staggered toward the gate and finally yanked off his remaining boot and cast it aside.

Brigit's bandits were dead, thanks to Thomas—how many others might be lurking about? Or worse? He wished he had a sword, a dagger, anything. But nothing would avail him against the mancer who used Elisha's own weapons and knew them better. Thomas was armed, but the danger he expected would be his brother's soldiers. If he saw Brigit coming, he might well count on his beggar's looks to disguise him and come out to see what he could learn from her.

How far had Rosalynn's plan extended? She arranged her rescue, saving Thomas at the same moment. The solution seemed obvious: hoping Elisha would get himself free, perhaps even believing it if she had felt the magic in the church or if she seen Alaric again without Elisha, she would send Thomas to safety in a place they could meet—the very village she suggested as a hiding place.

Casting a slight deflection to dodge any unwanted glances, Elisha walked toward the western road. A bell rang out from the church, calling the monks to Compline. Had so much time passed already? Elisha kept to the shadows, conserving his magic in case the eyes of ordinary men were not all that he must fear.

Torches blazed around the stable yard, illuminating a milling group of men, and he heard Alaric's voice. "Why aren't the horses ready? By Compline, we said. Where's that stable wretch?" The prince's tall, dark shadow sped along the wall and into the building. Elisha heard a child's shriek of pain and he froze, his fist locking around his surgical knife. By God, he had not taken twenty-seven lashes so that Alaric could abuse stable boys and insult women. He had to find Thomas, for more reasons than one.

The lay brothers who were meant to guard the gate had been distracted by the commotion at the stable, and Elisha ran through, free of the abbey grounds. He slogged as fast as he could down the muddy track and over the bridge where the abbey fields gave way to wattled yards, sheep folds, and huddled houses. Soon, the houses, too, fell behind. Before him, sunset lent a bloody murk to the clouded sky over the clustered darkness of the forest. The tilled fields ran out, leaving Elisha in thickets. Pigs snorted at his passage, and dogs barked as he left the last of the civilized land. Ahead, hills bulged against the skyline, topped with rustling brush. A flock of birds took flight with a scatter of cries.

A pond glinted dully to his right, and he turned onto an ancient lane, grassy and overhung with branches. A broken hut stood at the end of the pond with a ruined sty beside it, woven branches thrust up like ribs.

Elisha tried to calm his thundering heart. He slowed to a walk, ducking under the young trees growing thickly from tumbled pastures and the striped remains of furrows. Creatures rustled and started, fleeing his passage. Elisha hoped one of them would be Cerberus, ambling out to meet him, having recognized his scent. Instead, the trees grew closer.

Suddenly, the forest swept apart, revealing a clearing with a handful of houses a little more intact, and a low stone building topped by a little arch where a bell chain still hung, the bells from the nearby abbey filling in for the silence of this steeple.

Elisha stopped and his eyes slowly adjusted to the gloom. Six houses, their doors open or missing altogether, surrounded a meager yard, its earth so packed that few plants struggled up. The little church backed up to a larger building, probably a storehouse or tithing barn. Attunement. Immediately, if possible. Drawing a deep breath, Elisha stretched out with his other senses, letting his awareness fill in details: the patter of collected rain that trickled from the roofs, the scent of distant wood smoke. A crow cawed, then a chorus of them. As he reached out his awareness, he felt their slender heat. At the church, a patch of chill, then something colder brushed past. Elisha's gaze fixed upon the church. Light sprang up at his back. Elisha cried out, turning, yanking out his knife.

"You've wasted our time," drawled a voice nearby. "Sensitive? As sensitive as a clod, I'd say." A figure stood silhouetted by torchlight at the door of a ruined house.

"You leave her be!" screeched a second voice, from above. "Don't tease her." The crows chorused their support.

"Tell your friends to be quiet, or we'll be found," snapped the first. "We're not the only ones about tonight." A man, his presence cold instead of hot. It was not the cold of Death, but something smaller. It resembled the feel of the knife in Elisha's grip.

"You chose this place, Parsley, for us, or for your finer friends?" the second voice screeched back.

The patter of the dripping water grew suddenly louder and the torch sizzled with scattered droplets. "Let us at least learn a little more about our guest before dismissing him." The new voice, too, pattered, gentle as the drops. A mist hovered there. No, not a mist, a man as gray as rain.

"Who are you? What do you want from me?" Elisha called out, but he thought he could almost feel the answer as he tried to make sense of what he heard and touched.

"If he must ask ..." drawled the first man—Parsley. He let the words dangle.

Were they simply magi, or more necromancers? If so, they had little experience with Death—he felt it only by the church, in spite of cold Parsley's presence. Then he sensed a more familiar presence, though he could not place its origin at first. It suffused the earth around him. Elisha dropped to one knee, making contact, taking a gamble. *"Chanterelle,"* he said into the dirt, using the witch's way of speaking without words. All witches could use water, to make contact with one another. But Chanterelle—

"I'm here," she murmured. Then the ground before him bubbled, and she emerged slowly, as if mounting a staircase no other could see.

"Ah, finally she rises!" Parsley said.

"Because he knew to ask for me," Chanterelle said, her voice barely carrying in the air, though Elisha felt the anger it held. "And he knew how."

"He would, wouldn't he? He's met you before."

Then Chanterelle focused on Elisha, her gaze as well as her anger. "But he's just come from the mancer—and the mancer let him live."

"Shit," said Parsley, his presence colder than ever. Elisha glanced back, his memory stirred as the man spoke again. "You said he wasn't one of them."

"She said he wasn't. That doesn't mean he isn't," observed the misty form, the man gray as rain, who moved nearer. "Now that you've brought us together, Chanterelle," he murmured, "you need to go. They have already tried once to kill you. Now that they know you've been tracking them, they won't stop until they have you."

She gave the misty man a glance almost of pity. "I will not go until you have seen the truth about him." Returning her focus to Elisha, she said, "You have met the mancer."

"The necromancer asked me to join him. He—" but what could Elisha say? That he had been tempted? "He plans to kill me later, when he thinks I'm ready. Next time we meet won't be so easy."

"A coward, then, if not a mancer." Parsley shrugged. "Doesn't matter now he's failed your test."

Chanterelle continued to regard him from behind her curtain of hair, and finally spoke again. "He's not turned mancer," Chanterelle murmured. "I know their touch."

"He looked here," said the voice among the crows. They were clustered on the steps of the church, and a woman moved among them, hunched, old and ugly, clad in black. If ever a witch lived to give rise to the image of sorcery itself, it was she. Crows perched upon her shoulders and hopped along at her feet. "And we saw what he did on the road. Even you, Sundrop."

The misty figure—Sundrop?— gave a nod, but the cold man rejoined, "He hasn't got the knowledge, or the sensitivity. He is not one of us."

"If you haven't the time, Parsley, you shouldn't've come."

Elisha bristled to be left out of the conversation. For the moment, listening served him better than questioning. Let their private conflicts reveal them. *Indivisi*. Testing him, to try Chanterelle's claim. Knowledge and sensitivity.

"He hasn't been a magus very long," Chanterelle offered. "He hasn't learned much."

He knelt among them, ignorant as a child, despite the fact that she was half his age. Time to grow up—and fast. Parsley was not the only one who had other friends to look out for. Elisha rose to his feet. "The body in the church," he said. "Who is it?"

They fell silent, aside from the caw of a crow.

"You see?" Parsley, the cold man, folded his arms with a soft clang. "Any mancer's boy would know that much."

More, then. There was more for him to know. Elisha forced himself to relax and stretch his awareness. He found the body by the chill he'd felt when he reached out his awareness. Now, he reached up through the earth that gave him contact, however distant. The woman with crows cocked her head at him. Chanterelle slipped aside a fistful of her bedraggled hair to watch. The chill reached back, fitting him like his old, familiar boots. Elisha focused on the corpse they had brought to the church and recognized it. He swallowed past the ache of his throat. "I killed the man. Is that what you wanted?"

Shoving off from his doorframe, Parsley stalked nearer, his eyes glinting in the light. "Is it what you wanted?"

"He was a bandit, attacking an innocent woman. He

had to be stopped." Elisha thought to say more but held back. These people had no claim on him, no need to know his regrets.

"You had a talisman. An evil thing—"

"No," Elisha said, circling with him, meeting his eyes. "Terrible, yes. Not evil."

"A baby you killed—not evil?"

The crow woman hissed.

"The baby was dead." Tension knotted Elisha's shoulders.

"You did it," the man insisted.

"I knew it, I didn't *do* it," Elisha shot back. Then he straightened. "I *knew* it," he said again. The signs had been there, yes. Medically speaking, an experienced practitioner would have guessed the child would be stillborn. But Elisha did not need to guess. For a moment, he met Chanterelle's obscured gaze, and she smiled. Elisha turned from her. Nausea cramped his stomach. That same practitioner might guess it had been too long since he'd eaten, but Elisha's sickness went deeper than hunger. Could it be true? Could all of his training, all of his trying, have led up to this: that he made himself servant not to a necromancer, but to Death itself?

Chapter 19

❖

His wrist throbbed with every heartbeat, and he loosened his grip on the knife. No wonder Morag greeted him as friend, almost as a brother. "I am not with Death."

"You may not have chosen it," said Sundrop, the mistman, "but that doesn't mean it isn't true. Chanterelle did not choose her other self." Sundrop gestured toward her, and a spattering of rain fell. She sank down to her knees, hugging herself. In a soft, solemn voice he continued, "There are only so many times a girl can be forced to the floor before she sinks right through." The dirt that still clung to her body shifted and shivered on her flesh, forming a second skin from her shoulders to her knees.

Crows hopped down around her, tipping their heads, studying her, their mistress following. "Most don't choose, not at first, my pretties." She caressed one of the dark birds, and it bobbed up at her.

"Or they wouldn't choose such stupid things," Parsley, the cold man, snapped.

Elisha bristled at his harsh tone. The man must have

a heart of—"Iron," Elisha said aloud, leveling his knife at Parsley. "I'm surprised to find you in such company. Aren't you afraid of rust?"

Sundrop laughed as if storm clouds had broken. "Ignorant, but not a fool. Knowledge, I'll grant you. Sensitivity, yes—he's even spoken through raindrops. But I don't see how a man can be with Death. Even the mancers don't claim that." A speculative expression made the misty features suddenly acute—a young face, sharp and long-jawed. "Though the mancers might well wish to claim you."

"Why do you?"

"We don't." The iron-magus flicked Elisha's blade with a finger, bending it as if it were straw.

Sundrop splashed Parsley's hand and he cursed, snaking back his arm. Tiny pits of red showed against his skin as he wiped away the water, glaring. "If the magi are a race apart, we are apart from even them," Sundrop explained. "When Chanterelle suggested you might be one of us . . . well, some of us were curious." His gestures, graceful and gray, took in his companions. "Some of us were furious. Mancers are no man's friend. But a magus who walked with Death could be friend or foe—who could know?"

"How would I tell?" Elisha pressed. "How, if this were true?"

"How could it be?" Parsley the iron-man grated. "How can a man know death who hasn't died and lived again?"

Elisha's hand rose to the scar at his throat.

Sundrop's eyelids fluttered shut, and he stretched out

his hands. "There's a drought in the chalk—they could use me now, but I'd have to go closer. Drought," he repeated softly, with a subtle shift in posture. Elisha's eyes grew suddenly dry, and he coughed, the moisture drawn away, the mist sucked down toward Sundrop until Elisha couldn't swallow for the dryness of his mouth.

"Squalls along the channel," Sundrop continued. "Bad for shipping. And here,"—the fingers of his left-hand stirred—"in London, now, it's raining so gentle. Ah. Harder now. I can't quite reach that far . . . The storm will move this way. Already, it's raining harder, yes. Oh, yes." His fist clenched, and his body tremored as he panted, reaching for that distant rain. "Can you feel it, too, Chantie?"

Awareness could not spread so far, or could it? Could he feel the rain approaching from London? Elisha was starting to see why the magi claimed the *indivisi* were mad. The man before him writhed in ecstasy at the touch of a distant rain. The gathered moisture clouded over his head, then clothed him in a tiny, private storm, releasing the damp into the air around them as its master drank it in and groaned with pleasure, swaying his arms to let it sprinkle to the earth all around him, like a dance without music.

The iron-mage gave a snort of disgust, closing his fist with an audible clang. "The earth of this square contains fifty-eight links of mail, the fittings of a harness, including the horse's bit, a sword-hilt, broken, and seventeen nails." He did not close his eyes. "I feel strong steel and shod horses. We don't have much time."

"Twenty-one," whispered Chanterelle, staring at him. "Nails," she clarified.

Parsley glowered. "Don't make me summon them up for counting."

"You can't," she said. "The other ones are copper." She spread her fingers into the earth, the packed dirt accepting her as he stared her down.

"It's a blessing," the old woman cackled. "A blessing to know! A blessing to see with so many eyes, to hear, to ride the winds of near and far!" She thrust up her arms, and the flock of crows exploded upward, flapping around her.

"All these years," the iron-magus sighed, "and you still can't fly."

The woman croaked and drew back her head, shoulders humped.

A blessing that held its own curse. The iron-magus must hide from the rain. The earth's lover could be trapped by a fire set in her other flesh.

And Elisha? Did he truly know more of death than any other man? He had found the body, true enough, but it was fresh and personal. He called on Death only when he held the talisman—and that jar was a universal, a talisman so strong that any fool could use it to amplify magic, if not to such terrible ends. As Morag observed, he hadn't even created it a talisman on purpose. Could he sense a death approaching, the way that Sundrop knew a storm, or feel the deaths already present, like the iron-magus counting nails? Could it be his servant like the woman and her crows? Or would it, like the earth, devour him?

"You try too hard," Chanterelle said, coming nearer, moving as easily through the earth as he through the air. "You doubt and you deny and so you struggle."

Elisha glanced at the others and back to her. He needed to find Thomas, but he needed this, too, to be sure what he was and to know what he must do. Once more, he knelt before her, listening to her small voice. "Show me," he breathed.

She took his hand, a cool, gritty touch, and turned it, placing his palm upon the ground. "*You didn't kill the baby,*" she sighed into him, "*You knew its death. Knew it. What else do you know?*"

During his first lesson, under Brigit's care, she had asked him something similar: to catalog what he knew about the things he would transform, seeds and eggs. Now, he attuned himself to the young woman before him, growing aware of her stillness, her investment in the earth around them, the peculiar glinting quality of her eyes. Never again would he fail to recognize her presence or need to bring up corpses because he could not find her among them. She shared no emotion, he asked for none. They were together in a most intimate way, fully present, utterly without passion.

Then she sank into the earth, letting it flow up around her, inviting it closer, luxuriating in its touch as another woman might love furs. Her hand remained above the ground, still capturing his, her hair spread upon the earth like the fine roots of mushrooms. He felt the earth as never before, the layers of it, the richness of dead leaves mixed in and the questing strength of roots. Worms devoured the grains, making tiny spaces where air filtered in. Chanterelle tugged at his awareness through their contact, like a child pointing out fishes beneath a quiet pond, she showed him the chainmail, the scraps, the nails—both

iron and copper—and shared the tang of them upon the
skin, as if he touched them with his tongue. She found a
squirrel's den with the warm little creature startled, then
soothed by her touch. And there, a forgotten crop of tur-
nips. Withdrawing to her center for a moment, Chanterelle
murmured, "*It's everything I need.*"

He thought of the burning peat that trapped her with
the pain and the dead, but she pushed back the image.
"*The mancers changed my skill when they tried to trap
me, they perverted it, made it wicked. Like yours, when
you kill.*"

"*How can Death be anything but wicked?*"

A spasm of sadness and worry flickered through her,
and was gone. "*I thought you'd know.*"

He sensed the presences above them—no, around
them—but any magus could sense a living presence: it
proved nothing. He looked further. What did he know?
He knew the strength of his hands and the medical skill
that resided in him. He knew how to set bone and when
to cut it off instead. He knew his brother's baby was already dead. The talisman must be here, somewhere close.
He knew Brigit and how she had marked it with her
blood. Death, and blood that hinted at the death inherent in every life. A body lay in the broken church, and
the crow-woman let her friends pluck out its eyes. Elisha's hand clenched with the memory of killing, gripping
the handle of the now-useless knife he'd used to murder.
Chanterelle's presence unfurled through the earth
around him, kept him steady and warm, like an incubat-
ing seed. When he had sought her in the burning bog, she
was not all he found. He had sensed the presence of the

ancient dead, and in his panic, he could not discern between those corpses and the living woman. And she had seen them. No wonder she believed.

A little graveyard stood behind the tithing barn. Eight, ten, twenty-seven dead. Chanterelle's encouragement sprang through her touch. Others were buried here and there beyond the houses. As Chanterelle had shown him, he spread his awareness in all directions, moving from each discovery to the next. He ignored the presence of all the animals living and dead, their slight chills easy to pass over. Shod horses and fine steel, the ironmage claimed, and Elisha found them now, riding through the dark with a familiar presence at their head. It took a moment to sense the tension, the excitement, the strength and fickleness in that peculiar combination that was Prince Alaric. How far were they? Elisha started to track the distance between, but a sense of cold whispered through his senses. Alaric rode with a small guard, and Death rode with them. Elisha caught his breath, but he felt Chanterelle's triumph. *"You know it comes,"* she said.

"But I don't know who or how or when!" This half-knowledge galled him. He reached again, this time feeling the strain. Instead of growing stronger, the chill evaporated into nothing, as if he knew nothing. Angry, he snapped back his awareness, sending it scurrying behind, only to be jolted by a new presence, one he knew right away: Brigit. Was she coming out to meet her love? No, she came alone, on foot. She came for the talisman he had not found, probably sneaking out of the abbey now that Alaric had gone. Damn it!

Elisha shook himself, nearly breaking contact with Chanterelle. She shouldered upward, the earth moving aside until she sat upon the ground before him. Crows scattered from the fresh corpse in the church as their mistress flung wide her arms.

"Soldiers, aye," the crow-mage muttered. "Battle for us, my sweets, hmm?" Her body swayed, her arms lifting, straining for flight, then she swiveled her head and caught Elisha's gaze. "We like you, my flock and I. Where you go, Death is never far behind." She grinned, the gaps between her teeth as dark as crow's eyes.

"He can feel Death's approach," Chanterelle murmured aloud, and the iron-mage snorted again.

"You can't claim that," he said, "not until somebody dies. Not until he fingers the dead man before he's even bleeding." He held up his own hand, steady as a rod. "I can feel Death, too, when it's dripping down my hands."

From where he knelt, Elisha suddenly placed the voice, the single curse repeated twice as an assassin slew the Frenchman—with a weapon like a glove of knives. The cold man stared back, snicking his fingers together and folding his hands beneath his arms.

A crow swept suddenly back from the path with a sharp cry and dropped to the mage's shoulder. "Somebody's coming," she said and hustled away, snatching up handfuls of the black rags that flailed around her legs as she scurried into the woods.

Sundrop seemed to fade, his outline misty once again. "Welcome," he said, then, "We'll meet again." He gave a little bow and strolled away leaving the scent of rain.

The iron-mage stayed a moment longer, turning his

stance to aim the hardness of his hands down the path. "Shall I, Barber? Do you feel it now?" He was laughing as he retreated, leaving Elisha and Chanterelle alone, crouched on the ground in the flickering light.

"Thank you," Elisha breathed, although his knowledge felt a bitter gift.

"Power's never bad. If you've got it, and they don't." She smiled, but her eyes were hard. She tipped her head toward the silent church and the silent corpse within. With a gritty hand, she gripped his arm.

Images shot into him and he gasped. An inn and a barn with a hard dirt floor, a father too cruel, men who paid their money and thrust her down. "*Thank me, yes, oh master of Death. I wanted you to go to my father's home, to kill for me as you killed for Rosalynn. I can see now you never will.*"

Her touch throbbed as if her heart were broken all over again. She sank into the ground before him and rippled away through the earth and his awareness until she dove deep and was gone. Elisha sat back on his heels, stunned. For a moment, he wished she had stayed to talk—but he had no idea what he might have said. She had seemed the only reasonable one among the *indivisi*, but even she had her own motives. Each of them had come to their power through pain, and he had barely begun to imagine what his might mean.

Chapter 20

❖

Brigit was coming, seeking the talisman. Elisha reached out through his awareness, infusing it with death and tragedy and the memories of that day, crafting a false impression of the talisman itself. Brigit hesitated, her search turning aside at the clues that he provided. He could hear her approach now and scrambled to his feet, turning, at first holding out his ruined blade, then scowling as he thrust it back into his belt. No matter what he knew of Death and of Brigit, he could not kill her, for the child's sake if not her own.

She came along the path, a lantern in her hand that cast writhing shadows across her face and figure. Seeing him, she stopped short, raising the light, adding its glow to that of the guttering torch the *indivisi* had left behind.

"There's no point pretending surprise," he said, squaring his shoulders.

But Brigit did not even attempt it. "Oh, dear Elisha!" she cried and sprang forward, the lantern held aloft. "I was so afraid he'd kill you—then he said you'd escaped.

I was never so relieved." She was beaming as she came to him. Her free hand reached out and trailed across his throat, a touch that shivered his flesh with heat. "You're hurt."

He smacked her hand away. "No surprise there, either, Brigit. You hired the men who tried to rape Rosalynn and strangle me. Did you tell them my past, so they'd know how to scare me? Did you give them some help from the rope that hanged me?"

Her green eyes gleamed with tears as she brought her hand to her own lips—as if his blow had injured her, too. "They weren't to hurt you. Neither of you. Threats, only! I'm sure my orders—"

"Were to do whatever it took to make me use the talisman. Stop it, Brigit, just stop." He folded his arms, angry at himself for the way she still moved him, for good or ill. Any time she made him feel, she showed her power over him. He was the one who had to stop.

She swallowed hard, her pale skin and exposed throat making her seem vulnerable. Again, she reached for him. "Teach me, Elisha, please. Teach me as once I taught you."

This time, he seized her hand, turning it to reveal the scrape on her palm. "Did you not see enough? Didn't your blood show you every horror?"

"I know you've hidden it around here." She did not draw away, but let his grip bring her closer. "I saw," she murmured. "I felt, but I did not understand. There was cold . . . a darkness." She shook her head, biting her lip as she looked for words. "I remembered all that from when you first shared it with me—"

"I never. It was you who came, like a crow to a corpse. You who made me see what it was I carried."

"Yes, you're right." Brigit tipped her head from him, letting the lantern down to her side, her face shadowed. "I am so sorry for all the pain I've caused you."

"And the hanging rope? Dragging me down for your lord's pleasure? Are you sorry for that as well?"

At that, she frowned. "Just a memory. I didn't believe it would really be strong enough to hold you. Not you." She touched his arm, a shy stroke.

Elisha seized her to him and savagely kissed her, one hand cupping her head, the other snaked behind her, searching, drawn by the echo of his own pain embedded in the hanging rope. He steeled himself and snatched the rope from her belt even as she opened her lips to him, drawing him closer. Then he let himself remember. She wanted him closer, she wanted him to share—and share he did: the full force of the hanging rope.

He remembered terror that tore into his throat, the wrenching of his head as he was yanked upward and the tearing skin of his wrists as he struggled to free himself. He cataloged the darkness that throbbed over his vision, the desperation of his cries, even the feel of grass dropping from his bare toes as he kicked and fought for life. Brigit went rigid in his arms, breaking the kiss. He remembered how it felt to see her that day, to believe that she was coming to save him, the dread upon his heart when he knew she came to watch him die.

Brigit hit him, pounding against his chest, fighting away from his cruel embrace. She panted as she wiped her mouth, blinking back tears and shaking.

"Just a memory," he said bitterly, the taste of her upon his lips for the last time. He wrapped his fist around the few inches of hanging rope, a single strand of what must have been three at least. She had divided it, for future use.

Staring at him, still stunned, she asked, "Is that—was that—how it was for you?"

"Worse." The rope in his own hand still had power—but it was a power too easy to twist against him. He stepped away, holding the scrap to the torch's flame, wincing as, for a moment, his own skin flared. "Where's the rest?"

"I don't have it here," she stammered. "If I had known—I'm sorry."

Tense from his jaw to his toes, Elisha waited for her to twist the apology, to append her excuse, but she remained silent, her hair and cloak fluttering in the night breeze. For a moment he remembered how she came to him at what he then believed to be his darkest hour, bound to the whipping post, waiting to hang. She came to him with passion and hope, fulfilling his desires both body and soul, taking his child into herself. And the next morning, she came to watch him die.

"I told him not to kill you—I begged him, Elisha."

"So you can use me to gather the other magi." With an effort, Elisha let go and stood his ground, neither retreating nor giving in to the temptation to touch her again. "You should go. You will not get what you want."

"I want you." Her chin shot up, her eyes afire with lamplight. "I want you to join me. You watched my mother die, Elisha, and you hated yourself because you couldn't help her then. You can help her now, by bringing her dream to fruition. A kingdom where magi work and live without fear. You've not been one of us for very long, but you know what it could mean." She came to him again and laid her fingers on the back of his hand. "*We should not be killed for what we are, what we can do.*"

A land where witches need not fear? It was a pretty thought—but he thought, too, of all the witches he had met, those who derided the *indivisi*, those who refused to aid his healing of Mordecai because he was a Jew. Would the nation fare better with magi on the throne, with a woman on the throne who would betray her lover for her own ends? Two lovers, come to that. He thought instead of Thomas, alone somewhere in the darkness, and quickly brushed the thought aside before it could manifest in his emotions. "We should not be killed for it, no. Neither should we be crowned for it. Do you think an uprising of witches will convince the common folk to trust us, never mind the barons?"

Her brow furrowed, and she shook her head. "You would preach caution, then? Hiding in the shadows as we have done, hoping one day the *desolati* will suddenly find how helpful and friendly we've been?"

"Rather than seize the throne through underhanded means? Yes, I think I would."

For an instant, he thought she understood too much. "I am marrying it; there's nothing underhanded in that. It is the greatest moment our people have ever reached. My mother thought she could influence the court as the queen's companion, a tutor to princes. Instead, they put her to flames." A jolt of anger shot through their contact.

With it came the terrible vision, a woman the very image of Brigit bound to a stake while fire sprang up all around her. She grew magical wings, only to be struck full of arrows. Elisha turned the image away and stepped back from her, breaking the touch.

"You see, Elisha! You know what they'll do to us!" Her hand became a fist, trembling in the air between them. "Join us, Elisha, join your people. If you are with us, we cannot lose."

"You speak as if there's a war at hand—I'm no warrior."

"You need only stand at our side and show your strength. Who will dare defy us, with your power at our command?"

Yet Morag wielded so much more. Elisha shivered. "I will not kill for you."

"For all of us! You talk as if there's only yourself at risk here. I thought you worked for others, to help anyone who has need of you. We need you. Every witch that walks the earth, every witch unborn. You have an awful power, Elisha. So does every man who wields a blade. Will you run from it? Will you cower behind it? Or will you claim it and make it your own?" Her hand snatched strength from the air. "Will you wield it to defend your people?"

Her words rang inside of him, speaking to everything he thought that he believed. And yet, there was one thing he could not believe: Brigit herself. It wasn't Thomas who sought to kill his father and claim the throne. Yet somebody had. Somebody hired a physician as poisoner, somebody gave away the king's secrets, maneuvering the king into place for an assassination that Elisha himself unwittingly carried out. Did Brigit know? Or did she really believe that Thomas was the traitor?

Elisha spread his senses, carefully, lightly. Deliberately, he made contact, touching her face, smoothing back her hair, softening the words that he must speak, and searching for the truth. "Even if he regrets trying to kill me, Brigit, I can serve no king I cannot trust."

"Alaric will be swayed by me, given time." Then her face hardened. "It's not Alaric," she snapped, "It's me. You despise me, and so you turn your back upon our people. You would burn every witch in the kingdom if it meant they'd kill me, too!" Tears shimmered at her eyes and fell upon his thumb. Her lips trembled. "How many times must I apologize? How many times must I crawl to you, Elisha, before you relent?" Her tears touched him with anguish, her skin quivered with righteous pain, her muscles tensed, just a little, with the truth she tried to hide, deflecting his attention from Alaric back to her. He could not tell if she loved Alaric, but she knew her prince, knew what he was capable of and what he'd done. And Elisha could feel his horses drawing nearer. If Alaric caught him here, with her, there'd be one execution, that was certain. A swift death, a gravedigger, a mancer's blade. Elisha's skin shivered.

"I can never be what you want."

"Every witch who dies now dies for you."

He walked away, trying not to hurry, her words stinging him, burning in the place where her mother's wing had touched him long ago.

"Brigit!" called a voice that echoed in the night, and

Elisha heard her gasp. She had been so focused on him that she hadn't looked for any other. Elisha seized the moment, certain she would turn toward that familiar voice, and ran, sprinting for the nearest broken house and ducking behind the leaning door, his heart racing. Insensitive Brigit had missed her own betrothed's approach, surely she would overlook Elisha's presence? He wished he could let his awareness spread to feel as well as hear what they would say—but she would know if he did, and he dared not draw back her eye. He hid behind the door, trembling with each shallow breath. As he mastered himself, he practiced the skill of deflection, drawing upon the law of opposites: his presence implied the chance of his absence. He seized now upon this idea, suggesting that he had gone, erasing any trace of himself that might be felt by another.

Through the narrow gap, he saw Brigit turn about, scanning around her, searching for him, her face furrowed with shadows. She whirled back as hoof beats echoed into the square. "Alaric!" she squeaked as the prince dropped down from his mount, a few guards stamping their horses to a halt behind, lanterns casting bands of light that swung as they moved, making Elisha vaguely ill.

"I told you not to leave the abbey, Brigit," Alaric said, catching her arms, "not when the barber might get his accursed talisman."

"He wouldn't kill me, my prince."

"What happened to Ian and Patric?"

Elisha could hear her smile. "They're good men, your highness. They obey my orders, even if those orders are to remain behind. I can't get anything done while I am tended so diligently. But you did not come here to argue with me." Her shoulders softened, her body melting toward Alaric, as once she had melted toward Elisha. "Come, let us reconcile."

"My love," Alaric said, stroking back her hair, "you are not meant to accomplish anything. I am king—as good as, in any event. All you need do is show our people what an excellent queen you will be." He kept stroking in spite of the way her posture drew up, her shoulders squaring again beneath his touch. "And take care with our baby." His hand moved down her side, a gesture at once intimate and commanding. If Alaric thought Brigit would respond to any of this, he was a fool.

"Go on," Alaric called out. "Establish a perimeter."

"Aye, Highness!" Mortimer gestured sharply at the soldiers, directing them with his hands until each moved off in a different direction, one passing the corner of the house where Elisha was hiding.

"Do you know where the barber is or how he was taken? Was that your doing?"

Brigit gazed up at him. "I was as surprised as you— but his escape gives you a chance to reconsider. You cannot think you will be strong enough alone to take and keep this throne. Even Dunbury only supports you because he can't be sure about Thomas. If Thomas gets to him—or to the other barons—"

"Thomas won't be a problem much longer. I have other allies, allies your friends wouldn't like. I had hoped your barber might provide a balance against them." Alaric gave a shrug. "As it is, I must hope they don't know that."

"My friends already dislike most of your allies," she pointed out. "But you and I agreed we need to build a strong core, of both magi and *desolati*, especially when we strike down the laws against sorcery and make this kingdom free."

Alaric shook his head, bright hair lashing the rich velvet of his cloak. "Your ambition is one of the things I love about you, darling, but you still think too small." He cradled her face in his hands, his eyes tracing her features, then lifting. "If my plans succeed, you could be queen of much more than this little island. You're impatient for action, for your mother's sake if nothing else, and I understand that. I knew her, too, remember?"

"What do you want of me, then?" She jerked away from him, her skirts swirling with a hint of power. "You want me to ride a carriage to London and sit there with my stitching? Why? When you won't even tell me what you're planning? I thought we were together in everything, and now I find you stalking about in the forest, speaking of allies you will not name—" This time, Brigit interrupted herself, her breath caught, her profile sharp with sudden interest. "Allies," she breathed, turning back to him. "Let me stay, Your Majesty. Your allies might well wish to meet your queen."

For a moment, Alaric's soft, boyish features turned hard, his eyes with a glint of white. "No. Brigit, that I cannot do." He wet his lips, spreading his hands. "Negotiations are complicated, and these are dangerous people.

I had much rather you were a hundred miles away. I would not risk you, or the baby." He came to her, his hand spreading over her stomach, over Elisha's child growing inside.

Elisha forced his fingers to relax, taking a deep and quiet breath.

She pressed her hands over his, entwining their fingers as she brought his hand up to her lips. "I have things to offer, my love. Things they might desire."

His throat shivered, and Elisha did not need his extra senses to know the lust that must be firing through the prince's loins. His jaw clenched as he watched, not daring to look away, but Alaric met her eyes over their clasped hands. "And they would not hesitate to hurt you to get what they want. Trust me, darling, and we shall have so much more."

"Together," she murmured, almost too low for Elisha's ears, then she leaned forward, finding his lips with hers. Elisha did glance away now, suddenly fascinated by the dark recesses of the house around him, but he could not miss the man's groan of desire. Or Brigit's next words, "Let me stay. You will not regret it."

With an ostentatious rattle of sword and armor that brought Elisha back to attention, Mortimer returned, another figure trailing after. "Highness. You asked to see Farus when he returned." He gave a little bow before retreating to the perimeter, and the man he'd brought slipped back his hood. Parsley, the iron-mage, the assassin even his master did not understand. Was Alaric here to meet with the *indivisi*? Had they committed to his aid?

"Your Highness." The iron-magus, too, bowed, but stiffly—as he did everything. He glanced at Brigit with dull eyes, then back to the prince. "I trust you found the place without trouble."

"Thank you, Farus. I have a new task for you."

Parsley remained bowed, his lips down-turned. "I thought you might allow me to join the . . . hunting party, Majesty."

"Not now," said the prince firmly. Alaric stepped away from Brigit, bringing her forward on his hand with the grace of a dancing master. "Our future queen requires an escort back to London. Will you accompany her?"

"You cannot make me go," Brigit hissed, but Alaric offered a sad smile.

"My love, I'm afraid we can." He leaned as if to kiss her, but she turned her face from him.

"I have ways—"

"Please," said Alaric, and the magus stepped forward to wrap his hand around Brigit's wrist.

"The great barrows you asked about are just a little farther, Majesty, past a field of smaller mounds." Parsley gave a short bow, then nodded to Brigit. "Right this way, my lady. Let's get you back to London, shall we?"

She jerked against him, but his arm was rigid no matter how she tugged or twisted. "What are you?" Then she did not speak again, but locked her eyes to his, and Elisha guessed they were speaking through the contact. Fighting.

"Sergeant? Take four of the men. The others shall stay here. Keep her safe." Then to Brigit he said, "We'll speak again when I return." Alaric planted a kiss on her cheek though she writhed to escape him. But his body gave a sharp jerk, and he pulled away from her as if he'd been struck.

"Speak," she snarled, "but when you touch me again, I'll grant you no mercy."

Alaric looked hurt as the iron-magus climbed onto a horse, hauling Brigit up before him, still locked in his grip. "One day, Brigit, you'll understand."

"One day, you'll be sorry!" she flung over her shoulder as Farus galloped away with the soldiers.

Chapter 21

❖

In the wake of their departure, Mortimer strolled back to Alaric's side where he spent a long moment smoothing out his gloves, speaking as to no one. "The lady seems a bit . . . fiery."

Alaric scowled. "Leave my betrothed to me, Mortimer. She's safe, for now, and I have other business to attend to."

Elisha turned and sank down, his back against the wall, his heart thundering. Alaric was here to meet his allies. He still didn't know his brother was anywhere close by, and his arrival had prevented Brigit from locating the talisman, then removed her from the area, so Elisha had that to be grateful for, at least. But where was Thomas?

Elisha searched his memory for any clues about how Thomas thought and what he might do. It seemed a very long day. Had it been only that morning Elisha first felt Brigit's approach? He sat up straighter as it dawned on him that her blood might serve his uses as well.

Now that the other magi were gone, so far as he knew,

he risked expanding his awareness, reclaiming his attunement to this place. Thanks to his earlier efforts, it came easily, marking every house, the church, the soldiers, the prince, as vividly as day. Now, he sought Brigit. The fact that she had marked the talisman and tracked it this far showed it could be done. Elisha accepted this knowledge and stretched out. In other circumstances, he could search for the talisman itself, but if he activated it again, those earlier, eager minds, the ones who reached back when he used it against the bandits, could find them both.

The chill of death still hovered nearby—it had not gone with the retreating soldiers of the queen's unwanted retinue. He found the brightness of her presence moving quickly into the distance with the mounted men, hot with a fury he could feel even from here. What he knew of Brigit layered over this sense of her presence, a high spirit, a seductive touch, a hint of laughter, a depth of desire, a suggestion of her movement and her beauty. But the sign he searched for would be more subtle, older. Not far away to his left-hand side, he caught the slightest echo that reminded him of her, like the glimmer of light from a distant stream. By focusing his awareness in that direction, he honed the echo, it was dull, slight, but clear—a little patch upon the cold blackness of the talisman. His stomach tightened, and there, at last, he could sense the warmth of the man who still carried it. Thank God.

After such a brief acquaintance, he could not fully characterize Thomas from this distant sense of him, as he could Brigit, but it was him as surely as if Elisha beheld his lean form and vivid eyes and felt the weariness that overlaid the strength of his heart. Outside, the guards regrouped around their prince and moved back toward the trail they had come from. Elisha kept his awareness spread about him like tingling whiskers as he rose to a crouch and hurried across the darkened square to the woods on the other side. Chanterelle's patient sharing had shown him the precision that his attunement could achieve, and he used that knowledge now. By the time his eyes adjusted to the gloom, he already knew where the trees parted and where the rocks rose up. Cold shadows flicked among these shapes, shades he could not quite make out that rose at his approach and shrank back again as he passed by. These mysteries must wait. To the right, Alaric and his men nearly paralleled his own course. Damn.

Elisha ran faster as the fringe of woods fell back leaving him knee-deep in heather, then he stopped short in the deeper black by the hulk of a ruined house. The shadows rose higher here, and he could nearly see them with his open eyes: shades of the dead, as if the earth remembered them. Chanterelle's guidance had shown him how to look—and now he did not know how to filter what he found. He turned slowly, skin tingling. Thomas was nearby, his presence obscured by the leaping shades. The chill of Death hung heavily all around him. The rising moon showed brush-covered mounds before him. The village at the edge of the woods had given way to another of the ancient burial places that dotted the heather of the New Forest. Each mound echoed with the dull presence of the dead, but they rang as well with sharper notes, a taste of fear like blood upon the tongue, as if Death scattered the ground with scraps of dread.

Elisha's legs felt rooted, his body heavy with the pull of these sensations. An owl clacked its beak nearby, then a crow startled from the trees and flew off, cawing. The crow-woman watched him still, waiting for him to lead her to the carrion her companions craved.

"Thomas," he called, as loudly as he dared. Nearby, overhead it seemed, something stirred.

Elisha turned in the shadow of the broken house, then a man leapt down before him, sword drawn in a heart-beat, and its tip struck Elisha's breast. Thomas held a duelist's stance, the barest pressure needed to thrust home his blade. "Why did my brother take you aside, Barber? Why clear a church to meet with you?"

Elisha held out his hands, once more at the mercy of his king, but the long day and the weight of all that he had seen and done settled upon his shoulders. He could not see Thomas's face, only the hard determination of his form that shivered the sword's point against Elisha's heart. He stared down the long blade, recalling the ten-uous trust that they had found, and he felt like weeping. "He's afraid I'm working for the French. There was a man who came to see me back at Dunbury, a Frenchman. The man was killed in an attempt on my life, and the French are angry."

"Why should I believe you? A barber, a witch, my father's killer. You took communion second only to him."

The depth of Thomas's anger and his despair sim-mered along the sword, Elisha's awareness making contact at the length of a blade, the span that separated him from his own death. His next words could end that separation, but they must be said. "Your Highness, he's coming. Here. Now."

Thomas's eyes flared, his body tensed. "Judas," Thomas hissed.

"No!" Elisha winced at the sound of his own voice. "No. I came to find you, to warn you. He doesn't know you're here."

"How does he know where to come, if you're not leading him to me?"

"The heathen burial grounds are used by witches—one of them works for your brother's man, Mortimer. He guided your brother this far—please, Your Highness." Framed by his wild hair and beard, etched by burdens too great for one man, Thomas looked more like a bandit than those Elisha had killed, but it was the pain in his eyes that showed the truth. Elisha's heart pounded beneath his blade.

"Lady Rosalynn was scared for you," Thomas said. "It took all I had to keep her away from the church, and by the time I went back, you'd both gone. She swore he meant to kill you, and now I find you alive. Is she part of your plan?" In a moment, with a snarl of frustration, he had answered his own question. "She must be—she sent me to the village. She said you would find me there if you could, but when I got there I wasn't alone."

Gently, Thomas shook his head, then purpose returned to the sword, forcing Elisha back. The rough wall held him, the king's sword pinning him there. Thomas took a deep breath. "By God," he whispered, "I needed to trust you." His grief cut Elisha more sharply than any blade.

"Then trust me now. Rosalynn has no reason to ally with your brother, nor do I. He is your father's son, born a tyrant. I begged her to keep you from your brother, and she did." She had done brilliantly, and he would give her all due gratitude when they met again. If they met again. "I would swear upon the Cross, Your Highness. I would carry a bar of burning iron if that would convince you."

"And wouldn't the Devil give you strength. You've already told me you're not devout. Do you even feel pain?"

Elisha flinched and saw the hurt echoed in Thomas's own face. Betrayed again, just as he had dared to put his faith in another. Betrayed as Elisha had been the morning of his hanging. He swallowed, his own breathing pressing the sword's point harder, and met the prince's haunted gaze. At last, he spoke, carefully, quietly. "I swear upon your father's grave, as the man who put him there, that I mean you no harm."

Thomas's chin lifted, his breath caught as he searched Elisha's face. With the grace of a fallen angel, he stepped back, sliding his sword back into its sheath, his eyes downcast. "Forgive me," he whispered.

"Your Highness, we have no time for anger, or regret." Elisha wanted to touch him, to lay a healing hand upon his shoulder and mend the wounds his king carried so deeply, but there was no time for that, either. "The talisman, that thing I asked you to carry."

"It's here." Thomas fumbled at his waist a moment, then passed over the bundle.

Elisha stripped off the wrapping with numb fingers, removing Brigit's contact, and tossed it away. He should like to put the cloth to flame, but he dare not. "My enemies are looking for this. I should never have let you carry it."

A clatter of horses moved by, beyond the house, toward the heath of mounds.

Thomas regarded him across a great distance. He lowered his voice. "You trusted me. I should have done the same."

"No time," Elisha said, matching his hushed tone, though he thought the prince's men too far away to hear. Thomas gave a rueful smile, which vanished at Elisha's next words. "You need to go, to hide. I think they've left the lodge, you may be able to return there."

"And you?"

Elisha spoke the plan almost before he knew what he would do. "Your brother is going to meet someone—I need to know who."

"Oh, do you?" Thomas folded his arms. "If my usurper is gathering allies, it seems that I'm the one who needs to know." He spoke lightly, still treating his crown as a distant hope or folly.

"Let me be your scout, Highness, until you can afford a better one."

Thomas gave a firm shake of his head. "This was not meant to be your fight, Elisha, and you cannot win it alone."

Elisha tightened his grip on the talisman. Would Thomas be safer with or without him? It all depended on the roll of the dice—which enemy must he next

confront? Before he could say anything, Thomas had
stripped off his cloak and set out at a trot, moving low
through the heather in pursuit of his brother's horses.
Elisha hurried to catch him up. Thanks to the hilly
ground, they were able to parallel Alaric's course without being seen. Elisha spread his senses, trying to find
out if Alaric had other magi with him who might reveal
their pursuit. When he focused ahead, he stumbled and
nearly fell but for Thomas's hand upon his elbow, catching and holding him with its strength. Ahead, in a dell
nearer them than the road the prince followed, lay a
patch of frigid night where the layers of Death grew
dense upon the ground. It stung Elisha's awareness and
sent the shades of the mounds around them dancing as
if on the gibbet. For a moment, he fought for breath,
then glanced at his prince. "I know where he's going," he
whispered hoarsely. And, in knowing, he knew whom
Alaric must meet.

Somehow, he found his footing and led them around
to the west, coming up carefully atop a tall mound. At
its collapsing end rose a pair of huge stones, tilted to
one side beneath a broad capstone, the lintel where the
ancient heathens had gone to meet their dead. Elisha
found purchase on the rough, slanted stone and scrambled up. Thomas followed, and they lay on their backs,
side by side on the narrow slab. Elisha turned his head
to overlook the circle as Alaric and his men entered
and dismounted. The knights lit a pair of torches to
plant in the shaggy mounds to either side of the entrance before Alaric ordered them back. Leading his
horse, they complied, though Mortimer shook his head

and grumbled. The men spread out in all directions, moving away until they could not be seen, and Elisha could barely sense them.

"Twelve men, in a ring around us," he breathed.

"Holy Rood," Thomas lay back, resting his head against the stone, laid out as if for his funeral. "I'm a dead man."

"You won't die," Elisha told him, and nearly smiled. "I know a thing or two about Death." But even as he said it, the air thickened around him with a stabbing cold that sent his words out on a cloud of mist. Elisha's heart lurched, his grip tightening on Thomas's arm so the other man glanced back at him, face etched in a frown of moonlight and shadows.

"Something's changed for you," Thomas murmured. "And not for the better."

Elisha let him go, suddenly stung by their contact. He tried to deny what he felt, what he knew, but it was too late: Death stalked his king tonight.

Death seeped from the earth around them, buried in the mounds and creeping through the heather. Already, his fingers stuck just a little to the metal of his talisman, and he carefully set down the pot over his head, his arm passing before his face. Someone approached the lintel, alone: Alaric. The sense of death grew stronger, seeping out of the stone beneath him, up from the barrows and the torn bits that scattered them as if scavengers had been at the bodies they once contained. Elisha's throat closed over his misty breath. He should have made Thomas leave him. Rosalynn found a way to save the prince, why couldn't he? Instead, he brought him to the precipice from which no man returned. Tears burned at the back of his eyes—the only thing still warm.

"Always cold, you said." Thomas reached toward him, covering his shaking hand. "What's wrong?"

Elisha shook him off, touching Thomas's lips in warning. "As you live, Your Highness, don't speak. Your brother's below." The damp exhalation of Thomas's breath passed over his fingers. But Alaric was only one man. If they jumped now, they could cut him down and drag his body into the open mound. His guards hovered at the edge of Elisha's awareness—too far to come to their prince's aid. Why then was the dread so heavy on him? Every stalk of heather quivered with it. The earth throbbed with it. For a moment, the night split open, a slice of brilliance that shivered down his flesh, then slid shut, and Alaric was no longer alone. But how did anyone get here without Elisha feeling his approach? Unless he had felt the man's arrival, and it felt like death itself. He longed to turn and look down, but held back, waiting for the right moment rather than reveal their hiding place by moving without caution.

"Good Lord!" Alaric blurted. "Where did you come from?"

"I walked in places other men can't dream of, Your Highness," the newcomer drawled. "Or should I say, Your Majesty?"

"There's still one obstacle to that," Alaric snapped.

"That is your part, my prince." The speaker added a hiss. "We are occupied on other fronts."

"What, still working in Naples? I can understand the

Holy Roman Empire giving you a bit of trouble, but Naples? Really."

Elisha wished he could see the prince, to see whether his stance matched his brave words or if it revealed the fear that ran beneath them.

At his side, Thomas stirred, his eyes flaring. His wife had been from the Empire, Elisha recalled: daughter of the emperor himself. Elisha lay his hand over Thomas's, sending him a whisper of calm—the best he could manage for either of them.

"I see you have been paying attention, Your Highness," said the stranger in a long, slow tone. "Then you know we have made kings before. And unmade them. Your bravado does not impress me."

Even now that Elisha could hear the stranger and sense the stir of Alaric's emotions in response to him, Elisha felt nothing like the layering of physical and emotional humanity that defined the presence of another person. Where Morag's presence had been invisible, even when Elisha could see and touch him, this man projected an air of authority, demanding reverence. It reminded Elisha of nothing less than entering a church—that instant need for genuflection after a lifetime's indoctrination. The projection, however, did not show Elisha who the man was the way a presence ought to do—rather, it showed him how the man intended to be received. He did not merely deflect the senses, he manipulated them to his own ends, creating for himself an air more regal than mere royalty. Elisha had never realized such a deliberate manipulation was possible, until now.

No owl nor crow nor rustle of heather broke the silence now, until Alaric sighed. "Yes, forgive me. I do appreciate all you've done and will do."

"And all you have to do is kill one man. One man. Really."

"I could kill him gladly myself if —"

"If you knew where to find him."

"I see him everywhere — in every thief in the shadows, every beggar seeking alms." Alaric's voice held a note of hysteria, then he murmured, "He slipped the assassins. He dodged his own bodyguards and eluded the whole bloody Northern Army, and you think I am going to find him."

Thomas went rigid at Elisha's side, the words of his brother's confession stilling them both.

"It is not the first of your plans to go awry, Highness. Since early Spring, nay, since you changed your mind about your betrothal, events seem to have been slipping from your command."

"My father's still dead, isn't he?"

"Owing primarily to a barber and a baby's head."

Elisha flicked a glance toward Thomas, and found the other gazing back at him, silent and barely breathing.

"This is getting us nowhere. If you want me to rule, we need to find Thomas."

"Do we want you to rule? That is not so obvious as it once was."

Elisha shifted carefully, drawing back his awareness as he clothed himself in deflection, turning slowly until he could look down upon the scene. He did not break contact with Thomas, leaving his hand to rest upon a taut wrist, hoping the deflection could do for him as well.

Alaric swallowed, then he adjusted his golden chain. "What, would you raise up Thomas now? Everyone's heard he tried to hire out our father's death. The last thing the barons want is a king so eager and devious he'd kill his own father." His lips curled into a smile, as if he had the magus right where he wanted him, and Elisha wondered if his terror were as transparent to the other as it was to himself.

Alaric stood across the dell, a wary distance from the robed figure before him, who remained just below Elisha's hiding place. The edges of the robe furled and shifted in a sinuous pattern, obeying no mortal wind, even as they concealed him from head to toe. It resembled less a garment than a drapery of shadows. The regal projection faded, and dread hung upon the air, a creeping sensation that gave Elisha a sudden sympathy for the hare, quivering in the grass before a hound, uncertain if it could flee, desperately hoping that stillness could conceal it. If Sundrop had drawn the moisture from the air, this magus drew the light, creating a void of terror where even the breeze dare not stir.

"You are not the only candidates," the magus replied, and before Alaric could question him, the man went on: "But we do harbor a certain admiration for your daring." For a moment that miasma of fear lessened, and the robe of shadows warmed as if to an approaching dawn.

The shock of opening rippled once more against Elisha's skin, and he clamped his teeth against his cry. A brief flash and a chill wind ruffled the heather as if blowing from a long passage where a light was suddenly extinguished. Another magus stood there, shifting his hunched shoulders with a satisfied groan. "Never get 'nough o' that, I tell you. Better than fucking, init?"

"I shall ask you to keep your crudities to yourself," the master drawled.

At the voice, Elisha's skin felt suddenly colder. Morag, together with his mysterious master. But why did the master bring another magus? Then Elisha saw Alaric's throat bobbing, and his sharp exhalation blew frosty in the air. They played with power, taunting each other it seemed; even as the master exuded that hint of dawn, suggesting he approved of Alaric, he brought another to stand for night. Alaric's allies could come and go as they pleased. They could appear out of nowhere and summon one another. What else might they do? Alaric, faced now with two of them, was braver than Elisha had imagined. Even Elisha's presence at his side could not balance such allies.

"Morag, here, will help you . . . Highness. Myself, I have other matters to attend to." The tall, robed figure gave a wave of one hand and vanished with a shock of cold. Elisha thought Morag's technique too quick and powerful for him to follow, but it still released a sense of the passage—that howling turmoil of tortured wraiths. This man arrived and left with the deftness of a surgeon lancing the darkness.

"What'll it be then?" Morag asked. "Got another war for me?"

Alaric recoiled, but his tension eased, and the arrogance of his role returned. He'd been left with a servant, no longer worthy of the master's attention. Apparently, the sting of this insult couldn't outweigh his sheer relief. "I suppose

I shouldn't be surprised to find you in such company. What did you do with the barber?" Then he jerked forward, going pale. "You didn't bring him to your master, did you?" His glance flickered to where the master had vanished.

Morag chuckled. "Naw—yon barber wasn't havin' any of that."

Alaric covered this new relief with irritation, growling, "Then where is he? I thought you meant to help me bury him."

"Pfff. He weren't ripe yet." Morag flapped his hand. "I'll do it, Highness, in good time. That why you got me here?"

Was he ripe now? Elisha hoped not to find out.

"I should feel a good deal better if I—"

"Leave me the barber, Highness." For a moment, Morag's absurd guise slipped, and a hint of his dark power eddied in the air.

Alaric swallowed and gave a single nod. "I need you to search for someone—you are capable of that, I trust, and without any surprises? I need to know precisely where he is."

"Oh, it's precision you're wanting." Morag shifted with a creak of his leather jerkin. "You've got something of his, have you? Something close?"

Reaching into a pouch at his waist, Alaric produced a slender bundle and unwrapped it to reveal a short, sharp bodkin, easily concealed. "It's marked with his blood. Will it do?" but he asked coolly, and Elisha guessed he already knew the answer.

The other grinned. "Oh, aye, Highness. Blood's the best, next to flesh, eh?" He reached out for it and Elisha's heart sank. Morag would search for Thomas with his blood and find him—steps away from his brother's sword. Elisha's strongest deflection might conceal himself, but if Morag was any sort of sensitive, then Thomas was dead. Elisha searched his mind for some defense. Deflection was triggered by the law of opposites, inverting your own presence. If blood could be used to search, it could also conceal.

Elisha tugged on his shirt, and it pulled free from the dried blood at his chest. It stung, then trickled damp once more. He ran his fingers lightly over the wound, then turned swiftly to Thomas. "Don't move," he breathed. "Don't speak." He smeared his own blood across the prince's forehead, the mark of his hand staining the prince's cheek. "Whatever happens next, whatever you hear, do not move."

Thomas seized his arm, drawing him closer. "What are you doing?"

"Saving your life." He hoped. His blood might conceal the prince, at least to a casual search. Might. If he could tip the balance a little further.

Elisha broke away, rolled, and jumped down to meet the necromancer.

Chapter 22

❖

He landed, stumbling slightly, and caught himself with one hand against the stone, wincing as it jolted his injured wrist. Alaric cried, "Holy Mother!" followed swiftly by the swish of drawn steel.

"Hallo, what's this? Elisha Barber, init? Very pleased we meet again. And weren't we just speaking of you." He lifted his blunt hand as if tipping his cap, but he still held the assassin's knife.

"What are you doing here?" Alaric demanded, then he hesitated, his glance shifting over his shoulder, toward the village where he'd found Brigit. He glared at Elisha, shifting into a swordsman's stance.

"When I heard armed men approaching, hiding seemed like the best option." He met Alaric's hard stare. There were moments during the prince's conversation with the mysterious magus that Elisha had recalled the young prince's bravado and charm. Twice he had saved the prince's life and been repaid in kind when King Hugh sprang a trap to catch both himself and Duke Randall. In the church, Alaric pleaded for his aid, only to turn to his destruction when Brigit's brutal treatment fouled his attempt. Now, Alaric looked older, more fierce and yet more fragile, like a blade hammered a bit too hard. It might strike a killing blow or shatter on impact.

"You came here to meet Brigit, didn't you?"

"To take back what she stole from me, Your Highness."

"I see," the prince replied but with an arch of his brow that implied disbelief.

Morag chuckled, a throaty sound that jiggled his hunched shoulders. "Seems like maybe thanks are in order, yer Majesty. Given he did off your dad and all." His grin was tilted, his breath foul with rotten teeth.

"No doubt the country shall improve with better leadership—even for those of lesser rank. Serfs. Barbers. Common folk."

Morag prowled behind Alaric and back again, emerging from the darkness by Alaric's shoulder. He tipped up his scruffy chin. "Not a bad idea, yer Majesty, t'bring him in on your side."

They were a study in opposites: the prince tall, handsome, clad in riding clothes, but richly so, while his companion was stocky, lumpish, stinking. Elisha wondered if the man were leprous and had some putrefaction concealed beneath his sloppy clothes.

"He's already rejected that offer. Really, he leaves me no choice." Alaric held up his sword, but his glance flicked from Elisha to Morag, as if he couldn't decide which of them was more worrisome. And Thomas had thought Elisha bargained with the Devil.

The hunched magus watched him beneath bushy

brows, and Elisha felt the fleeting tingle of the man's awareness extended to him, like the touch of fleas in bedstraw. The brows gave a minute twitch. Somehow, Elisha had reacted to the invisible touch. Morag knew and it surprised him. Morag turned the assassin's knife in his hands, a trinket too small to deal death to princes.

"You heard all we said, didn't you?" Alaric smiled a little, the smile of a conspirator to his mates, resting back on one heel as he slipped his sword back into the scabbard. "I have nothing against you, really. Nothing that a marriage or two won't settle. We don't have to trust each other to work well together." He tipped his head a bit toward Morag, offering an example.

The invisible touch advanced again, this time so softly it was more of a change of atmosphere, like the opening of a distant door that disturbed the pattern of dust in the air. Elisha willed himself to stillness, to reveal nothing, clamping down on his emotions to be sure not a whisper of his heart could be read by another. His hand tingled, the fingers slightly numb, perhaps due to the binding that supported his sprained wrist.

"I don't think he's listening, Majesty. He's a bit distracted, eh?"

"It's this place," Elisha said, gesturing toward the mounds that made the darkness more complete. "It's not the best for conversation. Surely there's a tavern at Beaulieu with a private room? We could meet on equal ground, without soldiers or hostages."

"A good wine would ease my palate," the prince agreed, but Morag's furrowed face twisted.

"Not the best? This place? Why, I'da thought a man

like you, a magus full-blown and besotted with the dead would love it!"

Damn it. The prince might accept his misdirection, but Morag already suspected something. Elisha dropped his defensive skin and unfurled his awareness instead. With sickening clarity, the scene swelled inside his mind, the lurking presence of the dead in the mounds, the sprinkling of pain that echoed on the surface, the looming stones behind him with their terrible juncture: the heat of Thomas's presence marked by his blood, and the cold weight of the talisman, so close together that their edges blurred, and Elisha might not have known the living man from the sucking distraction of the dead. Pray God that Morag felt the same. Before him, the prince's cockiness returned. Untrained in the ways of witches, his emotions flickered out around him, eager now to go, hopeful that Elisha would go with him and give him some alternative to his unpleasant allies.

But from Morag himself, Elisha felt nothing. He could stare straight at the man, could feel the breeze of his passing as he stalked another circuit past Elisha, leaning closer, and feel nothing at all, not even the sense of an object, the way he felt the standing stones at his back. Every muscle in his body tightened, and he forced his hands not to make fists. "You're a gravedigger—I guess it means more to you than it does to me."

"Really." Morag rocked back. "I heard you were close with Death, like a lover, eh? Didn't notice it last we met."

"Maybe the *indivisi* should be talking to you."

Morag's laughter echoed around him. "Babies! Their

knowledge is shit. *Desolati*, like the rest. But maybe it takes a baby head for you to get a rise up, eh?"

The words shot straight to his memory. Morag still had contact with him, despite his own defenses—but how? He tried to shake off the vision, but still he saw his own hands take up the sorry thing, the remains of his brother's child, and pack the little head in a jar with some vain idea of healing it, bringing it back to life with the mystical Bone of Luz. But neither medicine nor magic could wake the dead. He swallowed, his chin dipping, but forced himself to watch Morag. Cold crept up his numbed fingers, insinuating itself into his flesh as if he held the copper jar, his skin sticking, the horror of its contents seeping into him. Elisha's stomach clenched, and his ribs felt too tight.

"No," he protested, but too quietly, trying to focus long enough to work out what Morag was doing to him, and how.

Morag watched him, a spectator at a bear pit, eyes alight, thick lips caught in a fascinated smile. Then he held out the little knife toward Alaric. "Hold this for us, Majesty. Your brother'll wait." He emphasized the word "brother," and Elisha shivered, his effort to focus shredding into nothing. In his mind, he opened the door to his brother's shop, searching, and found blood, pooled in his basin, spattered on the floor, oozing from the dead man's throat.

"Nathan," Elisha whispered, and his knees buckled. Morag caught his arm in a powerful grip, sinking down with him.

His brother lay dead, a suicide, blond hair tossed over his face, revealing the awful wound. Elisha held him, the body already growing cold, his guilt grown colder still. He steadied himself on the offered arm. The blood, his brother's life severed, as the child's had been. If only Elisha hadn't been so arrogant. If he hadn't been such a fool as to doubt his brother's love, if he—Christ, what a waste. His brother's life, his brother's blood allowed to drain away. For a moment, the talisman's power echoed in his chest with the horror of a life cut short. How much more powerful would his brother's head have been? Elisha gagged, turning away, trying to put off the image. It was not his thought! It never had been. He hated that power, hated the strength it gave him and the injury it made him capable of. And he hated most of all the way it made him feel: that sense as he moved to kill the king that he, Elisha, conquered all. "No," he whispered, or tried to, but his dry lips did not move.

Was it not enough that he hated it? That he renounced it at every step? But he could use it, too. Brigit's face drifted before him, Brigit's suggestion that this power might be harnessed against evil. What he might do in the name of justice. No witches need burn. No soldiers need die. No princes need hide. Elisha gasped, jerking out of the memory he was forced to imagine—and not a moment too soon. Morag's face thrust inches from his own, the man's breath clouding before him, the man's grip holding him steady. The face broke into silent laughter. "Go on, then, Barber. What else could you do with a dead man's blood?"

Morag was leading him, like a dog herding a sheep,

merely by suggesting which way to go. The miasma of grief and despair echoed in Elisha's memories, and all Morag need do was push him a step too far. The cold on Elisha's arm, where he caught himself as he stumbled in the grass. The cold of Death, and the slick, creeping sensation of another man's blood damp upon his hand. If he'd been less worried, he would have understood right away: the mancers had spattered the blood of a dead man all over the ground. It marked Elisha now and left him open. Morag kept his insidious contact, the insect-tingle of his awareness smothering Elisha's skin.

Elisha summoned up the cold of this stranger's death and struck back. The blood stung his arm, frost swirling out in tendrils, and he lashed them forward toward the other man's skin. Their misty breath between them turned to crystals that tinkled to the earth like rain. Morag twitched, but he didn't let go. His fingers dug in, welcoming the cold, and the frost evaporated back into mist. But the blood showed Elisha more, it shimmered around in his secret senses, marking the ground around the barrow, the area carefully prepared to enable the mancers to work their magic and insulate themselves from outsiders. If the stranger's blood gave him just a hint of death, it also gave him contact.

Elisha reached out through the earth to the next patch of blood and snatched at it, splashing the dirt away like water beneath Morag's feet, and he lurched, at first dragging Elisha toward him, then letting go as the earth rocked. Elisha sprang away from him, but Morag scrambled up again, growling. "A pretty trick for a sensitive child."

"Look," Alaric began, but Morag cut him off with a gesture. "Stay back, Majesty."

He reached toward his belt, and Elisha tensed, expecting a dagger, not the bottle that Morag pulled free. Again, he found the blood, the resonance around him of this one dead man. It came more easily now that he knew its touch, but it did not respond. No matter how he tried to twist it to his use. Instead, it cried out, as if his reaching awareness were a brand against the body that once contained it. He shied away, the wails of remembered death piercing his hearing from all around him. He wiped his hand against his trousers, trying to free himself from the dizzying shrieks that grew louder with every moment.

Something splashed across his face and throat. Elisha spun, wiping at his face. He had to find his balance, but the ground now tipped against him, sloshing at every step where it was marked with blood. His hand struck ground, scrabbling among the stones.

"I don't need the knife, yer Majesty," Morag said, his tone as ordinary as ever, "yer brother's—"

Before Morag could finish, Elisha launched his assault. Knowledge, Mystery, Affinity—and a handful of stones that flew like arrows.

Morag howled and danced, slapping down the missiles Elisha flung at him. One arrow streaked across his brow, spattering his face with blood. Another pierced his leg, another stuck into the hump at his back, quivering there like a feathered banner. They had little force without the bow to fire them, but the tips could still draw blood and strengthen Elisha's magic. Morag whirled, jerking free the shaft in his leg with a roar. "Stupid barber!" He flung up his hand.

Elisha's face and throat scorched with pain as the dead stranger's spattered blood sizzled with power. He screamed, staggering. Horror blazed to life through his skin, through the potency of the blood that marked him. It was not merely cold, but frigid. He could feel the work of Death.

It started with a lash of fear that built into a frenzy. He was attacked, beset, seized by a stranger in the dark. Strong hands tore his clothes and flung him down. Knives hacked into his arms and legs. He fought back with all his strength, bucking against the knees that bore him down, screaming against the knife that cut out his tongue, then choking on his own blood as he heard an awful ripping. Every inch of his body burned with pain.

Dimly, Elisha realized this death did not belong to him, but to another. Elisha fought it, but the force of the murder cascaded through him, carried by the victim's blood, reaching down from his face, covering the mark of the angel's wing.

He felt the rough stones of a path that scraped his body. "Help me!" he screamed aloud and gagged on the phantom blood that filled his mouth. He thrashed against the unseen, brutal hands. A blade carved into his belly and something burst. "Please," he sobbed through ruined lips. "Please," he begged, and he begged for death.

Chapter 23

———— ❖ ————

The horror vanished, like a smothering hand stripped away, and Elisha gasped for breath, coming back to himself with a vengeance. He felt a wave of gratitude, as if his prayer was answered—then realized that, if Morag had released him, it was not kindness but something else that drove him to it. Something had distracted him and forced his attention elsewhere.

Elisha rolled and scrambled to his knees, but he did not stand before he captured the dark vision that had gripped him. He knew Death, he knew injury inside and out, and he turned the cold upon itself, numbing his own sensitivity, insulating himself from the images the blood had conjured. He knew now how the man had died, and that knowledge was his shield. He worked quickly, plaiting that power with his memory of the icy, awful strength Death brought him. His ears still rang with the screams, and his raw throat recalled their terror.

Morag lay in a heap, his coat slashed, the arrow Elisha made from a stone fallen back to the earth, and Thomas crouched over him, sword in hand.

Even as Elisha spotted them in the gloom, Morag snarled, pushing against the earth and shaking himself. Thomas, still tensed from his attack, hefted his sword for a second blow, but it rang as Alaric struck his own against it, forcing him back. Their blades flashed silver in a flurry of blows, then they separated, wary, both in fighting stance.

Anger and worry over Thomas's presence warred with gratitude in Elisha's heart. If the king hadn't disobeyed when he did, answering Elisha's desperate call for help, Elisha had no doubt his own body would be left in ribbons, his blood drained for a talisman.

Morag heaved himself up, and whirled to where Thomas waited the next attack.

"Here, you bastard," Elisha whispered, and he sent his touch through the earth, to every patch of blood his art could reach. He sent them leaping from the dead man's pain. Fountains of earth. The mancer turned back to him with the slow, dread pace of the wolf to its prey.

Both princes recoiled from the spewing earth, then Thomas lunged forward. He thrust at Morag's chest. The magus brought up a hand, but Alaric's blade sang again, barely deflecting his brother's.

"Thank you, Morag—I'll take him." Alaric's boyish face twisted into a snarl as he whipped off his cloak and let it flutter to the ground.

Thomas wasted neither time nor breath. His unkempt hair lashed about him as he dodged the parry and sent a wicked thrust to his brother's off-side. His grim silence underscored the skill of his attack, but Morag's turning set loose the torn cloak to foul his blade, and Alaric slipped away left, seeing an opening.

The duel shifted from the shadow of the stones, leaving Morag revealed in moonlight, suddenly straighter. Elisha faced him, throbbing with the memory of pain. If he could reach his own talisman, he could touch Morag with a blast of death to wither him skin from bone. Instead, he searched the earth around them. The anonymous victim Morag carried in a bottle at his waist had no more power over Elisha, now that Elisha had such intimate knowledge of the man's murder, but neither could he summon the strength he needed past that particular defense. The first blood, which had marked the ground and touched his hand, lay scattered by the earth, degraded to fragments too small to use.

The ancient mounds sheltered their own dead, like the bodies he had called up out of the bog. Elisha thought of the shades that had marked his path from the village to this place, separating them now into slivers of cold, the residues of the dead. A fresh death was different, a piercing cold, a thick blackness almost palpable in his hands. These wisps, however, slipped through his awareness like vapor. He breathed them in, the scent of decay, and gathered them strand by strand, erasing the pain.

"I can feel it, Barber. I can feel you pulling—but there's nothing you can steal that I haven't already got." Morag rolled his shoulders. His hump rippled down, unrolling along his back in a wave of tattered shadow. "Better." He tipped his head toward the standing stones. "Mebbe I should let you fetch your baby head. That'd make this last a little longer. Little more fun, mebbe. I've got some friends, after all. Why not let you?" He pursed his lips as if considering, then shrugged. "Naw."

A shock of cold assaulted the stranger's blood, but Elisha ignored it. He heard the clash of steel and a cry from his left, but forced himself to ignore that, too. Thomas was a swordsman. It was in his hands and those of his distant God.

Elisha reached back through the contact, reflecting the cold until the blood in Morag's bottle froze. It slapped against Morag's leg when he moved, giving a thunk like a bludgeon, then the thong twisted hoary with ice and snapped, dropping the bottle to roll away.

"If ye had a proper master, ye could be something," Morag allowed. "As it is . . ." He took another step. The night ripped and sealed and he was gone. Elisha spun about, disbelieving.

"How long have you been in league?" Alaric shouted, dancing out of reach between the stones. "Did he kill the king for you indeed? What a victory if my little lies were true."

Thomas panted mist into the night. "Elisha! Where's Morag?" He stalked forward, but Alaric showed no sign of leaving the protection of the stones, holding his blade before him.

Gone, Elisha wished, but Morag wouldn't leave his chosen king unprotected. He did not speak, but searched the dale with all his senses. He could feel Alaric's men lurking in their perimeter, still too far away, still with no sign of tension. Whatever spell contained the battle, it was—

Something slammed into Elisha's back. He fell face first, skidding in the dirt, rolling fast to get up again. A bloody boot kicked hard into his ribs, knocking him flat once more.

"Sensitive," Morag sneered. "With Death, they say." He reached out and the frozen bottle leapt to his hand. He smacked Elisha's jaw with it, and a ringing rose inside Elisha's skull.

Thomas lunged, but Alaric burst from his refuge, slicing his brother's back as he spun to meet the assault.

Elisha raised his bloodied hand and shoved Morag, pushing his strength into the contact. The blood scattered on the ground marked Morag as well, and he tumbled as the earth protested and his boots flew from under him. Elisha pounced, reaching, the strands of Death he had been gathering now spread to every fingertip, crackling for company.

At his feet, Morag bent and wriggled, the movement so bizarre that it caught Elisha off guard. Morag's fist emerged, not with a weapon, but with a handful of his tattered cloak. He flung it up to snap before Elisha. The echo of Death throbbed, Elisha's power snatched from his very hand. Morag rose with a twirl that sent eddies of fear into his wake, Elisha's hoarded strength growing slippery once more.

The cloak flicked out, a thing long at the middle with two dangling straps and a fringe of—Elisha's stomach burned and twisted. Toes. They were not tatters of cloth but shreds of skin, flattened and strangely shaped, whorled as they had been in life, leathery as they reached out toward Elisha. It was no cloak that had been rolled in imitation of a hump, but a human skin.

The Frenchman. It must be. Elisha had seen his flayed corpse.

Elisha wrapped himself in knowledge, dodging Morag

as he remembered all he could of the messenger—how he spoke and acted, how he looked in life, how he felt in death, bleeding out in Elisha's arms. Elisha forced himself to remember, girding himself with the memories, knowing what to expect. Within his armor, Elisha gathered his power and felt a breath of triumph. Morag thought to use the murdered man against him. This time, he would fail. Elisha almost welcomed the contact, a hint of his old arrogance returning.

Retreating to give himself time, Elisha felt the slap of one long strap—not a strap, a leg, outflung by Morag's mad capers. Elisha gasped, the armor of his knowledge ripped aside. He staggered as if struck a body blow.

Morag clapped for himself now, a little jig like a drunken man. But the brush of the human skin swept away the last of Elisha's power, like a river drawing down a stream. Elisha struggled for breath, one hand pressed to his chest. Still pierced. By God, so the hide was not the Frenchman. Who? Not another stranger; the death, the sob of pain that struck him had an echo he should know, one that broke his own strength precisely because his strength had failed him before, when this victim had need of him. Guilt assailed him from within.

The skin was long and pale and pierced with holes that let the moonlight through. Its blond scalp fluttered at the back of Morag's head, doubling his own hair, its sorry arms pinned at his throat with a spike of bone.

"'s better to have 'em fresh and killed by me, but this fellow's got a whiff of betrayal—" Morag paused, letting one flayed leg dangle over his arm, and sniffed. "—mmm, jus' 'bout makes up for anyffin' else!"

Elisha gulped a breath, expecting to scent betrayal in the air. Morag's hand shot out toward him, the leg still wrapped over it. He seized Elisha's shirt and dragged him close. They grappled and the skin flapped around them. The touch shivered Elisha's skin, then struck him. His mouth filled with water. He was plunging under, tossed by a current, then trapped beneath branches. Every flailing attempt to escape brought streaks of pain. One, two, three bolts pierced him, back and lung. He gasped, struggling to free himself from branches, fighting the water, fighting the vision that gripped him. He knew this death! It was not his—then why could he not break free? Instead, it sank him deeper with each gulp of water. It burrowed into him with every touch of the dead man's skin. May sunshine gleamed overhead through the water that filled him, branches from a broken tree clawing at his face and chest.

As he sank, terror washed over him. His burning lungs strained; cut with the agony of the crossbow shots, the sense of his failing strength, the distant pang of longing for a girl he'd never see again, the astonishment at what he knew, that his trusted master would frame him with treason. His master who stood at his back and shot him, calmly re-loading to shoot again.

Benedict, the physician's assistant who suspected his master's treachery. The confrontation left Benedict shot in the river, a note in his belt to incriminate him. Elisha had pulled him free, fighting his death even as he felt it approaching. Helplessness rushed in once more. Elisha could not save him then—any more than he could save himself now.

He sputtered and gasped. In some distant shred of his awareness, Elisha felt the dirt at his back, the stones that scraped him, the weight of the man who pressed upon his chest, forcing contact with the dead man's hide. Morag the gravedigger must have been responsible for Benedict's sad remains and stripped the skin before burial. How many more victims did he carry, slung about his body like a peddler's pack? Who else's murder would Morag exploit? Elisha tried to cling to these real things, only to be sucked back into the vision, the dying repeated again and again.

Someone shouted. The weight upon him shifted. For a moment, Elisha could see the night sky, no longer overlaid with the river's run. Even as Elisha tried to push away the contact, his own bandage, leaping to the call of magic not his own, wound free of his wrist just long enough to bind it to the other. Morag rose, leaving him bound. "Son of a whore, Your Majesty—can't you see I'm busy?"

Not far away, Alaric yelped in pain.

Shadows flitted over Elisha's head, shadows with flickering blades. His breath burned, his lungs still fighting the battle he'd lost. A tall man with wild hair fought his wobbly opponent backward. A few more steps, and he'd be down.

"Here," said Morag. "This is the one." His hand went to his belt and pulled free a hank of hair. It fell in golden waves across his arm, as he held it up to the princes' gaze.

"Anna!" blurted Alaric, and Thomas froze. His sword arm wavered, he glanced away. For a moment, Elisha saw the blue of his eyes, edged with awful white. He gasped a single breath as if he, too, were drowning.

Thomas dodged in a daze, not near fast enough. Alaric, stumbling, bleeding, still clung to his sword. It slashed from behind, cutting deep at his brother's thigh.

In an arc of blood, Thomas twisted from the blade, for a moment still arrested by his dead wife's name.

Chapter 24

❖

Just too far out of reach, enemies between them, and Elisha's breath once more froze upon the air. The wind of dying rippled through the king's hair. Elisha reached out his bound and trembling hands.

For a moment, Alaric stood over, breathing hard, watching blood stream from his brother's thigh. "Fitting," Alaric murmured. Elisha's medical mind supplied the veins and arteries, the lateral slice.

A spasm passed Thomas's face, and he dropped to his knees, rocking in pain, groping for the wound. Pressure to the wound, Elisha thought, his voice too weak to speak. He tried to push himself up, but collapsed instead, gulping for breath.

Alaric reached out convulsively and cupped his brother's cheek. "I didn't do that, Thomas—you've got to understand." Thomas cried out at the touch, but Alaric did not let him go. "Anna—Alfleda—I didn't do that. They'd already done it, don't you see? Before they, before I—" His teeth flashed. "Before our alliance. I wanted you to know, before you—" He swallowed. "I don't kill women." A sound fled his lips that might have been laughter, and Alaric gave a little bob of his head. "This was a fair fight—you know that." His arm trembled as he made Thomas face him, but his brother's eyes and teeth clenched shut.

"Thomas." Alaric gave him a little shake, and his brother's eyes flared open.

Thomas winced in pain, wet his lips, and whispered, "God have mercy on your soul."

Alaric released him, jerking back, his face gone pale as he hurriedly crossed himself. He stumbled once more to his feet as his brother's head lolled to one side. "Mercy," Alaric panted. "I can give you that," and he raised his sword.

"Naw," said Morag, and he reached out to stay the blade. "Let him bleed out." Alaric gave a twitch, a movement of defiance despite the white gleam at his eyes, but Morag snorted. "When you're done showing the body, I'll be wanting the skin. The longer the death, the sweeter the skin." With the chuckle of a friend, Morag slapped Alaric's back, then he bent to collect the arrows that had struck him and slide them into the back of his belt: taking any trace of his own blood.

Elisha pushed hard and found his feet. Three staggering strides to Alaric's side. With a casual arm Morag swept him down. The blow stung with a river's cold and a dizzying pain. Elisha shook it off and tried again, hooking his numb fingers into Alaric's belt.

With a wince half of pity and half disgust, Alaric

gripped Elisha's hair and bent back his chin. "This one, too?" he asked.

"Thought he'd best me at my own game." Morag shrugged. "I'll deal with what's left of him." He resumed watching Thomas's death, greedy eyes watching the short, uneven breaths.

Elisha stared up at Alaric's face, the sword raised above him, Thomas's cold blood dripping on Elisha's lips. He could taste Death rising, his stunned awareness open to the dying prince's desperate, silent prayers, to the darkness seeping in through the gaping wound, to the dull, slender sense of an earlier pain. With a creeping of his fingers, Elisha's hands gripped the hilt tucked at Alaric's side. The assassin's dagger still wore Thomas's blood. Blood it had no right to.

Blood contact linked the assassin's wicked blade to the sword Alaric still bore. Elisha yanked free the dagger, Alaric moved to knock it away. Contact made, affinity stretched Elisha's blade to match Alaric's. It shivered in his grip and sprang upward into a princely sword, thrusting up beneath Alaric's ribcage, growing longer and sharper. Elisha's numb hands registered the soft severing of intestines, the piercing of the peritoneum, the final muscular thrust as it spiked into his heart.

Alaric's sword tumbled from his fist as his knees collapsed beneath him, his eyes gone vague. For a moment, Elisha felt the sharp, cold slash as if it cut him as well: Alaric's death, that shadow that hovered near as he rode, had come upon him. Elisha recoiled, and Alaric's dead hand slid free from Elisha's hair, settled briefly on his shoulder, and fluttered to the ground. The trapped sword scraped bone as it slipped from Elisha's hands.

"Damn you, Barber, you've killed our king!" Morag thrust between them, and unstoppered another bottle. Elisha braced himself for another onslaught of blood, but water drenched his face and hands. Washing away Elisha's latest crime—so he could not use the blood to turn this death to his advantage—if he had been strong enough. Morag hauled him up, his feet dangling, but his fury mingled with a wicked glint. "Those'll be some fine, fine skins." He gave a little snort of laughter. "Bleedin' shame I can't carry you all and do it proper. They may well 'ave my hide I tell 'em you killed their man. Mebbe let you live long 'nough to tell 'em yourself."

He tossed Elisha to the ground and kicked his back, forcing him to face the princes. Pulling a short, utilitarian knife from his belt, he lined up Elisha's hands, pinning his wrists. Then with a strong, efficient plunge, he rammed the knife home through both hands and into the earth below.

Elisha screamed, a raw, broken sound that trailed off to sobs.

Across the gap between them, Thomas's eyes slid open, unfocused, then shut.

"Not dead yet? Good." Morag knelt to snap the chain from Alaric's throat, the dead prince's head dropping back with a thump. "Can't take you, lad—not yet. Folks'll come looking." He patted Alaric's shoulder and gave a little sigh. "But him,"—he tipped his head toward Thomas— "nobody knows he's even close. Nobody but us."

Elisha stared, for a moment not understanding, as

Morag wrapped the chain around Thomas's thigh, cinching it, stopping the blood. Saving him?

Then Morag reached to the back of his belt for the answer: the half-moon blade already stained with filth except at its gleaming edge. Thomas lay before him, his hands unmoving, his chest giving the slightest shiver of breath. Morag turned and squatted, holding the blade before Elisha's blurred vision, superimposed over the mancer's reeking grin. "You killed mine, Barber. Bit a turnabout, eh?" He moved the blade ever so gently down Elisha's cheek. "Oh, you'll be sweet. Sweeter than a virgin's blood, after this."

The edge drew a frigid line, and Elisha twitched his face away, only to draw a thrust of pain from his impaled hands.

Morag ripped Thomas's shirt, revealing his chest, barely moving. He straddled the prince's crotch, crooning to himself as he sketched the carving strokes. Alaric lay nearby, crumpled, his knees bent and eyes staring at the sky. Where were his soldiers? Why didn't they come? The ground lay stained by strangers' blood—the mancers must have used it to cast a deflection around the space they claimed, containing the conflict within. How far out did the blood circle extend?

Elisha dragged at his power. He curled around his agony and pushed it aside, his fingers trembling. Could he strike again at Morag with the power they both knew? It evaded him. The mancer set one point of his blade at Thomas's navel and gave it a careful nudge. The prince twitched. Morag's rough tourniquet would keep him alive long enough to know what fate he suffered. In the memory of the stranger's blood, Elisha felt again the terrible ripping as skin was stripped from flesh.

It was not Elisha's battle, Thomas had said, and he could not fight it alone. Even Mortimer would be welcome. Elisha flung out his awareness into the earth, searching for the circle, the limit of Morag's magic beyond which Alaric's soldiers waited for their king.

He gasped in astonishment to find someone reaching back. "*Chanterelle*," he whispered to the bloodied earth.

"*It hurts*," she answered, soft and distant. "*Too much.*"

"*Break the circle*," he sighed. "*Let them in.*"

Thomas gave a whimper as Morag drew the blade up beneath his skin.

Elisha jerked against the knife that held him, clamping his teeth against the pain. But he could not stop the spatter of blood that sent his horror down below.

Chanterelle's touch, always shy, slipped away, and Elisha cried out in her absence.

Then the earth rumbled. Morag jerked upright, his knife dripping. Elisha dared not look away. He clutched his fingers together and jerked upward with all his strength, trapping his scream. The earth shuddered and roared behind him as Elisha tore the blade from the ground and tried to get his knees under him.

"Fuckin' dirt whore!" Morag shrieked.

From beyond, a voice called, "Your Majesty?"

With a growl, Morag flung himself away from Thomas and spun on Elisha just as he shook the knife free from the wounds that gaped in his hands. Morag kicked him hard in the gut, seized his arms, and dragged him up.

Shoving Elisha onto his shoulder, Morag locked him in place with one thick arm. Elisha shook his head, and let the throbbing in his dangling hands revive him. Morag cast about the ground. He took a step toward the standing stones where Thomas and Elisha first lay hidden and planted his feet.

For the first time, Elisha had a sense of the man who held him, a burst of awareness, as Morag ripped open the night. The gap rushed into being around them. This time, with his acute knowledge, his intimate kinship to the dead, the howl separated into voices, the shadows into faces. It screamed with a thousand voices: the tortured and the maimed, the soldiers and the seamen, the women torn by childbirth and their sad, wailing babes.

Unlike his sharp, efficient master, Morag hesitated, pausing to drink it all in. The shades of Benedict and the Frenchman clung to his shoulders, reaching toward Elisha, the man who once tried to help them. The man murdered in the alley held closer to his murderer, and the woman . . . Anna was faint and yet precise, an artist's drawing without the paint to bring it color. She was beautiful and terrible, trapped in her final pain.

It took Morag strength to stay there, filling the unnatural door that pushed to be closed. His arm trembled with the effort of holding the opening, as his body quaked with pleasure. He allowed the power of the place to rush through him. He was invigorated, reveling in the presence of so much pain, and just for that moment, his presence laid plain for Elisha's sight.

Elisha dangled at his back, turning his face from

Benedict's hide. He failed to save the young surgeon, it was true—but not because he didn't try. With his teeth he pulled free the binding at his wrists. His trembling fingers groped then grabbed the skin and it rose to his call, its arms around the villain's throat, its death an awful, willing tool. Elisha seized. The skin replied.

Morag cried out, scrabbling for his throat as the dead arms convulsed beneath his chin.

Elisha kicked, and the grip let free. He fell as Morag ripped the hide from his neck, bellowed, turned—and lost the focus that allowed him to open that terrible place. With a slam that resounded in Elisha's mind, the unnatural passage was gone into darkness and stars. Morag went with it, in spite of his rage.

Elisha rolled away, scraped and battered, and shook himself alert again. Across the dell, a fire roared in the heath where the twin mounds should have stood. Instead, they formed two pits, sucked down into the earth with a fierce strength. But the torches they supported had fallen as well and struck a blaze. Mortimer shouted for the men to rally to him, only to be answered by prayers and terror.

On elbows and knees, his hands clutched together and shaking, the bloody scrap of his cloth talisman trailing, Elisha scrambled back to where Thomas lay, his breath coming in tremors, shaking the line of blood that seeped from Morag's careful cutting, but he sobbed no more. Gritting his teeth, Elisha pressed his hands over the wound. Waves of dizziness assailed him, the sky wheeling now in darkness, now in stars. He once healed a man of worse than this, setting his hand back to his wrist, calling him home from the edge of death. But then he had the aid of the magi, channeling him their power through the river that they shared. He had to find a way to force the king to heal—and he had nothing, no strength, no spell, no hope. "God help me," he cried out.

And the wheeling darkness answered with a caw.

Chapter 25

❖

Crows settled around him. They hopped upon the earth and dropped onto the stones. They landed on his shoulders, claws pricking at his flesh.

In his secret senses, he found their presence, a shifting, fluttering form. A hundred lives both small and worthy, and somewhere beyond them, the lingering sense of their mistress, a woman who loved every feathery soul. Their swirling wings and patterns wove a screen of darkness, misleading the soldiers, giving him time.

Simple healing relied on the body's need to be whole, but it needed Thomas's strength, and the king's presence faded fast beneath his hands. He pressed harder, his own thighs straining as he pressed against the earth.

He had knowledge and affinity in plenty, if he dared to use it. His years of surgery in London, not to mention the hundred wounds of the battlefield, taught him the muscles, veins, and arteries he had envisioned in that flash when he understood the wound. He sought them now inside himself, drawing his awareness deep into his body until he could track the course of every vein.

Slipping his awareness to Thomas, Elisha caught his breath at the length and depth of the wound at the king's thigh. He felt it now as if it sliced his own skin. In his mind, he overlaid the images, Thomas's wound, his own whole flesh. Thomas's body wanted to heal, to be whole, but it had not the strength until Elisha showed the way.

He drew a deep breath, and drew down the strength of the crows, the mad woman's talismans in their thousands. Power echoed from one to the next with the magnification of magic and resonated through his flesh, steadying his shaking hands. Thomas's skin twitched, his muscles shivered. At the same time, Elisha felt a chill slice across his own thigh and gasped. He fought it, trying to hold the single image of unbroken flesh. Pain streaked through him. He convulsed against it, reaching for the birds. Something winked into darkness. Then another, and another. And each one sent a short, sharp energy into his hands. The pain eased and the shivering ceased. Elisha bowed over Thomas, his arms trembling and his hands slipping from their place. The gash in the fabric showed smooth skin, curled with hairs, barely a scar to reveal where Death had tried to mark him.

Elisha gave a breathless laugh, stronger now than when he started.

Crows burst into the air around him, cawing wildly. Those on his shoulders launched with a tearing of claws and Elisha reared back as they ripped his shirt and scraped his skin with stinging welts. It reminded him all too clearly of the day of his flogging. He waved his arms to scatter the rest.

A dozen black feathered forms littered the ground

around him, unmoving, their claws curled and eyes glinting.

"Necromancer!" shrilled a woman's voice. "We came to help, we did, and what did you do? You killed them and ate their lives like candies." The crow-mage stormed between the mounds. She dropped beside the dead birds, wailing, then gathering them, crooning over each one. Under her hood, her eyes and mouth crumpled in pain, tears streaking her face.

"Forgive me," Elisha said. "You came—they came—when I needed you. I never meant—"

"What you meant doesn't matter! It's not what you mean, it's what you are."

"Majesty!" called a distant voice. "Your Majesty, where are you?" Feet thumped, and the fire's glow died at the gap Chanterelle had made to break the circle of blood. The last of Morag's deflection was spent with his departure, the crow-mage snatched back her magic at Elisha's betrayal. Alaric's men would soon be searching, their master absent too long now.

Elisha turned to the crow-mage while testing the ragged pulse at Thomas's throat. "You and your friends saved his life, mother. I can never repay that."

She hissed at him, then rose up, her arms full of crows, her face buried in their bodies. Weeping, she stumbled away, leaving a drift of dark feathers.

Elisha gathered Thomas's head against him, catching him under the arms, and dragged him, stumbling, to the open end of the large barrow. He hauled them both inside and fell to his knees beneath the lintel where he and Thomas had lain earlier. The dead crows' strength lingered with him still, and Elisha worked a desperate deflection as Alaric's men spied their prince and ran. Elisha cast the last of the crows' power into his spreading awareness and found the soldiers' sense of despair, fear, a darkness too black for mere torches to penetrate.

"Your Majesty!" Mortimer and three others stumbled into view, their boots singed, and they dropped down by the fallen prince.

Clutching Thomas against his chest, hardly daring to breathe, Elisha stared as they checked Alaric's body, and Mortimer at last slumped onto his heels, shaking his head. He reached out to close the prince's still, blue eyes, then reached a little lower, noting the absence there. "Have they killed you for a chain?"

"By God—so much blood!" swore one of the guards, and crossed himself with a trembling hand. "Surely they are wounded, some even dead to have bled so much. We'll find them, my lord."

"Will we?" Mortimer looked up. "There was magic and devilry here. Or how should all this blood have been shed without our hearing?"

"And them mounds just . . . gone." The guard grimaced.

"Heathen things. I'm sure it's bound up with the demon that stole the barber," Mortimer said. "I fear our king moved away from the Lord this night, just when he was most in need."

A few others pounded up, breathing hard. "Nothing, my lord. No sign of anyone leaving." The leader frowned into the shadow of the standing stones, and Elisha held his breath. He strengthened the darkness as the soldier approached, calling up the layers of despair and grief that lingered there. Sheltered in the mouth of a tomb, he sat upon the precipice dividing life from death and turned that wicked edge to defend them.

The soldier leaned between the stones, his breath forming a mist as his gaze roved over Elisha's head. Finally, he drew back with a shiver and turned away, slumping in defeat.

"Come—we cannot leave him lie. In the morning, we shall conduct a thorough search and not a bandit nor a beggar shall remain. If the demon or the barber remains to be found, we shall find them." Mortimer directed the men to drape Alaric with his fine velvet cloak and lift him gently, the ermine trailing blood at his feet. As the bearers moved away ahead of him, Mortimer straightened and took another glance about. He slid his fingers beneath his doublet and took out a golden cross, gripping it. "Thy will be done," he murmured. Then he smiled at the darkness and strode away.

Chapter 26

❦lisha felt them withdraw even as he heard their footsteps retreat. Finally, he let the shield of despair sink back into nothing. He slumped against the stone, cradling the king against his chest. His arms shook, the gory holes still open at his palms, but he tried to breathe normally. He swore he would allow himself only a moment's rest, a blessed moment's peace upon the terrible night. His eyes slid shut.

Pain jolted him awake as his hand was briefly gripped, and he glanced down to find Thomas's eyes open, barely visible but for their liquid sheen. Thomas's hand released Elisha's, the fingers shifting to probe, but gently.

"What did he do to you?" Thomas murmured.

Elisha stared into the darkness, mastering his breath.

"What have I done to deserve such a defender?" Thomas whispered.

"Something very wicked indeed," Elisha told him. He wanted to smile, as if this were a jest, but he had known the thrill of taking the lives of crows and bending them to his own will. He knew the joy that Morag felt at opening his passage through Hell, and he knew the awful affinity between them.

"No," said Thomas, his voice still low, "Surely God has brought you to me."

"It wasn't God out there tonight. It was the very Devil." The very least of the Devils—and he had beaten Elisha to the gates of Hell. When next they met, he would strip Elisha's skin as a hunter strips a squirrel. Elisha tipped his head back against the stone and knew, with a stark cold truth, that the next time they met, he hadn't a prayer.

After a time, and with a muffled sound of pain, Thomas moved to sit up. His chest and back must still be hurting; next time, Elisha must be sure to heal his patient more thoroughly. When he could gather the strength, and find some light, he must see to his own pierced hands.

"You healed me?" There was a soft clatter of chain. "I remember . . . crows. I saw your open eyes and a dagger stood between us." And then, very softly, "I thought you were dead."

Thomas's warm hand found Elisha's hair, his shoulder, trailed down his arm. Ever so carefully, he took Elisha's damaged hand atop his own and gave a whisper of dismay. "Both?"

Elisha wet his lips, and whispered, "Aye."

Their careful breathing dominated the close chamber they shared. Beyond the door, stars twinkled, serene above the plain of blood. Thomas shifted and something tore, then his hands returned, wadded with cloth that he pressed to Elisha's wounds, his hands clasped between Thomas's own. "Can't you heal yourself?"

"Perhaps, had I one hand uninjured." His palms throbbed beneath the king's gentle pressure, as if they prayed together.

After a moment, Thomas said, "You have mine."

"It hurts," Elisha answered quickly, pushing away the king's compassion. "You'll feel the wounds as your own. If I'm not strong enough, they will be."

"You are." The king took a deeper breath. "You are strong enough. I know it."

Elisha swallowed hard, grateful for the gloom cast by the distant moonlight. He did not think he could look upon the king as he worked, or meet his eye. For Thomas's healing, he killed the crows, but he must rely upon the power around him for his own, the power of the dead who inhabited this place and those Morag had brought here, twisting them to terror. A final test, if a man could be with death.

The shades rose even as he began to reach, they echoed his call, growing more defined as he breathed, and Thomas's grip tightened, ever so slightly, frost tingling in the air. "Talk to me," Elisha said. "Distract yourself before it comes."

Thomas drew a breath and said, "What of my brother?"

Elisha thought of his own brother. Nathaniel should have placed the blame for his losses where it truly belonged: with Elisha himself. "Dead," Elisha told him, the word ringing in their little cavern as he reached his awareness down to his maimed hands, to the hands that covered them, still strong.

"I thought to curse him," Thomas murmured. "Then I thought of dying with hatred on my lips."

Alaric's stricken face flashed before Elisha's memory as his dying brother commended him to God. "It was curse enough for him to be blessed by you. Lord Mortimer seemed rather glad that Alaric was gone."

Holding the image of the healed flesh—even marked by branding, as Elisha's and Thomas's both had been—Elisha brought the power in, and Thomas cried out, his hands jerking, and then it passed, and both of them gasped for breath before Elisha slid his hands away. They still ached at the center, as if the flesh remembered.

Thomas let out a long breath. "In spite of everything, I am still sorry at my brother's death. Does that make me a fool?"

"Only in that you care too deeply." The shadows he had summoned frayed as he worked and then dissipated, trembling as they passed. Even after they sank into their rest, the darkness felt so very cold. Perhaps their souls had gone to Heaven or to Hell, as the church would have him believe, but the memory of death was captured in their fleshly remains—the pain, the grief, the suffering, the loss—all the echoes that endowed a place or a talisman with power. Was his use of it any more pure than Morag's? But Elisha had not slaughtered a stranger in an alley for the sake of the strength that he might steal, nor stripped the skin from the dead and sent them doubly naked to the grave. Elisha shivered, his head slumping, exhaustion passing through in giddy waves.

"I am a curse upon those I love, it's true." Thomas shifted a little away from Elisha, coming to sit beside him against the wall. "Do you know why my father burned the Lady Rowena?"

At Elisha's murmur, Thomas went on: "I used to dream of her. I dreamed of battles where she—or perhaps, I think now, her daughter—stood by me. I dreamed of . . . the things that young men do, I suppose, when a woman is beautiful and out of reach." His voice was halting, awkward in a way Elisha had not known him to be. Almost, Elisha was tempted to make contact and feel the king's emotions, but Elisha's awareness felt fragile, and Thomas's confession too personal already.

"Lady Rowena was wise. Kind. She tutored us in history. I was trying to keep her away, avoiding her because of my dreams. I think it worried her, it made her . . . pursue me. Certainly Alaric thought she did. He told my father she was bewitching me. I don't think Alaric meant for her to die—only to be sent away, to be punished for wanting me. For not wanting him." Another deep breath, a swallow, and he finished the tale. "Until the day of the stake, I wasn't ever sure she was a witch. She was the first to die for me."

Brigit couldn't possibly know this, that Alaric had betrayed her mother. She never would have seduced him if she knew the truth. What would become of her when she learned of Alaric's death? They were not even married yet. If she viewed the body, would she know what Elisha had done?

"That was my last witch, Elisha." Thomas spoke more firmly now. "And I did not even witness any magic—I closed my eyes at the stake and had to hear of it later. What happened tonight . . . it was . . ." His eyes focused past Elisha. "That Hell-spawn had my wife's face on his belt, like a favor from his lord."

In the slender moonlight that ebbed through their gruesome door, Elisha could see the pale cast to the king's face. "A necromancer."

At the word, Thomas recoiled and crossed himself.

"What all witches are said to be, he was in truth. He conjures magic from death. From murder, when he can get it. Mancers, the magi call them."

"The very Devil indeed." Then Thomas met his gaze. "And what are you?"

Elisha wanted to defend himself, to show himself unlike the mancers, but at the very least, Thomas deserved the truth. "In faith, I wish I knew." Elisha moved his scarred hands, the hands he once claimed were the only thing he trusted. "Magic is based first upon knowledge. I am a surgeon by training, a healer from the day the lady burned. But to work for life is to understand death. The rule of opposites, we call it. When I slew your father, Highness, I called upon the strength of death itself. I did the same when I healed you."

"You are with Death, the mancer said."

"It means I know so much about Death that I can summon it without a talisman—without another way to magnify my power."

"And the baby head?" Thomas asked, his voice sinking very low.

Elisha's shoulders slumped. "A talisman," he answered. "A very strong one. I did not mean it so."

"That's what I was carrying. The thing you thought would draw them to me."

Nodding, Elisha said, "I have to get it. I meant to bury it."

"I see." Thomas moved to face him, regarding Elisha with a level, hard gaze. Beneath the grubby beard and wild hair, beneath the fatigue of bleeding and battle, just for a moment, Elisha saw the king that could be, weighing what he knew and passing judgment. Twice now, they fought a common enemy, each drawing blows meant for the other. Either of them would be dead if not for the other. But the set of Thomas's jaw and the easy strength of his hands told the truth they both had been forgetting: this beggar, this branded thief, was the last man of the royal family in England. He had suffered too much already at the hands of those he could not trust, and he should consider Elisha to be among them.

Stiffly, Elisha rose to his knees. "I need to go fetch it, Your Majesty."

"And if the soldiers return?"

"There will be more of them tomorrow."

Thomas sighed in agreement.

"Besides, a witch has ways . . ." He gave a little shrug.

"You made sure they did not find us." Then the king, too, stood. "It seems, for now, we are safer together."

"In order to protect you, I need to have contact with you."

Thomas tipped his head, laying his fingers along the line drawn on his face with Elisha's blood. He watched from shadowed eyes until Elisha nodded. "You need contact as well to kill me," said Thomas carefully.

"I would see you to safety, if you will let me, Your Majesty."

"There is no safety for me here, Elisha. Nor anywhere."

Elisha pushed himself into motion and crawled out of the narrow passage, his hands pulsing with his weight. "I think you're wrong about Duke Randall, Your Majesty. I think he would serve you, if he knew you needed him."

Thomas did not respond and drifted after Elisha, both choosing their steps carefully as they straightened up from beneath the lintel. They walked slowly, as if they'd aged a hundred years that night. Where would they go for safety? Elisha could not afford his exhaustion. Shaking himself, letting the sting of scrapes and the ache of bruises wake him, he opened his senses to the world. He felt drained yet alert at the same instant, vigilant, acutely aware of the man who walked behind him. He was the sole retainer of the uncrowned king.

By the light of the lowering moon, the trampled ground was visible, partially scorched when the mounds collapsed. Dark places spattered the heather, stains Elisha knew to be blood, some of it his own, too much of it Thomas's. By now, the mancer's blood markings must be so intermingled as to be nearly worthless, but he stared down at them, wondering how Morag and his master appeared out of nowhere and vanished there again, down a corridor of the dead. Where had they gone—all the way to Rome? Maybe, if Elisha were willing to murder someone, he, too, could follow that road. He, too, might walk through Hell from one place to another, as easily as he had walked here from the abbey. Then he saw Thomas kneel by the place where Alaric had fallen, and nausea rose to sear his throat. The murder, at least, he had already done. The murder of his second king.

Clamping a hand over his mouth, afraid almost to

breathe, Elisha turned away and scrambled up the tilted stone. He spied the metal pot where he had left it the night before. Steeling himself, he took it up. Now that he had relaxed his intense awareness of Death, the pot lay in his palm without threat or chill. The Bone of Luz, the mystical bone said to allow resurrection, was a myth. But Elisha wondered if his recent experiences offered a new way to raise the dead. He thought of the pain captured in the shreds and blood of the men who Morag carried. If it were possible, Morag would have used his power to raise Alaric, perhaps using the blood the prince had spilled to enslave him just as he enslaved the ruins of his victims. If Morag, who reveled in power, could not do it, Elisha concluded, it could not be done.

Elisha rose to find his way down. Below him, kneeling in the trampled earth, Thomas prayed, his hands clasped together, his lips stirring with quiet words. The last nobleman to view the body, Lord Mortimer, had prayed as well, apparently giving gratitude to God for Alaric's death. Mortimer had other plans, but whether his plotting against Alaric would benefit Thomas remained to be seen. Mortimer seemed driven by his sense of godliness, and Thomas was nothing if not a God-fearing man.

Elisha lifted his gaze beyond, past the mounds and the road. The meadows beyond still bore the regular shape and furrowed texture of fields gone fallow these many years. A group of riders emerged from the trees that sheltered the ruined village, and he ducked down reflexively. They carried no light, as soldiers would, and something about the latter two struck him as strange. Cloaks flowed down in layers along their horses sides. Or rather, dresses. Two of the riders were women. Tentatively, he focused his awareness toward the road. The hoof beats grew instantly louder, and voices with them.

"Please, Father, I know he meant to come this way, if he wasn't—if Prince Alaric didn't—" Lady Rosalynn's voice held fear and urgency.

"Elisha's his own man, darling. And I daresay he can defend himself," said the other woman, Duchess Allyson, Elisha realized. "You told us that Alaric—God rest his soul—failed in his attempt."

"But Alaric is—" She took a breath. "He's lying in the church, and he wasn't even meant to be here!"

"We do not know what happened here—if mere theft is to blame, or if there is something else. Under the circumstances, Rosie, I do wonder if Elisha would even wish to be found," the duke offered.

He rather didn't, Elisha reflected, but he knew he must be, to see if the duke could be persuaded to support Thomas—else the king uncrowned would likely live as an outlaw until the verderers or whoever might be their new master struck him dead. Who would be next in line for the throne if the worst should happen? Would the heirs of King Edward's French princes be summoned back at last? Elisha had no idea. At the very least, the kingdom would plunge into chaos all the deeper with the loss of its entire royal family. Someone would step into that void, and likely someone worse than those who went before. The French king, who slew his own magi, stood ready to seize what advantage he could. Lord Mortimer himself clearly worked for other ends. Even the mancers said they already had another candidate. Elisha must not let it happen.

Elisha shed his deflection, certain that the magus Duchess Allyson would feel his presence, and clambered back down, making noise, hoping Thomas had finished praying. "Company's coming, Your Majesty," Elisha said, then put up a hand to stay Thomas's flight. "Duke Randall, his wife and daughter. They're looking for me. They know about Alaric."

"His men would have taken him to Beaulieu, to the church there." Thomas pressed his lips together, glancing away over the downs. "You believe that Randall would support me."

"And if he won't, I'll trip up his horse to give you a head start."

Bare-chested, a thread of blood marking his abdomen, still, Thomas let out a breath of laughter, his eyebrow arching as he glanced back.

The expression, the hint of humor, released a bit of the tension that clutched Elisha's ribs. He shrugged out of the silk shirt Rosalynn had borrowed on his behalf from the lodge and handed it to Thomas. "I'm afraid it's not so grand anymore."

Thomas's glance flickered down, rested on the dried blood at Elisha's chest. "How long—"

"Elisha!" Rosalynn cried out, already sliding down from her horse and running toward them, her skirts gathered up in both hands. "Thank God you're all right!"

"Rosie," her mother called after her. "Let him come away from there."

"Are you ready?" Elisha murmured.

"I must be," replied Thomas, and he slipped on the shirt, preparing himself as best he could.

They moved forward together, not quite side by side, to where Rosalynn stopped by the roadside, skirts swinging and breath caught. "You found your friend! Oh, I am so glad. I'm not sure I properly thanked you, sir, for saving my life. Surely if you had not . . . Father, are you quite well?"

Duke Randall slid down from his mount with a thump of unsteady feet, one hand reaching out, then drawn back to rest at his chin. "Oh, my," he whispered, shaking his head. "Oh, my."

"My lady Rosalynn Dunbury," Elisha said into the silence, "my . . . friend. Thomas, son of Hugh deSpenser. You've probably met before."

"DeSpenser? Gracious!" her hands flew to her lips, and she took a step back. "I should have seen," she whispered, "when you came for me."

Thomas swept into a bow both deep and graceful. "At your service, my lady."

"Of the House Plantagenet," the duke murmured. "Mustn't forget that."

"Elisha Barber," the Duchess said, still atop her horse, "my husband has always found you a surprising fellow, but I doubt even he expected such a surprise as this."

Elisha gave her a bow. "Your Grace," he told her, "Neither did I."

Chapter 27

$\diamondsuit$

By the time they reached the lodge so recently occupied by Brigit and her men, Elisha felt bone-weary. He stumbled down from the duke's pommel, envious of Thomas's ease in alighting from the horse Rosalynn had given up for him. The two ladies, sharing a horse, had turned back to fetch their retainers while the three men rode on ahead, searching for a refuge where Thomas could tell his story at some remove from his brother's corpse and the distraught soldiers who guarded it. By morning, a full sweep of the forest's outlaws would be on, with most of the duke's men involved along with any others who could be gathered. In spite of Mortimer's concerns over sorcery, speculation centered on the same band that had attacked Lady Rosalynn's party earlier. Randall informed Elisha that, before having left the abbey at dawn, Rosalynn had gone so far as to suggest to the prince's men that there might have been several more bandits who had escaped.

Duke Randall moved toward the lodge steps, but Elisha put out his hand, staying him with a speculative frown. Elisha tipped his head toward Thomas who stood a little apart, staring up at the plastered façade of his former home. He wavered and walked on at last, reaching the latch, hesitating, then opening the door. For a long moment, he just stood there, head bowed to rest upon the frame. Then his face turned aside, the gleam of his eye seeking Elisha's. He straightened and pushed inside, but not before Elisha caught a glimpse of his smile. He would have reached back through the blood to touch again the king's gratitude, but he refrained. It was not his place. It never had been.

A speculative "woof" emerged from the barn, then Cerberus barreled past them and clattered up the steps. Thomas's laughter echoed from the house.

Randall scratched his chin, listening, but he could not hide a smile of his own, and Elisha felt ever more certain he was right about the duke's loyalty, in spite of the accusations against Thomas. "Go on, Your Grace. I'll see to the horses."

"You're not a groom, Elisha," the duke protested, but only half-heartedly, then he followed the king inside. After a moment, a lamp lit the front window, and Elisha led the horses to the barn. It took far too long to unsaddle the beasts and work out the buckles of their bridles with his fumbling fingers. He wished he could just curl up in the hay at their hooves and sleep, but he doubted the duke would stand for that—and it would last only as long as it took Rosalynn to arrive and insist upon taking care of him. He hoped she would leave the suspicious Mary behind, now that her mother was with her. He brought water up from the river for the horses, then went back for another bucket, washing away the worst of his own filth. He wanted to leave behind the talisman, finding some supposedly safe place, but he dare not, and so it stayed in a new wrapping, dangling at his waist.

At last, he went inside, wiping his feet by the door, carrying the remainder of the water. "Hallo!"

"In the kitchen," Duke Randall called back. "The soldiers cleared out in a rush and left some provisions."

He stepped over the watchful shape of Cerberus in the passage. Thomas must be ravenous, Elisha reflected, but he found the two men at opposite ends of the table, neither one eating the dry sausage, cheese, and onions piled between them. The king looked up at his entry, firelight blending the smears of blood into the shadows on his face. Elisha held up the bucket. "Wash water, Your Majesty."

"Thank you." Thomas pushed over and came to the basin, noisily filled from Elisha's bucket. They shared a brief look, then Thomas splashed his face, scrubbing away the mark of Elisha's blood.

"I brought you a shirt," Thomas said, nodding to the cloth draping one end of the bench.

"Thanks," Elisha echoed as he pulled it on. "You should drink more. For the blood you've lost. Not wine— all the ancients agree on that."

Thomas reached for the hooks over his head, taking down two mugs and offering one to Elisha with a pointed stare.

"Thomas has told me how he came to the New Forest, but we've just come to recent events." Randall steepled his hands and asked evenly, "Which of you killed Alaric?"

"I did, Your Grace. Before he could kill Thomas." Elisha took the mug from the king, steadying it to be filled from a jug.

"After, really," Thomas observed. "My brother had already struck the fatal blow." Cleaner now, wiping his face with a cloth, the king stalked back to his place at the table with his draught of light ale. "I find I am hungry, in spite of everything. Do you mind?"

"Please," said Randall, pushing the provisions closer.

Seated at the side of the table, between the two, Elisha drank deeply, then tried a bit of sausage and found his stomach approved. The distance of the ride and the comfort of the small kitchen worked some magic of their own, allowing him to leave behind the most repulsive memories of the night. What he had instead was the fact he kept returning to, like a child picking at a scab: Morag was stronger, faster, more able to call upon his magic—simply better. Even with Chanterelle's intervention, Elisha lost the battle, and nearly lost their lives.

Morag's choice of Benedict's skin gave Elisha an advantage through the compassion he had shown the victim. Then, once he opened that dreadful passage, the mancer apparently couldn't help himself prolonging the sick pleasure of mingling with the misery of death. His distraction offered Elisha his chance to escape. A moment or two longer, and the soldiers would have imagined that the brothers had dueled to their deaths—while Morag's next battle would be won by calling on Elisha's own hide.

Elisha swallowed hard. So much for the peace of distance.

Horses trotted up outside, accompanied by the jingle of harness and the soft sound of voices.

"Well," said the duke. "The two of you should get some sleep. In the morning, we'll see what can be done. I'll have my men on guard at all times." He pushed back and bowed as he rose. "Well-met, Your Majesty. Welcome home." With his words, his scruffy king seemed to grow a few inches taller.

Elisha trailed Thomas upstairs to a low room that stretched the full length and width of the house. It contained four rope beds and a number of pallets on the floors where Brigit's soldiers had slept. It seemed too small and home-like for royalty. Thomas hung his lantern from a hook at the center of the room and gazed around. "We have much grander lodges," he said at last, "but my princesses liked this one." He wrapped himself in a cloak and lay down on the bed farthest from the stairs, facing into the room. For a moment, his blue eyes glinted sharply, then they slid shut, and he sighed.

Elisha, too, lay down, taking one of the pallets by the stairs. Soon, the ladies clattered in on the first floor, then came quietly up. "Duchess," Elisha whispered.

Allyson approached, settling on a nearby bed, while Rosalynn gave a little wave and took one at the far end with a number of blankets.

He sat up to face the Duchess, glanced at the others, then held out his hand, palm down. "Will you—?" But he did not know how to ask for the privilege of contact. They had never been so intimate before.

"You need to speak to me." She placed her hand over

his, so that her next words sank in through his flesh. "*I'm listening.*"

"*I fought a necromancer tonight, Your Grace. They are real—they're here.*"

She sent her understanding, radiating patience and concern.

"*He beat me badly. It's to luck alone that I survived, and he has a master even more powerful.*"

At that, the lady's face, so like her daughter's, furrowed with doubt. "*May I touch you more deeply?*"

Elisha nodded, then felt her awareness carefully extending over him, like a surgeon checking for unseen injury.

"*You seem well enough to me.*"

"*I drew upon the strength of crows, Your Grace, and more.*" Elisha sent her a few images from the night, the first encounter with Morag, his meeting with the *indivisi* and their testing of him, his collapse beneath the siege of terror, betrayal, and failure; he told her of reliving Benedict's death, of the moment he triggered Benedict's skin and fled the mancer's grip, letting her see how badly off he had been. Then he showed her the healing of Thomas. "*I did not mean to kill them, but each crow's death made me stronger.*"

"*You think the indivisi are right about you, that you are with Death, although the mancer denied it.*"

"*Twice at least I surprised him—when I gathered strength from the ancient dead and again when I used his talisman against him. Then the healing—I did not mean to kill them. I simply reached, and there it was, that power. The power I used to kill the king. Rosalynn told me that*

*mancers draw only from murder, from the fear and pain.
That might account for the crows but not for the rest.*" His
hand beneath hers balled into a fist, and his jaw ached
beneath the fresh bruise. "*I needed no crows to heal myself.*"

She studied him with her eyes, with her touch. "*What
do you want of me?*" she asked at last. "*Do you want me
to say that it's not true? That any magus could do those
things? That would be a lie. In the place of a recent killing,
I might feel the faintest chill. Could I gather the strength
of the departed? Certainly not, and I am a magus these
forty years and more.*"

She drew a breath then, as if she spoke aloud. "*Are
you then a necromancer? I have never heard that one of
them could heal.*" Her expression grew more serious.
"*And if you are with Death? The rule of polarity suggests
a man who knows death knows life as well.*"

"*It fits.*"

"*But what does it mean to be with Death?*"

They stared at each other in the gloom, then Allyson
said, "*Let us consider it and consult your learned surgeon.
It may be in his own search for knowledge that he has
found something to help us.*"

He nodded, but something more must have passed
between them, without his even willing it so, for she
drew back from him a little, allowing the lantern's light
to fall upon his face.

"*You're worried for him,*" she said.

"*I have killed two kings already, Your Grace, though I
never meant to kill at all. I could feel Alaric's death approaching. If I had been ready for it, I could have caught*

his death and held it in my heart, just like the crows. I think now, if I had taken it, what could I not have done?" Elisha's skin shivered. *"When the power is on me, I'm not always in control."*

Allyson bowed her head, but he felt the wave of her concern wash over him. *"It's one of the marks of the indivisi, that they become so devoted to their source that they can no longer distinguish its proper use. The source itself is enough for them. It . . . consumes them."*

In the dark, cool room, he heard the light breathing of Lady Rosalynn, the creak of the bed ropes as Thomas shifted his weight, still not at rest. *"Thank you, Your Grace. You've given me much to think on."* He slipped his hand away and pushed himself up, bowing.

"Elisha," she called softly after him, and he paused upon the stairs. "You still need rest."

"Yes, Your Grace," he told her, glancing back. "But not here."

He descended the narrow steps and startled the duke who stood by the entrance door muttering orders to a knight. "Not comfortable?" Duke Randall asked.

"Not really."

He frowned but said, "The kitchen's still warm, and there's a bench available. I thought I might . . . but you may as well."

"There's room for you upstairs, another bed."

The duke waved away his man and shut the door. "Tomorrow, you'll tell me everything. I need to know what's happened here. To you, as well as to him."

"Tomorrow, Your Grace." If he knew what to say. They nodded to each other, and Elisha found the bench while the duke creaked up the stairs. Cerberus occupied most of the tiled floor, sprawled in front of the dying flames, loyal and patient. If Elisha moved against Thomas, would the dog leap against him? Or would it stand in anxious confusion and let its master die? Beyond the sleeping dog, the kitchen door was shut against the darkness of the forest. If Elisha left now, he might slip past Alaric's men and the others who must be coming to find his killer. Instead, he settled on the bench, grateful for the heat. He might, himself, be a terrible threat, a formidable foe—but he knew now that there were others coming, others much stronger and more terrible than he. And nobody could know them better.

Chapter 28

———— ❖ ————

Elisha awoke to a furtive clatter in the kitchen and found Lady Rosalynn prying the lids from storage butts, and the fire already revived. "Good morning, my lady," he offered, and she turned to him.

"I was so hoping that it would be, but we haven't any eggs."

Elisha sat up, rubbing his aching jaw. "Sorry, I'm not quite awake yet. You need eggs?"

"At my brother's house, I learned to make biscuits, rather on a lark, and I thought I could make them today, you see, and that Prince Thomas might . . . well." She smoothed her hands down her skirts. "He's had such a difficult time of it, and I thought the biscuits would . . ." Her dark hair tumbled down around her face but not sufficiently to hide the hint of a blush at her cheeks.

Smiling to himself, Elisha recalled the sense he had, when he danced with her at the ball, that the disguised Thomas had more than a passing interest. "You like him."

Rosalynn turned quickly away. "I wouldn't say that,

simply that I appreciate what he did for me, with the bandits, and I know that he ..."

He crossed the room and lightly touched her shoulder. "My lady, I can get you eggs." She gazed up at him, her eyes wide, her smile wider. "Get your other ingredients ready. It won't be a moment."

Outside the kitchen door, he found the sun barely risen, and Cerberus stretching himself into a shaggy triangle. The dog trotted after as he went to the barn to find a few millet seeds. The last time he transformed seeds to eggs it had been to make a poultice for Thomas's branded palms. He should remember to check on the wounds, or tell someone else to do it. Eventually, the king would have his own physician in London with all sorts of expensive medicines Elisha could only imagine.

After seeing to his own needs, Elisha gathered a handful of seeds and brought them back to the kitchen where Rosalynn stood with a huge bowl of flour and a spoon in her hand. She was refreshingly unafraid of work. Elisha took a bowl of his own and set it on the table. He piled the seeds to the side, taking one. "How many?"

"I should say about five." Rosalynn stepped nearer, frowning. "I thought perhaps you'd seen chickens."

He pulled out a tattered talisman, barely remembering to clasp it tight in his fist so Rosalynn would not see it. The scrap was a bit of the fabric for Rosalynn's wedding dress—the one she never got to use after Alaric impugned her virginity and put her aside. Elisha let his talisman echo the magic, picturing the transformation, and there—an egg lay in his hand. She gasped, reaching out to touch it, then seemed to sag.

"I wish I had inherited my mother's skill."

Elisha made a dozen eggs, enough that he felt a tremor of weakness, to be expected after last night's adventures. He pushed the bowl toward her. "Witchcraft is hardly an easy legacy, my lady."

"I can see how hard it is for you, and I know what the terrible risks are, of course, but my father values it, doesn't he? It's not why they are together, but it's why they're glad they are." She gathered the bowl in her arms, gazing down at it, holding it as another woman might hold a baby.

In all his life, even when he might have hoped for daughters of his own, Elisha never imagined he might have such a conversation with a woman. She spoke of entering the convent, but she yearned for something else entirely and feared she would never have it. "You are generous, kind, and courageous, my lady. There are witches who should wish to be all that you are."

She smiled as she moved away, and he watched the tension ease out of her shoulders as she cracked the eggs and stirred her batter, beating at first too hard, then recalling herself and slowing. By the time they heard the household stirring around them, the smell of the biscuits drifted through every door.

"Good heavens, Mary, I didn't think—" The duke stopped short on the threshold. "Rosie?" He frowned as she looked up at him, the oven paddle in her hand. "I hardly expected you to—"

"'Thank you,' Your Grace," Elisha cut in. "I think the words you're looking for are 'thank you.'" It was too much, even given their relationship, but Randall accepted his intervention on his daughter's behalf.

Thomas followed him in, ducking beneath the lintel. "Thanks, indeed, my lady." He gave a bow, not too low as befit his higher rank but graceful enough. "It's been too long since this house felt a woman's presence."

She was blushing furiously but with her back toward the door; Elisha was the only one who knew. "I'll get the butter," he said. "And there's sausage as well."

Thomas noticed him then, with the slightest nod, as if he, too, had trouble knowing just who they were to each other: doctor and patient, comrades-in-arms, a king and a barber.

Thomas had begun to look his part, clad in some of his own old hunting clothes, an ensemble in green and brown, fine woolen trousers, silk shirt, a leather jerkin worked with patterns of leaves. His hair was combed back, at any rate, his beard still too long and wild, hiding his lips. His clothes hung a bit loose on his tall frame. Elisha, too, wore one of those shirts, borrowed from the king's possessions; but for Elisha, the sleeves were long, the shoulders a bit tight. The bruise on his jaw throbbed in time with a dozen other injuries. He must have looked like the last drunk standing at a tavern brawl. It was he who had brought these people together, and now it was he who should depart from where he did not belong.

Breakfast conversation was sporadic, and the meal seemed longer as the number of topics they avoided expanded as well. When the soldiers came in for their own mess, the little party adjourned to the solar with its diamond-paned windows and painted walls. Elisha trailed after and perched on a chest by the window. The ladies shared a long settee, leaving two cloth chairs for the duke and the king, but Thomas, restless, remained standing, running his fingers over the books that lay on his desk, his gaze finding one then another of the little things a prince might keep: a glass inkwell, an ivory miniature of the crucifixion, a sprig of dried herbs that hung from the rafters.

It was Duke Randall at last with his customary directness who broached the first difficult topic. "Your Highness, will you seek the throne?"

Thomas's blue gaze flicked to Elisha, then to the duke. "Your Grace, I am the heir, born and raised, but I have no army. You know better than I what the barons might think."

"They think you a traitor. They believe you hired that young physician Benedict to kill your father, even though the plan did not succeed." He held up his hand as Elisha moved to speak. "There was a note, Your Highness, offering to build a medical school if he obeyed you. The barons don't want such an eager prince. If you had tried to best Hugh by right of arms, they might have been swayed, but poison and subterfuge they won't countenance. The church, especially, is against you."

Head bowed, Thomas folded his arms, but Elisha said, "Alaric as much as admitted he wrote that note. He planned to frame Thomas for the killing and take advantage of the barons' anger."

"So you say, but who are your witnesses, now that Alaric is dead?" Randall's round face looked surprisingly stern. "There's none but you and Thomas. We can give out the story that Alaric hired out King Hugh's death, of course, and let that rumor spread, but neither of you is an uninterested party, and your association will only seem to substantiate the claims of those who believe the conspiracy. I've always been a supporter of yours, Your Highness, I think you know that, but I don't know that we can stand against the rest of England, especially not with the church backing the other side."

"They would need another candidate," Thomas pointed out.

"I can think of half a dozen in France alone who'd love to turn the bad blood over Hugh's succession into a chance to make their claim. They tried to woo Alaric into an alliance and are paying some calls on the barons as well. It'll be a few days at least before they hear of Alaric's death, but you'd best believe there will be French armies calling in a matter of months if we can't unite the barons at home."

"Lord Roger Mortimer has his own plans," Elisha pointed out. "If he hadn't broken their gift to Alaric, I'd guess he's involved with the French."

Randall cocked his head. "Unless he broke it to deflect suspicion? Hmm."

And the mancers had a candidate of their own, Elisha thought. But who it might be, and how they hoped to get so close to the throne again, he could not say. The idea that they would try it chilled him. He had not had much chance to sort through what Morag and his master had said. More to the point, he wanted to talk it over with Thomas, who knew more about royal politics than he did.

"If you had any surviving children—forgive me for saying it, Your Highness—that might make a difference to the barons. They might have been willing to accept a regency on behalf of the next generation." Duke Randall steepled his hands, elbows propped on his chair.

Thomas finally sank into the chair provided for him, and with such a weight that Elisha winced. He unfurled his awareness to the walls of the room, sensing the tremors of emotion.

"Really, dear," Allyson murmured, and Rosalynn looked as if she wanted to fly to Thomas's side to comfort him.

Thomas looked up, his expression bleak, but his words strong. "We can ride to London and seize the treasury. It's worked in the past. With your backing, we might make it stick long enough to sway some of the others. I'll need to find a way to make amends with the church. I can swear an oath in good faith that I had nothing to do with my father's death. With luck, we can build an army strong enough to match the French, especially if their support is divided among more than one candidate."

The duke sighed. "We've not fully recovered from the battle of Dunbury Ford, Your Highness. Neither in terms of army resources, nor goodwill among the barons. Some were my supporters, others sided with the king and transferred their loyalty to Alaric readily enough. We can field an army, we could even match a handful of French competitors. If they draw up behind a single candidate . . ." he spread his hands. "Your guess is as good as mine, Your Highness."

Thomas nodded. "Some of your men can ride for the treasury and seize it in my name, while I go to Canterbury and swear an oath. We gather up what support we can and plan for war. It's either that or I renounce my birthright and live in exile. My father-in-law might take me in."

"Would he support you in battle?"

"It's hard to say. He's under excommunication, and he's still fighting off the supporters of his rival emperor. I don't know that he has much to offer."

It took Elisha a moment to remember: Thomas's father-in-law, the Holy Roman Emperor. Elisha felt briefly dizzy at the level of the conversation. He shut his eyes, kneaded his temples. These men were planning the fate of their country, worrying over France, thinking to draw in the Emperor himself. Either way, it would be war: civil war among the barons, war with the various duchies of France. Against the backdrop of his closed eyes, he saw the battlefields of Dunbury, the houses burned, the pits of the bombards' strikes, the bodies burned and broken, some of them still screaming for release, crying for mercy from an unlistening God. Elisha would be there again, crawling among them. He had more tools now than sutures and saw, but even with magic he could heal only one man at a time, and there would always be too many. He could smell the blood, the burned skin, the foreboding reek of powder that hung in the sky. Last time, he did not know what the battle was for. This time, he might well know every little plan and goal and still be as helpless as ever. What was magic for, if it was powerless in the face of war?

"No," said Elisha, raising his head. "No, Your Grace. There need be no war."

The duke broke off his enumeration of the barons he

thought he might count on, and every eye turned to Elisha.

"Arrest me." Elisha swallowed hard, dodging Thomas's keen blue eyes and addressing the duke. "Bring me to trial for killing King Hugh. Let the new king bring me to justice and win his own reprieve." He knotted his hands together, the burn scars along his arm tingling as he spoke. "The church and the barons would unite for that—"

Thomas's voice came soft and hard, "They would unite to watch you die."

Chapter 29

"No!" cried Rosalynn, "It's too horrible!" Allyson wrapped her arms about her daughter's shoulders.

"It is horrible," the duke muttered, "but likely effective. It would deny that his highness played any role in the death and show his commitment to justice."

But Elisha ignored them. He stared at Thomas, who met his gaze. Elisha's heart thundered. This was what loyalty meant, the fealty they spoke of in poetry, that a man might be willing to die for his king. But it was rare for the man to claim his own choice in the matter.

"No," said Thomas, sitting up straighter. "There's got to be another way."

"You've just listed them, Your Majesty, and I didn't hear one that ends without war."

"I've just found you," Thomas murmured. "I wouldn't be here if not for you, and you want me to tie you to the stake. The answer is no."

At the suggestion of the stake, Elisha's throat went dry, and he nearly acquiesced, but the fact that Thomas cared enough to want to stop him gave him the strength to go on. His friends and neighbors, the peasants he served, deserved such a king. "I've been speaking to Duchess Allyson, among others, about this . . . power I have." The talisman in its jar rolled on its thong against his leg—an unconscious summoning? "My knowledge of healing and dying gives me affinities that others can't use. I can do things that surprised even the necromancer." He took a deep breath, and shared the last. "I think, given all that I've learned, there is a very real chance that I cannot die."

"What?" said the duke, but his wife made a little sound of discovery.

"'A very real chance'?" Thomas asked. "You seemed near enough to dying last night."

Elisha nodded. "But it also made me see I have a special relationship with Death. I can feel it coming, I can locate it around me, I can use it, as I did during the healing. If I know what I'm facing, Death cannot touch me." He held his breath, hoping he sounded more confident than he was.

"So I should put your head on the block, because there's a very real chance that you'll somehow survive? I can't do that, not to you." Thomas burst from his chair, his belt slapping as he turned away. He flung himself against the mantel, gripping it with both hands, his entire body tensed as if to push down the chimney. Cerberus emerged from the kitchen, already growling, looking for the threat to his master.

"Darling?" Duke Randall prompted his wife, drawing Elisha's gaze back to the settee the duchess shared with her daughter. Rosalynn's gaze stayed on Thomas, her brows drawn up.

Allyson tapped her cheek thoughtfully, studying Elisha. "I think it's possible. He has all the signs of becoming *indivisi*. He has little training yet, but if he can channel this skill, if he had knowledge of the circumstances, the mode of execution, we could plan for it. We must, of course, seek a method that—" She offered a faint smile. "One that leaves the body intact. Even a skilled healer would have difficulty overcoming certain kinds of wounds."

No matter how carefully she spoke, Elisha conjured images one after another of terrible ways to die: drawing and quartering, beheading, hanging, burning—by God, what had he talked himself in to?

"Even if we did it, there's the problem of myself," the duke mused. "Elisha's been living in my household at apparent liberty for better than a month. I can't suddenly throw him to the wolves, just because Thomas demands his arrest, especially knowing how weak is Your Highness's position with the other barons. They'd smell something rotten right away—they might even suspect Elisha's collusion. Most of them have heard that he's a witch. It might well look like a sorcerous conspiracy, or some undue influence. The whole thing would be tainted from the start."

Rosalynn was nodding her agreement, her dark hair glossy with combing, the house still smelling of her fresh-baked biscuits, then she stilled, watching Thomas. She spoke almost at a whisper, her eyes keen. "It needn't be, Father. Not if His Highness were able to persuade you to give up your retainer." She looked to Elisha then, her hands together, pleading and apologizing.

"Yes, Rosie, but how would he do that?" Randall smiled indulgently, but Elisha had begun to see where her thoughts were leading—where her dreams might be realized. "With all due respect, Your Highness," Randall said, "you don't really have much to offer at the moment. Not much that would convince the barons, in any case."

"He does, actually," said Rosalynn, then she bit her lip, and Elisha could feel her focus and her fear.

He wondered if Thomas himself were ready to hear of it. As much as he wanted the gift of the king's friendship, that was too great a gift to offer, far too great if it cost them the kingdom in another war. But, the conversation this morning had shown him that Thomas was a practical man—ready to lead, ready to rule, ready to make the choices that he must. Elisha released his clenched fingers, stretching his scarred palms, and gave Rosalynn a little nod.

She raised her brows, swallowed, took a deep breath, and finally said it. "His hand, Father."

Thomas's head shot up, his profile sharp as he stared back over his shoulder. The others still frowned for a long moment before Allyson raised her eyebrows at her daughter. Rosalynn ducked her head, looking anywhere but at Thomas, and finally met Elisha's gaze with a little flaring of her eyes, and the slightest curve of her generous lips. He could feel her nervousness giving way to a desperate hope.

"That is too bold," the duke remarked, but softly. "Really, quite extraordinary."

At the mantel, the portrait of his dead princesses

hanging over his head, Thomas merely stared. His grip now seemed to be saving him from falling.

Duke Randall went on slowly, in that same speculative tone. "The accused traitor Prince Thomas persuades me to give up my retainer, who killed his father, in exchange for marrying my daughter. Prince Thomas shows himself just, as well as prudent, and willing to serve the needs of his crown by remarrying. If I were another baron who heard this tale, I would believe it."

Thomas's jaw knotted. Finally, he blurted, "He's right. Damn it all!" He slapped his palms on the mantel, wincing, and shoved away, striding for the door. He glanced at Rosalynn. "Forgive me, ladies. He's right. And I would be proud to marry you. With your consent, of course."

For a moment, Thomas leveled at Elisha a furious gaze that blazed with the intensity of his thousand mixed emotions. With a distracted bow, he spun on his heel and strode away, Cerberus loping after. A moment later, a door slammed. Elisha had not known him long, but he had the sense that Thomas did not often use profanity. Even the burst of his anger held a pent-up quality that struck through Elisha's awareness. In the king's wake, the others seemed excited, the ideas coming together as Randall and Allyson picked out the details, and Rosalynn simply sat, her outer stillness belied by the humming that emanated from her presence. Thomas, the king, would have her! She hardly expected any man to be eager for her company after Alaric's denunciation, and now she would be queen. Elisha's two companions could marry, to the betterment of both, and all Elisha need do was die.

A soft rap at the door made them all turn, then Mordecai the Surgeon entered, giving a bow. "I apologize for my lateness, Your Graces. Had to see to some injuries at the abbey. Something about an earthquake." He raised his eyebrows. "How much have I missed? A good deal, I gather."

"An understatement," Elisha said, taking his friend's hand in greeting.

"Perhaps I should ...?" Rosalynn stood, smiling faintly, and her father dismissed her with a nod.

Her parents watched her go, and Elisha wondered if they saw what he did, the new assurance in her stride, the subdued way she spoke, her attentive listening.

"I do believe this journey has done her good," Duchess Allyson remarked. "In more ways than one."

Silently, in the way of the witches, Elisha laid out the plan for Mordecai. The surgeon's grip tightened. When he replied, he spoke aloud, "May well be right about death, Elisha. But cannot-be-killed is not the same as cannot-feel-pain."

Elisha scowled at him. "*You didn't need to tell them that.*"

"*If not your friends, they are at least your patrons. They should know what they have agreed to.*"

"I hadn't thought of that," the duke mused. "I know you're good, Elisha, but really, it's a bit much."

"If you have a better idea, Your Grace, I'll be glad to hear it."

"We may be able to arrange an escape. The key is for Prince Thomas to have you arrested for the murder. Many things can happen between arrest and execution,"

Duchess Allyson pointed out. "You might well escape and remain at large, as it were."

"Or appear to die prematurely, in prison." Mordecai released his hand and came to stand beside him, placing a warm hand on Elisha's shoulder, radiating calm. "Between the three of us magi, we ought to be able to find such a solution."

"Good," said the duke. "That's good. Thomas will be relieved. He can go to Canterbury afterward to swear his oath, if it still seems necessary. But we must act quickly, no matter our course. We'd like the French to hear of it as soon as possible on the heels of Alaric's death."

"And the mancers?" Elisha asked.

"What about them? Their man is dead. Even if they have another candidate, they'll be hard-pressed to put forward anyone with a clear claim. If we move fast to build Thomas's support, they would be facing the strength of the barons united."

"We'll need to watch out for the mancers," said Allyson. "We'll need to know how many there are, and who and where."

Elisha smiled grimly. "I'll have time to look for them when I'm dead. Morag, I would recognize. The other man probably not. But they have a way of travel like nothing I've heard of. They can appear and disappear at will." He described what he had experienced during Morag's flight from the abbey, and what he had seen the night before, concluding with Morag's delight in the horrible passage, drawing strength from the misery of the dead.

The hand went still upon his shoulder. Randall raised

an eyebrow at Allyson, but she shook her head. "I wish I knew what to say. There are rumors in the old texts about witches being carried great distances by devils."

"Might be worth some reading." Mordecai tapped one of his own collection of books swaying on their ropes at his waist.

Before him rose the fireplace where Thomas had stood, beneath the portrait of his wife and daughter. "There's more," he said. "Morag has a talisman of Thomas's wife."

"Oh, dear God!" Allyson crossed herself.

"But how?" asked the duke. "It's true enough Anna was murdered, but we all saw her buried. Her body was in a better state than poor Alfleda's."

He turned a bit pale, his lips pressed together, and Elisha did not need his extra senses to feel the duke's dread. Still, Elisha needed to know, now, while Thomas was out of earshot. "Was she skinned?"

"Good Gracious, no! But her face was . . ." the duke's hand moved before his own face, indicating terrible blows.

"Morag is a gravedigger. That's likely how he had access to get what he wanted from the princesses. He took the skin of the Frenchman—I saw that when I went down before the burial to study the man's wounds. The killer was a magus, too, but I'm not sure who he was working for."

Through their contact, Elisha felt Mordecai's fleeting pain at the memory of his murdered family—followed by gratitude that they need not suffer after death. Then the talisman at Elisha's belt grew heavy as he thought on the fate of families. He needed to take care of his nephew's remains. Soon he would leave here, in chains, for the Tower of London. If he would do something, it must be now.

Elisha rose, sending his gratitude to Mordecai for his support. "If you have no further need of me, Your Graces, there's something I should take care of." He bowed to each.

"Perhaps Mordecai Surgeon will consult with me on some methods to avoid execution," Allyson suggested, and the surgeon gave a nod.

"Elisha," said the duke, rising, his hand extended. He clasped Elisha's with both of his. "If I did not know Thomas would be the finest of kings . . ."

"I know," Elisha answered.

"Thank you." The duke managed a smile. "I still believe you'd have made me a fine son-in-law."

Chapter 30

◆

Elisha emerged into the sun and stood a moment, captured by the view. The lodge stood atop a fold of land with a spread of apple trees leading down the slope to a broad stream and a long pool at the bottom. Beyond this, patches of forest, downs, and fens rippled out in deep green, yellow, lavender, and brown. And there, at the horizon, he caught glimpses of the sea. No wonder the princesses had loved it here and that Thomas had returned to this, his last refuge. Where would Elisha go, when he escaped whatever punishment must be set for him? He had given up his home in London to his brother's widow, and he would give up his place at Dunbury for this mad scheme to succeed. He needed to search for the mancers, to learn what they were doing; he had no doubt they would act against Thomas. Whatever it was they wanted, a just king was not high upon their list.

He turned away, crossing the path to the barn where he found a small shovel. The downs would have been a good place to conceal the talisman, even the barrow where Brigit had kept it, except he felt sure she would be looking again soon. She would be seeking the truth of Alaric's death, and she was familiar enough with the talisman that she might discover it, even without marking it with her blood. Likewise, his own blood wouldn't serve. He had neither time nor liberty to find the best way to hide it forever. Elisha stretched his senses through the earth, searching. He stopped too soon, when he felt Thomas's approach. Stepping from the shadowed barn, Elisha felt too visible in the sunlight, carrying a shovel and the vessel of the child's head.

Thomas, too, stopped, rounding the corner of the house from the back where a stone wall rose. "Lady Rosalynn is in the kitchen, presiding over supper, I believe, but it won't be ready for some time. She is . . . kind. Also commanding, when she wants to be."

"I hope she has not overstepped her place," Elisha said.

Coming closer, Thomas shook his head. His hair and beard were damp, freshly washed. "I meant to consider the options dispassionately, but I did not think through what those options might be. The barons wanted me to marry after only a few months of mourning. Two years is a bit long."

"I guessed what she had in mind. You must be pleased . . ." But Elisha trailed off at Thomas's expression.

"Pleased?"

Elisha felt suddenly awkward, revealing what he had noticed, but he took a breath and said, "At the ball, when you watched us dancing . . . afterward, I could sense your attraction. I thought you would be pleased to know that Rosalynn returned the feeling."

"You could sense something like that?" Thomas looked wary, accompanied by a tremor of worry and something else. Bemusement?

"I meant nothing by it, Majesty. You were disguised, I was curious. I'm sorry." Elisha swallowed. Clearly, he had got something wrong. "You'll need to learn to guard your feelings more closely, Your Majesty. I'm not the only magus who can sense them."

"I see." Then Thomas gave a little smile. "I'm sure Lady Rosalynn will make an excellent wife and queen. Don't be concerned on that account." He spread his hands, still wrapped in their bandages.

"May I, Your Majesty?" Elisha gestured toward his hands, and Thomas held out the left to be unwrapped and inspected.

"I'd almost forgotten your more ordinary talents," Thomas murmured, the two of them looking at the brand, healing on his palm.

The warmth of Thomas's proximity jarred against his regal speech, as if he were putting back on the raiment of kingship. "I should have healed them last night, Your Majesty." Elisha glanced up. "I still could."

Thomas shook his head. "You need your strength. I'm not the only one who lost blood last night."

"They're healing well, Majesty. You may wish to keep them covered a few days longer." Elisha released him.

"I gave you the right to my name, Elisha. I wish you would accept it."

"It's hard for me to know how to act. On the great chain of being, a barber is the lowest link, a king . . ." he shrugged.

"It is difficult, but we shall make the best of it. Were you looking for something?" He stepped back, indicating the shovel.

With a sigh, Elisha told him the truth. "A graveyard." He carried the jar cradled in the crook of his elbow.

Thomas touched his arm. "In a few hours we must be enemies before the world. Until then, would you please let me be your friend?"

Beyond them, away from the sparkling sea, rose a thick stand of forest right up to the back of the barn, tangled with vines, the trees raised to be straight and tall, towering above. "If you knew the truth, you would not ask my friendship."

"Elisha, I know what's in the jar—the necromancers told me. What could you say to explain it that would be worse than anything I might imagine?"

The forest seemed to sway with memories and sadness, oak trees shaking their leaves in the shadows. "My brother's child was stillborn, or would have been. The midwife kept it secret for reasons of her own." He took a deep breath. "Nathaniel and I had quarreled, years before, so they did not ask for my help until she was in labor, and it was going badly. The only way to save the mother was to—" His jaw ached, and he forced himself to relax. "—to cut the baby. I don't know what madness was on me, but I thought I might bring it back to life, so I kept the head."

Thomas wore fine leather boots now, that was good. A king should not go unshod.

"There's more," Thomas prompted, but gently, his voice drifting over Elisha's bowed head.

Elisha's fist tightened on the shovel. "My brother thought his wife and child had both died." He came to the part of the story he had never told, the part that some suspected, but he never dared confirm. In a whisper, he said, "He killed himself. I took the blame for his murder, rather than have him buried outside the church. It's why I was sent to battle, expected to die." The hard weight of the jar pressed close to his chest. By the front door, the guards were talking. In the kitchen, Rosalynn's voice rose over whoever followed her bidding. Birds chattered in the trees and rushed from limb to limb upon the wind.

"Come with me." Thomas lightly touched Elisha's arm and walked toward the woods. Numbly, Elisha followed. He could sense the drift of Thomas's compassion, but he pushed it away, drawing back his awareness as they walked a narrow path behind the walled structure at the back of the lodge. Grapevines trailed over the top of the wall, snagging at his shirt. They continued past the wall and a short distance into the forest. The trees opened suddenly to a tiny church of stone, its peak barely the height of the wall they had left behind, smaller even than the barrow where he and Thomas hid from the soldiers. Even Elisha must stoop to enter the open arch. Alongside the chapel, two stones lay flat on the earth, carved with words and numbers.

"Alfleda was my second child." Thomas's voice was low, but even. "The first was stillborn. The two younger boys were carried off by a fever when Alfleda was four. She alone survived."

Elisha shut his eyes against the magnitude of such

grief. His king carried the deaths of four children, and the wife who had borne them.

"It was deemed better to bury them here than to take them to London and risk spreading the sickness." Thomas paused, and there was a shift of weight and mood. "I did not bring you here for your pity, Elisha. It is consecrated ground. Will it serve?"

He found the king watching him, frowning slightly, and Elisha found his voice. "It will. Thank you."

Thomas waited while Elisha dug a little hole, not too near the princes. He wasn't sure how much magic could linger once he had gone, but he worked a deflection on the jar, then sent his senses into the earth. The princes were longer dead, their presences muted, but noticeable. His nephew was in the best of company. Elisha covered over the jar, giving the little grave a scatter of old leaves.

In a clear voice over his head, Thomas recited, "*Pater Noster qui est in caelis, sanctificetur nomen tuum. Adveniat regnum tuum. Fiat voluntas tua, sicut in caelo et in terra. Panem nostrum quotidianum da nobis hodie, et dimitte nobis debita nostra, sicut et nos dimittimus debitoribus nostris. Et ne nos inducas in tentationem, sed libera nos a malo. Amen.*"

"Amen," Elisha echoed.

The forest and the church as well echoed the holy words, and Elisha wondered if the Lord might deign to listen to the prayers of a king, even on behalf of a sinner like himself.

After a moment, Thomas said, "If we buried you alive, would you survive?"

Elisha wiped the dirt from his hands, considering. "I

think so. I know a woman who can survive beneath the earth. I've witnessed her doing it. But it's an uncommon punishment."

"You'd prefer to be drawn and quartered?"

"Duchess Allyson thinks we can arrange for my escape before the execution."

"I pray to God you can, Elisha, but if something were to go wrong, I'd hate to know it too late."

Elisha nearly laughed. "Me, too."

"It's hard to say what influence I'll have on the trial, but I'll do what I can." Thomas shifted his weight, glancing at Elisha sidelong. "I was looking for you, when you came out of the barn. They weren't sure where you'd gone."

Taking the shovel, Elisha rose. "What's your will?"

Thomas ran a hand over his unruly beard. "I find myself in need of a barber." He reached in the front of his jerkin and took out a pair of shears and a folded razor, but his sharp eyes searched Elisha's face uncertainly.

Elisha shivered, studying the familiar objects.

"I need to be a king tomorrow," Thomas said, "and you're the best barber for miles around."

"And likely the only one," Elisha muttered. He had not held a razor since his brother had used one as the instrument of his death. He had known two kings and killed them both. A strong argument in its own right. Elisha shook his head. "I don't know, Thomas."

"You're afraid of killing me, yet I'm the one who will be killing you. You trusted me with the truth, Elisha. Now let me prove my trust in you."

Curiously, the determination in Thomas's sharp gaze

made him more like his father than Elisha had ever noticed before. If King Hugh's iron will had been harnessed for justice rather than arbitrary judgment, Elisha might not have had to kill him. As for killing Alaric, he would not have given up his ambitions so easily. Rather, those events would have passed without Elisha's knowledge: A king would die, his elder son accused of the crime, the younger prince taking command, and on the streets where Elisha lived and worked, he would have been none the wiser. The succession would have been a matter for gossip and hope—likely vain—that taxes wouldn't rise with the new king's accession. The rise of one prince instead of another would not be a cause for personal investment certainly not for sacrifice. Was Elisha better off before he knew the affairs of kings?

"I'll need a basin," he said, taking the tools into his hand, "a comb, and better light or I'm liable to cut your ear off."

Thomas brightened, lifting the shovel from Elisha's grip. "Have you seen the garden? This way."

At the back of the lodge, Thomas pointed Elisha toward an arch into the stone enclosure he had noticed earlier. "Won't be a moment."

Elisha ducked the arch and stepped through.

Inside, the place was a festival of color. A thousand flowers danced in the breeze, and on the cherry trees lining the back wall. The flowers took all shapes, long stems of open cups and delicate sprays of whiteness. Trailing vines of tiny purple blooms obscured the pathways while climbing roses scented the breeze. It looked as if this place alone, of all the house, thrived, even in its owners' absence. Owners who had so cared for it that it continued to blossom, sending forth flowers few had ever seen.

Elisha breathed in the fragrant air and held the breath, the blooms suffusing his blood. He had never seen so many flowers. Few villagers he knew had the resources to tend flower gardens, but contented themselves with those of the field, small, pale, hardy things compared with these. It reminded him of the ball where he first met Thomas, a room full of court ladies, bowing and flirting, brushing his arms as he walked further in to stand at the center, turning in wonder.

His gaze picked out the niches in the walls, bronze statues and marble offering secret glints among the brightness. Benches fitted the corners, covered with leaves and overgrown with all sorts of beauty.

"The princess garden," Thomas said, his face softened as he crossed the space between them, carrying a bowl of water in his hands. "Anna made this place. She was so happy to have a daughter to share it with."

"They must have loved it." Elisha set the bowl on one end of a bench gesturing for Thomas to sit.

The king produce a comb and handed it over. "Morag, the necromancer. Somehow, he . . ." Thomas trailed off, his face once more grim.

"I'll find him, Your Majesty." With deft strokes, he combed out the king's wet hair. "Shut your eyes." The comb and shears felt a bit awkward in his scarred hands, after months of wielding his surgical instruments instead, but he glided them over the king's skin, carefully trimming the fringe over his forehead back into fashion, a trickle of brown hair tumbling down. "After the trial, I'll search for him. The duke seems to think we've little to fear, now that their candidate for the crown is gone."

"He's wrong." Thomas's eyes snapped open. "What we heard last night—there is more at stake here than my crown. I need to know what." His hand traced a path along his sternum and clenched into a fist.

"I'll find out." Elisha moved around the bench, combing and snipping.

"I can't imagine who else could do it."

"You're not afraid they'll convert me?" Elisha asked lightly, trying to cover his lingering fear.

"Are you hoping to die, so you needn't live in fear of yourself?"

The question cut too close and Elisha hesitated, shears in hand, standing at Thomas's back.

"There was a time, not long ago," the king said softly, "that I would have been tempted to follow the easier road." For a time, both men were silent, fairy thimbles and bellflowers bobbing around them as if considering their words. "Whatever else you may have done, Elisha, you have healed me."

Elisha caught the tremor of that warm wave of gratitude, and he finished with the king's hair, moving on to trim his beard to a manageable length, still putting off the moment he must take up the razor. "You're lucky to have this place to return to, Thomas. I gave up my house in London. I'm not sure, actually, where I'll go, afterward." He shied away from mention of the execution.

"You'll come here," said Thomas firmly. "At least I'll know where to find you."

"Thank you."

Better groomed, better dressed, the prince had a high, clear brow and a lean, handsome face to frame those keen eyes, and hints of the honored King Edward showing in his build. Thomas tilted his chin back, exposing his throat, slivers of blue eyes watching Elisha.

Taking the razor, Elisha weighed it in his palm. He could not help seeing Nathaniel, his golden younger brother, lying dead by the cut of a similar blade.

"Next time we meet will likely be in court," Thomas murmured. "Whatever I say, whatever I do, you must remember that I am your friend. God grant me the strength to counterfeit hatred. I must play Judas and every moment I shall be living in Hell."

Elisha checked the blade and found it sharp. His stomach soured at the thought that he must face the king in court.

"Forgive me, Elisha, what I must do. I cannot help but hurt you."

Carefully, Elisha set the blade and made his first stroke.

Chapter 31

◈

By dawn the next day, everything had changed.

Elisha's borrowed tunic was replaced by a knee-length white linen garment, the reminder of his new status—or rather, the erasure of any status he might have had. A soldier took away his medical kit, handing it ceremoniously to Thomas, who gripped it a little too tightly. According to the plan, it should be hidden along with fresh clothes and other supplies to await his escape, but its loss made Elisha feel naked in spite of his gown. As a barber in London, he had owned little—never imagining he would lose it all, down to his dignity.

A fresh troop of soldiers arrived, drawing a cart. The duke's family had been moved away, the king arrayed in his finest clothes, tall and handsome as a king should be. His eyes shone, his beard trimmed to frame his mouth though it seemed set into a hard line. He stared at Elisha with disdain—a good act, though Elisha could feel the regret that surged beneath it. Other witches might be less sensitive, but the king should be more guarded with his emotions. When they brought up the chains, Thomas's fury and sorrow near exploded, then he made an effort to conceal his feelings, and the anger vanished. He suppressed it with a snarl that any other might have taken for his contempt at the criminal.

Elisha swallowed hard as the manacles closed upon him, and the soldiers urged him into the cart. Duke Randall stood nearby, allowed to show mixed emotions as evidence of the bargain he had made, to give up Elisha and see his daughter wed. Randall's right-hand man, Lord Robert, had arrived, shaking his head at this turn of events but still willing to obey the duke and take command of Elisha's passage to London. The duke and the king would ride on ahead in a display of solidarity, making way for the trial to come.

Mordecai had sent him a magical draught of strength and courage and then slipped away, still working on the plan that would set Elisha free.

The mists of the morning river curled around the cart as it creaked into motion, finding every pit and hump along the road. Elisha tried to find a comfortable position, but nothing would do. He rattled against the sides of the cart, his bare arms and legs scraped, his hands drawn down by the weight of the chains that bound him. The lodge dwindled behind him, trees closing in around the path. Four mounted soldiers rode behind, with more on foot. At first, Cerberus lagged behind as well, the cart about on a level with his tall head. He whimpered at Elisha, raising his ears, trying a tail wag from time to time. Then a whistle sounded from up ahead, and the dog gave a last wave of his tail before he trotted off to join his master. Elisha's heart sank. In some ways, his would be the easier part in this deception: He would be brought to London to face the charges. When he heard from Allyson or Mordecai, he would act on what they told him, or prepare to defeat the chosen punishment. They would smuggle him a talisman of some kind at the right time; he would be searched when he entered the Tower, so there was little point in carrying anything now. All he must do was tell the truth about his deeds. That, and endure.

A small shadow swept over him and circled back. A crow. The scratches on his back left by the angry crows on the night of the healing stung in some affinity with the circling bird. It let out a single "Caw!" The harsh sound made him flinch. Another crow joined the first. The leaves above rustled with a few more crows that jumped from tree to tree, black flitting shapes that broke off from the shadowed branches and merged back into them. They cackled together over his head, soaring and circling back again, over and over, a vortex of sharp beaks and black feathers. No apology would be enough for them or for their mistress. Elisha lowered his gaze, hunching against the front of the cart.

"What the bloody Hell?" one of the soldiers muttered, watching the birds above.

"They're his familiar animals, aren't they? He's drawn 'em out. We best be careful," his companion said darkly, training his gaze on Elisha.

With a sharp cry, one of the crows dove. Elisha dropped even lower, and the bird swept over him, pulling up and streaking away again.

"He sent 'em at me! Did you see?" the first soldier demanded.

The horses snorted, as much at their riders' nervousness as at the crows that came nearer with each dive. The next one grazed Elisha's arm as it defended his head. "I'm sorry!" he shouted after it.

"What's going on here? Where'd all these birds come from? Elisha?" Lord Robert rode alongside the cart, frowning down at him.

"Don't, my lord, he'll—"

"Shut up," Robert growled over his shoulder. "Come on, Elisha. Hugh's been dead for a month, and now they arrest you? I don't know what's come between you and the duke, and I don't have to like it, but I'm meant to get you there safe. What can you tell me?"

Elisha lifted his head. "I offended the mistress of the crows. They hate me."

A clutch of birds broke off, aiming for his face, and Robert drew his sword and with a harsh cry of his own, slashed through their midst before they reached Elisha. A few cut feathers drifted into the cart.

"You!" Robert pointed the sword at the fearful guard. "Ride back as quick as you can and fetch us a blanket. We'll cover the cart."

"Aye, my lord." The soldier turned his mount and kicked it into motion.

Robert rested the flat of his blade on his shoulder. Once, in defense of a fallen earl on the battlefield, that blade had crossed Elisha's throat when he was mistaken for a looter. Robert was quick to action, especially in defense of his comrades, but quick to forgive as well. They had been almost friends before now. "Thank you," Elisha said. Robert glanced back and gave a nod, his thinning hair ruffled by the breeze of wild wings. When the birds dove again, Robert's blade lashed out efficiently and returned to the guard position, a practiced move probably meant to slice the heads of standing enemies.

The crows shrieked their insults and shat upon his horse. Robert grimaced. They repeated this sally-and-retreat a few more times before the soldier returned with a horse blanket. Tremulously, he came up to drape it over the cart.

"Good work," said Robert, then Elisha watched the side of his horse trot back up toward the front. Beneath the cover, the cart quickly grew humid, but at least the crows couldn't reach him. Still, at every stop for bread or to see to his natural needs, they attacked with beaks and talons. He slept curled into the cart, smelling the straw, the horse that pulled him, and the stink of his own sweat. Every night, he heard the birds settling onto the cart rails, their claws scraping the thick material, and every morning he woke to early sun casting their shadows on his makeshift roof. If they could figure a way beneath it, they would have pecked out his eyes.

Their angry cries accompanied him all the way to London. Seven days? Elisha lost count in his fervent wish that it all be over. Just outside the city, a troop of yeomen from the Tower came out to meet the cart, and stripped off the blanket to expose the criminal to all the curious who came out from the farmsteads and gathered along the streets. A number of familiar faces watched him go by, some with fear, some with compassion, some who turned away when he caught their eye. The crows resumed their hectoring, and one sliced his brow with a

sharp beak just as they reached the Tower, leaving a
trickle of blood that oozed down his face. He wiped it
away with his chained and weary hands, looking up at
last to the rooftops of the king's castle. It gleamed in pale
gray stone with white edging, obscured by the flights of
dark birds that circled over him. The cart moved beneath
a gatehouse, wheels clattering over stone, the passage
interrupting the pattern of crows. The spikes of a portcullis stuck out overhead, then a smooth ceiling broken
by a square door which would allow boiling oil to be
splashed down on any trapped there. A second portcullis,
then an open yard where the cart groaned to a halt.

The Tower guard must have been warned not to touch
him, for they urged him down with shouts and pike
staves. Some gave wicked grins, wielding their pikes as if
to skewer him. Elisha rose, twisting away from the curled
and gleaming blades. He stumbled down from the cart,
catching himself, his legs feeling weak after the last several days of bread and water and limited movement.

Lord Robert kept his mount, dominating the soldiers.
"Leave off, you! Let the lords pass judgment!" He kneed
his horse into their midst, forcing them back before he
slid down and tossed his reins to one of them.

"Don't touch him, Lord!" called one of the yeoman.

Robert scowled as he came to Elisha's side. "I daresay
if he wanted my life, he'd've taken it." Robert cupped
Elisha's elbow and led him onward, his sympathy lend-
ing more strength than he could know. With his friend
beside him, Elisha walked taller, fighting down the rising
beat of his heart. In spite of the misery of the last few

days, this was not his only friend. He had not been abandoned—he would not be. He must believe it.

"The king's called for summary judgment," Robert muttered from the side of his mouth, "so we're straight to court. It's a damned shame King Thomas didn't get the chance to know you, nor you him. He's a good man, for all this. Trials like this, it's not customary for the accused even to speak."

"I can't claim innocence: there's too many witnesses," Elisha murmured back. "Including the duke."

"Blast it!" Robert's other hand slapped his sword hilt. "I doubt he'll testify against you, but the idea's probably enough." They stopped outside a tall, peaked door, and Robert faced him, with a slight bow. "I'm sorry it's ending this way."

"Not your fault," Elisha told him. "You've done what you could." He longed to give Robert more reassurance, to promise they would meet again, but the fewer people who knew about the plan, the safer they all would be.

Robert pulled out a kerchief and wiped the blood from Elisha's face, a gesture so motherly that Elisha smiled. Robert glowered back at him, snapping the kerchief away. He shoved open the door into the courtroom, gesturing Elisha through, but with his eyes averted, shining as he blinked repeatedly.

The courtroom glowed with candles on high rings of silver. Light glittered off the golden robes of the two attendant bishops, off the silver chains of office worn by the mayor and the gathering of lords, off the ruby rings on Duke Randall's right hand, off the gold and jeweled crown that graced the head of His Royal Majesty, Thomas, By Grace of God, the King of England.

The ermine of his collar turned buttery in that light, the velvet soft and near the color of flame. And all of this finery stood arrayed against Elisha so he had to squint a little in the shimmering hall. He bowed as best he could, and crossed with the yeomen to a wooden rail that faced the great company.

A herald stood forward. "Before all the witnesses here present, his most august majesty, King Thomas, does hereby accuse one Elisha of London, a barber-surgeon, of high treason in the death of his majesty's illustrious father and predecessor, King Hugh. There being seventeen sworn testimonies to this most foul murder, the lords of this court have found the defendant to be guilty, may God have mercy on his soul."

Thomas did not look at him as this document was read out. Duke Randall made fists with his ruby-decked fingers, and the man beside him, the slender Earl of Blackmere grimaced, his face pinched with concern, perhaps recalling how Elisha's intervention on the battlefield had saved his life. The bishops looked stern, and one of them crossed himself with slow reverence.

"Defendant to be hanged, cut down from the scaffold, drawn and quartered, each quarter to be sent to the four corners of the kingdom in warning against this grievous offence. Punishment to be carried out on the morrow."

Chapter 32

❧

Elisha's breath caught in his throat, his ears echoing the terrible laughter of crows. He clung to the wooden rail as his knees trembled.

With a sweep of velvet and a narrow glare, the king rose. "My lords, your graces," he inclined his head to the bishops and nobles, "I have not long been your king, but please indulge me a boon on behalf of my father."

The elder of the two bishops, a chubby man whose miter seemed to dig into his flesh, likewise inclined his head—a prince of the church acknowledging a secular ruler. "What is your request, Your Majesty?"

"I had reason to address the prisoner after his capture at the New Forest. At that time, he sought to sway my opinion in his favor. He spoke about his life here in London, and about his brother." Thomas paused. "I assume you know the details of the case, even more than I. I think it fair to say that he is haunted by his brother's death."

"Rightly so, given the circumstances, Your Majesty," the bishop sniffed.

"There is little so haunting, indeed, so disturbing as the thought of that untimely grave. This is what we find so appalling about murder—not merely the theft of the Lord's gift of life, but that long wait beneath the ground for judgment day, a wait made even longer for the sinner sent early beneath the earth, condemned to a few more days or months or years to suffer purgatory before he shall meet his maker." Thomas stood straight and fierce, staring directly at Elisha, his face impassive and blue eyes blazing as if he had never wished for anything more devoutly than this. "In honor of my father, and of the prisoner's brother, both gone untimely to their graves, I ask that the defendant be buried alive, cast into the cold bosom of the earth to plead with the Devil himself for his release."

The tide of Elisha's relief warred with the dread weight of the king's words. He had known the moment would come, but to hear Thomas argue for his execution still sent a spike of terror through Elisha's very soul.

"There, in the grave to which he cast his victim, he shall lose first the glory of God's creation and the warmth of His light, then the very air that sustains him, then any hope of freedom, trapped as he should be in a coffin made straight and narrow."

Every word he spoke seemed to craft that coffin, and Elisha forced himself to watch the king, to search for the signs of the compassion he knew lurked beneath this talk of God and the grave. Thomas strove to convince their audience it was, in fact, a fate worse than death. His crown gleamed, his eyes so sharp and blue, his stare so hard Elisha shivered.

"See!" Thomas cried, pointing. "See how he trembles at the very thought of it! Pain, hanging, cutting—all of that, he can withstand, for he has suffered such punishments before, but this is a thing no sane man can face."

Every eye in the courtroom was on Elisha, then the king.

"It's hardly customary, Your Majesty," remarked the other bishop, a tall man with a long face.

"True, true," the elder bishop replied, "but the king has spoken eloquently of his reason, and the prisoner does appear, at last, to have the fear of God upon him. If it is deemed vital to display his remains, he may always be exhumed at a later date."

"So you would submit to this whim? And what would the lords?"

"It's a travesty," snapped the Earl of Blackmere. "From beginning to brutal end, and you all know it." He surged from his seat with a swirl of his brocaded cloak, his left arm still held close and stiff.

At his side, Duke Randall said, "Phillip, please sit. You know it'll get no better." He gestured toward the vacated chair. "If it will satisfy the debt you think you owe, then His Majesty may see fit to make you jailor, that the prisoner's stay here be as brief and merciful as may be."

The Earl hesitated, dropping his gaze when he caught Elisha's eye. His shoulders slumped with a flutter of silk, and he sat again, heavily, taking back his arm from the duke's gentle grasp.

Duke Randall and Thomas exchanged a brief glance, and the duke spread his hands in apology. "Indeed, Your Majesty has spoken well. I harbor no objection."

"He survived the hanging and came back for his revenge, didn't he?" one of the other lords pointed out. "He can't get out of this—not if we pile enough rocks on top." A few in the back row shared a grim laugh. "No, Your Majesty, we're with you."

"Thank you, my lord Gloucester, and all of you, on behalf of my family." With all the grace of royalty, Thomas settled into his chair.

"Do you think it possible, Your Majesty," said Mortimer, leaning forward from his place at the back, "that he was involved with your brother's death?"

"His grudge against my father appears to have been personal." Thomas regarded him solemnly. "Much as I wish for justice, my lord Mortimer, I doubt the truth of my brother's death will ever be known."

Mortimer gave a nod, but a rumble of frustration echoed around the room until Thomas held up his palm for silence. "Please, my lords. We would all like to be certain what happened to Alaric, but the evidence is scant. Royal verderers and the soldiers of Dunbury shall finish their clearing of the New Forest, and no brigand will dare return—that shall have to suffice. Let us not delay our proceeding any longer than we must. Let our justice be swift that our enemies may fear and do us no wrong."

Gloucester gave a cheer to that, but settled down. The herald stamped the end of his staff against the floor. "Let the king's justice be pronounced and spread throughout the land!" This gave way to a louder cheer, and two yeoman caught Elisha's elbows to pull him away. Again, the Earl of Blackmere sprang to his feet, looking to the king, who gave a nod that sent him jogging from his place to push through the doors with Elisha's captors.

"Hear me now, the lot of you! There's to be no beatings, no torture, none of that."

"Yes, my lord," said the yeoman warder with a short grin, a clove clasped between his teeth, but he gave Elisha a dark look. "None of that, my lord."

"Phillip!" Duke Randall called, and the earl stopped, uncertain, and allowed them to go on without him.

As they walked, the corridors narrowed and darkened. The air grew damp, and they finally deposited Elisha in a small, stone chamber, a single slab of stone to serve him for bed, bench, and table. He suffered a moment's hope when they unlocked the chain at his wrists, but this was only to transfer him to a longer chain fixed to a ring on the wall. One man held the single torch while the warder shoved Elisha to his knees, then took a grip of his hair—still short from his last execution—and tipped Elisha's face toward the floor.

"Hold still, or don't—'s up to you." The warder pulled something from his belt and opened it not far from Elisha's face: a razor. He imagined the warder slitting his throat, pre-empting the execution and all that they had planned. Elisha's body went rigid, but he stretched out his senses, the one skill left him without any talisman. If he were indeed *indivisi*, he would need none. As it was, he hardly needed attunement to show him the warder's disgust, but there was no murderous intent. The razor sheared along his scalp, leaving a chill, black hair scattering before him, sprinkling the ground around his lowered head.

"Do you know what it's like to be buried alive?" said the warder conversationally. "My da was the village sexton. He had the opening of tombs from time to time."

The blade snicked Elisha's skin, and he winced, drawing a chuckle from the warder. "Get a fair number of people as weren't so dead as we thought. They scrape their hands to bits, trying to get out." He bent Elisha's ear to draw the razor along one side of his head. "They break their noses and their cheeks. They batter their brains right out of their skulls, what with the dark and the knowing what's coming. Imagine being trapped in there, the space getting closer and closer. They scream their throats bloody, but there's nobody to hear, is there?"

Elisha's own throat felt dry and tight, the space growing smaller with each word, quietly and precisely delivered as a nail.

"How long does a person live in the narrow box, you suppose? Couple hours, maybe? In a crypt, they last for days. Some of them get so thirsty, they start drinking their own piss. They bite off their own fingers and eat their own flesh. Was a pregnant girl once, died and laid out in the family tomb. We come back months later to lay down her brother, and we find her on the floor, her winding clothes ripped, her baby in her arms and both of them dead, huddled together like, their skin just hanging over their oozing guts."

When he had finished shaving, he nudged Elisha's chin back up again, admiring his handiwork. "But at least they weren't alone."

He met Elisha's gaze with a grin. "Now you look the proper killer." With his boot, he scraped the fallen locks together and kicked them into the stinking recess in one corner.

"Clear out." The warder commanded on a breath of clove, and they all trickled away, the iron grate clanging shut behind them, secured with a giant bolt. Elisha sank down on his heels, watching the light recede down the corridor until he was left in the dark, the cold biting his knees, the smell assaulting his nostrils, alone but for the echoes of those who had been there before him, and the lingering sound of the warder's voice.

Somewhere high above him, Thomas met with his barons, every conversation and handclasp cementing his crown. Or so Elisha made himself believe, for without that belief, all that happened would have no meaning. The image of a dead woman clinging to a dead baby hovered in his vision, haunting the darker recesses. He would not die alone, in the dark. He must believe that, too.

He had just begun to appraise his surroundings, the new chains that held him, and the grubby stones that entrapped him, when he turned to the sound of heavy treads and found a new light arriving. "Did they not even leave you the torch? I'll have a word." The Earl of Blackmere surveyed him with something like sadness. "The king's got to avenge his father, I suppose, but I do wish it'd been someone else." He wrinkled his nose.

Elisha rose and bowed. "It's kind of you to say so, my lord."

"Kind, nothing. Practical, more like. There's too few good medical men these days." Blackmere stepped closer to the grate. "There's a visitor who's asked to see you," he said, almost apologetically. "By law, you're not to have any, except the confessor who'll be by tomorrow, but, well, there it is. I am in charge, after all." He straightened and pushed his torch into a brace on the wall. "I'll send him," he said as he vanished into the gloom.

Him? Even before the visitor arrived, Elisha felt sure he'd guessed, and his anger grew when Martin Draper slipped back his hood and clutched the bars.

"Get out!" Elisha shouted. "You can't be here. Did anyone see you?"

Jolted, Martin jerked away, his sharp eyes darting. "No, Elisha, no. I'm not such a fool as that."

"By God, Martin, you should be denouncing me in every parlor down the merchant's row."

"If I denounced you too much, I'd only paint a worse picture for myself. Don't be cross, Elisha." He put his hand through the bars, and Elisha glowered at it, noticing that the usual array of jewels had been left behind. The Master of the Draper's Guild had even deigned to wear homespun wools to conceal himself. His eyebrows pinched together, and he beckoned with that hand.

With a snort of irritation, Elisha clasped it, his chain clattering. *"You have to get out of here, Martin,"* he warned. *"You can't afford to be associated with me."*

"Oh, tush," Martin replied, his inner voice clear and firm. *"I've got to get you out of here, if I could think of a way. I even dared appeal to the magi, and I haven't spoken to most of them in years."*

"Don't do that." Elisha quailed at the thought. If Martin drummed up a rescue attempt, the whole thing would fall in a shambles around his ears. Elisha had never imagined how their plan would affect his old friends.

"I tried to get a talisman I could smuggle to you, but the market in saints is off this season, and I know how you feel about hanged man's rope, besides which they searched me on the way in."

His agitation buzzing to the surface, Elisha fumed, *"Don't try anything, Martin. The crime is mine."*

"But you did it for the highest of reasons, Elisha! I thought Duke Randall, at least, understood that."

"Please don't blame the duke." Elisha shook his head. *"Every man must play at politics in this bloody kingdom."*

Martin raised a hand and touched Elisha's scalp, his finger a trace of regret on Elisha's skin. *"This is even worse than your last haircut, Eli."*

Turning his head away, Elisha broke the contact. "Please go."

"Something's going on here, Eli, I can see it, even if you won't own up to it. I thought Thomas was supposed to be the weak one, too merciful to be a good leader, but he won't even give you a decent trial."

"I don't want one," he snapped back, the pain on Martin's face telling him all that he refused to feel. "Why drag this out? Why not get it done and over?"

"Why do you want to die?" Martin asked, his voice childlike, as if the answer mattered more than he would admit.

Elisha stared at him through the bars, and chose the truth. "Because I would like to be wrong about who I am."

Furrowing his brow, Martin protested, "I don't understand you, Elisha."

"I know." With a sigh, Elisha softened. "Isn't that why you love me?"

Martin gave a rueful smile. "You know me too well."

"I do," he said, "and that is why you have to go. Now." He came up and set his hands on the bars.

Briefly, Martin clasped his hands over Elisha's. His dark eyes blinked back tears, then he pushed himself up on his toes and kissed him, a fleeting warmth and a breath of wine. Dropping back, shaking, Martin flipped the hood over his head and hurried away.

Letting his forehead rest on the grate, Elisha took a breath and let it out slow. He wet his lips, tasting a hint of orange and a touch of love. Come back, he wanted to say. Don't leave me with all of your regrets. Worse yet would be Elisha's betrayal of their friendship, if this were not his last night on earth. "Oh, God," he groaned to Martin's absence. In that moment, he understood polarity better than he ever had before: this absence was too thick with presence, too full of lost potential to ever seem empty.

Then he thought of Brigit. Wherever she was, in the shock of loss and mourning her prince, she would have heard the king's decree. Would she come to see him die? When he had been about to hang, he saw so clearly her face in the rain, peeking from under her cloak, giving him the secret smile that made him believe in her; she would save him, he was convinced. Instead, she failed him, as she had failed him ever since.

Disgusted with himself, Elisha pushed away from the bars and slumped on the stone slab. Despair seeped up through the stones. The pain of men who had been tortured, and the grief of those about to die, remained trapped here, compounded year after year in the two centuries or more since the castle had been raised. He was tempted to wallow in other men's griefs, to let himself go in favor of this emotional storm and not have to feel his own. Instead, he drew himself inside, deep and deep until he could not feel a thing, and he stayed that way until the worried Earl had him shaken from his apparent stupor and left him with his supper.

What was the point of eating? Shrugging the question aside, Elisha dug in. If Thomas and the duke wanted him well-treated, then they had chosen the best man for the job in the Earl of Blackmere. Rather than the usual prison fare, whatever that might be, the plate held a mound of parsnips in some sort of glaze with half a chicken similarly prepared. Elisha washed the meal down with the contents of a wooden bottle, which turned out to be a light mead. If all prisoners were so well-fed, more peasants would turn criminal.

When he was done, Elisha slipped back into that trance of un-being, conserving his strength for whatever would come in the morning.

Chapter 33

The day brought first a bowl of fresh berries—compliments of his keeper—and a half-loaf of filling bread. Restless with confinement and waiting, Elisha devoured it and returned to pacing. It seemed as if he had awaited this day for twenty years, ever since watching Rowena die had set him on his course. As if he had known at the back of his mind that there could be no other fate. Yesterday, he had tried to keep his hopes high, to regain that confidence he used to have—the arrogance that got him through as much trouble as it had gotten him into. Now, he tried simply to keep from screaming. His control ebbed away in nervousness until the cell once more echoed with the laments of those long dead.

On the other hand, this inadvertent awareness told him someone was approaching, and before long, he could hear shuffling steps, accompanied by others more sure. An elderly priest made his way down the hall, lurching against the wall with every second step, keeping himself on track. Beside him, a veiled nun provided escort and guidance, encouraging him with her quiet voice.

Joy surged up in Elisha as he came to greet them, a sloppy grin threatening to take over his face.

"Kneel," the priest commanded in a gravelly voice, his eyes focused somewhere to Elisha's left.

"Aye, Father." Elisha did as he was told, as Sister Lucretia set down a folding stool for her ward, then knelt beside him.

"Father Jerome has come to hear your confession," the nun announced, crossing herself. "He's deaf as a stone and as good as blind," she confessed in her turn, with a wavering smile. "I know you're not much for the Church."

"Just seeing you again does my soul good," he told her.

Eagerly, she reached through the bars to clasp his hands. "Oh, Eli, to find you again, only to find you here. How I have prayed for you, for God to find it in His Heart to forgive you."

Bringing the warmth of her hands close to his face, Elisha shut his eyes and breathed in her friendship, drawing her compassion from the contact they shared. Years before, Lucretia had been a young prostitute, desperately ill, and Elisha's intervention had saved her life. She had left the brothel in favor of the convent, believing that he had been the answer to a prayer. "Thank you," he murmured. "I don't think the Lord has time for me, but thanks for trying."

"Don't say that, Elisha. Even if you have not been faithful to the Lord, still there's no harm in asking for His aid, especially today." Fear shot through her, but she quelled it again with her faith.

"How's Helena? How is she taking this?"

Lucretia lowered her gaze, clinging a little more strongly to his hands. "She's upset. It's brought it all back for her, and of course, people will talk. I besought her to come see you, if they'd allow it since she is family, but ..." she let out a breath.

"Helena may have forgiven me, but I'm still a reminder that her husband is gone, and why. Will you tell her I'm sorry? I don't mean to dredge up all the pain for her." That sense of guilt which always hovered near Helena in his mind settled again over his shoulders, muffling the pleasure he took in seeing Lucretia.

"Have you anything else to confess?" Father Jerome demanded, swiveling his head to focus on some other unoccupied space.

Elisha stiffened at the question. It seemed not to be random, as if the old man had seen his guilt even through clouded eyes.

"It's the stories of witchcraft that have her most dismayed, Eli." She frowned at their hands. "Her sister has been telling her that you, well, you ... I do not know how to say this, or even if I should."

Quietly, he voiced what she could not bring herself to say. "Her sister thinks I had more to do with the baby's death?"

A quick nod. "She's claimed you had some need for infant's blood, and that's the real reason you fled. If you had been innocent, she says, wouldn't you have stayed to succor the widow."

"I had no choice! Aside from the fact that the widow cursed me to my face." He beat his forehead against the bars. He shouldn't have brought it up. He should have left Lucretia's visit untainted by these memories, for his own sake in preserving some guard against the growing fear.

She rested her forehead against his. After a moment of the quiet rhythm of her breathing, and the priest's shifting around on his seat, she said, "If you wish to confess, I will go off, for a while."

He felt the tingle of her curiosity in her skin. She had faith, she wanted to believe him innocent, but she had doubt as well. "No," he whispered, "not now."

"You are, aren't you?" she murmured, drawing away, her eyes roving across his face. "If you were not, you should have protested more."

"It isn't what you think, Lucy." He shook his head, wanting to explain it all and afraid to at the same time. He wanted to assure her he was no servant of evil, and yet how could he be sure? How could a man who drew strength from the dead claim to be in the service of God?

With a muffled cry, she released his hands, wriggling her arms back to her own side of the grate as she stared at him. Struggling with her heavy habit, she pulled herself to her feet.

"Please, Sister," he cried and bit down on his lip to stop the quaver in his voice. "Please, I need your prayers now more than ever."

She wavered, one hand on the silver cross at her neck. "Yes, I can see that you would," she said faintly. "I will not lecture you—you attended mass often enough to understand your sins. Is Helena's sister right about you? When did the Devil find you?" In the echo of her voice, he heard the question she did not ask: had she herself been so wrong?

Pulling himself up on the bars, he swallowed the tang of blood. "Sister, I have never been in league with the Devil, and the Church was all I knew of witches until weeks after I left here. We don't kill infants."

"No," she said, blinking. "Apparently you kill kings. I cannot reconcile this with the man that you were, Elisha."

Elisha grasped what hope he could. "Do you still work at the hospital?"

She nodded once.

"You use the medicines and treatments that you can, and you heal some, and some of them die. Some of them die no matter what you do. What if God gave you a way to heal them? Wouldn't you try it?"

Lucretia stepped a little further back. "You are trying to entrap me, aren't you? I've heard of moments like this."

"No, I am entreating you. You know me, Lucy, you know who I am and what I stand for. There's nothing to reconcile because I am still here, I'm still the man I always was."

Flicking a tear from her cheek, she said, "It isn't me you need to convince." Then she slipped a hand under the priest's arm and dragged him up. "Come, Father, we're done here."

"What, what?" he asked. "You've got to speak up." As she drew him into motion, he turned back over his shoulder and made a cross in the air. "Te absolvo," he muttered. "Te absolvo."

Absolved and abandoned, Elisha sank to the floor holding back tears. She was right, of course she was. He wanted to live, and yet no man could, not without unnatural power. He was meant to face a slow, terrifying death. And no one had come to give him the means to escape it. If he died, if he let go of his magic, could he face the judgment of God and of history?

Men came for him and led him down the dark corridor to stand blinking in the sunlight. The earl looked away, rocking on his heels as the cart was brought around. A phalanx of armed men glittered in the light of day, but Elisha hardly saw them. His mind turned over on itself. If he died, Thomas would blame himself. If he lived, he could never see any of his friends again. If he died, he was no servant of evil. If he lived—Was Allyson evil? Or Martin, who dared to love men instead of women and must, therefore, be more evil than the others? What about Brigit and her mother, desperate to save their people and willing to use any means? Were not ordinary princes taken by that same ambition?

They prodded him into the cart, his bound arms held before him. But if a soul as loving as Lucretia's could not allow for magic, then could it not be he who was deceived? The oxcart lurched into motion, and he swayed, but did not fall.

People lined the streets, jeering. Something smacked against his head and oozed down—an egg. Elisha almost laughed. Once, he had thrown an egg at King Hugh, a diversion to chase him away. Now it seemed his every deed would return to haunt him. Fitting, on this, the day he should die.

Rotten vegetables exploded on the cart and on his body, wetting him with the stink of decay.

Something brushed his hand, something piercingly hot in the chill of his turmoil. A man in a monk's robe and broad-brimmed hat walked alongside, a thick Bible in his hands. His lips moved, and Elisha caught the chant of Latin verses. *"You need to concentrate in order to go through with this,"* said Mordecai's voice inside his head. He did not look up.

Clamping his jaw, Elisha shook with fear and confusion. *"I can't—I don't know how any more."*

"You can," he said, his voice sharp and urgent. *"Listen to me, Elisha, listen. There is a torrent of emotion pouring from you."* His fingers dug into the wooden covers of his book. *"What has happened to you?"*

Gathering his wits, Elisha framed the moment in the cell with Lucretia, the loss of one of his dearest friends. His hand brushed Mordecai's raised fist wrapped around the book. In that contact, he projected his conflicts. He had no time to polish the sending, to make it more bearable, and he saw Mordecai reel with the shock of it.

"I'm sorry," he gasped to the air.

"Then hear your own words, Elisha. Why are we here? Why are there magi at all? Ha shem created the heavens and the earth and all the creatures who live here. We are a part of His work, Elisha. Some men are kings, and some are healers, and some of us are magic."

Mordecai jerked his head up, the Latin litany faltering as they approached the gate. *"There is no time."* The hat twitched aside as Mordecai met Elisha's eyes. Mordecai's stricken face begged for understanding, but he shoved the hat back into place. "*The talisman will be under your right hand. The headboard of the coffin is loosely nailed, you should be able to pull it in. There's a bundle of clothes at the Red Lion Inn, in the crook of the stable eaves.*" His shoulders hunched, and he clutched the book to his chest. "*You must not give up, Elisha, you're almost free!*"

But the cart bounced around the corner, forcing Mordecai back into the crowd as the crossroads came into view, and no words could have won Elisha back from the terror that swept through his heart.

He should have expected to be buried at a crossroads, the traditional place for suicides, murderers, witches. The crowd left an open yard around the area, broader in one patch where the king sat tall upon a wooden throne, his courtiers arrayed around him so that Elisha could not see his face as they approached. Clergymen of all ranks interspersed among them, prepared to defend their immortal souls and to be sure that God's justice, as well as the king's, should be served. On the packed earth, a coffin lay open atop a pair of ropes, ready to lower it down into the gaping pit. A man in an executioner's mask stood by, weighing a hammer in his gloved hands. A mound of dirt towered beside him, two men leaned on their shovels, waiting, and one of them was Morag.

Chapter 34

❖

Just for an instant, Elisha had seen his face, the blunt features, the crooked grin with its blackened teeth. Their eyes met, then the crowd shifted, crying out for Elisha's death, and the man was just a stranger, chewing on a stalk of grass, doing his job.

Morag! Even if Elisha had mistaken this stranger for that other, much stranger, gravedigger, enough of Morag's presence lingered here that it chilled Elisha, skin and bone. Whiffs of ruined flesh drifted on the air, the sting of old tortures and the faintest echo of dying moans. Morag had been here. By Christ, what had he done? Had he stolen the talisman, replaced the coffin, nailed the loose board so Elisha would suffocate under the dirt?

"No," Elisha shouted, resisting as the soldiers came around to grab his elbows and help him from the cart. He struggled against their grip. "No, Your Majesty, don't do this!" He flailed, and they pulled him down, tumbling to the ground at first, then hauled up again, their fingers digging into his arms. "Your Majesty, please!"

He stubbed his toes on the ground, anything to slow their pace as they dragged him forward. Thomas couldn't help him even if he wanted to, and Elisha felt sick knowing how his shouts must pierce the king's heart. "I'm sorry," he cried, and the threatening tears stung his eyes.

"Too late for that, Devilspawn!" a woman shrieked, her face contorted, her finger jabbing at him.

He tried to ignore her, searching the crowd. Where was Mordecai? If he could reach him—but what would the surgeon do? A Jew disguised as a monk, coming to his rescue with sorcery? They'd be for the fire for certain.

"The barber's bald!" shouted a man nearby, followed by the splat of a rotted onion that seeped into his thin garment. Elisha shivered, as much from the hatred as from the chill.

"Where's your brother's child, butcher?" someone called.

Elisha's eyes blurred the faces of the crowd. He racked his mind for someone who could help him, anyone. Focus! He forced himself to see, but he recognized too many of the faces: children whose births he had assisted, men whose bones he had set, women whose hair he cut just so. Or rather, he thought he recognized them until he saw the hatred that twisted their lips and the scraps of garbage in their hands. A group of the whores who used to come to him for cures opened their bodices and laughed, displaying the breasts he would never touch. He had steeled himself to be ignored by the king, but not to be so thoroughly reviled by those he always sought to aid.

Elisha bowed his head, forcing back tears that would only give them more fodder for their curses. He brought up his arms to cover his ears, but it did not matter, the disgust and fury of the crowd crashed over him. Their loathing cut him. Hoots and brays of laughter stung his skin.

Guards pushed back the crowd, struggling to do their duty. If anyone caught Elisha's eye, they thrust up sticks or fingers forming the cross. Shivering uncontrollably now, Elisha felt the cold tendrils of Death reaching out for him. His teeth chattered. His enemy had been there, and his friends could do nothing but watch, believing he would find the means they had provided for his escape. They would watch in vain, and his attempts to reach them now would only torture them later, when they realized they had failed him.

The calloused hands of his guards felt too hard, too angry or, worse, too uncaring, as if he were not a man about to be buried alive, but a corpse indeed, ready to be thrown to its rest.

His skin itched with the mounting hatred, the curses lashing against him. He had once withstood twenty-seven lashes without weeping, but that bravado dissolved beneath the weight of other men's emotions. He tried to curl back into himself as he had inside the cell, but the curses pierced him still, his defenses weakened first by Lucretia, then demolished by that sense of Morag. He tried to cling to Mordecai's voice inside his skull, the details of the plan he had proposed. Then his shadow touched the coffin laid out just for him.

The sky overhead went dark. Losing sight of his

shadow, Elisha looked up. Thousands of crows swirled in the air above. They croaked, mocking him from on high, come to see him fulfill their mistress's curse. More and more of them arrived from all directions, soaring and wheeling over the crowd, the black mass of their enormous flock centered over the coffin. A few of them perched on the edges and defecated on it, defiling the place of his death.

The human gathering, silent at the crows' appearance, began to murmur and huddle a little closer to each other.

"They'll think I am the Devil now for certain," Elisha muttered, glancing back up at the circling birds.

One of the guards spat at his feet. "You're not so high as that. I've heard how the Devil takes his witches."

Elisha swallowed the tide of nausea rising from his gut. He, too, had heard the stories, the Devil seducing his handmaidens for their evil work. No wonder the crowd was disgusted by him—men were supposed to be stronger than that. Thank God no one had seen the kiss in the dungeon last night, or they'd throw Martin in the grave as well.

The chubby bishop was arrayed in cloth-of-gold and decked with a jeweled scapular. The staff he carried gleamed with yet more wealth, especially the golden cross at its peak, glittering in the sunlight that shifted through the wings of the circling birds.

Raising his arms, the bishop began to mumble something in Latin. Many of those in the lords' echelon bowed their heads and folded their hands together, and the gathered clergymen, be they monks or priests, moved their lips in echo.

As he had in Father Michael's faith and Lucretia's compassion, Elisha felt the power of the Church, in a physical way. This time, the words of the liturgy rebounded all around him in a sort of binding and repelling spell, bent on casting him out, banning the Devil he was thought to serve. He could not understand the words, but their intention was plain enough, and they hummed in the air and in the earth beneath his feet. As the chant grew, it drowned out the excited peasant crowds beyond, then even the raucous crows. It beat upon his ears louder and louder.

The guards brought him to stand with his toes at the coffin's edge, facing the rough wood. It looked dark and mottled, as if they had expelled its last victim to make way for him. Could this be Morag's work? Elisha gulped for breath.

The force of the Church's mystic language died away, leaving a resounding silence, and Elisha brought his eyes back to the crowd. In his position, Rowena, knowing herself to be without escape, had used her final power to make an angel of herself. She tried to show her accusers that she held the power of God, not of the Devil, and they had shot her full of arrows for it. Elisha contemplated a similar attempt, drawing up the power he would have in that moment to sway the crowd with some spectacle even more astounding than his death. But when his death came, perhaps hours after they'd topped him with the final clod, he would be already buried, the coffin tight around him, the earth and stones piled upon him. Any casting he could make must reach beyond the grave in the most awful, literal sense.

It was too late for mercy or confession, for him to fall upon his knees and pray, or beg forgiveness, or whatever it would take to set him free.

His hands writhed, torn by the metal cuffs. His eyes cast about for help. And fell upon Thomas. King Thomas, with Rosalynn at his side. They sat on a raised daïs to his right, set back from the crossroads, with only the soldiers and the clergymen interrupting their view. The duke of Dunbury stood behind his daughter, his hand upon her shoulder, his face grim and mournful. Rosalynn had placed her hand over his, protectively. Even from here, he saw the darkness that rimmed her eyes.

Thomas sat rigid, his eyes vacant, his lips drawn together. His expression held a severe concentration, as if he were forced to sit through a performance he did not enjoy but could not leave. There was nothing of compassion in the face beneath the crown.

The prayers finished, the herald pronounced Elisha's fate. The yeoman warder shoved his back, and Elisha fell into the coffin, face down so that he would never see the Kingdom of Heaven. Horror slapped his skin, a dread beyond the mere moment. Morag had been here. In some awful, creeping way, Elisha was not alone.

Immediately, he tried to scramble up, his bound hands under him, scraping the wood, his toes already bloody as he heaved himself to his knees. The heavy shaft of a pike slammed into his back, knocking the breath out of him as he fell. Blood ran from his nose and lips. His cry of pain became a blood-spattered cough. The sharp point of the weapon pinned him down, piercing his shoulder.

Crows cackled, the only light that reached him broken by the swirl and flap of their wings. With a scrape of wood and a cheer from the crowd, the darkness encroached and was suddenly complete, the pike snatched back, that pressure gone, only to be replaced by the amplified sound of a pounding hammer driving nails into his coffin.

Elisha gasped and coughed and finally caught his breath. His hands ached, trapped beneath him. His own blood confused the signs and he thrust out his awareness, hurrying, desperate to counter whatever Morag had planned. He could feel the stamping of the crowd, the victory of the priests and lords, the bouncing feet of the children, trying to see.

Elisha's questing fingers, seeking a more comfortable place, found an edge of wood beneath his right hand. The talisman, just as Mordecai had told him. Thank God! He had just enough room to shift to one side, his back pressing the coffin's lid, his left shoulder giving a stab of pain. His stubby nails pried loose the scrap of wood, and something slipped into his hand. His fingers closed around it, and all that was outside of him was swept away by horror and remorse.

In his hand, he held his own razor, closed, its bone handle smoothed by years of use. The rivets that held it formed cool dimples against his skin. Something interrupted the flow of the thing, a bond holding it shut, but Elisha barely felt it as the stored emotions it held swarmed up through his hand. His brother had died with this razor.

Just for a moment, he caught a glimpse of Nathaniel—no, he was inside of him, feeling the tension of waiting, the fear for his wife almost more than he could bear. In his tinsmith's shop, he worked endlessly over a cooking pot, smoothing down a repair. Footsteps hurried up, and the midwife appeared in the workshop door, her hair wild, her hands bloody.

"He's done it," she spat through shriveled lips. "Your damned brother's killed your baby, and your wife, too. I told you to wait for the physician, but you—"

Nathaniel staggered to his feet, the file and pot clattering to the floor, forgotten in an instant as disbelief and grief welled up in him. He ran for the door, shoving past the little woman. "Helena! Sweet Lord, Helena!"

In a few of his long strides, he came to the door of the house they shared. He mounted the first step and froze, for he heard his brother's voice. Elisha sounded furious and exhausted in the same breath, his insufferable arrogance finally pushed aside for a problem he could not solve. "If he'd only got to me sooner, maybe then. Or the hospital . . ."

Gasping on the steps, unable to get enough air in his lungs, Nathaniel trapped a cry in his throat. It was true. Elisha had always known what to do, while he floundered along, too poor to support the wife he'd taken, not to mention the child. His baby. Dead and butchered. Sweet Jesus, what had he done to deserve this day?

"Nothing!" Elisha wanted to cry out. "Nothing! It wasn't your fault. I was wrong, Nate—" But the events witnessed through his brother's eyes had happened months before, and he was as helpless now as he had been then. Through his brother's ears, he hated the sound of his own voice.

Nathaniel fell back from the stairs. He had lost it all, everything in one terrible moment when he had done the wrong thing. Swallowing his grief, he turned away and saw the razor and basin set aside upon the heap of their furniture, moved out of the way for the failed operation inside. The razor winked in the sun, the brass basin an inviting empty vessel, waiting once again to be filled. The tools of Elisha's ostensible trade. Nathaniel knew better. He knew that Eli's true work was the healing, stitching up wounds and setting bones. Even as he despised his brother's unholy pride, he knew, too, that it was justified. Elisha had healed a thousand men, while Nathaniel could only mend their pots.

He took up the tools and returned to his own place, the dark calm of the workshop that was his domain. His beautiful Helena was dead because he couldn't accept his brother's apology, couldn't accept it because he might have to admit that he, too, had doubted his wife, had doubted why she would marry someone like him, poor and hopeless. If he could have bowed to his brother a long time ago, everything would be different now. His family might have lived. Nathaniel laughed in a way that Elisha found achingly familiar. Hadn't Nathaniel's own pride been just as great?

One of the seven deadly sins, the ones you could not just atone for, the ones the apostle Paul himself reported would prevent the sinner from entering Heaven. Nathaniel opened the razor, tilting it in the shaft of sunlight that split his workshop wall. It didn't matter now what God would think of him: his Helena was dead, sacrificed to his stupid pride. He opened the razor and leaned over the waiting gleam of the empty basin.

Chapter 35

❖

Elisha jerked himself out of the memory. They had provided a talisman all right, but one too strong. He couldn't control it, it overran his own awareness. He caught gasping breaths, trying to find his balance, but it was gone. His brother's guilt rushed through him, mingling with and mirroring his own. His hand cramped from gripping the razor so tightly.

Finally he noticed the texture of the bond that held it, his fingers edging the loop back, still working on escape. The loop was a thin braid of human hair. Elisha wrapped his fingers around it, a bare quarter-inch of compassion in the captured horror exuded by the weapon of his brother's death. Thomas's hair, a trimming from that haircut Elisha had given him in the garden.

Now he remembered Thomas's hand clinging to Rosalynn's and the lines of worry around his eyes. The expression was neither boredom nor irritation, but concentration. He had given Elisha the means to make contact, and Elisha leapt at the chance, the slender ray of hope in the thundering dread that surrounded him. At once, Thomas's presence filled him, Thomas's thoughts focused on him, urging him to succeed, to live.

Suddenly, like his brother at the moment he had chosen death, Elisha didn't care what God thought, whether his talent was good or evil, whether every other person he had helped had left him on this day. Thomas remained, steadfast, as he had lent his own strong hands to heal Elisha's in the ancient tomb they shared. Trapped by his crown, he could not say a word, but he had sent the message nonetheless. Thomas needed him to live.

With careful wriggling, Elisha managed to slide free the strands of hair, the braid looped in his palm, clinging there by virtue of the blood and sweat that had slicked his hands. He drew himself back in, mastering his fear. First he must be strong enough to resist the suffocation of the grave, then he must work his way to freedom. And still he did not understand the threat of Morag's presence.

Taking a deep breath, Elisha shut his eyes. He drew upon Thomas's compassion and the fears and regrets that surrounded his brother's death. He brought them together like that braid, entwining strands of power. A new idea glimmered in the midst of darkness; a way, without showing his strength, to make room for hope in the midst of the anger surrounding him and thus find the balance he so desperately needed.

He slipped his senses out through the wood of the coffin that pressed in on him, sensing the dedicated stance of monks and priests, the attentive presence of the soldiers. Four strong men seized the ropes beneath his prison. They heaved the coffin up and lowered it down. He rocked and struck bottom with a thump. The first shovel of earth rattled down upon the lid. Elisha's heart thundered in the tight space of his tomb—the warder's voice insinuated itself into his memory, describing the tortures of live burial. Out, out he crept from his mind, summoning up that insidious power. Come, Death, if it would serve him. By the bonds of blood and grief, he commanded it. The cold unfurled within him, as if it had been waiting for his call. Shivers of death ran along his skin, tickling like a thousand crawling things.

From the writhing braid of his power, he drew the bleak and unforgiving permanence of Death. He could not be smothered—he was already gone, he told the darkness. Death was his servant as was the darkness.

Yes, he would be cold—the cold of the grave, the cold of despair and of those bereft of hope. The cold of his brother, and colder still, but that very cold could preserve his life.

As he enveloped himself in Death, he nearly lost the thread of Thomas's compassion. He searched, gripping the razor, so that the braid of hair pressed into the scar at his palm. On that terrible night, Thomas joined their hands together, allowing Elisha to heal. This spark found space among the shadows, and Elisha cast its light out along the paths that he had laid, out among the excited lords and their dismayed ladies, out further still among the merchants and their clients, out beyond that to the workmen and tradesmen and prostitutes, to the people he had dedicated himself to serving. He took that compassion and suffused it with his memories, glancing back over his life, the children he had saved, the workmen who kept their jobs because of him, the women healed of their wounds and sickness by his hands, the babies born whole and healthy.

His eyes shut, breathing in the already stale air of his doom, he called upon his incipient panic and blew forth these memories like the wind that uplifted the crows overhead.

Everyone who had been touched by Death, now was touched by him. He touched them not with the awe that Rowena had sought, but with the intimate moments they already knew.

Little by little, they fell silent. A woman touched the scars on her arm, remembering how he had bound the wound, and turned away. A father remembered the medicine given to his fevered child, and bowed his head. The mistress of a brothel ran her fingers through her hair while her girls embraced each other and wept. Malcolm Carter, who had brought Elisha to Dunbury, thought of his son's broken leg and crossed himself. Somewhere on the outskirts, Arthur Mason, who fought in the battle of Dunbury Ford, studied the stump of his leg and spoke a prayer in Elisha's name.

Elisha's spirit soared. It was true; he had not been for Death all these years, but Life. He laughed as the power surged through him. The Law of Polarity fleeted through his mind. It was not Death he fought for, but Life. Life that he preserved and tended and might have died for. And if that were not God's battle, what could ever be?

At last he had broken the hold of fear and hatred that had mired him in doubt. Focus, Mordecai had reminded him. At last, he just might manage it. The sound of falling earth grew dim and distant, its weight groaning against the wood. It was time. Elisha's elation spread, tingling through his fingers and toes. He could do it. He was unstoppable.

In spite of his surging confidence, somewhere in his belly lodged a knot of terror he could not dispel, a foreign fear he was determined not to feel, a lingering sense of Morag's presence. With a will, Elisha squeezed away that fear and got to work. He sought affinity, imagining all the similarities between the bound lock of hair in his fingers and the locked chain around his wrists. With a roll of his fingers, he let the hair fall straight, and the manacles clattered free. For a time, he rested his forehead on the wood floor, working his fingers, shaking out his aching wrists. He allowed himself to drift, waiting, allowing the audience time to disperse before he began his real work.

When he judged that an hour or so had gone by, Elisha stretched his awareness beyond the skin, feeling the priests and nobles above him recede toward the city. A number of people lingered, devoid of hatred now but uncertain what to say or do. A few of them were crying. "I'm sorry," Elisha whispered, though they could not hear him. He had not meant to cause them grief, only to stop the terrible waves of their hatred long enough to find his focus.

In that moment of regret, Elisha felt a familiar step approaching, a presence he knew so well he could almost taste it. He snapped back his own awareness, gathering his power deep inside, revealing only the fear and the pain, the things anyone might expect to find. Brigit was no sensitive—he did not know how far she could even attune herself. Could she feel him through the earth? Not likely. Certainly not clearly enough to communicate through rock and wood. But he could feel her coming. Then she stood over him, crying.

Tears struck the earth over his coffin and seeped down through, tears of genuine grief. For Alaric? He was recently lost, and Brigit's claim to the throne lost along with him. These tears shone not with ambition, but with love. Each tear carried with it a moment, a smile, a look, a touch. It was not Alaric she mourned.

Elisha gasped, his fingers spread upon the wood as the memories sank through. He had seen them all before—but from the other view, his own. Once again, he was given the strange blessing of seeing how another saw him. His brother saw him competent, arrogant, distant. Brigit saw him strong, desperate, furious. She saw him struggle with the rules he was given, saw his discovery of magic and shared it with him. She saw him take the flogging he earned by his defiance of his superior's orders, and felt a shock of dismay when she realized the man he defied orders to save was Alaric, the prince who loved her. Brigit remembered the moment she showed Elisha the talisman, his ignorance and naivety: he did not understand what he had, what he might be. But she did. With her help, he could become great. With his help, she could achieve her mother's dream. No witch need ever burn again. If he would only recognize who he really was.

They shared a kiss that night, a kiss of such passion that it swept her away along with him. It swelled through her body—and inspired a new idea. She broke the kiss—

hating the need to delay. But they would come together again. She would have him—when her body was ripe and her womb was ready. He wanted her, and she would make sure he enjoyed her—he wouldn't even think of what he gave her in return.

Elisha barely breathed. Her tears showed him all he had resisted. How could he believe she loved him, when she would have let him hang for the sake of creating a greater talisman for her own use? She still had the hanging rope; she savored it as a part of him. She savored everything about him, treasured every memory, acknowledging that his sacrifices made her stronger. He wanted to hate her, to punish her with a vision of all he had gone through, touching her as he had touched the others. Slapping her back from her obscene grief.

Yet it was true, in its own way. She loved him with a passionate desire that made Martin Draper's attraction seem a weak and pale thing. She loved him, though it shook the vision of what her life should be and that was a distraction she could not afford if she would win her kingdom. Her love was commanding and cruel, like a master willing to beat a loyal hound who ignores an order. Her tears rebuked his doubt, and Elisha let her be. He let her weep over him, but he withdrew even further into himself, removing the perceptible fear and replacing it with cold. If she could feel him there at all, let her believe that he lay already dead beneath her feet.

It seemed a long time before she left, but that effect was caused more by the shroud of his brother's death that he used to conceal himself. That day when he killed his first king, time had passed strangely, his awareness almost outside of time, as if he could minutely observe everything around him in the instant of another man's death.

When he next unfurled his senses, the dread kindled again at the back of his mind. In the shock of Brigit's coming, he had forgotten about Morag, but still there was no sign of what the mancer had done. As Chanterelle had taught Elisha, he allowed his focus to become particular. He wasn't merely looking around as he used to, he was looking deep—as if he had moved from the examination of a patient to the diagnosis of their specific ills. The roughness of the wood became a series of fine lines, some raised, some depressed, like ridges of hills infinitely small. The piercing wound in his shoulder resolved into a small, sharp triangle, its point pressing against his shoulder blade, a stream of blood winding between the fine hairs on his skin. It severed only muscle, and he knew where to place the sutures. When he was free, he could heal it—but that nagging worry kept him from expending the strength just now. He was not out of the ground, not even out of the coffin. Focus.

Elisha deepened his awareness a little further from himself and found the panel over his head, the one Mordecai told him would be loose. Tucking the talismans close to his body, Elisha wriggled his hands upward, wincing as they scraped the wood. He felt over the panel with his fingers. The board gave beneath his fingertips with the slick sensation of rotten wood, a faint hum of magic concealing the fault from those who prepared the grave. Elisha dug his fingers in and pulled, tearing free a few slivers, then yanking the board inside as it gave way. It rapped his head, stinging his naked scalp. He brought it in front of him, working it down his body out of the way. A bit of loose earth trickled in after it, touching his head with a lashing cold. Elisha stopped, releasing the rotten wood.

He let out a breath, his chest aching slightly. Did he still need to breathe? What was the operation of his affinity with Death? Always, it maintained an uneasy balance with his body's own needs. Chanterelle had shown him how she found breath within the dirt. He needed to get free of the constricting coffin and use what he knew. He was not Chanterelle, of course, and did not have her connection with the earth, to move effortlessly among the grains and pebbles. The best he could hope for was a sort of swimming, like a fish. The earth might shift over him, but it couldn't be helped. If a passerby saw movement, they would imagine the dirt shifted due to the recent excavation.

He took up his talismans, wishing he had some better way to carry them. He would need at least one hand, and the idea of placing either the hair or the razor in his mouth revolted him. Transferring them to his left, Elisha rolled back onto his stomach, relieving the pressure on his shoulders. He took a deep breath, his last within the coffin, and pushed himself toward the dirt. Feeling ahead for the minute spaces Chanterelle had shown him were always there, Elisha moved the dirt. Thankfully, it was freshly turned, loose, rather than packed. He moved as carefully as he could, his right hand extended before him, keeping his eyes closed against this rough, new darkness. Again, he felt the chill. It must be someone else had died near here, leaving a trace.

Elisha kept his awareness tighter. He had strength enough for this without taking on that terrible power. The crossroads was clear toward the city but had some clumps of brush toward the west. It should be safe to emerge there, and not so far that it would tax his strength completely. When he found the roots of those bushes, he would know to rise. In between, the ground would be hard, unturned, and he would need a greater extension of power. He crept forward, his knees and toes pushing against the wood of the coffin, then scraping the small stones, grinding in the dirt. Elisha gritted his teeth and went on, until his battered toes touched the soil, the coffin left behind him. The pressure increased, the weight of earth bearing down on him, and it was a continual process using the contact of every grain of dirt against any surface of his body to push the earth away and behind, allowing it to tumble into the coffin.

His right hand shivered. He inched it forward again, but the cold grew worse, creeping up his hand until his fingers felt numb and cramped. Now his wrist and arm trembled.

Cursing inwardly, Elisha released a bit of his focus, taking his attention from the tiny grains to the cold earth that stretched before him. Something mixed with the dirt here, making it lighter than it should be. Elisha snapped back his hand. His stomach roiled. He felt the earth reaching back toward him, felt the terrible sense of loss, like the fury of the crows, but close, so close. Chanterelle. Now that his focus wavered, he could feel her, all around him, mingled with the earth. Morag had slain her and ground her into the dirt she knew. Every bit of soil, every stone, stung with the taint of her death.

Chapter 36

❖

Elisha's lungs burned, tears trapped behind the squeezed lids of his eyes. He kept his jaw clamped shut against the urge to gulp for air—there was none but the tiny pockets trapped between the grains of earth. Not enough. His chest couldn't expand, his ribs groaned. All around him, the dirt grew dense, pressing in on him. He remembered the comfort Chanterelle used to take from this contact, but all he felt now were the echoes of her terror and the irretrievable union of her flesh with the dirt. Dirt-whore, Morag called her, when she came to answer Elisha's need. And he had hunted her down.

Elisha could not move forward. Even from here, his skin recoiled, and his hand rebelled against thrusting through her. To continue would be a violation as cruel and sickening as that of the men who drove her to earth to begin with. He tried to retreat, inching backward by digging in his toes, but the way behind was already filled with the earth he had displaced. His body cramped into the smaller space, pulling back from the edge of what he now recognized as another grave. He guessed if he moved aside and tried again, he would find the shreds of her mingled in a circle all around. He might probe deeper and try to go beneath—surely, in only one night, Morag could not have dug too far down. But going down meant doubling his effort for he would have to rise again. His nostrils itched from the effort of breathing. In fact, he itched from the soles of his feet to his battered toes and legs, to his aching sides to the top of his scraped and shaven head. The longer he delayed, the harder it would be to ignore the mounting unpleasantness of the sensations that built up in his flesh. He had to go up, right now, or die in truth only a few feet short of the grave.

Morag wanted him to rise. Elisha squeezed his eyes shut so hard that he saw red now instead of black, a dancing red like the carpet page of a rich manuscript furling with poisonous vines.

How long had he been down here? It felt like ages. Thomas and the rest must be gone by now, the road abandoned to those who knew nothing of what had happened or else could not afford to avoid the place.

Even changing direction was an arduous process, digging his fingers upward and pushing at the earth, turning his body and wrenching his wounded shoulder. He sobbed with the effort, and with the knowledge that he was doing what his enemy wanted, and he had no choice.

But the thought of Morag presented a tantalizing option. Somehow, the mancers could appear and disappear, travelling a secret corridor of Death. Elisha might be able to use it, if he only knew how. It was something to do with using blood to seed the ground, as they had at the arch where Alaric met them, and at the stone where Morag had dragged him from the abbey. It needed preparation then, and what? Death? But Morag did not seem aware of the death already around him, in those mounds of ancient burials. Murder? Did it truly take them to another place, or straight to Hell like the demons that they were? Had Morag shown him Rome, or merely told him that? In spite of the horror they inspired, the mancers did not seem any more supernatural than he himself.

When he touched his old razor, he had triggered the memory of his brother's last moments. It had been that effortless for Morag the night they met. He had seized Elisha, draped him over a shoulder, and opened a door that didn't exist. Tentatively, Elisha reached out again toward Chanterelle. He had known her, surely better than the mancer who slew her; if there were a door she could open, would she not open it for him?

His fingers sifted through the soil and the remnants of her. Ash struck like a thorny vine, tearing along his skin with a prickling pain. It surrounded him, scraping at him, entwining about his trembling arm. He aimed his awareness to this end: to bring all the focus he could spare, from the process of keeping back the dirt, into those outstretched fingertips. The cold insinuated itself through contact, but he had little sense of Chanterelle. She was fragmented, her body and self so broken he could not find her center. She surrounded him, pulsing with pain and terror so that his skin crawled, but the sensation was so pervasive he could not bring his awareness to bear upon it. Unlike that connection he briefly shared with his dead brother, this was as thin and dreadful as mist, binding, clinging—not a thing he could push away or avoid without shedding his awareness completely. And if he did that, he was doomed to die beneath the ground. Up, then. Up to face whatever monsters lay in wait.

Elisha steeled himself to thrust in a new direction, and his muscles protested. Already, he weakened from the efforts expended. Dear God. He might come bursting from the earth to collapse at Morag's feet, ripe for the skinning. And whoever else witnessed his emergence would acknowledge Morag the hero of the scene, killing the fiend that dodged his own death.

His left hand gripped his talismans a little tighter. Thomas's compassion, Nathaniel's sacrifice. His tutors among the magi always chided him for failing to build more strength with his talisman, rather than allowing it to resonate with the focus of his power. He practiced now, recreating the braid of strength he had earlier drawn on, but damping the full intensity of the razor. His situation was too precarious for that. The grief alone would overwhelm him.

Armed as best he could be, Elisha moved upward, wriggling and pushing through the earth like a mandrake root being harvested. He wished he could spring forth from the ground with a shriek. Pressure built up within as well as around him. As he moved despite the protest of his twitching muscles and burning lungs, the urgency transformed his progress from escape to confrontation. The sooner he rose, the sooner he would know what threat awaited him; to meet it with his strength or fall before it into nothing. *We are each of us soldiers, fighting our own enemy until we fall and do not rise again.* Mordecai's words, before Elisha knew who and what he was. At the time, in his arrogance and excitement, Elisha's reply had been to suggest that he might rise again in a way that none expected. Today, he would be lucky to rise at all.

The earth above grew lighter, the pressure slowly releasing, and Elisha moved more carefully, until his fingertip touched air and he froze, praying it had not been noticed. He mustered his scattered thoughts first on searching the ground around him, reaching for attunement. He could feel no one, but he was not fooled. Morag would be here, whether he waited so well concealed that Elisha could not sense him, or whether he would appear from nothing in a howl of the ravening dead.

Deflection would not alone suffice against an enemy magus who expected him, but it might buy a few minutes for Elisha to understand the situation and find some advantage. He sucked back his senses, projecting his own absence as he wriggled the last few feet and pushed his right arm, then his head free of the earth. Dirt scattered down over his shoulders, and he fought the urge to shake himself—any further sound or disturbance would make the deflection that much more difficult.

The dull light of an overcast afternoon showed him little but the nearby mound that covered his grave. He heaved and shoved against the surface, kicking and finally had his knees on the broken ground. He gulped a breath, reeling in the sudden release.

A familiar acrid odor reached his nose, but it was out of place here, so much so that he did not immediately place it. He started to get his feet under him, and the edges of his tunnel trickled away with a soft rumble.

A slithering rattle followed by the tap of metal. Then he realized that he had smelled smoke, but not from the wood fires that would heat any local houses, and he froze, eyes wide. The air was so dry it hurt his eyes and nose and throat. This unnatural dry felt like Sundrop's doing, taking the rain from the site of Elisha's grave. Mud would have made Elisha's escape all the more difficult. But if Sundrop meant to help him, he must not know about the offended crows, or what had happened to Chanterelle. Sundrop had urged her to flee out of fear she would be discovered by the mancers. Did he now search for her with the touch of his soft rains upon her earth?

When he heard the blast, Elisha first thought of thunder. But the percussive force of something shot past him from the left in a rolling wave of smoke. Instinctively, Elisha threw himself to the ground. A bombardelle. Someone had shot at him. Why not arrows or the sword, something sure to strike, at the very least?

It came from behind, and he scrambled to his hands and knees, peering into the smoke that swirled around him.

Why not an arrow? Because he couldn't be seen. Until now.

Another rattle of metal on metal, the hiss of flame. Elisha flattened himself, only to draw down a wraith of smoke like a pointing finger over his head. Deflection might fool the eye but not the air. Instead, he sprang up and dodged right. A second shot cracked the air, and

Elisha dove away as the lead ball slammed into the dirt where he had emerged. Smoke roiled out, spilling down in the wake of the thunder.

Elisha projected his breath, pushing the smoke briefly away, and caught a glimpse of the bombardier, standing in the open on the ring of earth despoiled by Chanterelle's ashes, leaning slightly back on one foot as he braced the bottom of the staff where his weapon was mounted. Unhurriedly, he drew something small from a pouch at his side, stuffed it into the mouth of the tube with that rattle of metal as he drew out the slender shaft he used to pack it. A bit of flame flickered at his hand, obscured by smoke into a pale light.

"So, this's how a death-mage dies: shot full o' lead on the dirt-whore's grave." Morag's head swung like a hunting hound, scenting his prey. His form shifted slightly, the flame crackled.

Elisha dove as the shot thundered by. He struck hard, his injured shoulder grinding into the dirt, and he bit back a cry. The smoke allowed him to be tracked, but it also made the aiming that much more difficult. A few running steps and he'd be free, beyond the range of the wicked instrument. He floundered up again, panting, then used his breath to make contact, gathering the smoke rather than letting it disperse. He thickened it around him, between himself and Morag, then leapt first left, then right, improvising a dance to confuse the eddies and the ears.

"Hah!" Morag laughed. A rattle, and another shot that punched a brief hole in Elisha's smoky defense.

No matter, Elisha ran, easily avoiding the direction of

the shot. One, two, three, four, steps—and then stuck fast, his sole rooted to the spot so that he wrenched his ankle and fell to his knees, crumpling sideways with a cry. The earth sucked at his foot, wrapping it like a gripping hand that dug in its fingers as he tried to move. It seized him like ice, a burning agony that pulled at every inch of exposed skin. Chanterelle's ashes awakened to her killer. Morag used his own trick against him, but instead of moving the tainted earth, the ashes marked Elisha heel and hand and dragged him down. He twisted, looking back.

Beyond the turbulence of Elisha's passage, Morag laughed again. The smoke began to clear from the last shot. Elisha tried to gather it once more, but Morag's presence shone through like a beacon in a fog. He braced his weapon, stuffed in the shot, and slowly drew out the tamping rod, then lifted his head to stare directly at Elisha. He slipped the rod into his belt and raised a wick that sputtered flame.

"You think someone might hear? Somebody might come a'runnin' to find out what's on? Not to a witch's grave at a crossroads. Not to the sight of smoke and the smell of brimstone." Morag drew a deep sniff, like a lady with a nosegay. "'ave no fears about the common folk. They think I'm the Devil come to take you home."

He chuckled. "Come to think of it, mebbe they're right." He touched off the flame with a sound like thunder.

———————— ✦ ————————

Chapter 37

Elisha grabbed at the smoke with all of his strength. He flung his awareness through the writhing space between them and felt the impact of the ball striking through. Contact. He struck back with a ferocious need, but smoke alone was not enough. The ball slipped just a little, streaking through his smoky grasp with a sizzle, burning a furrow down his side. Elisha winced. It saved him for a moment, but it wasn't enough.

"You're quick, I'll grant ye that." Morag propped the staff to begin his ritual of reloading.

Crouched on the ground, a bare ten yards from his enemy, his foot clamped down, Elisha didn't feel quick. But Morag took his time, letting the smoke disperse, moving no nearer. He, too, needed contact, and the band of ruined earth gave it to him—enough to keep Elisha in his grip. Elisha groped through the contact, forcing himself to face the thousand piercing grains of Chanterelle's suffering. Every grain diminished him, striking another tiny blow against his crumbling strength. He panted, pushing as hard as he had under ground, with barely greater results. He could feel the pressure of Morag's feet upon the dirt, but he could not sense him at all. Just as before, Morag's presence and absence were one: He had as little character as a stone, and he gave as little hint of what lay inside. Without that, Elisha's awareness slipped around him, broken into useless eddies like a river pierced by bridges. Rage as he would, he could not strike a man he could not sense. He felt only the iron pressure of those boots that held him, too, upon the ruined ring.

Magic pinned Elisha down, but simple lead could kill him. He recoiled his senses, fleeing the dread of Chanterelle's destruction. Every gasping breath brought a stinging pain from his latest wound. But if he would not die for Brigit's use, he would be damned if he died for Morag's. He reached out again and found the lead ball marked with his blood, burrowed into the earth not far away. He clung tighter to his talismans and borrowed the racing speed of his heart. Quick, Morag had called him. He would see about that.

Morag braced the weapon and brought up his flame. Elisha flung his shot. With every urgency of his being, he sent it home, back to the barrel that launched it.

Steadying the staff, Morag touched off the flame. Elisha's shot slammed into the hollow core, and the thing exploded with a ferocious blast. Shards of smoking metal flew. One of them slashed Elisha's face, leaving a burning trail, as he ducked for cover. Across the ring, Morag staggered with the impact, stumbling free of the ruined earth. For a moment, Elisha was free. He scrambled to his feet, limping a few steps beyond the ring, the smoke searing his nostrils and throat as he tried to catch his breath.

With a snarl Morag flung away the broken staff with its smoldering shape of bronze petalled like a flower from Hell. Blood streamed down his face and arm from a dozen rents in his clothing, and one ear dangled. "Oh, barber, ye'll regret that shot."

Elisha stumbled as he ran, trying to think of some way to defeat the mancer. He screamed as he unwillingly stopped again, his knees buckling at the terrible sucking at his soles that held him down. His right hand dragged backward, pulled everywhere the tainted earth touched him. Morag had regained his circle. He not only had contact with the dirt, but also intimate knowledge of Chanterelle's death and desecration. He called out to the dirt with the force of that knowledge, and Elisha was held like a deer at a net, waiting for the hunter, and the hunter came, boots scuffing the ground.

Elisha reached back through that same contact, but he didn't have the knowledge. For him, it was still too faint and fragmentary.

"I met a woman at your graveside, oh, barber mine. Weeping she was for love of you." His breath rasped, then bubbled as he coughed. Elisha stilled his struggle, listening.

Morag grabbed his arm, fingers digging in and dragged him, Elisha's back pressed to Morag's thighs, the other thick hand clamping Elisha's jaw. Morag pulled him up, smearing him with blood, squeezing Elisha's head until his teeth ached, and the mancer stared down from his burned, battered face. "Pay for that, ye will. I had to leave my pretties home, 'cause I was that worried what you might do with 'em. Needn't've worried, eh?" He chuckled in Elisha's ear, his own dangling against Elisha's forehead. "You haven't learned shit since last we met."

Elisha reached up with his left, flicked open the razor, and snapped it across Morag's throat, but the mancer turned with the cut, spinning like a dancer, and seized Elisha's hand, crushing it.

With a fierce lunge, Morag bit down on the razor's back and tore it free of Elisha's grip. He spat it aside and flung his captive down, slamming a knee into Elisha's chest, holding him spread like Christ on the cross. "You can't beat me," he spat, and Elisha felt the mancer's blood, mingled now with Nathaniel's dried remains. His stomach clenched with nausea. The new wound gaped at the side of Morag's throat, but too shallow to kill. Why couldn't his brother have failed so dismally? Failed—and lived.

The mancer bore down on him, and his ribs cracked. He could no longer draw breath. "I tasted your brother's death," Morag murmured, his voice gone soft now with something like lust. "Ooh, it tasted good. Steeped in despair." He licked his lips, lingering on a gash that cut the lower one. His gruesome glee was the first emotion Elisha had felt in him. Hoping to overwhelm Elisha with repulsion, Morag sent him this, making a breach in the utter lack of presence he affected. Morag's shield had a flaw.

He tasted Nathaniel's death, but he did not know it. And so, Elisha showed him. He ripped open his memories, his own and the awful vision captured by the razor. He could not vanquish this demon with horror; he didn't even try. But there was more to dying than that. From the flickering memories of that moment, Elisha chose the thread of guilt, the layers of his own remorse from his doubt of Helena to his silent acceptance of his sentence. He sent Nathaniel's mistrust, his late action, his realization at what must be done to save his wife, and the moment he was sure both wife and child had died and might have lived if not for him.

Morag shivered, his tongue protruding. He blinked a few times and Elisha felt the rush of unaccustomed emotion, a feeling so foreign to Morag that he had prepared no defense against it. Tears streamed down his captor's face. Impatiently, Morag shook them away. He shifted his grip, blood flying as he shook his head again, trying to shake off the emotions. His loose ear flapped, but his lips curled now with sorrow rather than hate. Morag stared at Elisha with tear-stained eyes, a mixture of guilt and wonder on his face.

Elisha called Death. He called it quick and sharp from the flecks of his brother's blood and slipped it like a razor through this fracture in Morag's defenses. The mancer thought he knew death, but he was wrong. His knowledge was inflicting it, torture, murder, shock, and horror. Pain, to him, was power, but this . . . he struggled to understand, and Elisha undermined his struggle. Elisha summoned up the howling blast, the cold, the cracked abyss. There was no control as there had been with King Hugh, there was only desperation. Morag's labored lungs seized, his torn face split as he realized his danger. He thrashed and kicked, but Elisha held on. The two of them rolled, the cold of dying lashing between them until it lanced home through the blackened shard of bronze from the bombardelle that lodged behind the ruined ear. Elisha sought for Morag's death and found it there. A nudge and the shard drove inward, eager.

Morag's body convulsed, his eyes flaring, tears drying, then he finally stilled, sagging onto Elisha, pinning him and dribbling brains.

Elisha shoved him away, and vomited. He rested his forehead on his trembling arm. King Hugh's death seemed so easy now, so distant, thanks to the numbness he had cultivated. Then, he had called on the body's natural decay, turning the flesh against itself, using his talisman to bring out what was already there—the death inherent in the idea of birth. Alaric's death was different, true, but it had come in battle, as a king should wish to die. Morag's death was murder. Personal and ugly.

He gagged, wiped his mouth, and crawled a little further away to the fringe of brush around the milestone where he had planned his emergence as overhead, something cawed.

Slumped against the stone, Elisha groaned, pulling his legs closer, curled into himself. "Take him," he croaked in answer as another bird circled by. "At least, you can't tell your mistress I left you with nothing."

"Sundrop knows she was killed for you."

Elisha bolted upright and grabbed the stone to steady himself as he turned.

"He couldn't bear to touch her grave." The crows' mistress shuffled toward him. With a bob of her head, she sent on her friends, and he could hear the suck and splat of fresh meat being torn by beaks and talons.

"I'm sorry, Mistress," he tried again, swaying, but she flapped her hands.

"We're watching," she said. "Don't forget us." She shut her mouth with a click.

"Never," he sighed.

She shuffled past, crooning to her black darlings.

Elisha straightened slowly in her wake. The cold still lingered, and he drew it upward, taking it in, reluctantly, as a hunter accepts an ugly whelp: it was not wanted, but it was his. The strength of Morag's death tangled inside him from every tingling patch of blood and every salted, starry tear. Elisha drew a deeper breath and showed his ribs how to heal. He closed the wound at his shoulder, sealed the furrow of the bombardelle's shot, and eased the ache of his twisted ankle. With halting steps, he approached the scene. His razor lay on the ground, still open, one patch of the old blade clean where Morag's lips had pressed. Numbing his hand to the memories, both new and old, Elisha reached out for it and shut the blade. He cast about in the gathering gloom, and finally spread his senses, leery of feeling either Chanterelle's agony or the gory victory of crows. But he found what he was looking for and pinched it close: the lock of Thomas's hair.

Now that the battle was done, the smoke clearing, someone would come, and he must be gone. How they would explain the fresh corpse at the crossroads—and how much of it would remain—he did not know.

Enough strength lingered from Morag's death to sustain his walk, and he cast a deflection to keep him safe, though he was so tired that it hardly seemed worth it to try. Thomas was enthroned, with the support of bishops and barons, and soon he would be wed. Rosalynn would have the prince she deserved, faithful and strong. Elisha lived, in spite of his enemies. Truly, it had been a victory. He wondered how long it would take before he felt it so.

His leaden feet kept moving, his aching lungs yet breathed, and so he found the inn as Mordecai said, and the bundle tucked in the rafters there. The clothes were fine but not too rich; plain linen, new and clean. Elisha breathed in Thomas's concern. He found the packet of food, but could not consider eating just yet, not with the taste of death still there upon his tongue. A belt curled underneath, with a softly clinking purse and Elisha's medical pouch. Tucked at its back, he found a new knife, short, sharp, its blade with the swirl of metal that showed the smith had layered it over and again. A Damascene blade worth all the rest, and then some. At the bottom lay a pair of boots more supple than any he had ever owned. When Elisha first met Thomas, they had been nearly equals: two men apart from others and barefoot. For a long moment, Elisha gathered his gifts to him and breathed in his gratitude.

After scrubbing away the last of the dirt at a trough by the back, Elisha dressed carefully in the privacy of the stable and stepped out again, refreshed. Before him stretched the road back to London, past the crossroads that should have been his grave. Beyond the clusters of houses and shops, the highest steeples, towers, and walls of the city stood rosy in the last of the sun's light. And over the gate, snapping proudly in the wind, waved the pennants of the king.

Saladin Ahmed

Throne of the Crescent Moon

978-0-7564-0778-0

"An arresting, sumptuous and thoroughly satisfying debut."
— *Kirkus* (starred)

"Set in a quasi–Middle Eastern city and populated with the supernatural creatures of Arab folklore, this long-awaited debut by a finalist for the Nebula and Campbell awards brings *The Arabian Nights* to sensuous life. The maturity and wisdom of Ahmed's older protagonists are a delightful contrast to the brave impulsiveness of their younger companions. This trilogy launch will delight fantasy lovers who enjoy flawed but honorable protagonists and a touch of the exotic." — *Library Journal* (starred)

"Ahmed's debut masterfully paints a world both bright and terrible. Unobtrusive hints of backstory contribute to the sense that this novel is part of a larger ongoing tale, and the Arab-influenced setting is full of vibrant description, characters, and religious expressions that will delight readers weary of pseudo-European epics."
— *Publishers Weekly* (starred)

To Order Call: 1-800-788-6262
www.dawbooks.com

Deborah J. Ross
The Seven-Petaled Shield

An all-new high fantasy trilogy of magic, myth, and war—from a co-author of the Darkover novels!

THE SEVEN-PETALED SHIELD
978-0-7564-0621-9

SHANNIVAR
978-0-7564-0920-3

THE HEIR OF KHORED
978-0-7564-0921-0

To Order Call: 1-800-788-6262
www.dawbooks.com

Kari Sperring

Living with Ghosts

978-0-7564-0675-2

Finalist for the Crawford Award for First Novel

A Tiptree Award Honor Book

Locus Recommended First Novel

"This is an enthralling fantasy that contains horror elements interwoven into the story line. This reviewer predicts Kari Sperring will have quite a future as a renowned fantasist."
—*Midwest Book Review*

"A satisfying blend of well-developed characters and intriguing worldbuilding. The richly realized Renaissance style city is a perfect backdrop for the blend of ghostly magic and intrigue. The characters are wonderfully flawed, complex and multi-dimensional. Highly recommended!"
—*Patricia Bray, author of The Sword of Change Trilogy*

And now available:

The Grass King's Concubine

978-0-7564-0755-1

To Order Call: 1-800-788-6262
www.dawbooks.com

Violette Malan

The Novels of Dhulyn and Parno:

"Believable characters and graceful storytelling."
—*Library Journal*

"Fantasy fans should brace themselves:
the world is about to discover Violette Malan."
—*The Barnes & Noble Review*

THE SLEEPING GOD
978-0-7564-0484-0

THE SOLDIER KING
978-0-7564-0569-4

THE STORM WITCH
978-0-7564-0574-8

and

PATH OF THE SUN
978-0-7564-0680-6

C.S. Friedman
The *Magister* Trilogy

"Powerful, intricate plotting and gripping characters
distinguish a book in which ethical dilemmas
are essential and engrossing."
—*Booklist*

"Imaginative, deftly plotted fantasy...
Readers will eagerly await the next installment."
—*Publishers Weekly*

FEAST OF SOULS
978-0-7564-0463-5

WINGS OF WRATH
978-0-7564-0594-6

LEGACY OF KINGS
978-0-7564-0748-3

To Order Call: 1-800-788-6262
www.dawbooks.com

John Marco
The Bronze Knight